The Needle's Eye

MARGARET DRABBLE

The Needle's Eye

A HARVEST BOOK • HARCOURT, INC.

Orlando Austin New York San Diego Toronto London

www.HarcourtBooks.com

Library of Congress Cataloging-in-Publication Data
Drabble, Margaret, 1939–
The needle's eye/Margaret Drabble.—1st Harvest ed.
p.   cm.—(A Harvest book)
ISBN 0-15-602935-9
1. Custody of children—Fiction.   2. Separated people—Fiction.
3. Single mothers—Fiction.   4. England—Fiction.
5. Slums—Fiction.   I. Title.
PR6054.R25N44   2004
823'.914—dc22   2004007300

Text set in Bulmer MT
Designed by Linda Lockowitz

Printed in the United States of America

First Harvest edition 2004
A C E G I K J H F D B

For my parents

I would like to thank
all the lawyers who talked to me about this book,
and also Hilary Dunkley,
who introduced me to the identification of flora.

The fascination of what's difficult
Has dried the sap out of my veins, and rent
My heart from all its natural content.

—W. B. YEATS

FOREWORD

I'VE SOMETIMES WONDERED why I find Margaret Drabble's novels so peculiarly pleasurable. One reason may be that she combines what are usually disparate delights: the skills of those writers who, like Arnold Bennett (about whom she's written a fine biography), deftly detail the social fabric and capture the texture of a specific time and place; and those of writers who, like Virginia Woolf, render with great precision the subtle movements of the interior life. Such balance is rare; Woolf considered Bennett her antithesis. But I see it in George Eliot and also, among more recent British writers, in Elizabeth Bowen, in Pat Barker, and in Drabble herself.

Born in Sheffield, England, in 1939, Drabble has written fifteen novels to date, most recently *The Seven Sisters* (2002) and the just-published *The Red Queen.* I missed her early novels the first time around; I didn't "discover" her until the late 1980s, by which time I was already struggling to write myself. When I found her work I fell on it greedily, reading out of order and nearly simultaneously everything of hers I could find. Here was a writer—a living writer, a woman writer—who was unafraid to tackle large subjects, and who did well the things I so loved in late nineteenth- and early twentieth-century novels while at the same time brilliantly conveying life as we lived it right now. The intensity, the seriousness, the playfulness—I loved, and still love, these characteristics of Drabble's work, as I do the sense of a writer continually interrogating the nature of the world, and of our place in it.

Since then Drabble's novels have continued to inspire and delight me, but my favorite remains her sixth, *The Needle's Eye,* which was first published in 1972 and is set a few years earlier. Intricately plotted, rich in compelling characters, it's told in a dense, seductive, omniscient voice that beautifully balances inner and outer lives. It offers a complex social portrait of London, from the customers in a neighborhood off-license to, among others, a discontented couple in their posh London town house, the students and teachers in a scrappy, underfunded urban school, and a group of smug barristers in their chambers. At the same time it also reveals, with startling clarity and intensity, the central characters' souls.

A long set piece lures us into the novel's world, a twenty-five-page account of an upper-middle-class London dinner party that, in its precise social comedy, penetrating interiority, and psychological acuity, suggests both Virginia Woolf's *Mrs. Dalloway* and Arnold Bennett's *The Old Wives' Tale.* During the party, the central characters—Simon Camish and Rose Vassiliou—are introduced to each other, and also to us, through an extended conversation that manages to be funny, touching, and completely human. Rose is in her early thirties, Simon a few years older; both are living in ways directly opposed to their upbringing and both have just reached a moment of crisis.

Simon, the working-class son of a widowed and impoverished mother in northern England, has scrabbled his way to a career as a successful barrister, married a wealthy woman, and moved to a fancy house in a fashionable neighborhood, where he's a hostage to his wife's social ambitions and completely disconnected from his roots. In an inversion of his journey, Rose, heiress to a substantial fortune, now lives with her three children in a shabby house in a grimy northern London neighborhood, which her friends find squalid and dangerous but which she adores. She's never outgrown either her own impassioned sense of justice or the Biblical lessons of her childhood nanny, and having taken quite literally the stricture "For it is easier for a camel to go through a needle's eye, than for a rich man to enter the kingdom of God," she's divested herself of a substantial fortune, with the intent of living as austerely as possible. Although she's made herself notorious in the process— an underage engagement, several lawsuits, and a hurried marriage followed by a messy divorce have all been splashed across the newspapers—she's created a peaceful and happy life.

A letter from her ex-husband's solicitor, announcing that he wants custody of the children, shatters that peace and initiates the plot, which as it unfurls ties Rose and Simon ever more tightly together. Rose needs her new acquaintance's legal help, his steadiness, and his sympathy. Simon needs Rose's warmth and ease to counteract the dryness afflicting him, which he thinks of as "a feeling in me, in my brain, in my heart, so dull, so cold, so persistent, so ancient, that I am growing fond of it." (14). Their oppositions— he's as deeply conventional as Rose is unconventional, standing for law and justice as she stands for love and mercy—allow Drabble to explore the intersection of public and private morality in unusual depth. How sharply, we'll learn over the course of this novel, do the soul's deepest yearnings conflict with the messy, urgent needs of the world and of those we love.

The non-ironic use of the word "soul" isn't very common in literary fiction these days, nor are such passages as this, in which Simon confronts himself:

With a faint sudden recurring shock of astonishment he would recognise, in his own behaviour, an eternal human pattern of corruption. This is it, he would think to himself, this is I, doing what all men do, I am enacting those old and pre-ordained movements of the spirit, those ancient patterns of decay, I, who had thought myself different. I, who had (surely) other intentions. Corrupt, humanly corrupt if not professionally so, and humanly embittered.... He was caught. And his spirit would hunch its feathered bony shoulders, and grip its branch, and fold itself up and shrink within itself, until it could no longer brush against the net, until it could no longer entangle itself, painfully, in the surrounding circumstantial mesh. (144)

Or this, Rose's analogous experience:

She had seen her soul, suddenly, as she spoke; it was dark and crying and bloody, like a bat or an embryo, and it was not very nice at all, not an agreeable thing, and it flapped and squeaked inside her angrily whenever Christopher touched or spoke to her. (423)

The intertwined spiritual journeys of Rose and Simon hark back to the central question of Bunyan's *Pilgrim's Progress* (a text Rose knows well): *What shall I do to be saved?* Pilgrim's question, broadened beyond its specifically Christian context, is also Rose's and Simon's: *What shall I do to lead a good life? What does it mean to be good?*

When the novel was first published, Joyce Carol Oates wrote on the front page of the *New York Times Book Review* that Drabble, like Doris Lessing, had "taken upon herself the task, largely ignored today, of attempting the active, vital, energetic, mysterious re-creation of a set of values by which human beings can live." I can't better that description, except to add that Drabble's work always offers not only instruction but delight. *The Needle's Eye* is a funny, lively, lovely but ultimately serious novel (all the best ones are), which teaches us in the end not how to live—who could teach us that?—but that there are reasons to ask the question and accept the consequences.

—Andrea Barrett

Part One

H E STOOD THERE AND WAITED. He was good at that. There was no hurry. There was plenty of time. He always had time. He was a punctual and polite person, and that was why he was standing there, buying a gift for his hostess. Politeness was an emotion—could one call it an emotion, he wondered? that was how he regarded it, certainly—an emotion that he both feared and understood.

There was only one woman in front of him in the off-licence, and she was certainly in no hurry either. She had not even got round to asking for anything yet, because she was too busy telling the man behind the counter about her granddaughter. Two weeks old, this child was, and the lady had just finished knitting her a pram-cover in stripes of white and blue: it didn't matter that it was blue and not pink, the daughter had said, she didn't like pink anyway. The man behind the counter was interested in the story: not merely polite, but interested. One can tell the difference. The woman was short and broad and she was wearing bedroom slippers. What raffish districts of London his friends inhabited: NW1, this was, with all its smart contrasts. They depressed him unbearably, the well-arranged gulfs and divisions of life, the frivolity with which his friends took in these contrasts, the pleasure they took in such abrasions. It appalled him, the complacency with which such friends would describe the advantages of living in a mixed area. As though they licenced seedy old ladies and black men to walk their streets, teaching their children of poverty and despair, as their pet hamsters and guinea pigs taught them of sex and death. He thought of these things, sadly.

Though the old lady did not seem sad. On the contrary, she seemed happy enough, this new grandmother: pleased with herself, pleased with her pram-cover, pleased at the prospect of the evening she was just about to set up for herself—for she embarked, now, on the purchase of one bottle of Guinness, two of pale ale, and one of fizzy orange. The man wrapped them up for her carefully in tissue paper, while she thought about other things that she might want. A box of matches, she decided on, and then (curious order of choice) a packet of ten Players: one might have thought that that would be all, but it wasn't, because her eyes then lit upon the plastic display of crisps, and she thought she'd have one of cheese and onion and one of salt and vinegar. Also a bar of chocolate. And while she was at it, a small packet of aspirin. Listening to her, watching her look around this obviously familiar spot for yet more purchases—(nuts? tobacco? small cherries in a jar?)—he felt such violent waves of nostalgia possess him that he nearly spoke. He knew where she came from, this woman: it was a world from which he was forever exiled. But he knew it: he knew its domestic interiors, its pleasures, its horizons. And he knew what she was doing, with her purchases: she was trying to get out of being in that shop the exact experience of being in it, she wanted to exploit it to the full. But imagination failed her: she had to admit defeat. That'll be all, she said, regretfully. In front of them on the counter stood a small gyrating plastic advertisement for a brand of lager: while the man added up her purchases she inspected it, and when he had finished she asked him how it worked. It worked off the light, he said: no battery, no switches, nothing, it just went round and round for ever as long as the shop lights were on. He was proud of it: a new acquisition. She was impressed. She gathered up her bits and pieces and thrust them into her large shabby peeling bag, nodding her approval as she did so. What will they make next, she said. Marvellous, isn't it, said the man. Thanks a lot, Mrs Donovan. Thank *you*, Mr White. Give my regards to your daughter, Mrs Donovan. She'll be in herself shortly, Mr White, that I'll be sure, said Mrs Donovan, and they both smiled and she shuffled out. Her legs, for so stout a woman, were thin and twiglike, her stockings wrinkled. He felt a pang of loss as she left, and the man turned to him, politely, his expression entirely changed, businesslike, inhuman, obsequious, almost but not quite repudiating the quality of his previous transaction: 'What would you like, sir?' he asked, and Simon, politely, said, 'Could I have a bottle of Vermouth, please, and twenty Gold Leaf?'

There was no point in making any effort: no point in commenting on the weather, or the revolving lager advertisement. He received his purchase in silence, paid in silence, said thank you as one must, and left.

Diana and Nick lived just round the corner, but he thought that he might as well take the car right there with him, so he got back into it and drove himself fifty yards and parked. Diana and Nick: Nick and Diana. Perhaps he would enjoy himself after all. Better than eating alone at home, anyway, and that was surely why they had invited him: or was it out of some more positive desire to corrupt? That would be setting their interest in him too high perhaps, but he couldn't conceal from himself the fact that he had noticed that they (and one or two others) were always pretty quick off the mark to ask him round whenever his wife was away. He would have been touched, if he hadn't been slightly shamed by their alacrity: how had he let them in on it, how had they guessed, when had he so carelessly revealed himself? Not at all, maybe, not at all, surely: it was simple goodwill on their part, there was no need to be suspicious, or if they had an intention to corrupt it was so universal, so benevolent, that it implied no particular knowledge of him or of his circumstances. Old friends, they were, and what more natural than that they should invite him round for an evening while his wife was abroad? Julie herself had probably put them up to it: she had probably given Diana a ring and explained that she was off to New York for a fortnight and what about keeping an eye on poor Simon. The rage that possessed him as he thought of this was so acute and so bitter that he wished he hadn't allowed himself to speculate: though it was not rage against her, but a raging defence of her naïveté that so stuck in his throat. How could he protect her, when she was a free and adult woman, quite capable, all too capable, of lifting telephones and ringing up anyone to ask for anything? Ah well, forget it, he said to himself, and lifted his hand to ring the doorbell. He rang it, but there seemed to be remarkably little response: no answering sound within, and only the dullest sensation of indentation, so he decided that the bell was broken and lifted his hand once more to the knocker—an attractive knocker, a new one, a smiling and serene brass woman's face with grapes in her hair, a standard pattern but one that he had always liked. But before he had time to knock, the door opened, and there, silent and noiseless on the polished wooden floor (silent because of small gold cloth slippers) stood Diana, smiling with an equal calm.

'Simon, hello,' she said, and he stepped forward and kissed her on the cheek: a cheek which she offered, always, with no prospect of refusal, and anyway one would not be likely to wish to refuse such a nice brown even surface. A generous attitude, hers.

'I do like your new knocker,' he said, when he had greeted her and handed her his gift: following her up the stairs to their first-floor drawing-room. 'I was going to use it, I thought your bell didn't work.'

'One can't hear the bell from outside,' she said, 'we made it ring upstairs because we could never hear it.'

'How well organised you are,' he said, following her into the room: where their conversation immediately lost itself in faces, drinks, introductions and the soft bright interior of the room itself, which glowed diffusely, elegantly inhabitable, fashionably quaint, modern with a modernity that had no hard edges, no offence, no bravura in it. He had always liked the room, bearing signs, as it did, of so much in both of them, as well as of the hard-earned affluence that kept them together: for who could have guessed, watching the pair of them as they circled attentively with drinks and olives, so blending and agreeably harmonising with their choice in colours, their framed pictures by their own three rather talented small children, that this time a year ago they had parted for ever, with the great and customary acrimony that attends such separations? There had been much speculation both about their parting and their reunion: he himself had always had faith that a genuine affection had brought them back together, an affection supported not too ignobly by a reluctance to abandon so much comfortable bourgeois texture. What would Nick have done, in a horrid little flat away from all these deep piled carpets, or Diana, drifting desolate around a house that did not interest her as a refuge, but only as a meeting place, a place to receive in, a place to display? It was not, he felt, weakness that had brought them back to one another (though he thought this perhaps with bias)—it was more a sense that they augmented rather than diminished each other, they were better, more operative together. He had seen them both, singly, over their months apart, and though neither of them had confided in him (for he knew himself to be too discreet to invite real confidence) he had noticed that there was no sense of relief in either of them, but rather an exasperated self-assertion so unnecessary and so unnatural to both that he was sure it was the responsibility of independence that they had abandoned with a sigh of relief, rather than, in the first place, each other's company. They flourished, in this setting: even Nick, whose impatience at monogamous domestic claims had been real enough, thrived on it. It was not surprising, it was a setting that would encourage most kinds of growth: Simon, sinking into the corner of a deeply-upholstered off-white settee, and resting his feet on a luxuriantly waving, almost grotesquely verdant, silky rug, reflected how much affluence was, quite

7

simply, a question of texture—a point that both he and Nick, with their similar histories of success, and their similar points of origin, were well placed to appreciate. The threadbare carpets of infancy, the coconut matting, the ill-laid linoleum, the utility furniture, the curious upholstery (running his fingers as he reflected, over the dense knobbly undyed tweed of the chair-arm on which his arm, itself softly if soberly clothed, now lay)—they had all spoken of a life too near the bones of subsistence, too little padded, too severely worn. Of gloss there had been a certain amount, for polish had been cheap enough: in Nick's semi-detached it had glowed on trolley and sideboard and peach-coloured mirror, hiding poor quality in *éclat*, and in his own home it had been a veneer, a thin and penetrable barrier against scorn and decay. Cleanliness costs you nothing, his mother used to say: a statement not wholly accurate, as she must have observed herself when adding up her grocery bills. Bleach, disinfectant, furniture polish, shoe polish.

Polish on the furniture in this room, now he thought about it, was noticeably absent: the upright chairs were not polished but painted, the sideboard was a dusky gilt, the occasional tables on which people rested their glasses were painted metal, or marble. The glasses themselves, in opposition, shone; they were thick and modern, they enclosed strange shaped bubbles of air or dark refractions. There were even one or two pieces of Waterford crystal at large, gleaming in a more traditional manner, but thick, too, and heavy, with no sparing of substance, as there had been in the brittle pretty pre-war mock cut-glass best sherry glasses and best tumblers with which he had been familiar as a small child. All the garments in the room showed the same symptoms as well, from Diana's golden slippers upwards: there was an abundance, on the women, of velvet and lace and of fashionable peasant embroidery— so far removed, the peasant embroidery, in price and in effect, from anything that a real peasant might be expected to wear. How rich they all were. He sighed. It amazed him. Where did it all come from, this money, in this society that complained so often in its newspapers of its ailing economy, its national debts, its crippling taxes? He sighed again. He should have accustomed himself by now to these manifestations, but they remained obstinately foreign to him. And he himself, by what strange turns had he come to be sitting there, as well turned out as any of them, with shoes of their quality, and wads of bank notes stuffed carelessly in his pocket? Did any of them, in that room, share his surprise, his suspicion, his sad mistrust? Or was it that nowadays he knew only such people, like clinging to like? He had done what he had done, and it was a natural consequence that he should be sitting here, as he now was. Nick and he had both succeeded, though Nick's ascent had indeed been more honourable, for he had made money, not married it. He had made money, though by such easy lazy careless methods that Simon was inclined to think that Nick's world was a garden of idleness compared with the hours that he, at his different pursuits, was expected and obliged to work. A garden of idleness, the television world, where bright young middle-aged people stood about on burgeoning, sprouting carpets and drank large drinks and watched their own reflections, discreetly, in mirrors and eyes, and laughed at themselves with great good nature as though their simple wit (their only marketable commodity, and what a price it fetched) could buy them off, could buy them off from judgement. Amusing they were, amusing they knew themselves to be, but since when had a slight facility been a guarantee of an income such as his father and Nick's father had never dreamed of?

Diana had a cut-glass bowl full of marble eggs: she was holding one up now to the light, showing a man whom he thought to be a journalist the way in which the light shone through it, forbidding him, prettily, to admire another egg of a light orange because it was painted, but confessing to an affection for a blue egg—'it's not real either, but it was my first, my very first'—and permitting him, for sentiment's sake, to admire it too. 'But this,' she said, 'this—' diving to the bottom of the bowl, fishing out an egg that looked, from where Simon was sitting, to be quite black, 'this is the rarest of all.

9

Look, you see those markings? An uncle of mine brought it for me from Afghanistan, it was given to him by...' and her voice fell and faded, so that he could not hear the history of the egg—a history so characteristic of such gatherings, he knew without hearing it, quaint, charming, fey, old world, entirely pointless. And he knew, as he watched her standing there, her little hands clasping the egg, her head on one side, her face soft and radiant with the effort to please, that she and Nick could be making no great effort in their reunion—(apart from any other reasons, how could they be, when one of them was so thoroughly nice and likeable and desirable a woman)—because they were incapable of any real effort, any un-natural effort, as gracefully incapable as a climbing plant would be of growing erect alone. They had parted because it seemed the eas-iest thing to do, and because it seemed the easiest thing to do, they had come together again: and so again they would part, should cir-cumstances alter.

What a strange way of living. Perhaps he wronged them. Per-haps they were not like that at all. Significant, though, that this room should be so full of climbing plants: but how silly to say significant, for now he thought of it so was his own house, Julie was always buy-ing them, they must be the fashion. *It will not climb up on an arti-ficial host.* That was a phrase (he forgot what plant it described) that he had found in his bed-side gardening book. Which was Nick, an artificial or a natural host? The idea amused him so much that he turned to the girl sitting by him, thinking he could share it with her, but she, turning simultaneously towards him, embarked upon trade-union reform, no doubt having been pre-informed that he had a professional interest in such matters, so he was obliged to listen to her and to answer her, but he had heard and said it all so often be-fore that he was able to do it all with a very small part of his con-sciousness, leaving the rest free to continue to inspect the room. He assumed from the size of the gathering that he was nearly the last to arrive: not the last, however, for the numbers were not yet even. There would be another woman expected: another woman for him.

He wondered what they would try on him this time, remembering the last occasion when he had been invited out to dinner without his wife and had found there, like a risen ghost, a woman whom he had once admired for two whole years, hopelessly mildly and unrequited, and produced for him so much too late, laid on his plate like a peach or a slice of pineapple, yet still, even served up, with a ghost-like and sullen aspect, as unwilling and hopeless a prospect as ever, with the added disadvantage (unlike the comparable peach) of being no longer loved and no longer desired. What more useless than an image of a past goal, never attained and no longer wanted? It was an indictment of both past and present, like a dreadful dream he had once had, in which he had found himself in a room full of unread Dandys and Beanos—hundreds and hundreds of them, piles and piles of them, all virgin, all untouched, and had woken to find himself thirty, and the Beanos not even there. Surely she would not arise again, this ghostly creature, expecting to be wooed across such a muddy ditch? He would not put it past Nick and Diana: they knew her, she was unmarried, they were schemers, all of them. And then, as suddenly as the idea had arisen, he dismissed it: it was impossible, they would not wish so gloomy a creature upon their friend Julie his wife, they would be too frightened that they would never hear the end of it from her, they had not invited him with any motive at all, but simply to make up numbers, to fill a gap, because he was accidentally and conveniently spare, a polite and useful man. Nothing wrong with that either, nothing wrong with that: he was getting paranoid, he must do something about it: and the something that he did was to bend the whole of his attention to the earnest young woman, who was, amazingly enough, trying with an appearance of sincerity at least to persuade him to explain the elements of Rookes *v.* Barnard.

Nick and Diana must have given me a pleasant build-up, he thought, as he started to explain: she listened, intelligently, asking intelligent questions, nodding, smiling, thinking herself very good to be so interested, although so pretty, and he watched her pale oval face and her blinking false lashes—he hated false lashes, he really hated them—and wondered why she bothered. They moved on, shortly, to penal sanctions and contracts and discipline, and in a rash moment he made some analogy between parental and judicial discipline, and he saw her well-intentioned attention waver and struggle and finally lose itself: she had children, and she wanted to talk about children and how one should treat them, so they started to talk about that instead, and whether or not she should threaten her children with punishments that would never be fulfilled and whether such threats had any value: she was overcome with guilt, he drily noted, she had to confess, she had told one of her children before coming out to dinner that if it didn't shut up and get back into bed she would lock it in its bedroom—'I didn't *mean* it,' she was saying, 'I really didn't *mean* it, but I lost my temper . . .' and he knew that she needed condoning, and that she would have wrested any conversation on any topic whatever to this end: so he condoned, politely, confessing to parallel misdemeanours, doing in fact what was required of him, but as he did it he felt suddenly sick with himself, because he did not care, he did not really care, in fact he objected to being used as a confessional, he objected to the whole mechanism of self-denigration and comforting admissions that they were engaged in, because one had no right to cheer oneself up by such means, one had no right to sit so comfortably assuaging one's conscience and asking for forgiveness. Despite himself, he felt welling up within him an emotion so familiar and so unpleasant that it quite frightened him: he had not yet learnt how to forestall it, though with time he hoped he might (but what a long discipline ahead) and it was too bad to confess, too bad to share, it was not, like this girl's loss of temper, pardonable. It was an emotion of hatred. He hated it, he hated feeling it, but the hatred remained. He had come to hate people, even the people that he liked, like Nick and Diana and this pleasant pale girl, and he hated them, ignobly, because they were not his and he could not have them. They might smile and offer him invitations, but he hated them for it. He was filled with resentment, a resentment that respected no distinctions and no loyalties. It was impossible to struggle against it, impossible to remind himself that it was his fault, not theirs,—or rather not impossible to remind himself, because he did, constantly, he did, even now—but impossible to *feel* the reminder, impossible to feel sympathy even though he knew quite well the forms and words of it. He felt nothing, nothing but dislike and bitterness; unless to tell himself that the fault was his. It altered nothing, such knowledge. One could order one's features and one's responses so that it did not show, so that it caused no positive offence, but that was no salvation: one might behave impeccably, and still, if one had not charity, it would be of no avail. And he no longer had any charity, it had all dried up in him.

Suddenly, as he sat there talking about something quite different, he thought, 'I am embittered.'

And he knew that what he was, was precisely what the word meant, and that it was what he was. When people described other people as embittered, they were describing people like himself—embittered through failure, of one kind or another, and bitterly resenting those more fortunate. He could, as yet, conceal it, but what would happen when he became like those colleagues of his who could not mention a name without a disparaging remark, who saw the whole world as a sour conspiracy to despoil them of any satisfaction or success? And even if he managed to conceal it for ever, what a fate was that, to suffer and not to speak, to subdue one's resentment by reason, to exhaust oneself in concealment and the forms of charity? The continual suppression of impulse seemed an unredeeming activity, but he could not think of anything better to do, the impulses being so base.

He could pretend, perhaps, not to recognise them, but a suspension of recognition was beyond him: what had once been honesty, and what was now an unrelenting habit of introspection, denied a simple refusal to admit. He had to admit it: he disliked this girl for smiling at him, he disliked Nick because he was an old friend, and Diana because she was so kind to him, and the financial journalist talking to Diana because he was not married, and that other woman in the long velvet dress because she was divorced, and the man talking to Nick because he was married to the girl talking to him. He disliked them all, childishly, simply for being what they were, and he liked disliking them, he did not want to like them, he did not want people to be pleasant or generous or remarkable, because if they were, they too much condemned his cold heart for not warming to them. They put him in the wrong, either way, by their virtues, by their failings, and he resented them because they aroused his own meanness of spirit: there was a wicked flow from him, a contaminating flow, and all those people, and the pretty room with its candles and fringed shades and oval mirrors and embroidered carpets and peacock feathers was swamped by his ill-will, by his not liking his own liking of it.

But no, the room was not swamped, it was quite unaffected: he must remember that.

It was he himself that was swamped. A bad word, swamped: because what he was, was dry, dry as a bone. And he wanted everything to be as dry as himself so that he would not be reminded of thirst. That woman in the off-licence, how her evening's plans had rejected and excluded and judged him. There was nothing to be done about it, nothing, there was nothing in himself that could save him: there was nothing to be done in life, but to keep going, keep working—and work, yes, he always came back to this point because work could be done, adequately, even well, and without the need for the justification of tenderness he could still perform the acts—the laborious, technical, tedious, legal acts of care. It wasn't even the work that he wanted to do, but it was an approximation, it was satisfactory. He could, anyway, continue to do it, that at least was something. He knew where he had arrived, in his thoughts. He always came to the same place. He was familiar with the journey. And having got there, he said to himself; there is a feeling in me, in my brain, in my heart, so dull, so cold, so persistent, so ancient, that

I am growing fond of it, I look to it, I look forward to taking it out, at the end of this journey, I take it out and polish it like an old stone, I warm my hands on its coldness and it grows faintly warm from my hands and its much handling. If it weren't there, I would have nothing, I would be destitute: if I couldn't feel it now, as I sit here holding this clinking drink and lighting her cigarette, I would cease to be. It is precious to me, this dull and ordinary stone. It is always there. It is called resolution.

'HOW UNLIKE ROSE to be so late,' said Diana, uneasily, half an hour later: and it was evident, immediately, from the tone in which these words were spoken, that Rose was the honoured guest, the star, the sanction for the evening's gathering, and that her presence, thus transformed into absence, was threatening to turn itself into as great an embarrassment as her arrival would have been a triumph. 'I can't think what can have happened, should I give her a ring, Nick?'

'I don't know,' said Nick, who was helping himself to another drink, reluctant to allow his wife's anxiety to spread, but not quite sure, because himself anxious, of how he could contain it. 'Let's give her another five minutes, should we?'

'All right,' said Diana, brightly, thinking with panic of the cassoulet slowly drying, the salad slowly crumpling into its dressing, and, worst horror, the mousse beginning to sink. She was never very sure about mousse, it was usually all right but she didn't trust it, nor did she trust herself not to have another drink, out of desperation, and if she did she knew that she would probably start dropping things in the kitchen and burning her hands when she got things out of the oven. One disastrous dinner-party, just before Nick had left her, she had dropped the lid of the iron casserole on her foot, under the influence of a whisky too many, an accident which had proved amazingly painful, and which had in fact precipitated his departure, because when the guests had gone she had accused him of never helping to carry anything, and they had had a dreadful row, because he had said that when he did carry things she got equally angry with him for not staying and amusing their guests. She couldn't decide, either, and was becoming increasingly incapable of deciding whether she ought to go and start warming up the soup now, or whether that would ruin the soup too, and moreover make it too clear to Rose, when she did come, if she did come, that she was very late. On the whole she much preferred people not to realise that they were late because it upset her so much when they had to apologise. She ate an olive and tried to sit still. Nick, meanwhile, was embarking on the subject of Rose: she wished he wouldn't, because if Rose didn't come it would make them look so silly, like boasting that one had invited the Queen but unfortunately she hadn't been able to come. Not that Rose's status was exactly queenly, of course, and she really ought to trust Nick's instincts in these matters, because he usually did things all right, so she tried to say nothing as she heard him say to Simon, 'Do you know Rose Vassiliou?', as she watched Simon's very sad polite blank smile, as she heard Nick continue confidentially, 'Rose Bryanston that was, if you remember—' and watched, so expertly aroused, the faint responsive flicker of recollection in Simon's eyes—(Simon, surely, no reader of gossip columns, and yet surely not so removed from the world? No, not so removed, for he was replying in the affirmative, admitting his consciousness of Rose's existence—poor Rose, wherever could she have got to? and what a disaster that she was so late, when her chief card, as a guest, was her perfect unassuming propriety, her calm diligence, her—if one could use so portentous a word—her humility, and to be late was not humble, could not be called so)—and then, after all, she could suddenly sit still no longer, and had to rise up and drift, she hoped unnoticed, off into the kitchen, where she stared at the cold green soup in a mixture of disgust and hungry apprehension, leaving Nick, struggling as he was with a delicate evocation (possibly at any moment to be interrupted by its subject) of Rose's notorious past, to reflect upon her almost offensive calm and social tact.

Simon, listening to this highly allusive discourse, began by not bothering to try to connect with it, so sure was he that Rose Vassiliou was yet another visiting Greek singer or Portuguese actress or American intellectual, whose existence could in no possible way interest his own life (except as material to report to Julie, and that was the kind of obligation he tried to resist, seeing no reason why he should feed too often the passions in her that he disapproved, in much the way that one resents buying as Christmas gifts objects that one intensely dislikes oneself, despite the pleasure that one knows they would give to the recipient.) But as Nick continued to explain, evoking the absent Rose's virtues, he did begin, dimly, almost despite himself, to remember something of what he was being told: from ten years back or more, the story was, when they had all been young, and this Rose herself a little younger than they had been, because she had been under age, and that was what all the fuss had been about: she had been made a ward-of-court, being an heiress to some kind of hard commodity like steel or ships or glass, and having set her heart on marrying an unsuitable man. The results and details of this scandal he had quite forgotten: whether she had married, eloped, or submitted, he no longer knew: but he was aware that her name was still current, that the intervening ten years had not passed quite without event, though he could not work out what her name was now connected with—meths drinkers, prison reform, he vaguely thought it might be something of this kind— and yes, that was it, he had it now, it was all coming back to him, she was the girl who had given all her money away to the poor, or something ridiculous like that. He couldn't remember the details, but it had been something like that. Rose Vassiliou, yes, that was the name. Though who Vassiliou was, he had no idea—had he been the adventurer, from whom she had been so dramatically protected? The name sounded vaguely adventurous, and he pictured to himself a handsome Greek sailor, seducing a young, pretty, and impressionable heiress: though possibly quite wrongly, he knew, for there was nothing to prove that Vassiliou had not on the contrary been some subsequent shipping magnate, the punitive choice of an angry father. Whoever he was, he was clearly not expected to dinner this evening: he would have made the numbers odd. And Nick and Diana, for all their charming informality—Nick would never wear a suit, had not been seen in one for years—would never have permitted that.

Simon was speculating about wardship, and the possibility of family relations so bad that such dire acts of legal aggression could take place within them, and penal clauses in industrial relations bills, and the relations of law and goodwill, when the door-bell rang, and Nick, only just able to conceal his extreme relief, abandoned him a moment too hastily to answer it: and when Nick reascended the stairs with the well-heralded Rose, his first thought upon seeing her was a sudden, treacherous recollection of a remark that had been bandied about at the time of her wardship—that it was easy enough to see what the man in question was after, because it was certainly not her beauty. He had remembered the remark, because such remarks always obscurely pained him, making him more aware of his own lack of beauty: having a moral and sophisticated mind, he would endlessly discuss to himself the problem of whether the pain caused by such casual remarks about others was true sympathy, or really a transferred sympathy that was at its dark heart masochistic. And with these anxieties as a background, he was relieved to note that Rose Vassiliou's plainness—as she advanced towards him, her hand extended—was not pathetic, it did not move the heart to pity or to its sinister reverse: she touched at once something that was more like tenderness. She was small, her hand itself was small, and her face, childish yet anxious, was delicately mazed with the young wrinkles of her age—which, from the accidents of her publicised past, he could have accurately calculated, placing her in her early thirties, a little younger than himself

18

for he had read of her elopement (was it?) while at Oxford. She frowned as she smiled in greeting, her brow raising itself anxiously, nervously polite, aware that she had been late, remiss; and the wrinkles gathered into the descending thin curls—a row of them, lying straight across her high forehead, and her mouth strained slightly, with its pale lips, as though smiling were an effort of true goodwill rather than a natural effect of pleasure. Her hair was a pale and faded brown, that might once have been blonde, or which might even, prematurely, be a darker brown upon the verge of grey, and her eyes were grey: her whole face was so affectingly uneccentric, so conscientiously pleasant (so unadorned with lipstick or eye-lashes) that it was some moments before he noticed that her clothes were less complaisant, or if complaisant, then complaisant, to her hosts, in a different sense—for she was wearing a long dress eccentric enough by any standards, a tatty off-white embroidered and beaded dress, with fraying sleeves and an irregular hem line, and on her feet were very old fiat red leather shoes, bursting at the seams, and extremely worn. There was nothing dowdy or ugly about her dress: on the contrary, he had to recognise, once he noticed it at all, that she had a certain private elegance, an elegance so unworldly that it made the whole room, and all the other beaded dresses and peacock feathers and gold slippers in it, look suddenly too new, too bright, too good: too recent imitations of the gently decayed image that she so unostentatiously presented. She looked, because of age and softness, authentic, as ancient frescoes look in churches, frescoes which in their very dimness offer a promise of truth that a more brilliant (however beautiful) restoration denies. And yet it was almost impossible to resent her curious distinction: impossible even for him, so schooled in resentment: because she carried with her such an air of sadness, of lack of certainty, that to resent it would have been not an act of self-defence, but an act of aggression, of violent reproach. He would never have noticed her, had she not been drawn to his attention, deliberately, by Nick's carefully designed preamble—Nick, a perfect judge of such matters, had known that she required explanation, that her qualities would not speak for themselves, that an untrained or uninformed eye would never recognise her rarity without a label to point it out. Because she was insignificant. A modest, unremarkable looking person. So how could one resent a distinction that one might so easily have missed altogether?

Perhaps, astonishingly, she disarmed self-defence: or so he found himself thinking, as she took his hand, and smiled, and turned from him, slightly, to Diana, to accept a drink, and to say, as she drank a large mouthful of it, that she was sorry she was so late, and that she would take her drink in with her to dinner should dinner be ready, as she had delayed everyone, and that she nevertheless had to have the drink because she was so tired and so overwrought at being so late, though she was feeling better already at the very sight of alcohol and other people's faces. Diana, at this gesture of permission, disappeared to heat the soup, and Rose Vassiliou had time to expatiate upon her apology, though so delicately that she seemed to convey a sense of true pleasure in having at last arrived—'I couldn't get a taxi, you know, Nick,' she said, laying her hand on Nick's sleeve, a hand mazed he could see with fine dry lines—'I couldn't get a taxi because I live in such a ridiculous place—' and she laughed, expecting Nick to laugh, and turned to Simon, expecting the question which he duly asked. 'I live in such an absurd place,' she said. 'You wouldn't believe. It's way up behind the Alexandra Palace, have you ever been that way at all? No? Nobody ever has, it's quite astonishing. The taxi men don't believe my address when I give it to them, and so they forget to come— they say they're coming, but they don't come.'

He knew better, for some reason—for some clue she had given him, some covert signal—than to ask her why she lived where she lived: the interesting fact was interesting only if self-sufficient, it would bear no explaining—and so he had time only to make a comment or so upon the unreliable behavior of taxis before she was removed from him, and taken to talk to other people—other people who knew her already, he noted, from the tone of the greeting, and then in a moment, before he had time to do more than reflect on the insatiable congregating sociability of misanthropes like himself and people who lived behind Alexandra Palace, Diana appeared to summon them, at last, to dine. He was very hungry, as he had not eaten since lunch: an inadequate and hurried lunch on Fleet Street. And he found himself hoping, as they descended the stairs, that he might perhaps find himself sitting next to Rose Vassiliou.

He had not for so long experienced something like preference, something like a faintly favourable emotion, that he dispelled it from his consciousness most consciously: it would not do to fall too eagerly upon the neck of so shy and rare a visitant. He talked, instead on the way down the stairs, to the man who was a journalist: but nevertheless, at the table, it was beside Rose that he found himself requested to take his place. She was turned from him, as he sat, towards Nick, on whose right she was seated, and she remained so turned, except for a few brief swervings for salt or bread, until the soup was over: so he concentrated his attention upon his other neighbour, a tall divorced woman who said that she ran an agency for disseminating news upon artistic and social events: 'an official grapevine, you might say,' she said to him, flashing at him some very white and even teeth, and he could not tell if she were truly commercial in spirit, which he might have understood if not respected: or whether she truly interested herself in such matters. He suspected the latter, for there was something of the enthusiast in her manner, something both excitable and gullible, that he recognised from his domestic experiences: though this was perhaps merely a front, an attractive shine, upon the harder business of making gossip pay. He contented himself in listening to her, for he had little to say, being well aware that a mention of his own profession, even if offered in a spirit of polite exchange of information, would have created in her a response of instant, pitying boredom: so he listened, and asked questions—being quite well enough informed, alas, to ask the right questions—and from time to time, as he looked down at his green soup, he also looked slightly askance at Rose Vassiliou's hand, which was crumbling to pieces, with an untiring restless purposeless motion, the brown wholemeal bread on her plate. It interested him, this hand, and he remembered the touch of it in greeting: it had been light and dry, and the back of it was brown and slightly crazed like an old earthenware pot. He could not recollect that he had ever seen so fine a mesh of wrinkles, that had about them no suggestion of age, or of loosening of the skin: they were of the surface, like small scratches. The hand looked not old, but childlike. One nail only had been bitten: a confined neurosis, attached to the index finger. There was a ring on the middle finger with a white stone in it: a sardonyx. The hand hovered over the bread, restlessly plucking and seizing and crumbling, like a friend or a small bird.

When the soup plates had been removed, amidst conventional cries of appreciation, which Diana accepted quite graciously, already convinced that the casserole would prove inedible, Rose Vassiliou turned to Simon, correctly, and smiled a little anxiously— (eyestrain, perhaps, had caused that look of concentration, those hair-like crowsfeet)—and said to him, 'You were at college with Nick, I believe?' and he said that yes, indeed he had been, and at school too, oddly enough: 'You come from the North, then?' she said, 'I would not have known it'—and he and Nick exchanged glances, and both agreed that they had camouflaged themselves well. 'The North East, it was,' said Nick. 'The North East. Simon never goes back, do you, Simon?'

'I have no cause to go back,' said Simon. 'Everyone has moved. My mother lives near Hastings now, so there is no cause to go back.'

'You don't dislike it, then?' she said, left in dialogue with him because Nick's other neighbour had claimed his attention: and he replied, 'No, not particularly, but my wife does, and so we don't go—'

'Why does she dislike it?' said Rose, and then, thinking better of the question, attempted to disguise it by helping herself to some vegetables. But it was too late. He replied, saying that she disliked it because she too was from the same region, and had always hated it with a real passion, and now could hardly be dragged there for any reason. 'Sad, to hate the place where one was born,' said Rose, and he agreed that it was sad, but common, and asked her, aware of rashness, where she had been born herself. 'In the country,' she said, sighing, as though the phrase explained itself. 'In the country.' He found it difficult to interrogate her, aware that there were facts about her that he might have been expected to know, but she continued, after a pause, and after a sip of wine: 'I was born at our house in Norfolk.'

'And did you like it there?' he asked, wondering what violent wave had thrown her thence to the back of Alexandra Palace—a journey so much the reverse of his own, so different a shore upon which, in the middle of life, to find oneself cast—and she said, through a mouthful of beans, 'Oh yes, I liked it, how could one not like it? That's the trouble with nice places, one can't help liking them,'—and then she smiled, a smile full of a wish to please, and said to him, changing the subject from herself, afraid to bore (a sign he recognised) and said—'And you, what do you do here in London? You're not in television like Nick, are you?'

'How can you tell I'm not in television?'

'It's your suit, I think, it's too respectable. You're not offended, are you? I like respectable suits—and your hair, too, no, I can tell you're not in television. I don't *want* you to be in television, I want you to tell me about something quite different. You're not offended, are you?'—and her hand hovered near his sleeve, placating and gentle, and then returned to its dry crumbs—'Tell me what you do,' she said, managing to sound as though she might almost want to know. 'Tell me something new.'

'I could tell you about Trades Union legislation,' he said, 'for instance. I tried to explain it to somebody before you arrived, but she found it as dull as I'm sure you would.'

'Not at all, not at all,' she said, 'I am most interested in Trades

Unions, I am even not uninformed on the subject—but you're not a Trades Union man, are you? Surely not?'

'What will you allow me to be?' he said, watching her profile as she ate, watching her as she turned back to him, quite unusually susceptible to her interest, hardly yet beginning to guard himself against its ease, so careful was its expression: 'Why, you can be what you like,' she said, laughing, gesticulating with her free hand, 'you can be what you like, but tell me what you are, and in exchange I will tell you the story of my many careers—' and he, lured on by this truly interesting bargain, said, 'Well' (for how could such a statement go unprefaced)—'well, I'm a barrister.' And her smiling face, turned towards him, flickered and flinched as though a bright light had suddenly dazzled her fading eyes. It was unmistakeable: he saw it happen. She looked down at her plate, and he saw the food through her gaze suddenly unpalatable, though she had been eating with hunger until that moment: she pushed petulantly at a lump of chicken skin, she prodded a bean, she struggled quietly, and then she looked up again, chewing a piece of sausage the texture of which communicated itself to his own mouth, and said 'Ah yes, a barrister, that I wouldn't have guessed. And what have barristers to do with Trades Unions?'

It was so quick a transition, so cool a recovery, so useful an assumption of quite spurious naïveté, that he in turn wanted to lay his hand upon her sleeve, but he was not given to such gestures, so he made his own: and his own consisted of explaining quite seriously his own connections with industrial law. She listened, gravely, assenting now and then to some query, but so quietly that he could not tell whether or not she appeared to agree with him through politeness, through a genuine similarity of conviction, or because she was thinking about something else, about that something else into which the name of his profession had obtruded so disturbingly. He could still sense in her a whole area of sensitivity that he had unwittingly exposed and was now afraid to touch, so it was with some relief that he enlisted Nick's help—having seen Nick's head turn slightly as he heard the word 'compensation'—and Nick, sure enough, was quite happy to turn round and recount the only piece of litigation that had ever interested him, which was the consequence of an accident that his aunt had had while bicycling to work at a biscuit factory near Tynemouth in 1938.

Simon had heard the story many times before, but one could not deny that Nick recounted it with real wit: his aunt's pride in her important position, her delight at finding herself a precedent, her Cuttings Book of all the newspaper reports on her case, made a good anecdote. Simon always enjoyed it twice over—once, because he was the only person there who really appreciated the technical details and significance of the case—and then all over again, maliciously, because again, he was the only person there who knew exactly what this particular aunt meant in Nick's delicate social presentation of himself. Nick's social background was simple enough to describe in real terms: his father was a dispensing chemist in a miserable working-class district in Gateshead, and as such had enjoyed considerable local prestige, being, comparatively, a man of substance and learning. His mother had been a dressmaker, and her four sisters, of whom the bicycling aunt was one, had all been factory workers. Nick, throughout grammar school, where Simon had first met him, had laboured endlessly to upgrade his own background: the aunts were concealed, rejected, utterly denied. The more affluent aspects of his home life were peddled mercilessly: he had done a good trade, Nick had, during the war, at primary school, with Horlicks tablets, soda bombs, vitamin sweets, and other such lures for sweet-rationed youth. By the time he reached grammar school, he had stopped trading in sweets, officially, and started trading in his father's interest in nuclear disarmament, an interest which his schoolfriends found amazingly avant-garde and chic, for a father. Then he arrived at Oxford, sized the situation up in a trice, dropped his emancipated father, and started to trade in his working-class aunts. They were invaluable to him. He flaunted them at debates, bandied them about at parties, flung them at insolent girls at balls, crushed friends with them over a quiet drink in the pub. They were never, of course, allowed near the place: they worked better from afar. Simon was the only person who had ever met any of them. He wondered, sometimes, how Nick could bear to know what Simon knew about him. Was it connivance? For there were things that Nick knew about Simon as well, perhaps.

From industrial compensation, the conversation moved vaguely and generally on to the validity of cherished grievances: the North versus the South, workman and employer, Arabs and Israel, Northern Ireland, the rights of women. The journalist, who was sitting next to Diana, defended most ably the view that one cannot endure more than what passes in one's own lifetime, and that any claim to hereditary woe is a luxury: it was so much what Simon had once believed, and better put than he could have put it, that he listened with real interest. It was a good subject, the conversation was good, and yet at the back of his mind nagged the knowledge that he no longer thought it to be true, the line taken, and that people endure not one lifetime but many, layers and layers of evolved suffering handed down, worse than anything Freud had ever proposed in the way of predestination, and into his mind, as he tried, inadequately, to formulate something of this conviction, came a whole recollection so vivid that it startled him—his mother, standing next to him in church, looking down at him when she saw what the psalm for the day was, and saying to him crossly and primly and vehemently, her brow wrinkled with outrage, her hat bobbing insecurely as she bent to his low level—'Pay no attention to this psalm, it's wicked, it's ungodly, Simon. They shouldn't sing it in this day and age, they shouldn't really.' The psalm was the 137th Psalm, about the waters of Babylon, and its message was that the sins of the fathers shall be visited upon the children, and that the brains of the children of one's enemy should be dashed out upon the rocks. He too had believed the psalm wicked: wicked it was: but true. She had tried to undo it for him, his mother, she had tried to break the chain and untie the knot, but how uselessly, to what avail.

There was another dissertation on the same theme, in Ezekiel. She had pointed it out to him. Ezekiel too had tried to arrest the course of destruction. Thousands of years ago. Ezekiel had said, 'What do you mean, by repeating this proverb concerning the land of Israel "The fathers have eaten sour grapes, and the children's teeth are set on edge"? As I live, says the Lord God, this proverb shall no more be used by you in Israel. Behold, all souls are mine, the soul of the father as well as the soul of the son is mine!' He had made a brave attempt, that ancient prophet. The sour grapes, the crushing of grapes, and the battering of babies' soft skulls. Israel and Egypt, from generation unto generation.

When they had finished talking about Israel, he asked them what they understood by the term radical. What does it have to do with roots, he wanted to know—a cutting of roots, a planting of roots, a discovery of roots? They picked it up with interest, and went over it: he sat back and listened. Carrots and turnips, Cobbett and Burke, he was no historian, but it did seem to him that he and Nick had travelled rather too far too quickly. A radical ought to believe, must believe it possible to convert a nation within a generation, but could that ever be so? Where would he have been if his mother had not fed him pelican-like with her own blood? It was all very well, free higher education, education acts, grammar schools—was it not significant that of all the people round this table, he and Nick (Nick only by maternal descent) were the only two who might with any justice be called working class, and that they had arrived there because their parents—Nick's father, his own mother—had bent on their sons the peculiar weight of their own thwarted ambitions? From generation unto generation. Men do not spring out of the earth like soldiers from dragons' teeth, nor do they spring into and out of grammar schools with such abandon.

He found himself thinking like this more often these days. A sign of age, no doubt.

The others round this table, no doubt about it, had all had it made from birth. Some more than others, but they had all been born into possibility, into affluence. It was easy enough to tell. He was good at picking out masqueraders, being one himself. It was less easy with women, it was true—he saw less well the shades of their past, their pursuing furies, for they were obscured to him by their nice clothes and their nice bodies. But one could still tell.

So what, therefore, did it mean, that their views were so correct, so liberal, so progressive: what did it mean, that hardly a breath of dissension ruffled their faith in the progress of equality? Only the journalist demurred, and he was an economist, and therefore obliged, these days, it would seem, to breathe a note of sober pessimism: economists, Simon could not help noticing, had moved slowly to the right over the last year or so, like a moving backcloth, against which he stood, himself a stationary object: they rippled past, row after row, or so he thought, but maybe it was not so, maybe he met different people these days, or maybe, it was not inconceivable, maybe he had himself moved imperceptibly, without noticing it, towards the left? That could not be so, surely, one became reactionary with age. It must be the acceleration of the warned and the wise, fleeing some real or imagined disaster, that had left him standing. But he was in good company. All the rest of them, save the economist, were with him: there they sat, well-dressed, liberal, enlightened on the massive National Debt. Would it ever sink beneath them? There seemed little danger of such an event.

And he and Nick, two from amongst all those millions, had made it, after all.

The conversation fell to pieces when the woman who ran an agency could not resist introducing the fact (while they were on the subject of *Roots*) that there was to be a new production of *Roots* at the Oxford next month with of all people Myra Hallam in the lead, could one imagine: no, one could *not* imagine, yes, one would quite like some chocolate mousse, thank you very much, and did *she* know that Richard Boot was signed up to play the lead in Miroslav's new film? Simon tipped some cream on to his mousse and felt himself, unhappily, at home: so much at home that he even contributed some transatlantic news of the same nature, relayed to him the night before by his wife, news pertaining not to the theatrical but to the artistic world (could one distinguish, on such a level of operation, the two) and he was quite glad that the news, such as it was, had managed to find a more suitable resting place than his own memory. Little did he care what Adam had said to Julie about Paolo, or what prices were being asked for Cather's new pieces, or why Hannah set up on her own: but others cared or appeared to care, and he noticed with a faint rustle of apprehension that Rose Vassiliou, nibbling delicately at a leaf of watercress salad, its stalk pinched between two fingers like a flower, attached herself with as much curiosity to such news as anyone round the table: he had lost in her an ally, and yet he knew quite well that he would have been yet more alarmed had she withdrawn herself and silently denounced the tone of the conversation, for who had introduced it but himself? And how was she to know, how was anyone to know, that the kind of pleasure that he had once taken in such subjects had been converted, long ago and thoroughly, into an irretrievable boredom, in view of the fact that he spent a lot of energy in trying to conceal just such an impression? He concealed it too well by half, perhaps: a good job well done, and to his own undoing. But there was no harm in appearing to be interested in such cultural junk as was now being discussed avidly: it hurt nobody but himself. It was even an act of loyalty to absent Julie. He might as well demonstrate himself a husband in her absence as in her presence: in her presence, anyway, the act was no longer very effective, as she had learned to see through him, had indeed heard too many of his real views in private, to be taken in by a politely assumed attention. She knew perfectly well by now that his attitude towards many of her interests amounted to loathing: he loathed pop art, modern plays, television, owners of art galleries, interior decorators and modern furnishings with an almost undiscriminating passion. He loathed, in fact, people like this agency woman, facing him across the table with her dreadful braying toothridden bosom shaking laughter: and as he sat there, politely, at dinner, eating the last mouthful of his chocolate mousse, and trying to smile at some name-dropping tale about a well-known actress, he felt himself plunging into misanthropy, as a drunken man plunges suddenly into an awareness of being drunk. He tried hard to stop it, and its inevitable distortions, as a drunken man tries to still the waverings of trees and stony walls and picture rails and cornices: knowing it to spring from himself, ignobly: but such visitations are beyond the realm of the will, he could do nothing, he was helpless, he lowered his eyes to his plate and sat there, and it was with a sensation of profound physical relief that he saw Diana rise to her feet, and lead the way up the stairs.

Over coffee, he began to calm down a little: he made himself useful by handing round the coffee cups: and found when he had done so that there was only one possible place left for him to sit, which was next to the agency woman who was talking, in a low and intimate voice, to Rose Vassiliou. So he sat by her, yet again, and he could not help overhearing the conversation, so strident were her low tones: she was talking about her ex-husband, he gathered, and he was so confidently sure that it was one of those tedious, unsolicited, boring after-dinner confessions from one stranger to another that he was shocked—shocked, or in some way threatened—when he heard Rose respond to this confidence in terms not of polite sympathy but of familiarity and affection. He did not know why he had supposed these women strangers to one another, but when he heard Rose speak,—and what she said was 'But Maisie, you poor thing, you shouldn't put up with it, you should have rung me, you know—' he was shocked, as though his judgement were being judged, for one or both of these women he had maligned, they were friends, or at least concerned for one another, and he did not know whether he had to condemn himself for his judgement of the woman called Maisie, or whether to condemn Rose Vassiliou herself for the hopeless easy promiscuity of her sympathies, for her tone of genuine understanding, which must be assumed, which could not be real, or if real, how much more harshly was he himself excluded, to how dry a world was he more rigorously condemned by his own condemnations. They were friends, these two unlikely women: friends, interested in one another's affairs. He hated them both for it. He ached, he turned away. He had no affairs that could bear the violence of discussion, none that he could expose to the bright light of sympathy. He ached with loneliness. It was a good transition. Loneliness, dreadful enough, was in every way preferable to hatred. He envied those women their conversation and their sorrows. He envied them, he liked them for liking each other. He turned away, and talked to Nick about the new board room dramas in ITV.

DIANA, HER DUTIES AS A provider of food over, sat down in a corner of the settee and started to worry about how to get rid of her guests. Maisie was the only person likely to stay for ever, but as she lived more or less next door to the Wilsons she could surely pack her off with them in their car—what a mercy it was that Maisie had given up driving after that accident, when she drove herself she used to make a habit of sitting about until three in the morning waiting to get sober, under the impression that she was thereby relieving her hosts of a great anxiety—and Julian could probably be relied upon to leave quite promptly as she had heard him say to Nick that he had to fly to Frankfurt in the morning. It was only at this stage in the evening, however, that she really began to face the problem of what to do with Rose. Rose was mad, there was no doubt about it. There was no reason, of course, why one could not get a taxi for her, but it seemed so impolite, and also there was the money problem. The last time she had come Nick had driven her home, and

Diana hadn't liked that either, because he had done it with a little too good a grace. She had, now, to admit to herself that she had expected Simon would drive her home: it had seemed all right, last week, as a concept: but as the reality of it drew nearer it really did seem rather an imposition, to ask him to go miles out of his way. Most men it is true would probably quite like a chance to drive Rose home, but Simon was not like most men, and she found it quite impossible to tell whether he had taken to Rose or not: but hell, so what, at least one could always rely on him to be polite and do the right thing, she might just as well consign him to five miles of extra journey or whatever it was, as there was no other way out. He looked dreadful tonight, did Simon: as incapable of enjoying himself without Julie as he was incapable with her. She wondered whether he knew how miserable he looked—how offensively bored. She found time, now, to worry about him a little—though it was pointless, worrying about someone like him, he would never tell one anything, in a way she rather resented the real obduracy of his silence. Why didn't he forget about it one day and just complain? Everyone else did. But even to Nick, Nick said, he didn't complain. It was annoying of him, this discretion, it was inhuman, it even made one suspect from time to time that after all he hadn't got any feelings, that he was not so much suffering (which would be understandable and vaguely pleasing) as insensitive (which would have reflected no credit upon anyone). And then, as if to counteract such a suspicion, he would give one of those anguished glances, or crack one of those very slightly bitter jokes, or make one of those generalised but savage remarks about the futility of progress or the turpitude of mankind, and she would know again where she was, happy again, for she found such remarks (she didn't quite know why) exhilarating. She took such remarks, such glances, as signs of vulnerability, as appeals, and she prided herself on her sensitivity to them. She liked, passionately, to be liked, to be thought worthy of confidence, and having despaired of any more intimate confessions she was happy to accept such moments of emotion as came her way: guessing (correctly?) that such was his only method of communication, that no others were more honoured or more favoured than she, and that she herself, because more awake to him, because more awake to people altogether, saw more than most.

She was tired. She was beginning to think it was time that people left, but they were all talking about Germany, a subject that did not interest her at all. It did not interest Maisie, either, she could see, for Maisie had gone unnaturally quiet and was starting to heave restlessly in the depths of her chair. The men, of course, were absorbed in the topic: she often wondered what satisfaction they found in exchanging such dry pieces of information, such probably inaccurate platitudes. Gwenda, of course, was rigid with intention, with the effort to show that she was taking an intelligent interest, and really she wasn't holding her own too badly: although a glaze of boredom had covered her eyes, she was still managing to ask apposite questions, and even at one point was able to volunteer a small fact. Rose was listening, simply listening, she too looked tired, but she was too well bred (quite literally so, thought Diana with great satisfaction at the thought) to fidget or sigh. I will offer her another drink, thought Diana, but didn't, because she knew that any move on her part at this juncture would be interpreted as a signal for departure, and although she was exhausted and longing for them to go, she needed them too much to want to stay to be able to take any steps to precipitate their going. They would leave, in the end, of their own accord, she only had to sit and wait: so she sat and waited, and in the end the Wilsons said they must get back to their baby-sitter, and everyone started to struggle to their feet—and amazingly enough, now the note of reprieve had sounded, she suddenly found herself anxious to retain them, to retain at least some of them (though it was with relief that she heard someone offer and Maisie accept a lift)—because she could not bear to think of them all going away, their separate ways, and discussing with one another as they went her cooking, her house, her dress, her marital problems, and leaving her out of these discussions, leaving her with the cigarette ends and the unwashed dishes, leaving her, quite simply, because they had had enough of her and wanted to go home. So she started, hopefully, to offer more drinks, but it was too late, they were all determined upon departure, except Rose, who sat quite still in her chair, evidently not knowing how to set about leaving. Simon was on his feet, and she wondered, as she received the Wilsons' thanks, whether she should say anything to him about giving Rose a lift, but luckily she did not have to, because she saw that he had noticed the situation, that he was waiting to offer, politely, as she had always known he would. And when the others had all gone, there he still was, looking anxious and obliging. 'Are you sure you won't have another drink?' she said to Rose, thinking that perhaps after all she might detain these two for a little while, but Rose shook her head and smiled and said that no, she really ought to be going, she didn't like to be out too late because one of the children was always waking in the night and she ought to be there in case. And Simon, hearing this, said, let me drive you home, and Rose said of course not, she would get a taxi, and Simon said that it would be no trouble, and Rose said that it was miles and miles away, but she was looking so tired that it was clear that at the next offer she would accept, as indeed she did. So she had to relinquish them, though they stayed for a few moments to talk to Nick, who had come upstairs again from seeing the others off at the door: and then they departed together, as she had arranged, and left her feeling obscurely cheated.

She went into the kitchen to pour herself a glass of water, as she was dying of thirst—perhaps everyone had been dying of thirst, perhaps that was why they had all gone home, to get themselves from their own taps the drinks of water which she had not thought of offering. And as she stood there, gazing into the debris in the sink, a wave of panic filled her: so pointless it was, such an evening, such a stupid life she led, such stupid frivolous aspirations, and they had all gone away and left her, her part was finished, she would drop from their minds as casually as a leaf from a tree, as naturally unregretted, having played her part, having fulfilled her role, she would drop from their minds as from this story, having accomplished nothing, set nothing in motion—or if something had been set in motion, how terrifying, how alarming, she was not able to cope with consequences, she did not like to think that anything would happen, nor that nothing would happen. What was it for, she asked herself, as she rinsed out the clean watery glass, what was it for, and why would she do it again the week after next?

IN THE CAR, driving northward, Simon wondered silently to himself if he should make conversation. She looked tired, this woman, perhaps she did not want to talk. Perhaps, on the other hand, she did. How could one possibly tell? It would not have crossed his mind to resolve the problem by speaking because he himself preferred to speak, by maintaining silence because he himself preferred silence. He had never known such elementary simplicity, it was so alien to him that he could not even conceive of it in others, though he had from time to time, with faint astonishment, observed its existence. He imagined to himself, in his embarrassment, that her mind must too be occupied embarrassingly with the same preoccupation, and he hated the proximity of two anxious people in so small a space. So that when, finally, after five minutes or so, she spoke, the sound of her voice took him aback no less than her words. She sounded as though she had been thinking, not of something or anything to say, but of how to say exactly what she now came out with. With deliberation she said, as though she had been working on it in those five minutes.

'You're a lawyer, you said? A barrister?'

'That's right.'

She sighed, heavily, and then said, 'What I need is a lawyer.'

'I don't suppose I'd be able to help you,' he said. 'I don't suppose industrial law would be of much use to you.'

'Not exactly,' she said, vaguely, pursuing her own thoughts. 'No, not exactly.' And then she said, recklessly, horribly, as though throwing herself off a height, or upon his stony mercy, 'I had a letter today from my solicitor. About the children. My husband says he wants them back. And another one from him, half an hour later. He says he's going to make them wards-of-court.'

'To make them what?' he said, hardly able to believe that he had heard aright.

'Wards-of-court,' she repeated. And as she said no more, he was left to comment.

'It's not possible,' he said, inadequately. And then, more helpfully, 'It can't be serious, it must be some kind of threat.'

'That's what I try to tell myself,' she said. 'But it might be serious, after all. You don't know my husband. The kind of things he does.'

This was so evidently true that he did not think himself equipped to comment. So there was silence again, until she continued.

'The letters were sent round,' she said, 'by messenger. Which made it seem serious. And also urgent. But I haven't done anything. I didn't know what to do.'

'Perhaps,' he suggested, 'it was just an impulse?'

'It probably was,' she agreed. 'But you have no idea how he persists in his impulses. Once he has had one he is so loyal to it, it is quite terrifying. Once these things have been set in motion there is no stopping them. They go on and on, and everything is quite caught up in the process.'

'A lot of people,' he said, without much faith, 'make gestures. Start things they have no intention of finishing. They threaten something they have no wish whatsoever to do. Or so I have often found.'

'Yes,' she said, 'I know some people are like that. But we have never been like that, we have always pursued everything to the bitter end. It's something about the law, it makes it so hard to stop once one has started. I sometimes fear...'—and her voice, which had up to this point been remarkably steady, began now to thicken and dampen—'I sometimes fear that we have gone too far ever to restrain ourselves from anything. For him, every threat becomes immediately a reality. There seems to him no point in not doing anything. He is not reasonable.' She began to cry. 'I am afraid,' she said, 'that he actually likes it now. The solicitors. The letters. The publicity. He is determined to win, in the end. Oh dear, oh help, I am so sorry to cry like this, I feel so sorry for you, I knew I was going to do this to you the moment you offered me a lift home, in fact quite considerably before because it was obvious much earlier that you were going to have to offer me a lift, and there I sat knowing that the moment I got away from Nick's I'd start to cry all over the place. I can't help it, I always tell everybody everything, it's a terrible habit, it really is.'

'That's all right,' he said, 'I don't mind.'

'You probably do mind,' she said, 'but you're too polite to say so and I quite frankly am too miserable to care.'

She blew her nose, and looked at him, the tears pouring down her cheeks quite copiously. 'Well, no,' she said, amending her last statement as she briefly met his eye, 'I'm not too miserable to care, but I'm too miserable to stop. And I really am sorry. But I must tell somebody, I had to tell somebody, and I couldn't there, with all those people there.'

'I don't mind,' he said again, foolishly, but this time she took him up on it, saying almost eagerly, as though it were some rare generosity that had prompted him, 'Don't you really? That is so kind of you.'

Then there was a silence: she was still weeping, and in fact her sobs seemed to be gathering momentum, not slackening, so he said, a little late perhaps, as though he had sensed at once, though dimly, the length, if not the sorrow or delights of what lay ahead, knowing as he sat there that he must give himself over to it, that he must allow it to happen, this quite accidental connection—he said, 'You'd better tell me all about it.'

'Would you mind very much if I did? Perhaps we could wait until we got back and then I could show you the letter and you can tell me what you think of it.'

'That would seem a sensible thing to do,' he said. 'And now, please do stop crying, it is beginning to make me feel quite dreadful.'

'Is it really? I am sorry. Have a cigarette.' She fumbled in her bag and produced a packet of Woodbines, an offering from which he would in any other circumstances have withdrawn, but as it was he took one. She watched the trembling of his hand as he lit it.

'On the other hand,' she said, 'perhaps I could begin to tell you about it now, as I have made it quite impossible to talk about anything else.'

'If you would like to.'

'I wouldn't know where to begin.'

'At the beginning?'

'How could one possibly remember the beginning? It seems to have been going on for ever, I seem to have been struggling through legal nightmares all my life, first that awful business when I wanted to marry him, and then the divorce, and the rows about the money, and then this business, I can't face any more of it. I'll have to get another solicitor, I could never look mine in the face again. Perhaps you can recommend me a solicitor. Oh hell, I've completely finished off this handkerchief, you haven't got a Kleenex or anything have you?'

'There's a whole box in the back,' he said, and she reached for it, and then sat there, pulling pieces out and dabbing and recommencing.

'I've never seen anything like it,' he said, with admiration. 'You really do know how to cry, don't you?'

'It's a special talent,' she said. 'Very good for me, and I always feel much better after it, but it makes everything terribly wet.'

'Come on, now,' he said, starting forward from some wet and gleaming traffic lights. 'Tell me. When were you divorced, who divorced whom for what, and what did the court say about the children?'

'How business-like you are,' she said, gratefully. 'Say all that again.'

'Who divorced whom for what?'

'I divorced him. For cruelty.'

'Did he defend it?'

'He did, actually. It was a horrible scandal.'

'I'm sorry. I know that you might feel that I ought to know. But I never read much about scandals.'

'Don't you really? I read every divorce case I ever see. And every custody case. Whenever they reach the papers. I must have known it, you see, I must have been expecting this all the time...'

'Why did he defend it?'

'I don't know. Why do people? Out of vindictiveness. Out of outrage. I don't know, but he was quite right, something always sticks, however innocent one is, and anyway, he knew how to make me suffer, I can't really blame him for wanting to make me suffer, can I?'

'I wouldn't know. I don't know much about it yet.'

She smiled at him, suddenly, very nicely.

'You poor thing, I bet you don't want to, either, do you? I bet you wish you were safely home in bed, don't you?'

'Well, not exactly. I can't deny that you're upsetting me, but then you probably wouldn't like it much if I were quite indifferent, would you?'

'No, not really. But you needn't get too upset, after all, it's such an accident that it's you here and not anyone else, isn't it?'

He was silent at that, not quite sure that he cared for her diminishing of his arbitrary role, especially as its accidental nature seemed in no way to restrain her from the most violent onslaught upon his sympathy—a claim, a demand, politely and diffidently enough expressed, but evidently quite relentless and insatiable. And she, sensing his reserve, continued.

'Of course, I would like you to be sympathetic, but I wanted you to know that I see that you have to be. I wouldn't like you to think that I am in the habit of making a nuisance of myself. Though perhaps I am, really, perhaps I am. And also—' and here her voice stuck, as though she couldn't get the sentence out, and it came out very coldly and a little high, '—Also, I am aware that there are different points of view, there are two sides to every case. You might not necessarily agree with my way of looking at it at all. And if you don't agree, you must say so.'

'My dear lady,' he said (for some unknown reason), 'you needn't feel that I will be interested in seeing any side of the case but yours. Why should I? But if you were to bring yourself to tell me a few facts, I might be able to offer you a more useful form of sympathy, don't you think?'

'In the form of legal advice, you mean? I'm terrified of lawyers, you know, when you said you were a barrister at that dinner I nearly fainted, I thought—I don't know what I thought, I thought you'd been planted there by him, or else that Nick and Diana somehow knew all about it and had invited you for just such a purpose as this, and then I told myself not to be so silly, it only happened today, nobody could possibly know, and then that journalist as well, I don't trust journalists either.'

'You'll have to start giving me directions soon,' he said, looking ahead at the unfamiliar streets. 'I don't know this part of London.'

'No,' she said. 'Nobody does.' She started to laugh. 'That's one of the things everyone's got against me, they think I'm mad to live in such a place, but I like it, I really like it. Left, here.'

'How long have you lived here?'

'Ever since I was married. Eleven years. We came here at the beginning. I couldn't leave, now. Next on the right.'

'Don't you find it depressing?' he said, depressed himself by the rows of identical houses, the endless curving streets, the ugly squat inelegantly-gabled terraces, the dark breath of urban uniformity, petty eccentricity and decay.

'Depressing? No, not at all. I know it, you see.'

'And that makes a difference?'

'Of course it makes a difference. I hated it at first, I hated it for years, but I believed in it, and now I love it.' She gestured, suddenly, with her small light hand towards the passing streets, and said, 'All this, you see, I created it for myself. Stone by stone and step by step. I carved it out, I created it by faith, I believed in it, and then very slowly, it began to exist. And now it exists. It's like God. It requires faith.'

He was silenced. Listening to his silence, she said, equally suddenly and quite diffidently, as though used to defeat, 'If you see what I mean.'

'I don't see what you mean,' he said, 'but it's quite astonishing to hear you say it.'

'I'm not boring you?' she said, anxiously, but without any real fear. 'It is interesting, isn't it? And anyway, even if it isn't, you must listen to me. Please.'

'Yes,' he said.

'It's the next turning on the left,' she said. 'Number eighteen.'

THE HOUSE, INSIDE, was not what he had expected: it could not have been, for he had expected nothing, his mind having ceased to project any images upon this woman, who dealt him so lavishly such an alarming series of blows, who offered him so generously such surprising gifts. Gifts, her words were, her confidences. They could not be rejected: he sat there, in the shabby armchair, quite burdened with them, holding a cup of tea and a piece of fruit cake and copies of her various legal wrangles. He could hardly concentrate on these latter objects, so taken was he with everything else about him, with Rose herself sitting in a rocking-chair with a mangy cat upon her knee, with the flowered walls and litter of teddy bears and unwashed cups, with the crocheted tea-cosy on the teapot, with the peculiar objects upon the mantelpiece. He couldn't at first work out why the room was at once so strange and so familiar: it was so entirely unlike his own home, or the homes of any of his friends or colleagues, but at the same time he recognised it, it was a known landscape, its very dimensions—for it was small, low, overcrowded with furniture—were reminiscent of somewhere intensely remembered. He sat there, his eyes resting blankly upon the names of Christopher Vassiliou and Rose Bryanston, and their painful efforts to engage and disengage themselves, and suddenly he had it: it reminded him, this room, of his grandmother's house. The tea-cosy, the bundle of knitting, the ticking clock, the armchairs, the round tin tray, they were all objects that he had not seen for years, and here they all were, well worn, well used, lived with. He could not have said why the similarity, or rather the perception and recognition of it, so pleased him, as he had never cared for his grandmother's house after very early infancy: he had found it cramped, oppressive, smelling of cats and bad cooking, and too full of deadly whiskery unfeeling menacing embraces. Perhaps it was the absence of embraces that made Rose's house, in contrast, so soothing: she for sure was not going to seize his head and pinch his cheek and grind his nose upon her buttoned cardigan, and he did not see that he was called upon to make towards her advances that would have been only slightly less shocking. Sitting there in her rocking-chair she looked untouchable in some way that at this stage was a vast relief: she looked contained within herself, her body—hands, arms, head, neatly-crossed legs—all a part of its own self, not reaching out or pleading in any direction. She was miserable, it was true, and had, in the car, been almost distraught: she had moreover appealed for assistance and thrown herself upon his goodwill in a way that should have been disquieting, but the fact remained that there was nothing unquiet about her, and he could sense nothing underground or subversive in her appeal. Some people, simply by existing, struck him as subversive, and he recoiled from them in alarm, knowing himself quite unable to respond to their dark calls and silent conspiracies—unable, unwilling, he was never sure which, and it was this uncertainty that he disliked most of all. But this woman, although in a sense imposing quite brazenly upon his time at this time of night, was in some other sense most reassuring: her tears in the car, which he had found distressing at the time, were now completely over, and she felt, as she had said she would, clearly better for them. Her distress, her sorrow, her embarrassing confessions were not embarrassing at all, because it was as though she had so come to terms with them that she could afford to sit there, rocking gently backwards and forwards, while he read or pretended to read these painful documents about her private life. Her manner in distress, like her lack of beauty, held no threat, no offence, no violence. He envied her: sometimes he thought that his very appearance was an affront to others, as that of others was to him.

And then again, he said to himself, how useless are these speculations: perhaps I am merely rationalising to myself the relief of finding that I am not expected to make a pass at her. It was so difficult to know, these days, as a man, what was expected of one: he had little sympathy with women who would moan at him from time to time that they found themselves living in a world without rules, because the one rule that seemed quite clearly to remain was the rule that instructed a man to make the first move. The circumstances in which the move could be made had altered vastly, it was true, and took some learning, but then in his case they would have taken some learning anyway, so different were all the circumstances in London from those in which he had been reared. It would have been as difficult, or as easy, for him to have learned the rules of Victorian or Edwardian London as those by which Nick and Diana and other such friends appeared to conduct their lives. It did not often happen to him to find himself driving a woman home from parties, but when, occasionally, he did, he found it little use to know that one might casually embrace any single, divorced, separated or accidentally solitary person—because that solitary person, for any mixture of reasons, including simple reluctance and dislike, might quite easily refuse the embrace in a quite painful way. Not that he had ever tried it, but he knew himself well enough to know that women must find him as unquieting and ambivalent and underhand in intention as he found them. He had quite often wanted to try it, but had never done so, afraid both that he might like it and might not like it if they said yes, and knowing that he would quite disproportionately hate it if they said no. Even Diana, an old friend and wife of an older friend, afflicted him in this manner: it was not for a moment that he expected that she expected or wanted him to make any step towards her, it was just that he felt in her such an area of dissatisfaction, at times, such a pull of inadmissable emotional craving, that he could not be at ease with her. Nor, he knew, could she with him, because he was the same as she was: dissatisfied, uncontained. He repressed these dissatisfactions more rigorously than most, but feared that the repression made him even worse company. Because he disliked the lack of ease. Some people, he knew, thrived on it, and could not support any relationship that was not uneasy, tense, unfulfilled. But he, denied both peace and pleasure in lack of peace, was obliged to live in negation. It was not very good for him. But he did not see what else he could do. There was nothing else he could do. And it was for these reasons that he felt something unusually like contentment as he sat there, fulfilling a legitimate need, helpfully attempting to apply his mind to Rose Vassiliou's problems: problems that seemed to him, the more he read of her papers, to be quite severe. It was a wonder that she could sit there so calmly, without fidgeting, calmly stroking her dirty grey cat.

'What do you make of it?' she said, when, finally, he looked up. 'Do you make anything of it? It's a bit late to get one's mind round that kind of thing, I suppose.'

'It is a bit late,' he said, 'and also very complicated. I should have to think about it, before I could really say anything helpful.'

'But I ought to do something, oughtn't I, about that letter that came today?'

'You should really have handed it straight over to your solicitors. You'd better send it round in the morning.'

She sighed.

'Yes, I suppose I should. I can't really face them again, but I suppose I'll have to.'

'They seem to me,' he said, 'to have looked after you quite well. They're a good firm, you know.'

'Do you know them?'

'I know Jeremy Alford, slightly. Do you get on with him all right?'

'Yes, I suppose so.' She waved her hand about and then started to tug anxiously at an escaping lock of hair.

'It's just,' she said, 'that one does hate to bother them again. They were so helpful and nice, it seems awful to start bothering them all over again.'

'But that's absurd, you mustn't look at it like that. That's what they're there for, it's their living, it's their bread and butter, that's how they keep going. It's money to them, you know, not trouble.' He looked at her, and then, hoping he had got her right, taking a slight chance, said, 'In fact, you know, this kind of thing, I'm afraid to say, lawyers find peculiarly interesting. They actually enjoy an interesting case like this. It's not very nice of them, in one way, but quite useful, in another.'

She brightened: he had been right. 'Yes,' she said, 'I did used to notice that other people enjoyed it. The barrister thought my divorce case was frightfully interesting, it made me feel much less of a nuisance, in a way. At least somebody was getting something out of it. Like doctors and rare diseases, I suppose.'

'They'll probably be delighted to hear from you again. In their sadistic way.' She smiled, amused. 'It will be to them,' he said, presuming on success, 'like the sequel in some particularly thrilling serial.'

'Yes,' she said. 'I suppose that they might quite reasonably look at it like that. That's quite comforting. I only hope—' and she hesitated, at some genuine anxiety—'that the press don't come to look at it that way. There's no reason why they should get to hear of it, is there? They are always so interested in everything I do, for some reason.'

'I can quite see why they are interested,' he said, looking back at the papers, as though for confirmation. 'What you have done is, really, rather strange, you know. But I don't imagine they will get on to this. It will probably come to nothing, anyway. Your husband— wouldn't tell them, would he?'

'How well you seem to know him already,' she said, with a faint wash of despair, that dislodged the cat from her knee. 'But no, I don't think so. He would have done, once, but now he's become far too respectable. And too clever, too, I imagine. He is very good at picking up the proper ways of doing things. You should have seen how quickly he learned about witness boxes. If people did get to know, now, he wouldn't let it be known that he had told them.'

'I don't think, then, that there is much danger.'

'And do you think—' and here she leant her head back, and shut her eyes, '—do you think that there is any chance, any chance at all, of his getting the children? There isn't, is there? Could there be?'

'I wouldn't have thought it possible,' he said, quickly, instantly, not allowing himself to think about how to reply. And then, thinking a little more, of something to say—'Do you think he really wants them back?'

She shook her head, rocking it backwards and forwards on the back of the chair, not opening her eyes.

'I don't know. I really don't know. I've been asking myself, all day. I don't know.'

The subject having been opened, he had to go on with it, though he would rather have left it and continued to reassure.

'Had you any suspicion that this kind of thing would happen? How has he been towards the children since the divorce? He had,

I assume—' and again he pretended to consult the papers on his knee '—reasonable access?'

'Yes. He used to come and take them out. Every other Sunday. And he used to take them on holidays sometimes. He wasn't really allowed to, I don't think, but how could I stop him? It was—not very good. He used to spend so much money on them. And with my not having it, and not wanting them to have it, it was . . . very difficult.'

'And so you protested?'

'No, I didn't protest. I don't protest. How could I? I could only go on doing what I was doing. I don't expect every one else to do the same. I don't expect it. But sometimes—it becomes impossible to go on doing what one has to do. If other people are determined to prevent one.' She paused, and sighed. 'He took them out last Sunday. I wasn't here. I left them with the woman next door, for him to collect. And he brought them back to her. That's how it was.'

'I see,' he said, this time genuinely consulting the wad of correspondence, 'that you refused to apply for maintenance, against your solicitor's advice?' At this, to his relief, she smiled, with true amusement.

'Yes, I did, I refused. It would have been too silly, really, me having maintenance from him, wouldn't it? I simply couldn't see why they wanted me to apply, it was too absurd, in the circumstances, and they kept saying it was normal and would make things easier and that if I didn't want the money I could give it back again or not take it or something. But I've had enough of giving money back again.' She started to laugh. 'I must have got rid of more money than anyone my age ever has. It's quite a problem, I can tell you, though so different from most people's that I never get very much sympathy for it. But when I thought of the terrible time I had getting rid of all those thousands, and what a disaster it all turned out to be, I really couldn't face claiming ten pounds a week or whatever it would have been from Christopher. It's not as though I've managed to get rid of everything yet. There's another great lump due in a few years, when I'm thirty-five, that nobody could do anything about, and then I've got hundreds of square miles of pineforest or whatever it is in Norfolk. I must go and have another look at it some day. Not that it brings me anything in, that was the whole point of it, that was why my father bought it, so I wouldn't be able to touch it, but it's all there, growing away, and some day somebody's going to have to do something about it.'

'Then what, may I ask, do you live on?'

'You may *ask*,' she said, still laughing, 'you may well *ask*, and I might as well tell you that there was a day when I'd have been deeply embarrassed to tell you, I thought it was so embarrassing to be able to live at all, in this world. But I've grown up a bit since then, I'm not quite as mad as I used to be, you know. No, the truth is, that when I gave all that money away, eight years ago or whatever it is, I kept enough to give me enough to live on, in income. Or I thought it was enough, the idea was that it would be just enough. It was so farcical, you should have seen me, sitting down and working out what the national average income was, and what the level of national assistance was, and all that kind of thing—so stupid, I always had to do it all myself because no accountant would ever help me, accountants really can't bear to let one give one's money away, they simply wouldn't be a party to such a ridiculous enterprise, so in fact I made some rather strange miscalculations, and I meant to leave myself with fifteen pounds a week and in fact left myself with more like eighteen pounds ten. But even that, as you can well imagine—or as I can *now* imagine you can imagine, though it's the kind of calculation I was as bad at as I was bad at investments—that really wasn't enough, so in fact since Christopher left I've been doing a variety of odd jobs. I did dinners at the school, and I supervised the launderette, and stuff like that—bloody badly paid jobs, they were— once I thought I ought to do something a bit more ambitious and I worked for the publicity man on Act for Racial Harmony, but it was so horrid and everyone pestered me so much that I gave it up. But in fact, you see, one can live quite magnificently on eighteen pounds ten, especially when one has wealthy friends like me. I get asked to so many things, I could live for free, I sometimes think. And I *have* to go to a lot of the things because they're all good causes, and I can't say no. And also I have a lot of good friends who are really intelligent like Nick and Diana, who don't seem to want anything from me, and at the same time are very good at helping me to deal with the rest of the world.

'So I live quite well. Though some people might not think so.'

He had tried hard to follow this, while she was speaking, but had already recognised that he would have to study her past transactions in peace and quiet if he was ever to understand them: and he truly failed to understand her reference to the intelligence of Nick and Diana, though perhaps it had been an oblique compliment to his own polite attention. Or perhaps she had seriously intended it.

Perhaps she judged Nick and Diana from a standpoint utterly different from his own. Perhaps he had failed, himself, to appreciate them. Though what right had she, suddenly, like this, out of the blue, to imply superior intimacies, superior illuminations? He felt once more, welling up in him, uncontrollably, suspicion, distaste, anger. If Nick and Diana understood her so well, and she them, why had she not stayed behind to talk to them, instead of forcing him into the role of confidant, instead of conning him by her doubtless professional confidences into movements of true sympathy?

One would have had to be hard-hearted enough to resist, as she had quite well known: but then that was what he was: hard-hearted. Hard-hearted and also weak. She had probably seen it at once. He cleared his throat, shuffled the papers back into their battered folder, and said, nastily enough, picking up her last remark.

'Yes, I daresay you do manage quite well, but nevertheless I think you ought to get in touch with your solicitor first thing in the morning. I think that's the best advice I can possibly give.'

She did not look at him: she looked at her hands folded in her lap.

'Yes,' she said, evenly. 'Yes, I am sure you are right. It is very kind of you—to have taken so much trouble.'

And she looked up at him: their eyes met. He could see that the change in his tone had registered profoundly, and he wished, immediately, that it had not.

'I am so sorry,' she continued, 'I ought never to have kept you up so late. But I can't tell you how grateful I am to you, for having listened to me. I had to talk about it, and it was so kind of you to listen. But one ought not to inflict one's problems on other people, I suppose, it is very inconsiderate.'

'Of course not,' he said, attempting warmth, to no avail. 'I am very glad that you told me. I am only sorry that I cannot be of more use.'

'You have been very helpful,' she said, hopelessly. She had abandoned him, she had cast him out, and it was by his own choice that he had been expelled, from this warm room and intimate, redeeming, cluttered pool of light. She had had no choice: he had demanded it. He saw it very clearly. It was this, his damnation: to know the bias of his nature, to know its dangerous weighting, and to be quite incapable, quite helpless to redress it. He had known he had misjudged her: he had known himself to be neither conned nor trapped but on the contrary trusted: and he had nevertheless rejected trust, and had thus pointlessly hurt her. He struggled: it was too late, but he struggled, he tried to go back, and when he spoke it was to make the only amends he could, the amends of dry justice.

'Perhaps,' he said, 'there is something more that I could do. If I think of anything, I will let you know. Of you could give me a ring, if you needed me. Anyway, I hope you will let me know what happens.'

It would have taken a miraculous generosity to respond to the coldness of this offer, and he hardly expected her to do anything other than flinch, having once recognised, as she so clearly had, his treacherous withdrawal, and being unable to recognise, as she must surely be, his desire to withdraw his withdrawal: but, amazingly, she looked at him again, and smiled with an extraordinary niceness, and said, warmly, with enthusiasm,

'You *are* nice, you really are so kind, and I have been so awful, dragging you out here and giving you nothing but a cup of tea. How awful I am, I am so selfish, and I try so hard not to be.'

'You gave me a very nice piece of cake, too,' he said, in a neutral, hopeful tone.

'Did you like it? Have another slice. I made it myself. I like making cakes, it is lovely now that the children will eat them, little children don't eat cake, you know, whatever people say, only big children eat cake. How old are your children? Have another slice.'

'I really couldn't,' he said. 'I must go.'

'I suppose you must,' she said. 'Do you have far to go? I hardly dare ask, in case it turns out you live in Dulwich or something dreadful like that.'

'Nothing like as bad as that,' he said. 'Only Hampstead. It's quite near, really.'

'Yes, that's not too bad, that could have been a lot worse. What a relief.'

He rose to his feet, still holding the folder, and said, indicating it, 'Perhaps I might keep these, for a day or two? I could go through them and see if anything occurs to me? Would you mind?'

'Not at all, of course I wouldn't mind. How very nice of you.' She too rose to her feet, and then said, a little anxiously,

'You know, you could stay the night if you like. If you don't feel like driving. I could easily put one of the children in my bed, it wouldn't be any trouble.'

'That's very kind of you,' he said, meaning it, and managing to sound as though he meant it. 'But I don't think I should. I have to be at work early in the morning, so I'd have to get up even earlier and get home to collect my things. It wouldn't be worth it.'

'No, I can see that. Oh dear. Oh well, never mind. You will forgive me, won't you?'

She followed him into the hall, where he unhooked his hat and coat.

'There's nothing to forgive,' he said, about to go. 'I'm afraid that I too, like other inquisitive lawyers, find such affairs quite interesting. Quite unusual, the whole case, really, you know.'

'Yes, it is, isn't it?' she said, frowning slightly at him. 'Odd, really, how unusual it all is. When all my life I've tried so hard to be normal. But perhaps an abnormal person trying to be normal is bound to produce very unorthodox results, do you think?'

'I am not yet qualified,' he said, 'to express a view, as to your normality or abnormality.'

'The judge who divorced me,' said Rose, 'said I was highly eccentric. I thought that very unkind. You will read that, you have it all there, there's a copy of the transcript.'

'I will read it,' he said, 'with great interest.'

And so they shook hands, and he left her, and drove back to his empty house. As he drove he thought of the child's warm bed that he might have slept in. The opportunity was not to recur.

He also thought that perhaps there was a natural progression, an inevitable progression, for people like himself, from his background, who had grown up amidst too much physical intimacy—houses too small, settees too narrow, bedrooms too full, kisses (like his grandparents') too brutal and forceful—from this world they could only wish to grow apart, into the thinner air of non-touching, into larger rooms and spaces. And having reached this clear, empty space, they would wish once more to find touching, to find chosen, not accidental warmth, to find intimacy and contact. And it would no longer be possible, the world of touch would be lost for ever, and they, the refugees, the sensitive ones who had found the noises and the pushing unendurable and had fought their way out on to a clear drawing-room carpet with empty yards on either side, would eye each other across the spaces, isolated, marooned, unable to approach or touch, or share a bodily warmth, having lost for ever this capacity. He thought of his mother, in the large high rooms of her

Victorian boarding-house on the South Coast, living her South Coast life, breathing the unpolluted inhuman air: his sympathies were with her, for he too had recoiled where she had recoiled (she had taught him to do so), and yet where was she now, where was he now, what had they lost in gaining so much?

He thought, too, of Rose Vassiliou. She had been christened Rose Vertue Bryanston, or so it said on various documents. He wondered where the name Vertue had come from. If he saw her again, he would ask her. He was sure to see her again. Why else had he kept her papers, but as a hostage for that possibility? He was rather frightened by her papers. She should never have let him have them, it was indiscreet and unprofessional of him to have taken them, he felt: though he could not have said why.

When he got home he locked them away in a drawer and pretended for a whole day that they were not there.

ROSE, LYING AWAKE IN BED after Simon Camish had left, got up in the end and got a child and took it into bed with her. It was the middle child of the three, the one that never woke. She held on to it both for comfort for herself and to protect it. She was worried to death about three things and she did not know which worried her most, as two of them were serious and one was not, but the non-serious one being the most recent was naturally uppermost in her mind, out of all proportion to its gravity. She was dreadfully worried about the man called Simon Camish and the dreadful way she had inflicted her problems upon him, and the entirely stupid way she had let him go off with her papers when she could see that he had only offered to take them because he was afraid that otherwise she would think that he was not interested (which he probably was not). If he was interested, that was dreadful, because he would be able to work out all the very bad things about her and Christopher and all the reasons why she might lose the children, and if he was not, then that was worse. Anyway, it had been incredibly foolish to tell such things to a total stranger (however well known to Nick and Diana, and however often discussed by them, and however obviously trustworthy and reliable, quite agonizingly reliable, from Diana's accounts). Whatever Nick and Diana thought of him, and she could see that they thought a lot, the fact remained that to her he was a total stranger, who had been bullied unmercifully into driving her home and listening to her difficulties and reading her incredibly boring and confusing and incomprehensible documents. There was no excuse, she should not have done it, it had been not at all kind of her, and very stupid of her to have assumed so simply that he would see her point, would be on her side. She ought to have learned by then that many people found it very difficult to see her point. It was far more common, she reflected, for people to see her husband's point, when they thought about it: but then she herself did not reflect or think enough, she was hopelessly impulsive, and thinking about this and the reasons for it brought her onto her second and more serious anxiety, which was the complete and hopeless irredeemability of her own nature. She was so weak, she was so shockingly weak and trusting and shallow, spilling herself like that to any stranger who did not firmly enough drive away: she was simply incapable, and had always been so, of behaving in a rational and considered manner. The events of the whole day had borne witness to this: first of all she had been so silly about the child next door, when Mrs Flanagan had asked her to mind it, she should have said straight out, No, I'm sorry I can't, I've got to take Maria to buy some new shoes, but instead as usual she'd said Oh yes, fine, and had found herself dragging around with Maria moaning and the Flanagan baby yelling and the result had been that she'd had to leave the shoe shop without buying anything, and Maria's lace-ups had got holes in the toes, real holes. And then Dickie White had rung her, the moment she got back, from Bush House, and asked her if she'd go and take part in a discussion about the Urumbi uprising, and she'd said no, and he'd said oh dear I'd been counting on you this time, you couldn't do it last time I asked you, and so she had said yes, and when she put the phone down and started to think about it she had realised that in fact last time Dickie had rung she had in fact said yes, because he had used exactly the same line on her, and had clearly found it totally effective. Then, just as she was cooking the lunch, the letter had arrived from the solicitors, and she had tried for hours without success to pretend that she had neither received nor read it, shoving it behind the plant on the mantelpiece and willing it not to be there, but it was there, and when the children were watching Huckleberry Hound and were quite busily occupied she had furtively got it down again and read it again, and it seemed suddenly very serious, and she knew quite well (as Simon Camish had said) that she should communicate immediately with her solicitors, but she hadn't dared, so instead she had rung up Emily and had told her all about it, and Emily had been as kind, witty, sympathetic and practically useless as ever—in fact even more useless because by the time Rose had got off the phone to her the solicitors were shut, though she supposed it was also true that even had she not rung Emily or had she talked to Emily for less long, she would still have taken great care not to ring the solicitors until too late, as she could not really face speaking to them at all. So she had then braced herself to re-read yet again the letter from Dawson, Mead and Woodbrooke, and had found this time, what she had not noticed before, which was that their client (meaning her husband) had simply instructed them that he wished the question of custody to be reconsidered. The wards-of-court threat was in Christopher's letter only, and he was not reliable. So there was some time left, perhaps, to think about it. She wondered if Dawson, Mead and Woodbrooke had enjoyed writing this letter. She thought, from what Simon Camish had said, that they would be sure to have advised against it, but perhaps solicitors have to do what they are told, and that is why they use that word 'instructed', to avoid responsibility. They never say 'we would like to' or even 'we must' but always 'we are instructed'. She recalled her father's solicitors, who had not at all liked doing to her what he had made them do: in fact the younger Mr Sykes of Sykes and Son had been moved almost to tears by her plight, when she had confronted him, at twenty years of age, robed in her hideous discredited shaming certainties. They must have been beautiful then, or he would not have been so kind, he would not have blown his nose so often and told her to be brave and sensible as he was sure she really was, in quite that tone of voice. Poor Mr Sykes, she hoped he had not grieved too much over her fate, perhaps she should go and see him again to show him how well she was, how well she was doing, despite all.

And then, after she had re-read the letter, and found that it was not quite as bad as she feared, that the children were not to be ripped from her by bailiffs or children's officers, for some reason she began to get sadder and sadder: bathing the little child and chasing the big ones up to bed was even more of an ordeal than usual, because added to the usual irritations was the panic fear of losing these irritations, which made her, she was aware, behave quite oddly, and her behaving quite oddly made the children behave quite oddly, too, and so, as ever with children the process was cumulative and self-perpetuating, and by the time Mrs Sharkey's Eileen arrived to baby-sit they were all resolutely refusing to go to bed at all. And Mrs Sharkey's Eileen was quite incapable of organising them, as well as being very pregnant and miserable and betrayed and talkative, so Rose had been very late getting out of the house at all. And when she had got out she had to face another character problem: knowing herself already late for Nick and Diana's, where she could hardly bring herself to go, so dreadfully worried was she, she knew that she ought to get a taxi, and she had been half-thinking in her characteristic way that she might, but as soon as she emerged into the street she knew that it was out of the question, in a way, because she would never pick one up in that district in a hundred years (as she should well know, having inhabited it for eleven) and that she had not the energy to walk to the nearest place where she might pick one up, which was a good quarter of an hour away, and even then not certain. On the other hand, the bus could not fail to take less than forty minutes, which would make her embarrassingly late, and she hated causing inconvenience. So she stood there on the pavement at the end of her road, hesitating, not knowing which way to go, whether towards the bus and certain lateness, or towards the taxi road, and a long walk, and possible speed and possible even greater lateness.

She stood there, racked by indecision, and began to cry, and finally walked off and caught the bus, because she could not really afford to pay both Eileen and a taxi, even though she had promised to talk about the Urumbi uprising for Dickie, for which she ought to get at least eight guineas: blood money, that, if ever there was such a thing. On the bus she continued to weep because she knew she would be late, and Diana would be upset and not knowing what to do with her supper, and she did so hate causing offence: and she wept also because of her character, because she was always like this, always indecisive, meaning to oblige, but finally, inevitably, causing inconvenience to all. Eileen, for instance, whom she had asked to baby-sit because she needed the cash, was really no longer capable of doing it, and had always been feckless—once she had put Vick on Maria's bottom when she was a baby, instead of Vaseline, with awful results—and now was so far gone in pregnancy that if Maria fell out of bed, which she did sometimes, Eileen would have the utmost difficulty in heaving her back in again.

Luckily Maria hadn't fallen out. This had been the one good thing about the day, thought Rose, as she lay there, holding Marcus's warm squashy body, as it so gently and regularly heaved. She tried hard not to think about her third grave anxiety, which was that she might lose the children. She did not really believe it possible, but she feared the opening of old wounds, the carving of new ones. Her life had settled down, all things considered, so well, and why could they not leave her alone? She was doing no harm, she was contented, she was even, most of the time, happy. The children too were happy, as far as one could see. Her life had at last become, as she had so long willed it to be, innocuous. She had settled in, after all these sorrows and trials, she had become, slowly, what she had once so long ago willed herself to be: she was settled now, and her nature, though it saddened her at times as it had done this evening, she had on the whole so accepted and understood that she felt she could look at its vagaries quite equably, she could watch it panicking over the choice between taxis and buses with something like a maternal amusement. She was what she was: she had learned to go along with it, she had learned to say yes to Dickie White and to notice that she had been conned and not to object to that perception: she would, instead, go along and do the job. There was no need for them to disturb her any more. She was no longer a threat, she was a quiet person, they could surely, now, leave her alone. She did not think that even if they tortured her, now, she would very amusingly or gratifyingly cry out. She would be more likely, she hoped, to cry rather quietly until they stopped. But how could she tell? One cannot trust oneself too far.

She lay awake a little while longer, thinking these things, and looking around the dark room. It was dark, but one could see the objects in it quite well, because there was a street lamp outside Mrs Flanagan's next door, and the light entered the room through the thin cheap floating curtains. There was a flowery pattern on the curtains of which she had grown extremely fond, and she could hardly now believe that she had once disliked them. They had been there long enough, they had come with the house. At first she had been unable to understand why anyone should have bought curtains of such ineffective material, and the light through them had kept her awake. Then she had come to realise that it was a question of expense. Thin materials were cheaper than thick ones, and that was that. It had dawned on her like a slow revelation, and now the light filtered through them with the same revelation perpetually embodied. It satisfied her, it assuaged her. The whole room satisfied her—the wardrobe, also left behind by previous owners who had been unable to get it through the door, the creaking bed, big enough, now she was on her own, for herself and all the children at once when they wanted to come, the pictures stuck on the walls, the rug that she had made herself, the dark green walls that she had painted herself four years ago, and really ought to do again soon when she could face it. She loved it: it was peaceful, it was safe, it was what she had wanted. She could hardly now believe that she had once lain here in such panic, so terrified of what she had undertaken, so inadequate to take possession of it, so frightened by what had then seemed its wilfully chosen menace. She looked back on those early days, sometimes, and they were a measure of how far she had travelled, how surely, despite all, she had made herself advance into safety. Because if one has an image, however dim and romantic, of a journey's end, one may, in the end, surely reach it, after no matter how many detours and deceptions and abandonings of hope. And hope could never have been entirely abandoned, even in the worst days. Thinking this, with some comfort, she fell asleep.

ELEVEN YEARS BEFORE, if questioned, but there was nobody who dared to question her, she would not have been able to describe her image with any fitting confidence. She had herself lost sight of it and, lying in that same room, upon that same bed, she had been cold with the terror of that loss, and more frightened than she could ever have admitted. She had been frightened, in those days, of everything she had found about her: the long drab streets, the hard-faced suspicious old ladies in the shops, the gas works, the bedding factory, the shabby children in the streets, the house itself, which she would have to think of as her home. She hated the house, its very architecture appalled her, she hated its low narrow rooms and its sagging ceilings and its hacked, planed, untrue, ill-fitting doors. It stank of fleas, a dark red smell of blood and of sawdust, and the mattress of the bed, on which she threw herself in despondency, exhaled at her the vicious defeats of generations. Dirt poured into the place through every badly carpentered crack. Decades of what she had first taken for neglect had left the whole building riddled with holes and irregularities: it took her years to realise that it was not neglect that had patched up the sash cords and filled the cracks in the walls with putty and stuck pieces of varnished paper over major structural faults, but on the contrary a yearning, anxious, impoverished solicitude, the solicitude without money that can never rebuild or reconstruct, but can merely patch and cover and stop up each breach as it occurs. The house, far from speaking of despair, spoke of the unflagging efforts of nearly a century: a little cement here, a new bit of wiring there, a new knob on a door (albeit a nasty bakelite one to replace the irreplaceable brass original) they all bore witness to effort, not to defeat. But how should she have known this, brought up as she had been? She had no eye for such things, and what was around her she could not see. She lay on the bed, sick from her first pregnancy, and thought that there was nothing, nothing in the world that she could do. There was no action possible for her. She had no money, apart from the five pounds that Christopher had given her for a week's housekeeping; she had not the faintest idea of how to set about earning any. She was almost uneducated, and completely untrained in any useful sense. Without money, there was nothing to do: one could sit, like a tramp in the park, or in the library, but the library was not accommodating. It was not a district that felt much need of libraries. And it was too cold for the park. It was cold enough in the house: she was too frightened of the electricity bill to switch on the electric fire, so in the mornings when Christopher had gone out, she would get back into bed and pull the blanket over her and wonder if she had enough strength to survive. They had married in November, on her twenty-first birthday, as she had always threatened that she would do, but now, because of the cold, she thought it would have been better to have waited until the spring. In the spring, things would surely be more tolerable.

Later in the morning, at lunch-time, she would go out to the shops, braving the unfamiliarity and hostility, and buy herself something to eat. These excursions braced her, and would bring her to some sense of what she was and what she was doing, because, quite often, as she was buying a tin of beans or a box of eggs, she would see an old lady buying herself a single egg. The grocer would calmly take down a box of half a dozen, and take out one, and put it in a paper bag.

On one of these expeditions, fortified momentarily by the sight of human distress, she bought herself a packet of a patent cement mix from the do-it-yourself shop on the corner, and she went home with it and mixed some of it in a tea cup, and began, herself, to fill in some holes. It was an activity, it soothed her. The holes, when filled, did not look very elegant, but, looking at her work, she began to feel that there was at least a possibility that she might learn.

Fleas, holes, cold, single eggs. Behind these threatening entities there loomed a shadowy edifice, an inhabited house, a hope for the future: she shivered, she trembled, she flinched, but she persevered, she had faith, she built up brick by brick the holy city of her childhood, the holy city in the shape of that patched subsiding house. It was slow, it was very slow, but gradually the ideal and the real merged and swam together, so that there were times, when, after five years or so, she would sit there not knowing which she inhabited, irritated at one moment beyond measure by the noise of the radio next door and the fraying edge of the carpet and the way the cats had ripped the braid off the armchairs, and the next moment invaded by such visionary peace at her acceptance of and familiarity with these things. Her alliance with the objects around had irradiated her, transformed her. But her friends, or such friends as continued, through loyalty or love or curiosity or desire for profit to make the long journey, continued to think that she was mad. Hardly a gleam of her vision reached them. They would visit her, all her friends but one, and shake their heads, and go home and say that Rose was mad.

IT WAS DIFFICULT not to assume that Rose must be mad, if judged on the evidence of her actions, thought Simon Camish, sitting by himself the following evening in the luxury of an empty house, staring at the papers with which she had so confidently entrusted him. Her parents had clearly considered her dangerously mad, as had her husband and her solicitors: so had the judge in the divorce case, though he had nevertheless found (a little reluctantly) that a passionate desire to rid oneself of one's money is technically not as grave a matrimonial offence as the inflicting of black-eyes, split lips, cuts and manifold bruises. The judge had not liked his own decisions: it was easy to tell from the tone of his pronouncements. He had not approved the eccentricity of Rose's behaviour. Simon was not sure how far he approved it himself. There were certain aspects of the case that he did not begin to understand. It seemed clear enough to him, from his reading of the matter and from the bias of his own judgement, that Christopher Vassiliou had married her for her money, and that part at least of the bitter disagreements of their marriage had sprung from her wilful determination to disinherit herself, against his will and expectations: but that did not begin to explain why she had married him. What impulse could have led a woman like Rose to ally herself with the qualities she professed most to despise—avarice, brutality, showiness, ambition? Perhaps they had not appeared as such to her when she was innocent, nineteen and wealthy: perhaps she had then been gullible and in love. Or perhaps, in those days, they had really not been so, perhaps they had not existed: perhaps it was she that had brought them out. He knew all too well the extraordinary facility that people have for marrying, for the wrong reasons, those who appear to possess qualities the very opposite of those with which they are in fact endowed: qualities which gradually reveal themselves in their true light, or are gradually created, by the agency of their new ally, in a form utterly disastrous, utterly opposed to any possible harmony. Christopher might have been all right when she married him: it might have been she herself that had ruined him, by the dizzy height of her ridiculous expectations.

It was, of course, his own marriage of which he was thinking. It always was. How else could one think of marriage? He was sure, now, as he had not been ten years ago, that he had steered so clear of divorce law largely because of its horrible fascination. He had friends who were drawn to it as a drunkard to a bottle: protesting all the while their innocence, as novelists protest that their characters have no connection with, are in no way drawn from life. He thought of Julie. He had not intended to do so, he did not like to recognise the immensity of the relief of her temporary absence. He had married her for her money, or so it had been said: as Christopher Vassiliou had married Rose Bryanston. That fact in itself should give him some sympathy with Christopher, for he alone knew of his own degree of innocence, his own degree of guilt. Julie too had been an heiress (though on a much more modest scale than Rose, and not an only child), and there was no point in saying that that was not why he had married her, because who would believe him? So he did not bother to say it. Though it was, in fact, true. He knew, by now, more or less exactly why he had married her: he did not expect that the next few years of introspection would lead him radically to alter his opinion on this matter, and if he did, it would not be because of new light, but because of growing forgetfulness. He had not married Julie for her money, directly. He had become involved with her because of it, perhaps—or because of what it represented. It had represented, in her, the very opposite of his own cold, overwrought, conscience-stricken, guilt-ridden childhood, where every mouthful of food had been taken from his mother's very plate, or torn (figuratively) from her bleeding breast: Julie, at nineteen, had possessed warmth, gaiety, vitality, family feeling, an easy affection, an easy enjoyment, all the things he had never hoped to have—an unquestioning pleasure in food and cars and holidays and comfort, a large house full of endless guests, lavish unthinking expenditure on clothes, meals out, meals for friends, a lavish generosity, charmingly combined with an aptitude for gratitude for the smallest favour, the smallest kindness. He had, he supposed, fallen in love with a way of life. He had found everything about it charming, even the things that he knew to be vulgar, like the thatched cottage and gardens painted on the white walls of Julie's parents' dining-room, and the heart-shaped cover on the lavatory seat—objects which made his mother's impoverished, sensitive heart shudder with alarm. His mother had not approved of Julie, nor of the Phillips, nor of their house. And that, of course, was in part why he had liked them so much.

It had become a second home to him, that large mock-Tudor house, scenically situated in splendid isolation at the outer limit of commuter land. The Phillips could not have taken the country proper, being townsfolk at heart, but they humbly acknowledged that they were now too grand and too rich to live in town itself, and had moved out, obeying the laws of nature, to a spot where they could have their own quaking blue eyesore of a swimming bath and their own tennis court. How Simon loved that hideous swimming bath, and how he lived to repent his early love and all its ill-aimed defiance. Julie's disapproval of the swimming bath was as intense as his mother's, at times: she was ashamed of it, she sulked. Simon found such pique amusing, he did not take it seriously, he laughed at it. Julie's ambition was to go to Art College: there was a very chic Art College in the district, and Julie wanted to disown her swimming bath and go to it and move in the fast set. She had a very clear conception of the fast set: it hung around in the Bongo Basement Club in Newcastle, wearing beards and duffle coats and jeans and large sweaters, and it was there that Simon, in Nick's company, had first met her. She had blossomed weirdly there in the underground light, glowing in her white fur jacket, her orange silk scarf, her tight black sweater. She was popular in that circle: she could always pay the bill. But she wanted to be more than a hangeron, a camp follower: she wanted to be a full member of the club, and that was why she wanted to go to Art College.

It was Mr Phillips's behaviour over the Art College that gave Simon his first shock about the Phillips ménage, a shock which was to reverberate through the whole of his married life. He had always liked Mr Phillips, if only because Mr Phillips had always seemed to like him, and he had always assumed that Julie could do with him whatever she wanted. He was an indulgent father, ever ready to provide new clothes, a holiday, a lift in the car. Moreover, like many self-made men, he had an exaggerated respect for the powers of culture and education—he forced the children to attend concerts, plays, local events of every kind. He had paid out good money to educate Julie at a boarding school in Yorkshire: the two younger boys (one of whose weddings Julie was now attending in New York) were at that time still at Sedburgh. So it seemed probable that he would view Julie's request to go to Art College with favour, involving as it did a project combining both culture and education. Julie, however, had clearly sensed trouble, and had waited around for nearly a whole year after leaving school—the year during which she took up with Simon, himself now at Oxford—before daring to broach the subject. Simon could not see what she was nervous about: Mr Phillips was a cheery man, as far as he could see, uncritical, unfussy, easy to amuse, easy to persuade. Simon had enjoyed his hospitality—his bad jokes, his childish pride in his latest gadgets, his continuing satisfaction in being himself, so well set up in life. When Julie confided in him her desire to go to college, he encouraged her, telling her that her father would surely approve, that she must have the courage to ask at once, or she would be too late for the next year's applications. She looked uneasy, but promised to follow his advice.

The next time he saw her, she was in tears. Her father had refused, she said, to hear of such a thing. He had flatly refused. He had no intention, he said, of allowing her to go around with those scruffy parasites, and if she didn't keep out of their way he would come and drag her away by the scruff of her neck.

The volte face was total. Mr Phillips meant what he had said. When he calmed down, he explained himself on two counts, at least: the first being that he did not believe in educating women, it was a waste of money, if she wanted to do something she could go to a secretarial college, but that was that, that was all he offered, he had spent more than was good for her already on teaching her things that were going to be no use. The second explanation really explained the first, which must have been triggered off by something: and the something was a scandal at the Art College, of which Julie and Simon knew little, and which they would have been too naive to consider, had they known. Not so the local press and Mr Phillips, who took such things seriously. It was mild enough, thought Simon, looking back with the insight of more than a decade of student troubles, but it had been a first-class scandal, in those days. Two girls pregnant, a lecturer dismissed, rumours of grouped nude poses (the Young Spartans) and a threat of a withdrawn local grant. The very thought of it had driven the nice, good-natured Mr Phillips into a blind rage. And there lay Julie's hopes, shattered. She was heartbroken. Her friends in the Coffee Bongo tried to cheer her up, telling her she wasn't missing much, it was a lousy place, it was no good anyway, but the fact that it had produced a scandal made Julie pine for it all the more. She knew her father wouldn't dare to stop her associating with her friends, but she had wanted to be one of them, she had wanted to be accepted.

(Odd, during the whole business, thought Simon, that he had not once bothered to ask himself whether or not she had any talent. He had simply assumed that she had not. And he had been wrong in that, as in so many other things.)

After her disappointment over the Art College, Julie had seemed to depend upon Simon more and more. And it was at this point, long before their marriage, that he began to feel himself trapped. He had thought her gay, insensitive, extrovert: he found her increasingly vulnerable, suffering, suspicious. He would willingly, at this point, have ditched her, swimming bath, tennis court, wealthy father and all, but it was too late. She wouldn't let him go. She knew, somehow, with that horrible knowledge of one's own limitations, that she couldn't make the grade of those nonchalant dirty young men, that it was no good trying to get off with Mike Boyd or Johnny Featherstone: she knew that Simon Camish, with his adam's apple and his poor eyesight, was in her range. And so she clung to him and blackmailed him. Simon alone knew the truth of her manoeuvres, and he was too chivalrous to impart it: so there he stood, indicted, judged, condemned by his own actions of mercenary motives. He well might feel for Christopher Vassiliou.

Time threw up some amusing patterns, though, in all the dirt. One of those bearded boys had made good, he had become a big name, a real pop hero: one of his works glowered now at Simon from the wall, across the room. He had made good and gone to the States, where he was doing even better. Julie had visited him, last week: he had taken her out to dinner, he had been delighted to see her again, she had been one of his first buyers.

It was all very well knowing now, about Julie, about oneself. It was then that one had needed to know. He had thought Julie warm and open: she had proved, like her father, irrational, bigoted and cold. The gaiety had revealed itself as a manic fear of solitude, the gregariousness as an inability to make any friends at all, the desire for a fast life as a symptom of a profound, irremediable crippling social ambition, founded on the insecurity of her own provincial background. It took Simon some time to work out what she must have suffered, at boarding school, as she trained her accent successfully to bridge the gap between her own and her father's, as she tried to emulate the graces of more polished homes. Ironically, he had loved in her family the vulgarity that she had been set to leave. And she had left it with a vengeance. She had insisted that they should live in London, despite his plea that he could practise more fruitfully and usefully elsewhere: she had surrounded them with friends whose lack of friendship or any other kind of appeal had driven him out of the house for more evenings than he could count: she had spent money—at first her own, and then, gradually, as he had begun to acquire it, his—with an ease that made his hair stand on end. Whatever she had wished to reject in her background, it had not been its affluence. He really judged himself, now, for having ever admired the easy spending of money. A golden mean there might be, in such matters as in all, but the longer he lived the surer he was that the golden mean had more to do with meanness than with extravagance. And with all this, she was profoundly, painfully, evidently unhappy. He had thought her a naturally happy person, once. And now she was as profoundly miserable as anyone he knew. Her state afflicted him beyond bearing. He could not, he supposed, be entirely responsible for her unhappiness, but he felt himself to be so: he had failed her, he had been inadequate, he had not even been able to satisfy her simple needs, and now he would have to go on and on failing her, because there was no way out, and he would have to go on and on helplessly witnessing the deterioration of her temper and her manner. If she could herself have been happy with the life she had imposed on him, then he would, obviously, have resented it less: it was the pointlessness of his loyalty to her that most depressed him. She needed him, he was indispensable to her, and that was that: there was no joy in it, and no reciprocation, and no possibility of release. He fulfilled, for her, the highest attainable point of the acceptable—way, way below the desirable, way below anything that her voracious nature would have desired for its satisfaction—and as such, too adequate to be rejected, but utterly unsatisfactory to her, he would have to continue to exist. She did not dare to reject him. She knew she would never get anything that more closely resembled what she wanted. He should have known that she was forcing herself to accept him, as second best, in those distant days up North, when he had been forcing himself, out of pity and compromise, to accept her. No. That was not it. He had known. And it was because he had known that there had been the pity. He had sacrificed himself to her needs.

She had been completely perverted, poor Julie, somewhere, by someone, given desires that could never be assuaged, given the knowledge to know what she was missing, the sensitivity to suffer at the loss. Like talentless artists or writers, whose lack of talent in no way kindly diminishes their insatiable craving to succeed, she was doomed to disappointment. He was too moved by her to betray her. A stronger man than himself would not, in the first place, have married her, as he had done, but at least he had the strength to stick it out.

Her looks had not deteriorated as much as her temper, however. She still looked quite presentable. He thought of her, as a girl, in that white jacket, her reddish hair all bouncy round her face. Now, as a woman, shiny with good health and lipstick, driving along in her big fat car. Julie on the telephone, giggling like a schoolgirl to her so-called friends: Julie betrayed by those same friends, furious about the betrayal, abusing them as wantonly as she had praised them, resorting to the gross terms of childhood—'Stinking bitch,' she would say, violently, 'Great fat old cow—' referring to some smart young woman who had withdrawn her attendance or stood her up at some lunch date in favour of a more profitable, wealthier, more sophisticated host. And the childish crudity of these terms would horrify him: they reminded him of his own grandfather, if of anything, and of his mother's pained wincing and refined agonies beneath such abuse—abuse directed not at her, because his grandfather was afraid of his mother, as who would not be, but at all the undistinguished world around. There was in Julie a coarseness and a lack of discrimination that must have attracted him to her, as one is attracted, compelled, to approach one's own doom, to live out one's own hereditary destiny: coarseness she had from his grandfather, coldness from his mother, and their good qualities she lacked. She must have good qualities of her own, he would tell himself, but he was too deeply entrenched in her, in his own past, to perceive them. He grieved for her: her disappointments and childish enthusiasms grieved him: but what could one do about them? She lacked all judgement, all reserve: her emotions swung violently, creaking and screeching like a weather vane in uncertain weather. He longed at times to point out that such a young man, such a woman could not possibly be all that she saw them to be, because the facts did not support such a construction, but she refused to listen, trusting what she called her intuition, so he had ceased to comment, and had withdrawn himself. Even with the children he rarely intervened, but would watch her yell at them and indulge them, irrationally, wantonly, destructively: the two girls seemed, miraculously, to have survived this treatment fairly well, and to have adopted a fairly cynical attitude to their mother's inconsistencies, but the boy, the eldest, had become, he sometimes feared, psychotic. At the age of nine he either could not or would not read: he was destructive, sullen, infantile. He could not do anything about it. He had tried, but he did not know what to do.

Her language, now he came to think about it, afflicted him as much as anything about her. He hated the way she talked. He knew that her classy friends, and indeed his, spoke as crudely, but to them the words came naturally, whereas to her they came with an air of defiance and genuine venom. He sometimes thought that if he heard her once more describe the colour of the drawing-room walls as goose-shit he would drop dead upon the carpet, or take off his glasses and fling them at the wall, or kick in the china cupboard door. In vain to tell himself that nobody else minded: that others, in fact, smiled obsequiously when she said such things, and that it was only his own fastidiousness, dubious enough itself, that protested. He did protest. He said nothing, but he eternally protested: he could not accept, he could not reconcile himself. Once he had said to her that he wished she would not spend so much of the day with her hair in curlers, but she had laughed at him, and, later, when she had had time to think about it, reviled him for such a suggestion, saying, truly enough, that there was absolutely nothing wrong with wearing curlers, she always looked fine when she went out, and that it was only because he had seen too many curlers as a child that he now found the sight of them unacceptable. True enough, but if people cannot accommodate each other's prejudices, then what was the point in attempting to live together? No point at all, and yet it had to be done. It had to be done, and that was that, and there was not much point in thinking about it. And yet how could one resist thinking about it? He really did think he could see it all now: he had been attracted to her because his life with his mother was so appalling, and she to him because he was the only possible acceptable escape from her father—the only escape acceptable *to* her father, that meant, for she would never have had the courage to defy his expressed will. For Simon had been acceptable to Mr Phillips, mysteriously: Mr Phillips had always had faith in him: naively, he had liked the idea of his daughter marrying an Oxford man, a barrister. He had given them a lot of money, to set up house. A dowry. Simon had almost been pleased to think that others might assume he was marrying for money. At least such an assumption concealed the truth. He would, at that age, have preferred to appear as cynic than as fool.

Who knows, he thought, perhaps when I am fifty I will have forgotten the extreme gloom into which I sank when the engagement was settled, the deep depression I inhabited from that day on, and I will conclude that it was the money I married, after all.

Perhaps the gloom had been, after all, a fraud. Who knows?

He had read his Freud, with interest. He particularly liked the description of the lady who had married three husbands, each of whom had subsequently died, shortly afterwards, of a fatal illness contracted after the date of the marriage. Interesting, that was. Interesting, too, that one could always tell which of one's friends were being analysed or seeing too much of psychiatric friends by the way in which they would suddenly, out of the blue, for no reason at all, start abusing their mothers. One really had to watch that kind of thing. The time element was the catch. As Proust and Bergson said. At times he thought that he could sort the whole thing out if only he could formulate it in some kind of Proustian concept: as by saying: he had been drawn to Julie, mistakenly, by what he had mistakenly taken her to be, not by what she in fact was, which had, in the fullness of time, attached him to her in a much more serious manner: for he, when young, could not truly have wanted what he had thought he had wanted, he had wanted instead the underlying doom, the concealed and underlying reality, which alone could have presented an appearance attractive and possible to him, as he then was, in a manner that reality could never have achieved, being too far from him as beholder, him as participant.

Which made it all come down to the same thing, and excused everybody, except himself, acquitting everybody of deceit, and his mother of guilt. Very satisfactory. And yet none of that made any difference to the fact that he had known, when, *at that point in time when,* he had offered to marry Julie, that he ought not to have done so, and that by doing so he was condemning himself and her to unhappiness. Why, then, had he done it? He had wondered even then, but there had seemed no possible choice. Inevitability had held him in its grip: psychological determinism had really got its claws into him, on that day when he had stood in front of her father, in his so-called study. He was sitting in a crushed gold armchair, Mr Phillips, with his legs up on his fox-and-pheasant embossed brass fender, contemplating a magnificent iridescently rainbow-gleaming electric fire, smoking a cigarette, his grey moustache puffing with emotion, his kindly little eyes glittering hard with friendliness and bonhomie. That's fine by me, my boy, he had said, I've been expecting you to come up with something like this, you know. I bet you bloody well have, said Simon to himself, as he drearily embarked on his speech about being poor but hardworking: he had sensed well enough, though never witnessed, Julie's appalling domestic behaviour since her failure over Art College. She had sulked and moaned and made herself intolerable to live with. Mr Phillips was glad to get rid of her so easily: he could hardly conceal his relief. Simon, who had as yet seen Julie only on her best outdoors behaviour, was frightened to witness thus the faint reflections of her true self, in her father's shifting looks. And as he tried to explain his prospects to Mr Phillips, he felt all the life drain out of him, out through the soles of his shoes, in a most boring dreary way, as though he at that instant resigned himself to the future. His father-in-law, realising perhaps that it would not be wise to allow Simon to dwell in too much detail on the realities ahead, cut short his speech, with a gruff 'That's all very well, that's all very well, there's no need for all that'—and had then led Simon, grotesquely, off to the bathroom to inspect his latest acquisition. It was startling, it was alarming, the speed of the transition. The purchase was a white plastic pillow, with a blue frill round it, that stuck on to the end of the bath by suction pads.

'It's a new line, you see,' said Pa Phillips. 'You lie in the bath—I read a lot in the bath, I'm a great reader, you know—you lie in the bath and you rest your head on it. Ideal for reading. Get it?'

Simon did indeed get it. He nodded, stupefied. The plastic pillow took on a symbolic significance: like a ring, it cemented the contract, it embodied his engagement to Julie, and was never more to be dissociated from that moment—though it was still there, that pillow, more than a decade later, the very same one, a little less plump perhaps, a little less ridiculous, but still there, witness to many a reading of many a *Financial Times*. 'Get it?' repeated Mr Phillips, and Simon nodded yet more vigorously, afraid that its proud owner, now gazing at it in solemn pleasure, might suddenly turn gay and jokey, as he was wont to do, and leap into the empty bath to give a demonstration. He did not know how to forestall this demonstration, should it to be truly threatened, so he continued to nod and smile: one of the difficulties of his father-in-law was that he always elicited a violent response, was never satisfied with a mild assent, insisted upon an almost physical reaction to every question he asked—and as the questions were for the most part of the unanswerable quality of that particular 'Get it?', Simon found it very hard to provide satisfaction, and would be subjected to an endless battery of 'Hey? what do you say? That's right, isn't it? I'm right, aren't I?' Some people, notably his business associates, had learned to deal with his technique by thumping him violently on the back at each of these queries, but Simon had never managed that, so he was always left, as then, laughing somewhat foolishly, grinning overeagerly, nodding his head on his long neck until it ached with motion. He had never got much better at it, through all these years. Then, staring at that pillow, nodding like an automaton, or like a toy dog in the back of a car, he had not known whether he wanted to laugh or cry. But he knew that he had had it.

And now Julie had three children, and had gone with them and her parents to New York for the wedding of her youngest brother. And, such was the effect of time, he suspected that despite her protestations she had been quite looking forward to a bit of the vulgar old parental life, in posh hotels, for a few days, especially as she was managing to thin it out with a few more chic engagements of her own. She hadn't been away without him for a long time: a few days reversion to the life she had so hated, when she had had it, might be quite enjoyable. She might even come home in a better temper. Though that was a great deal to hope for. Too much, probably. He sighed, got up, shut his desk, and began to walk restlessly round the room. He was tired of sitting still, and worrying.

It was, really, in many ways, a nice room. Even the goose-shit walls were attractive enough. She had a flair for these things. It was spotless, smart, and trendy, full of plants and attractive little knick-knacks. (That, he was sure, was not what she would have called them, but that was what they nevertheless were.) It was a nice house, in a nice district of Hampstead, a period house, bought at a period when prices must surely have reached an all-time height: a house in a pretty, elegant, fashionable terrace. As a house, he had nothing against it. He could see why she liked it: brought up as she had been in that vast bulging ugly stockbroker's mansion, she had longed for the support of a terrace of elegant neighbours in an acceptable district of town. She had caught the coloring of her surroundings well enough: when she took her curlers out she even looked right in herself. Khaki, mustard and a dark greeny-brown predominated, and he knew that these colours were right because even people like Diana, who knew about such things, admired them with a genuine admiration, and did not seem to notice that some underlying coldness or some hidden crime, undetectable to the eye, must surely destroy the whole effect. A house built upon sand, he said to himself crossly and peevishly, will not stand, though his didn't do much in the way of crumbling, so lavishly propped, repaired, pointed and maintained it had been: and he went and poured himself a drink. He very rarely drank anything when alone and the action unnerved him slightly. He thought of his mother, reared in a dark terrace: a detached house down south was what she had wanted, and she had got it, a detached boarding house on the bleak south coast, where the cold waves flung handfulls of pebbles angrily at her windows and rotting facade, day after day, night after night, in endless, everlasting, moaning attrition. She had made a north country of her own in that desolate spot. Amazing, the power of the spirit over the waves and mists and elements. His mother, by a divining instinct, had sought and drawn towards her those batteries of grit.

The whisky was going down quite well. He looked out at the dark garden, and decided to stop thinking about Julie. He would think, instead, once more, about Rose Vassiliou. He knew a great deal more about her now than he had done upon meeting her: he knew even the day and date of her birth. In 1937 she had been born, daughter of Janice and William Bryanston, in Norfolk, where her mother's family had lived for generations in rural dignity. Her father had made a fortune in scrap metal, cranes, bulldozers, heavy plant of every sort: his company now had interests in building, contracting, property development all over Europe. His father had owned a garage in Leicester. Rose had been brought up (most inadequately, it seemed) by a succession of nannies and governesses:

her schooling had been highly irregular. She had engaged herself at the age of twenty, without her parents' consent, to a Greek from Camden Town, Christopher Vassiliou. She had threatened to marry without her parents' consent if they wouldn't give it, which they wouldn't: whereupon she was made a ward-of-court, and Christopher was forbidden to see her. She undertook not to see Vassiliou, and the wardship was lifted: nevertheless she was sent abroad for several months. When she came back—she was by this time twenty-one—she was met by Vassiliou and married him in Camden Register Office. Her father then disowned and disinherited her, as thoroughly as he could—but alas, owing to his own foresight and desire to evade paying unnecessary tax, he could not prevent certain trust funds coming to her, though the first of them was not due to mature for another couple of years. So for a couple of years she and her husband had lived in comparative poverty in a flat in a house belonging to his uncle, in Middle Road, behind Alexandra Palace. Vassiliou worked at first in his father's travel agency, then set up a small travel business of his own. Rose had three children, Konstantin, Marcus, and Maria—the youngest now aged five. After three years of marriage she had inherited part of a Trust Fund, amounting to thirty thousand pounds, which her father, despite every effort (his ill-will had not faded with time and the birth of a grandchild) had been unable to alienate from her. Most of this sum she had given away, within months, in a lump donation, to an African charity. In the divorce proceedings much was made of the donation of this sum of money, Vassiliou claiming, in reasonable and measured language—he had been a good witness, the judge had been impressed by his manner—that she had had no right, in the circumstances, to alienate so large a sum of money from her children and his. However, in the following years Vassiliou's fortunes had improved considerably: he had begun to earn a very respectable income. In 1967 he had left her—he claimed in the proceedings that she had driven him out of the house. She had decided, after some months, to divorce him, and was granted a decree at the end of the following year. The grounds were cruelty, with the usual complaints of physical violence (medical evidence produced, neighbour's evidence, and a permanent scar on Rose's wrist), abusive language, violent and unreasonable demands, incessant and unmotivated jealousy. Vassiliou, in defence, said that it was his wife that was violent and abusive: and that moreover she was a thoroughly unreasonable person. By this he meant that she had refused to move house when he wanted her to, and had refused to reconcile herself with her family even when, through his agency, reconciliation was offered. Vassiliou, oddly enough, had by this stage managed to get on good terms with her family, and had even called several members of it to witness to his wife's unnatural obstinacy. There had been a great deal of sympathy for him—the judge clearly felt that it was hard luck, to have been through so much for so little—but it was decided that he had over-reached himself. His aims had been reasonable, in trying to make his wife live as he wanted, but his methods unfortunately not. And so he had lost the case. Neither side had cited adultery. Vassiliou's jealousy, which had manifested itself by ringing his wife every hour from work to see that she was where she said she was, or by locking her in the house from time to time, had been completely generalised, attaching itself, for lack of a better object, to a woman friend called Emily Offenbach with whom Rose used to go for walks in the park with the children. Rose, for her part, had not accused her husband of any form of infidelity. This was one of the points that Vassiliou seized upon with some force. 'I know,' he said in the witness box, 'that as a young man I was not a sensible person, but I have reformed myself, since I married her I have been entirely devoted to her and to my family. If a man is to be judged by what he was ten years ago, where would we all be?' It is not up to you to ask questions, said Rose's counsel, predictably enough, but the point had been made: and made even to me, Simon thought, as he reflected upon this curious fact.

Perhaps, of course, there had been adultery, and Rose had not had evidence, or had not wished to call it: she might well have been more sensitive towards it than towards the violence, which would have been enough, as she had rightly been advised, to win her the case. All the same, the omission was interesting. It was impossible to tell, from the evidence, what the nature of their relationship had been. They had been through enough for it. Was it true, as Rose's barrister had implied, that he had married her simply for the money, and had ceased to interest himself in her when he found he could not get it? It could not after all be as simple as that, because the whole thing had happened so slowly, over so many years. And was still going on. He suddenly knew, or felt that he knew, why this man had written her such a letter; it was to keep things going. Why should he want his children back? They had not featured largely in his defence during the divorce, beyond the conventional pleas for the preservation of family life, and he had seemed satisfied with an arrangement for reasonable access. But perhaps, after all, whatever she had said, she had not allowed him reasonable access? He ought to have asked her, though perhaps she would not have said. Difficult, to ask such things, and yet she had seemed in a sense to request interrogation. Why else should she have trusted him with her affairs?

Why else, indeed, and how could he, how should he respond? He was not good at responses, so many had he of necessity curbed. The dark garden lay out there beyond the glass, and he stared into it. He was struck, as his thoughts suddenly collapsed softly and mutely, like a pack of cards, in his head, by the house's unnatural silence. He had not spent so long alone in it since they had bought it. There were not even any sleeping children upstairs. There was nobody but himself. He could do anything, this evening, unobserved. But of course there was nothing to do. He could have another drink, he supposed. But it did not seem a very exciting idea. He could switch on the radio, or go to bed. He stared out into the darkness, and suddenly it came to him that he would go into the garden. The idea dropped into his mind: mild, harmless, eccentric. An adequate substitute for whatever else he vaguely yearned for.

He went down the stairs, to the garden floor, and opened the back kitchen door. It was January: he had not been out in the garden, save to retrieve a rotting chair and a child's bicycle, for months. He was not a keen gardener; he tried to teach himself, from books, as he taught himself most things, but had no natural aptitude. The air, as he stood there on the back step, met him with a mild soft damp tenderness: it was a warm night. He went out. It was not a large garden: paved with old stone for the most part, and in the spring surrounded with a border of plants that flowered and trees that blossomed. Somebody had cared for it, once. Over the low wall at the other end of it was another much larger garden with tall trees.

The night was not dark. The light from the house illuminated the garden, and the sky itself, although a winter sky, was not black but luminous with stars and a faint pale grey glow overhead: low over the horizon, through the tree tops, there was that familiar pink radiance, the source of which he had never been able to identify. As a child, his mother had told him that this red glow was the glow of the fires of factories, where men toiled all through the night, and perhaps it had been, up in Newcastle, but it looked just the same down here, and as far as he knew there were no blazing furnaces on Hampstead Heath. Much more likely, he supposed, that it was the reflected glow of the lights of the city, the accumulation of fluorescence.

He walked down to the end, to the wall; the earth and stones breathed, for they would fulfil again their ancient bargain. He listened to their breath. At his feet were the green shoots and grey flat spears of bulbs, and the foliage of such small-leaved plants as never perish, plants so modest that they never die. He did not know the names of them, but he stood carefully, on the earthy border, so that they should not be crushed. By his shoulder nodded a ghostly white crumpled bud of a rose: it had been there for weeks, he had noticed it through the window, through frost and snow, frozen into an everlasting flower, never to open, never to die, a witness, a signal, a heroic pledge. The mildness of the air astonished him, as, each year, did the year's relenting. A perpetual winter was what he expected: he would, he felt, experience no surprise should, one spring, the trees refuse to bud, and the flowers to blossom. Why should those branches not remain for ever bare, the earth for ever hard and inhospitable? By what grace did these green hopes and gentle exhalations perpetually recur? He had done nothing to deserve so munificent a resurgence. He touched, with his hand, the damp, raw, pitted cells of the brick wall, themselves weathered into a semblance of organic life, and the smoky leaves of the ivy: in acknowledgement. Then he went back into the house and looked for her number, and telephoned.

She answered, at the third ring.

'Hello,' he said. 'Is that Mrs Vassiliou? This is Simon Camish here.'

'Oh, hello,' she said, nicely. 'I was hoping you might ring.'

'How are you?'

'Oh, me, I'm fine—' and she gathered breath, and continued, 'but I've been feeling so guilty, so awful about imposing all that on you last night, when you must have been so tired, I meant to ring you to say I was sorry but I felt *so* sorry I couldn't, and anyway I was hoping you might ring me.'

'It didn't matter,' he said, 'it didn't matter at all.'

'Then tell me,' she said, 'what did you think? What did you think about it all?'

'You must tell me, first, what happened to you today.'

'Today? Oh yes, I see what you mean. It seems a long time ago. Well, I rang the solicitors, as you said, and they rang his solicitors, and everybody said there was no need to do anything about anything for the moment. Apparently he's forgetting about the wards-of-court bit and is only applying for custody. Would that be right?'

'I imagine that would be right. Have you any idea, yet, what made him do it?'

'No, not really.'

'You weren't, for instance, planning to take the children abroad, were you? Or get married again? Or do anything decisive like that?'

She laughed. 'Good heavens no. Nothing like that at all. Why should I?'

'You can't think of any other reason?'

'No, I really can't.' She hesitated. 'Do you think it matters?'

'No, not really. It's just that when people start behaving foolishly for no reason they are quite likely to go on. It would be convenient if one could think of a reason.' He too, in his turn, hesitated. 'You hadn't, for instance, been preventing him from seeing the children, had you?'

'No,' she said, 'no I haven't. It was difficult at times, you know. But he saw them whenever he wanted to. More often than he was supposed to, in fact. I never liked to say no.'

'Then we needn't worry about that.'

'No, I don't think it was that.' She paused, again, on the verge of confidence. 'There have been other things, though,' she said, 'that he hasn't liked. About the way I bring them up. He might be able to make out some kind of case. I can't deny it. What do you think, they don't ever take the children away from the mother, do they?'

'No, hardly ever,' he said, not quite truthfully, remembering a few nasty precedents.

'I don't know,' said Rose. 'I don't know.' And then suddenly she gathered courage, and came out with it. 'Actually,' she said, 'I do know why he made the solicitors write that letter. I know what started it all off. I had another letter from him myself this morning. Well, it wasn't really a letter, it was more a sort of collage. He must have been reading lots of old stuff. He's got a whole suitcase of it. Letters from me, letters from my father, bits of the divorce case, press cuttings. And I think he must have spent the evening reading it. Because he sent me this thing, with bits cut out and all stuck together.'

'What was it meant to convey?'

'Oh, you know,' she said, miserably. 'What an incompetent I am. And how I let him down. And what he went through for me. I think he'd been brooding over how furious he was with my father about all that scene before we got married.'

'Then why doesn't he take it out of your father?'

'God knows. He really gets on with my father these days. He works for him now, you know.'

'But why should going back over all that make him want the children back, all of a sudden?'

'I don't know. Perhaps he really does think I'm incompetent. Or perhaps he didn't like sitting on his own and reading about it.'

'He probably doesn't really want them at all. The more I hear of it, the more it sounds to me as though he's just doing it out of ill-will. And if that's so, you needn't worry. Not that you need worry for a moment anyway, because he couldn't possibly get custody— he hasn't got a suitable home to offer them, has he? What on earth would he do with them if he did get them?'

'What would he do with them? Christ only knows. Let them lounge around in bed all day reading comics, and then one day he'd suddenly leap up and pack them all off to Eton, or Harrow, or Rugby, or something.' She laughed: and how could he not assume affection, in so appealing a description. 'Anyway,' she continued, 'it's quite out of the question, he lives in a quite unsuitable flat in somebody else's house, they'd never have the kids as well as him, I should think they're getting pretty fed-up with him by now.

'Actually,' she said, lowering her voice as though she might be overheard, 'he lives just down the road from you. I took the liberty of looking you up in the phone book when I got worried about sending you off with all those documents, and I saw that you lived just up the road from him. Odd, isn't it?'

'Yes,' he said, 'odd.'

'I've just thought,' she said. 'He might be planning to take them to his mother's. He couldn't, could he? He couldn't do such a thing?'

'What's wrong with his mother?'

'More or less everything. She hates me. She thinks I drag him down.'

'And where does she live? Would she have the accommodation to take them in?'

'What a very practical mind you have. I would never have thought of things like that. I'd somehow pictured all three of them snatched from their beds and all crowded in a row into Christopher's boot cupboard. I suppose the law wouldn't let a thing like that happen, would it?'

'No, certainly not. The law takes a serious view of things like accommodation.'

'Interesting, isn't it, things that the law takes seriously. Like bruises and adultery. It's a kind of code, I suppose, for what really goes on.'

'One has to have a code.'

'Oh yes, oh yes, that's one of the things I've learned. So you think the fact that I've got three bedrooms, even in this desolate dump, will be in my favour? My mother-in-law's got three bedrooms too, but come to think of it he'd never dare introduce her into a court of law again, not after what I know about her.'

'What do you know about her?'

'Too much by half. Christopher's parents are in fact crooks, you know. I don't think any other word would cover all their activities. It's amusing, when I first knew Christopher I used rather to hope that they were, because it seemed an exciting idea, and then when I found out what they used to get up to I was absolutely horrified. But now I've got used to it. It seems normal, now. Christopher's father runs a travel agency and he made a packet out of getting people out of Cyprus in various rather shady ways. There was a wine fiddle too. I think the new thing is trafficking in computer trainees—you won't tell anyone else all this, will you? When I first met Christopher they'd hardly got going, but you could see they thought big, you know, second-hand jags and nightclubs and things, and then they made some kind of big deal in 1959, just before Independence. And there was another thing about selling a house. They'd got this seedy house just north of the Euston Road, crammed full of lodgers and relations, and Christopher's uncle wised up to the fact that the whole district was being bought up by private buyers for a big property company, and so he refused to sell, and kept on raising the price and in the end he got thirty thousand for it. Amazing, isn't it?'

'Yes,' he said.

'And as a result of all that, if you managed to follow it, Christopher's Ma has now got a very nice residence in Finchley, gaping with empty rooms. But on the other hand she hasn't got a very moral character to produce in court. Christopher's side wouldn't let her speak at the divorce even though she wanted to. Though the funny thing about that house deal was that it was all above board. Or crooks on both sides. It upset me no end. Christopher thought it was funny. But it upset me. I've always had such a horror of speculation.'

'Tell me,' he said, 'why?'

'What do you mean, why?'

'I mean, why? Not everyone has, you know.'

'Haven't they? No, I suppose you're right. What a very basic question. Do you really want an answer?'

'Supposing that you had one.'

'Oh yes, I've got one. I've worked it all out, over the years.'

'Tell me, then.'

'Well, all right. But it makes me sound a fool. I am a fool. Did you happen to note that my middle name is Vertue?'

'Yes, I did. One couldn't miss it.'

'It was quite ordinary, really, for me to be called Vertue, it's just a family name, everybody is, but when I was a child'—she started to laugh—'when I was a child, I used to take it terribly seriously. I thought it was a special sign. I was a dreadfully religious child, you know. I went through a stage'—she giggled, nervously—'when I thought I was Jesus Christ reincarnated, and everybody would notice it and be nice to me at last. Though that was a silly hope, when one looks at what happened to him. Sad, really, wasn't it?'

'Very touching. But I don't see where the speculation comes in.'

'I was coming to that. That was the fault of this woman that looked after me. Actually, I can't remember now if I was religious before she got hold of me or whether it was her that did it, but anyway, whichever it was, she made things much worse. Noreen, she was called. She came from the village. Awful, she was, she had a dreadful effect on me. Very puritanical. Religion is hot stuff in East Anglia, you know. Why nobody stopped her corrupting me I can't imagine. They probably never noticed. Anyway, she used to nag me endlessly about the family's money and my father's wickedness in being so rich, and usury and interest rates and gambling and shares and the stock market, and I just used to listen and take it. And one day when she took me to church, the sermon was about that text about it's being easier for camels to get through needles' eyes than for rich people to get into the kingdom of heaven—and it was an absolutely absurd sermon, all about how Christ hadn't really meant it, and the eye of a needle not being really an eye of a needle but a Hebrew phrase meaning a gate in the walls of Jerusalem, and of course camels could get through it, or small ones anyway, though it was a bit of a squeeze—casuistry, in fact, that's what it was, but to me it was like the Road to Damascus, a horribly heavenly light shone upon me and I knew what life was like, endless prevarication and shuffling and squeezing and self-excusing and trying to cram oneself into grace without losing anything on the way—and on the way home I asked Noreen, what did she think of the sermon, and she sniffed and looked down at me—I was very small at the time, only about eight, I think—and said that if I wanted to believe that kind of soft soap then I could. Oh, she was a dreadful woman, Noreen. But she was right.'

'It sounds as though she shouldn't have been allowed near a small child,' he said.

'No, maybe not. But as she was right, that wasn't much of an argument. And since I could take it, I did. How can one say, excuse me, excuse me, I'm only a small child, if one recognises the truth in one's bones?'

'It was an odd way to find out.'

'Yes. But I was destined to be some kind of freak anyway. As well that sort as any other. Even by other people's standards.'

'You don't think of yourself as a freak.'

'No, of course I don't. I know I'm right. But I'm not so mad that I don't notice what other people think, you know.'

'And you really have Noreen to thank for the way you are?'

'No, not wholly. There were other things too. It was very funny, you know, when we got home from church that Sunday after the camel sermon, do you know what my parents were discussing at lunch? Insurance. There'd been a burglary in the neighbourhood, and quite a lot of stuff had been taken, paintings and things, and silver, and my father was telling my mother that it was worth overinsuring, there was such a good risk of being robbed. He loves that kind of conversation. Mother wasn't listening, she never listens, but I listened. And I remember vowing to myself over the roast beef, I'll never possess anything, I said to myself, that I fear to lose. It was a very solemn vow. After dinner I went upstairs and made myself a special prayer to God—there wasn't a suitable one so I cut bits out of other prayers and joined them all together, just like Christopher's horrible letter, now I come to think of it—and then I went out into the garden and vowed, under a tree that I thought was specially sacred. And that was that.'

'And you actually lived up to it?'

'Oh, I don't know about that. I gave some money away, but that's nothing. There are still plenty of things I wouldn't like to part with. The children, for instance. Cruel, isn't it, the way one has to keep wanting things.'

'They are hostages to fortune,' he said.

'Yes,' she said, 'that's just about it.'

'You won't lose them,' he said, 'don't worry.'

'I daresay I won't. But I don't like the thought that I might. It's bad enough having to worry about them dying, without this as well.'

'I wish I could see you,' he said. 'I don't like the telephone.'

'You wouldn't like to see me at the moment. I don't look very nice. My hair is wrapped up in a towel, because I'd just washed it when you rang. But do come and see me, some other time.'

'May I?'

'It would be very kind of you.'

'Not at all. It would be kind of you.'

'When will you come? Come tomorrow.'

'No, tomorrow I can't come.' He hesitated, and then he said it. 'I can't come tomorrow because my wife is coming home from America.'

'Oh. I see. Then that would not be convenient,' she said—embracing, encompassing his excuse, so directly, and yet not failing to accept the implications, the fact that he had named his wife in such a context—familiar, she must be, a single woman, with this world of implications, and delicately, carefully, taking no step beyond them. 'When, then, would be possible?'

'I could come the day after,' he said, working out that the day after he had a case in Southampton, and that nobody would care much about the time of his return. 'In the evening.'

'In the evening, that would be very kind. What time could you come?'

'I'm not sure, whenever I get back, I am out for the day and I will come to see you on my way home.'

'Yes,' she said. 'Yes, that would be very kind of you. And now, I suppose, I must let you go to bed.'

And he agreed, of course, that this might be so, and gave her his Chambers telephone number, and they said good night to one another, politely, and severed their connection. And he, for his part, went to bed and thought about the things that she had told him.

SHE, ON THE OTHER HAND, sat up for some time, kneeling on the hearth rug in front of the gas fire and drying her hair. The gas dried it up and frizzled the ends but she didn't much care. She was thinking about that year when the money had come in, so long ago, when she had been twenty-four. It always distressed her, the callousness with which one discarded one's past self, the alacrity with which one embraced the wisdom of the present. Looking back upon one's past, one could disown it, with knowledge, experience, and judgement all augmented: but what if one had once been right and ceased to be so? And what were those years, if they ceased to exist? Foundation stones, in her better moments she hoped, but what if one were burying beneath rubble some priceless intuition? One thing one could be sure of, that one would never know, because, beneath the rubble, it would be lost for ever: it could no longer be examined. So many passions could never be re-created: better lost, most of them, but either way one would never know, and the distressing thing was that in looking back, some of the necessity seemed to have gone from one's actions: knowing, as she now did, what had happened to that money and what had been the consequences of her parting with it, she thought that she knew better, would know better next time, would not repeat such a dreadful mistake, such a flamboyant, histrionic, disastrous, ruinous gesture. But at the time, at the age of twenty-four, it had been the only thing to do. She could no longer imagine herself so rash and foolish—sitting there, at that very table, with her dog-eared little cheque book full of meagrely-pared electricity payments, writing out with a shilling biro, Pay Akisoferi Nyoka twenty thousand pounds—her hand trembling, her heart beating loudly in her frightened chest, exhilarated beyond bearing by the extremity, the irrevocability of the act, by its irreversible determining quality, by its implications, by its very size. (In much the same spirit she had married Christopher, trembling, afraid, mad and blinkered by a suicidal commitment, haunted by an image that had to be made flesh.) But the fact that she could no longer remember the self that had married Christopher, nor the self that had signed that cheque, did not mean that they had not been necessary: and one had to go on, wearily continuing to make mistakes, believing them to be acts of truth and faith and righteousness, at the time having faith in them, and yet all the time knowing that in ten years one would look back and say, Christ, how could I have done that, believed that, been that, with any conviction? And yet, what about those past selves, what permanence, what validity were they ensured? Foundation stones, was an image that had risen to her mind, because she liked the thought of building, but one of those selves, in endeavouring to build, had been quite literally bombed and blasted out of existence, it had gone up in real flames and fire and smoke, and doubtless lay there now in real ruins, real dust and ashes. Those thousands of pounds, donated for the construction of a school in Central Africa, had gone up in smoke: the school had been built, it had stood for some months, and then it had been obliterated in an unfortunate outbreak of civil war. The thousands of pounds had gone, and so had a hundred children or so, but for them Rose knew that she could take no responsibility: they would have died anyway, and the location of their death was the last aspect of it to concern her.

She knew that, even objectively, even in Brechtian terms of product, the money had provided work for builders, schooling for children, however briefly, however tragically concluded. A few months may be as significant as a building's natural span, in the scale of eternity. And anyway, that was not the end of it. Rose, despite herself, had to admit that she was much exercised by an ancient orthodoxy, a modern heresy: she believed in faith as well as in works, she believed that giving is not simply for the benefit of the receiver. So perhaps she had not been so foolish, after all. On faith, on works, on spiritual progress, on all these counts she was quit, even by such a disaster.

She thought of that piece in the Bible, about building on the sand, and about the crumbling plaster (particularly in the lavatory behind the cistern) in her own house, and about Noreen also she thought, connecting her with the Bible, and remembering, also, what she had said of her to Simon Camish. Noreen, really, was at the back of it all. She would have liked to think that the information about Noreen had been imparted for the first time, virginally, but of course it was not so: she was a great spiller of facts, a gossip, no less, she could keep nothing back. But however often she gave Noreen away, the woman remained dourly with her: a gift that nobody would accept, a gift that nobody knew how to accept, an encumbrance, a possession, that had set her apart where she now was, crouched upon this home-made rug. Simon Camish had responded to Noreen more than some: there was either religion or self-denial in his background, she could tell, or he would not at all have known what she was talking about. Funny to think of her still alive, an old woman now, not a witch or a saint but an old woman, perhaps even a little mellowed with age. She hadn't seen her for years. She remembered her face: long, pale, horse-like; with permed yellowish hair in rigid waves surrounding it, in her memory, as the hair surrounds the face of an out-of-date advertisement, glossy and laminated but dust-collecting, in a small hairdresser's shop. The hair might have changed by now, in the last twenty years—it was a postwar, austerity image of the woman that she preserved, not having seen her for fifteen years or so. She wondered (for the first time, a novel thought, so there was some purpose in thinking) if it had occurred to any of her family to blame Noreen on the occasion of her marriage, and all its preceding and succeeding sorrows and embarrassments: probably not, because few people would have been able to make the connection between Noreen, grim, evangelical, life-denying, pinched and priggish and retreating, and Christopher, beautiful, dirty, seedy Christopher (as he then was) his hands in his pockets, his dark glasses glinting, his extravagant hair drooping, his aggressive slouch, Christopher, flashily kicking a tin can down Camden High Street, clever, sharp, and foul and bitter, demanding, taking, deceiving, getting: the one discipline as rigorous as the other, and she had wanted him for so many reasons, all directly or perversely Noreen-inspired: because he was sexy and undeniable, and crude about it, and anybody less crude she would have been obliged to deny—but with Christopher one abandoned judgement, one fell, hopelessly, enchanted, into whatever mud or gutter or dark corner or creaking second-hand bed that one could find—that was a perverse reason, a reason that rejected Noreen (as she would have had to be rejected, because she herself, Rose Vertue, could never have made much of a virtue of chastity, as Noreen did, she was not made of the right kind of flesh or spirit) but there were other reasons more directly descended, though Noreen would not have liked to acknowledge them as her offspring. She had, after all, first wanted and meekly followed Christopher because he was one of the dispossessed—doubly so, financially and racially—and Noreen had taught her to despise possessions. She could not, however, have foreseen, as she indoctrinated that small impressionable child so many years ago with a sense of the wickedness of riches, that it would end like that—Rose pale, in tears, confronting solicitor after solicitor, Rose exiled, Rose returning and weeping in the pages of the *News of the World,* Rose married, Rose locked into bedrooms, beaten up, bleeding, scarred, divorced, threatened, and really very happy now, at last, if only people would allow her to continue with her own admittedly curious theory of living. No, there was no doubt about it, Noreen would not have made much of these developments. She would not have regarded Christopher Vassiliou as one of the meek, the poor in spirit, the lowly. She had had a different, more static and silent and sexless picture of that kind of person. She would not have liked Christopher at all.

So many thoughts of Christopher were now crowding into her mind, all at once, that she could hardly organise them: they flocked and gathered. Some of them were to do with violence, and some of them were to do with blood, and some of them were to do with the Bible—two of the subjects seemed related but not the third, and she couldn't work it out, she couldn't straighten it, until she remembered that scene—in this very room, it had taken place, years ago, one of those scenes about money it had been, and about why Rose had not wanted it, and she herself had been crying and screaming and had finally thrown her plate of fish and chips at his head and missed, yelling all the while, distraught with fury and quite confused, about the rich not getting into heaven, and the needle's eye, and unless you give all that you have to the poor ye shall not etc. etc., and Christopher had thrown the tomato ketchup bottle at her and it had broken and gone all over, and the children had woken and stood at the top of the stairs shivering, as was their habit on such occasions, and Rose had gone on yelling these demented Biblical tags until Christopher, understandably beside himself with rage, had kicked over the table and grabbed at her and said (frightening her into silence), Don't you quote the fucking Bible at me, they used to quote it to us at school, don't think I don't remember that cunt standing up there and telling us the parable of the talents and bloody wrong he got it too, I remember him droning on to this collection of morons and misfits and telling us that no matter how bloody thick we were we all had our little talents and we could use them if we wanted, and nobody was without anything—the idiot, standing there looking at that dim crowd of eleven-year-olds, our last term at primary it was, and he looked at them—and Christ if ever you saw a group of finished dead no-good human beings it was there, and he went on about how we all had good we could do in us, no matter what fools we were, and how people like me who were going on to Grammar needn't think we were any better than the rest of them, and that our greater gifts we should use to greater good, and then he read that bit, that bit of

Bible, and it was all about making money, that's what it was about, so don't you quote the Bible at me, and don't you expect me to sympathise with all the subnormal races of Africa, there's enough subnormality on the very doorstep here, why don't you go out and drop fivers from the top of a double decker bus, you histrionic bitch?

And then she had tried to get away from him, to comfort the child, knowing he was right, and she had trodden on the broken ketchup bottle, blind as she was with tears and rage and moral confusion, and she had cut her foot, a curious cut between the toes, God knows how it had happened but it bled like nothing on earth, and what with the blood and the ketchup and the damp chips trodden into the carpet she had wished to die, but had gone up instead to comfort the child, and having reached the child Christopher had shouted something at her—oddly enough she could not remember what it was, that had thus proved the last straw, but he could always do it, he could always manage it, with unfailing monotonous regularity, with pre-ordained finality, and this time she had been quite overcome with an upsurge of such violence that she had flung the smaller of the two children down the stairs at him, and he had caught the child but only just, and it too was covered in ketchup and looked as though bleeding, and she had managed, in the end, to comfort the other one, and had retired to bed with it, trembling with shame and self-contempt and a profound, unceasing misery, because she knew—at each of these moments she knew, and forgot now less often in between them—that all was up with herself and Christopher, whom she had so wanted, for whom she had endured so much, and that they had reached a point beyond any hope of repair, they had reached such depths now that the walls behind them—to that flat plateau of mutual co-existence, of occasionally sunny tolerance—were no longer scalable, they were down for ever now, and unless they parted—dirty, dishevelled, undesirable—they would kill each other, perhaps even literally.

It was so difficult, looking back, to remember how things had ever reached such an extremity. It had happened gradually, at first—the hard word, the suspicions, the intolerance, the endless distrust on both sides, the foul temper about ruined meals (on his part) or no outings to the cinema (on hers), and suddenly there had seemed no point in ever watching one's temper, in ever trying to control one's foul resentments. But it had been the first blow that had done it. She did rather tend to agree with the courts about physical violence. It was a serious matter, a more than technical offence. If he had hit her when she had still, passionately, loved him, she would not have minded it, she would have enjoyed it, even, but of course he had not done so, on the contrary, when she had loved him he had loved her and he had been, accordingly, good to her. And she could not help thinking (though she could not be sure) that it was she herself that had struck the first blow. He had struck her only in self-defence, but he had done this more and more frequently, having more to defend himself from, having committed more offences, and therefore having induced more attacks: and his defence had become violent out of all proportion to the odd kick or slap or bite or broken glass which she had inflicted on him, until she was always the loser. There was no going back, for her, after such a pattern had been established. Yet how could they live together, with such knowledge, in such a mire, and being in the mire, why should they ever restrain themselves from kicking, biting, and breaking plates and windows? There was nothing to be salvaged, nothing at all. So she had agreed with her barrister at the divorce, she had politely produced her evidence of wounds: 'this is a mere technicality, you know, but it is one of the most convenient matrimonial offences' he had said, smiling urbanely, and she had smiled and thought Christ, what is he talking about, convenient, does he think I liked being beaten black and blue, does he think I liked bleeding, and having my hair pulled out (in such large patches that it was confused with another nervous disease she developed at around the same period, the disease of alopecia)? Christ, she had said to herself, he must meet some sophisticated couples, if they can bear all this without resentment, and recall it merely as a convenience and a technicality. Similarly, the judge's attitudes had confused her: her own judge's, but even more the judge of a completely disconnected case that she had gone to watch in order to brace herself for her own forthcoming ordeal. Curiously enough, that too had been a mixed marriage, a defended divorce, between a Turkish-, not a Greek-Cypriot and an English girl: Rose had sat there, suffering from the very look of the room, feeling grotesquely conspicuous in the Public Gallery, and God knows what it would be like in the witness box, and she had heard this story of grief and woe and violence, not dissimilar, in several respects, from her own, though the sums of money involved in their joint deposit account book had been smaller: the Turk had been a good witness and had won his case, which depressed her enormously, as she had felt obliged (through the loyalty of sex) to identify with the feckless wife, who had deserted husband and children because she wanted (her own words) a bit more fun out of life. And her chief complaint against the husband had been his violence: he made, it appeared, a regular habit of flinging things at her, slapping her, punching her and so on. If he had done these things, Rose thought, the woman might indeed legitimately have objected, but the judge did not think so: he spoke of things that any man might do under provocation, and seemed to think that a few blows one way or the other were the normal fare of married life. Indeed, he had said, of the abusive words of which the lady complained, that she must not be shy to repeat them in his presence, that he had heard anything she might be likely to say and worse, and that surely such words (extremely familiar, it had to be admitted, to Rose's ears and lips) were common enough in the give and take of daily matrimonial intercourse, and could hardly be taken as grounds for divorce for cruelty. He also said that it was funny that the lady in question hadn't had a few more bruises to show: and hearing this Rose had looked down on the battle scar upon her wrist with a loving gratitude. And the judge had found for the husband, describing him not as cruel but as deserted. This may well, Rose thought, have been so, but she remained perplexed by the nonchalance with which abuse and blows had been disregarded by this elderly man, the kind of man, she imagined, who would consider it an act of violence, in his own domestic situation, if a guest were to put down a glass on a polished wooden surface, or drop ash upon a parquet floor.

The Turk had said, from time to time, that he loved his wife. In much the same way as Christopher, not much later, was to declare in court that he loved Rose. Love. The word fell uneasily on the official air. But nobody queried it. And she had a strange sense, as she sat there, both times, as spectator and as plaintiff, of love as some huge white deformed and not very lovely god, lying there beneath the questions and the formality, caught in a net of which points alone touched and confined him—points, blows, matrimonial offences, desertions, legalities, all binding love down though he shapelessly overflowed and struggled—and necessarily bound, the net being entirely necessary, because without it there was violence and terror and warfare. She had invoked the law, she had invoked it herself, in her own defence, in the defence of her children, in much the way that it had been invoked against her in her minority, and then as now she would abide by its decisions.

But what would happen to her, this time, over the custody? There were some decisions she could never accept, though the loss of her children, the threatened one, was the only one she could imagine. This time too there must be technicalities—education, religion, drink, responsibility, she dimly guessed what the issues would be—and this time might she not find herself there mumbling shamefully of love, while Christopher and his lawyers called upon the voice of reason and tightened the net over her struggling passions? It was not possible, she refused to think it possible. Simon Camish had said that they very rarely took the child from the mother, unless the mother were grossly defective. But she knew wherein her gross defects lay. She knew it already. And those defects being her virtues, her faith, her way of life, she could not even, without losing all, offer even a promise of reform.

SIMON CAMISH, driving back from Southampton, having lost his case, had a headache. He was on his way to Rose Vassiliou's, and did not want to go there. He wanted, however, to go home even less. And in any case, duty bound him. He was incapable of breaking an arrangement. But, he thought to himself, there is really little good that I can do, the whole business is not at all serious, clearly this woman's husband is a trouble-maker, whereas she is (as I have seen her) quiet, domestic, a conscientious mother, and there is no conceivable reason why there should be any difficulty over the children. She wants reassurance, that is all, and really I see no reason why I should be obliged to offer unpaid reassurance to any woman I happen to meet. She has a nerve to request it, and I am a fool to offer it.

This is what he was telling himself, which was much the same as what she, waiting for him, was telling herself. But both were uneasy, she because she knew better, and he because he had taken the trouble to send for some newspaper files on her (God knows why curiosity should have led him so far) and he had found there things that did not make sense, that one could not possibly like. He could not face, he had not the energy for the encounter, so he repressed the uneasiness of his investigations, promising himself that he would deal with the whole matter as superficially and sensibly as possible, and then get out of it quick before anything uncomfortable presented itself. It was a familiar professional mode, and quite often it was all that was required. He hoped that it would be so in this case.

But unfortunately, when he arrived there, the scene that he found was not exactly susceptible to such an approach. The children, for one thing, were still up. Having calculated that the one real advantage of visiting her first would be that he would miss his own, he was rather put out to hear, as the door was opened to him, the noise of hers.

'I'm sorry,' she said, standing there in her apron in the narrow passage, 'I'm afraid I haven't managed to get them to bed yet, but they'll be going soon. Do come in.'

'That's quite all right,' he said, bravely, putting down his umbrella and his brief case, and following her into the living-room, which seemed remarkably, uncomfortably full of people. A pregnant young woman, of a sullen and sultry aspect, was sitting on the settee in a kind of trance, for she did not look round when he entered, and at her feet two smallish children (mercifully, he noted wearing pyjamas and nightdress) were rolling around fighting. The television was on, but competing with it was a large child, who was playing the oboe.

'Come along now, little ones, off to bed,' said Rose, as though expecting no response, and indeed getting none, for the children continued to fight, but the eldest child put down his oboe and offered his hand to be shaken, when introduced. 'This is Konstantin,' said Rose, and he looked at the child's face, and felt his determination waver, and also his resentment. Because, after all, anyone would worry about losing a real child: worry was an entirely natural response, and reassurance an entirely natural desire, however trivial the grounds for anxiety—and seeing the object of anxiety, the grounds no longer seemed trivial, the whole matter became serious, even as a suggestion. The child was quite striking. He had long fair hair and a face of the most delicate frail politeness.

'You play the oboe, I see,' said Simon, fatuously, as Rose behind his back removed the two little ones, and the pregnant girl dislodged herself and disappeared without a word.

'Yes,' said Konstantin.

'How long have you been learning for?' he asked, unable to think of anything else to say.

'Since I was six, I think.'

'Do they teach you at school?'

'There's a man who comes round. A peripatetic teacher, he's called.'

'Oh, is he?'

'He teaches three of us. We do it together.'

'You could play me a tune,' said Simon, sitting down. His head was splitting. The child played him a tune. When the tune was over Rose came down again and told him to go and have his bath, which he did, without a murmur of protest.

'He's a very polite child,' said Simon, to Rose, carefully.

'Yes, he is,' said Rose.

'And very—striking.'

'It's his hair,' said Rose. 'Mine used to be like that, at his age. Funny that he's inherited it.' She looked worn out.

'You look worn out,' he said.

And she looked at him, sharply, and said, 'So do you,' and they both laughed.

After that she offered him a meal, and he offered to take her out for a meal, and she said that she had nobody to babysit, so she cooked for him, instead—a nice meal, though he did not much notice what he was eating—and while they were doing this they talked. There were various questions he wanted to ask, and so he asked them, because it seemed the best thing to do. He asked her about her marriage, her parents, her exile to the Continent, her divorce: but first of all he asked the first thing, the reason for which was the act that seemed to have set the whole thing in motion. He, like her, had come to accept that it must have been some notion of revenge that had led Christopher to think of applying for the wardship or custody of the children—a notion reinforced by the sight of the collage letter which Christopher had sent Rose the morning after Simon had first met her, which contained a cut-out headline from a popular daily, saying WARDS-OF-COURT: ANYONE COULD MAKE ANYONE A WARD-OF-COURT followed by a picture of a girl who had been made one, as a joke, by a total stranger who had seen her dancing in a nightclub. So he said to Rose, now, still sitting at the table with the letter on her sideplate—'What was it, why ever did your parents do such a thing to you? You wouldn't really have married without their consent, would you?'

'Oh, I don't know,' said Rose. 'I might have done. I really had provoked them rather a lot, you know. Perhaps I wanted to provoke them into doing something awful, do you think? I've often wondered. They're a funny couple, you know, they brought me up very oddly, I don't know what they can have expected. My father's father had a garage, perhaps you know all this, and my father made all this money, and married my mother when they were both quite old, well, in their mid-thirties, and she must have been talked into it by her family, I think. Because now they keep the house up. Not that she's there very much, she goes abroad for most of the winter. She doesn't really do anything, she hasn't got any friends or anything. She's got a companion, now. She's a very sad person. Bored all the time. My father's quite different, he works all the time, he never stops, I can't see what there is in it for him now but he just can't stop. So neither of them had much time for me—I bored her, and he wouldn't talk to me because all he could talk about was business and I didn't understand about it... I suppose I was a disappointment to them, but on the other hand it's hard to imagine what they could actually have *wanted* me to be, they never tried to make me take an interest in anything, they didn't try to encourage me to go out or do anything.

'When I was a child I was lonely, of course, but then we were most of the time in the country, and I liked the country, I used to find things to do. And then, suddenly, when I was fifteen, they took it into their heads to send me off to boarding school—God knows why they didn't send me earlier, you'd have thought they would have been glad to have me out of the house, perhaps they just didn't think of it. I hated it at first when I got there, but then I made this friend, Emily, I still see a lot of her, and things began to look up. She used to take me about, and look after me, and said why didn't I do some exams and go up to University with her, but it was far too late by then because I was far too ignorant, but it was nice that she'd thought of it . . . I cheered up so easily, once I met Emily. She went to London University, and while she was there I used to live more and more in the London house, and met her friends, and went out with some of her men, and they all used to tell me what to do with my life—they were very left wing, all of them, perhaps all students are, but it was odd really because Emily has never had the slightest interest in politics, in fact Emily's a bit of a Fascist, I've always thought. But anyway, there were all these friends of hers, telling me what to do with my money.

'I had quite a lot of money, you know, they gave me a massive allowance, for a girl of my age I had an enormous amount of cash, and I used to pay for everything wherever we went, it was always me that paid, so they were always pleased to have me about, and they used to work out for me what I ought to do with my money, and what I ought to give it to, and that's when the trouble really started because I gave quite a large sum for a political magazine, it wasn't really a student one, it was a semi-professional job, but somehow the story got into the papers and my father was extremely angry. They printed some story about strikes, actually, the magazine did and he thought I'd given them the information, though where he thinks I'd have got hold of it one can't imagine, but I remember he asked to see me one evening—oh, it was too frightening, not what he said, but the total unacknowledgement of me as he looked at me, and I remember saying, "But what do you think I *do,* how do you imagine I get through the days, I have to do something," and he said, why. And I said I hadn't thought he would mind, I hadn't thought he would care, and he said he didn't care as long as I kept my name out of the papers, but that if I was going to waste my money on anarchists then I couldn't have any more. So he cut my allowance, but the poor man, he really didn't know, he cut it by half and I was still doing fine. Perhaps he thought I bought clothes, or something. Perhaps he thought that was the kind of thing women had to do. And then he asked the only shrewd question he'd ever asked me, which was if I'd joined the Party, and I said no, which was the truth, though I'd thought of it. I think, after that, he'd have liked to keep me at home, to stop me going about, but he couldn't do anything about it, he was so used to letting me go my own way, to ignoring me in fact, he couldn't set up any mechanism for stopping me, he didn't know how to, mother being so useless and disinterested, and anyway she was in Nice at the time. She was in Nice quite a lot. Her health wasn't very good. It never has been.'

And here she seemed to run down, obliging him to employ more than the encouraging interjections with which he had punctuated this monologue.

'And it was with these students that you met your husband, was it?'

'Christopher? No, it wasn't, not really. Well yes, in a sense it was, because I was there when I met him, I was in the office of that magazine, it wasn't really an office, it was more a basement room, in Bloomsbury, that was also somebody's flat, but they used it for an office. You know, to tell you the truth about that strike story, I did give it to them, but I hadn't meant to, I simply didn't realise the implications of what I was saying—but still, anyway, to get back to Christopher, I was sitting in this dump listening to a friend going on about something or other, South Africa I think it was, when Christopher arrived with a whole load of printed stickers. He had a van, he was driving a van, in those days. Amongst other things. And this friend of mine, taking one look at Christopher, said have a cup of coffee, in his comradely way, because he thought Christopher looked like a potential comrade, and because he was a nice-looking fellow, and because it made him feel good to give cups of coffee to people who drive vans, and because it was the kind of office where clearly not much else went on'—(Simon, listening to this last sentence, was astonished by something so familiar in others and so odd in Rose, and took some time to work out that it was merely a breath of simple malice)—'and so Christopher had a cup of coffee, and I watched him, and I suppose he watched me, because when I said I had to be going he said, naturally enough that he'd give me a lift. Naturally, having the van, I mean. And so I went off with him, and I hadn't really anywhere I ought to be going, I never had, in those days, so he drove me home, and I asked him in because there was nobody there, and we had some tea, and then we had a drink and then I went out with him and had some supper with him, and so it went on.

'How old was I? I was nineteen, and he was twenty-one.

'I loved him. I fell completely in love with him. He completely seduced me. He really knew what he was doing, did Christopher. He was working two nights a week in a Greek restaurant in Char- lotte Street and I used to go there and sit in the kitchen and wait for him. That's how it was. I didn't really—it's amazing how little I knew about him. I didn't want to know because I suspected I mightn't understand. He was no fool, obviously, or I couldn't have—well, I don't wish to imply that I wasn't a fool, because I was, about him, completely, but at least I knew it. He'd been to Gram- mar School, but when I met him I assumed that he'd started work- ing as soon as he left, and it took me years, well months at least to realise that he'd actually started off at University but he got kicked out, or dropped it—I think he couldn't stand it, he genuinely hated being in anything like a traditional institution, he had nothing but contempt for it—I should have put it together earlier, he left it be- cause he was ambitious, not because he was unambitious, and he couldn't bear to waste three years or so on a students' grant find- ing out not very much, and all that van driving and waiting and dealing and double-dealing he used to go in for was really the foun- dation of something much more lucrative, in the end, for him— well, indeed, for anyone. But Christopher was attractive. Dirty, he was, and he smelt of oil from the van, and he lived on bacon sand- wiches, it was something I'd never set eyes on before, and to find that such a person actually seemed to want me—'

'I would have thought that a lot of people might have wanted you. You were a very desirable property.'

'Oh no no, not at all, not any of my and Emily's friends, anyway, they were far too altruistic, they wanted my money, but only for meals and donations and drinks, and loans and abortions, they never had anything as grandiose as a scheme for marrying me, they simply wouldn't have thought of it, and I was no beauty, you know, I was a miserable-looking creature in those days, I probably still am for that matter—no no, I don't think anybody else would have dreamed of having that kind of intention on me. There were— there were kind of official suitors, sort of dynastic suitors, but one couldn't take them seriously. Or rather, they couldn't take me seriously. They were far too young to be wised up to that kind of thing.'

'So Christopher and his bacon sandwiches found you a willing victim?'

'He certainly did. Willing and eager.' She pushed at her hair, and laughed. 'We used to spend a lot of time in a Greek club. In Camden Town. Its windows were all stuck over with paper, it was very secret. They played card games and billiards, and I sat around and watched. There weren't many girls allowed in. I was allowed in because I was Christopher's. It was a real élite I'd hit at last, I used to think. I felt really privileged, sitting around there and drinking cups of coffee. It's funny, really, looking back on it. Or almost funny. It would be funny, if I could think I had survived it all.'

'You look as though you've survived it,' he said, with meaningless gallantry.

'I don't know about that,' she said.

'Tell me,' he said, 'what made you decide to get married? What made you think you wanted to get married?'

'Well,' she said, 'it's hard to know, really. I think I—for my part, this is, I'm speaking only for myself—I wanted to make some kind of declaration. I don't know. I felt it so much, I wanted to show I was serious. That must be why most people do it, isn't it? Out of gratitude. Partly. I don't remember very well how the subject of getting married came up, I think I was saying something about Emily, who'd just got herself engaged to Offenbach, and Christopher said, oh, very politely, perhaps you would think of marrying me. You couldn't possibly want to, I kept saying, but as soon as he'd suggested it I knew it was irresistible, that I had to do it. And then also you must remember that I was hopelessly in love with him at this stage, I used to trail around after him like a small child. So we decided to get married. I couldn't believe it. I couldn't believe my luck.'

'So what did you do?'

'What did we do? Well, first of all Christopher wrote to my father, and my father wrote back saying you must be joking, and so Christopher and I went to see him, and there was a scene, and father called Christopher a dirty Greek, and Christopher called father a Jewish swine, knowing quite well father isn't Jewish and never has been, and I cried, and then I walked out of the house with Christopher and wouldn't go home. And then it all started to happen. As a matter of fact I'd been fairly discreet about him up till this point, but now it seemed necessary to assert ourselves, so we started going around together in public or whatever bits of the public we could find—we went to nightclubs, and restaurants, and I took him to all the dreary parties I used to get invited to and never went to, and we made a bit of a stir. It was quite exciting. You look very shocked. You don't like the idea of making a bit of a stir.'

'I'm not sure that what shocks me most isn't the idea or *your* liking to make, as you put it, a bit of a stir.'

'Ah, but I've changed, you see. This was many years ago. I have changed.'

'Can one change, so much?'

'That,' she said, sadly and anxiously, 'is what I sometimes wonder.'

'Don't worry about it now,' he said, regretting what he had said.

'No, all right,' she said, more cheerfully, 'I won't. I must finish this story, mustn't I? Where was I?'

'You were at the bit where you and Christopher were provoking parental opposition. Where were you living at the time?'

'Well, oddly enough, we were living in that basement where I first met him, I said we'd be caretakers for the magazine because the fellow that lived there moved out without trace, and we used to sleep there on a mattress on the floor amidst a lot of bales of newsprint. It was a nice house, one of those old houses in a little terrace, and nobody knew we were there except people who'd promised not to say. And every day I'd ring up home and ask if they'd changed their minds—father had got mother home by this time—and they'd yell at me that they'd get the police on to me and cut me off without a penny and God knows what.'

'And did you make any efforts at conciliation?'

'Yes, of course I did, I said I'd come home as soon as they allowed me to marry Christopher, I said they could cut me off if they liked, I even said I'd wait till I was twenty-one, which would have been a good eight months. I'd known Christopher nearly a year, by this time, you know. A year's a long time. We couldn't have been accused of not knowing each other.'

'But the circumstances were hardly normal.'

'No. Hardly. I suppose not.'

'It must have been from this that this cutting dates?' he said, producing from his pocket a slip of newspaper.

She took it, and looked at it, with a mixture of pride, disgust, embarrassment and amusement that seemed to him an extraordinarily finely-constituted response. 'Oh Christ,' she said, 'wherever did you get this?'

It was a photograph of herself, and Christopher, many years younger, sitting in a restaurant. Roses and a candle featured. Christopher looked vicious but satisfied, Rose plain and anxious to please. The headline was 'Tycoon's Red Daughter Rose with Greek Croupier.'

'Where did you get it?' she repeated, returning it to him.

'I stole it from a file on you,' he said. 'I liked it so much. Why does it say croupier? Was this another career he adopted?'

'No, no, not at all, that was just a mistake, a friend of mine was rung up by the press and said he was a courier, because that was the politest way he could think of saying van-driver, though actually by this time Christopher had got rid of the van and had got himself a car, with a deposit of my money, of course, and he used to drive American ladies around sightseeing, so perhaps he was a courier after all. Whatever one of those is. But not a croupier, no. Though he'd have been good at it. He was a really good gambler, was Christopher. Really good. Anyway, that car was the last thing he had out of me because my father shut the bank account. That was the first warning I had that things were turning nasty. I went to the local branch, in Russell Square, and told it to ring up my branch at Marble Arch and let me have some cash and they said no. I couldn't believe it.'

'Were you alarmed?'

'To tell you the truth,' she said, thoughtfully, carefully, 'I think I was—relieved. Really. Relieved. It sounds silly, but that's how it was. I was—partly, I suppose, gratified to find that I'd had some effect, and also, oh it sounds absurd, I was glad to have cut myself off from all that stuff. I'd always at the bottom of my heart believed that one couldn't get rid of money, that it would stick like a leech or a parasite, and breed and breed even if one tried to cut it out—and I was right, that was a real premonition, because look at me now, living here in this little house, it's nothing but a mockery, you know, in some ways, all right, so I pay my way and live as modestly as I can, but there are always people to ask me out, and newspapers to pay me or at least feed me and give me drinks when I want them, and even my clothes—well, that dress I was wearing when you first met me, I'd had that for twelve years, you know, and I can *afford* to wear it, I can go around in that kind of thing, but the girls round here, they can't do it, they couldn't do it—Oh Lord, I don't know what I'm talking about, but yes, there's another thing, it suddenly struck me one day that no matter how energetically I get rid of whatever money comes my way, there's nothing on earth to prevent my father from leaving it to the children. How can I stop him, after all? They're his only grandchildren. How can I stop him?'

'Why should you wish to stop him?'

'Isn't it obvious?'

'Not unmistakably so. But don't bother about that now, that's another issue, go back to the business about the closing of the bank account. And the relief.'

'Yes. Well. I've forgotten where I was. The relief. I went out into the road and I looked in my bag and counted what we'd got between us. Fifteen pounds ten, it was. Quite a lot.'

'It wouldn't last long, though.'

'No, it didn't, we went straight off to the club to have a game to improve our finances and lost the lot.'

'That was silly.'

'Yes, it was, wasn't it? It seemed very funny at the time. So we went back to our room to sleep it off, and when we got there there was a man waiting for Christopher and me. At first I thought it was the police raiding the magazine, it was always having that kind of trouble, but it was us he wanted, and he explained to us about me having been made a ward-of-court and Christopher being warned to keep off and all that. I didn't know whether to believe him or not, but it seemed deadly serious, and moreover Christopher seemed to take it very seriously, so I agreed to go home and talk things over with my father, and Christopher was driven off by a policeman, and I heard them saying that an injunction had been granted, I think that was the word, and that if he attempted to contact me he'd be jailed for contempt of court. And that was what I couldn't face, it was the separation, because I really couldn't live without him, you know, I couldn't get through the time when he wasn't there, even an hour without him was like a lifetime. So I didn't see what I was going to do. Oh God, it was awful, that stretch of time before I knew the worst, I was so lonely, and more or less housebound in that mausoleum of a house—it was like being a child again, ill with boredom waiting to grow up. And yet at the same time I knew that whatever they did they couldn't make me wait more than eight months. I wanted to write to Christopher, or ring him and tell him I'd wait, but they watched me so closely, it was amazing, it was historic, and I suppose that what really kept me going was the feeling of being martyred. In fact they could hardly have treated me more unwisely, me being what I was, but then I wouldn't have been what I was if they'd ever known how to handle me. The only positive comfort I had was that my father very unwisely let me know that he'd tried to buy Christopher off, and Christopher had refused whatever he'd been offered, which demonstrated some kind of faith in me, at least.'

'A faith that was not misplaced.'

'No, as it happened. But he couldn't have been certain of that, could he? Not absolutely certain? He might have lost, mightn't he? Anyway, what happened was that they decided to send me abroad, until I was twenty-one. Eight whole months of exile. I really thought I wouldn't be able to bear it. And the worst thing was that I thought I'd have to go without telling Christopher, but I managed to bribe somebody to send him a letter—well not really bribe exactly, simply persuade, because I'd nothing left to bribe with—and Christopher came round one night and threw stones at a window, and we managed to have half an hour before anyone heard us, and I promised to come back and he promised to wait for me, and then we were interrupted, and my father said he'd send for the police and have him put in prison, and I said if he did that I'd kill myself, and that if he'd leave Christopher alone I'd go meekly off to Paris as I was supposed to, and so I did. I can think of all sorts of things now that we might have done—we could simply have eloped, or I could have said I was having a baby, or something, but I didn't think of them at that time, and I couldn't see Christopher to work anything out with him, and that half hour we did get we spent on love and promises, not on plans. We made a mess of it, I suppose. But there wasn't much—guidance. One simply doesn't know how to behave in such a situation, one doesn't know the rules, and I never understood the legal business, although father kept getting his solicitor in, poor fellow, to explain it to me. God, he was embarrassed about it, that poor man, he really couldn't look me in the eye.'

'So you were sent abroad.'

'Yes. That's right. It was a nightmare. I went with a cousin, more like an aunt she was I suppose, she was so much older, and we dragged around Europe. She watched me all the time, she took her duties very seriously, and we kept moving around without my knowing ever where we were going, so I couldn't contact Christopher and get him to come out to rescue me, I suppose. She kept my passport in her handbag. It was awful, I was bored like death, I can't bear to look back on it. Living through those days, without a word. We went to Paris, and Rome, and Amsterdam, Brussels and Prague, and Bavaria. That wretched cousin, what she went through God knows, she must have been bored to death too, though she put on a good show of looking interested. But really she wanted someone to talk to as badly as I did, and as soon as she struck up any kind of acquaintance, in a hotel for instance, she clearly felt it was time to move, in case I started seducing or bribing them. Really, I can't quite now think why I put up with it, why I didn't just walk out, except that after a month or two I began to make a virtue of endurance and promise myself I'd stick it out if it killed me. Also, there was nowhere much to walk to, without a passport or any money. I read an awful lot of books. They shouldn't have sent me to Italy, there were people there who kept reminding me of Christopher. They treated me very badly, you know. One would hardly believe it. Do you know what my father did? For one thing, he vowed quite solemnly that if I did marry Christopher when I was twenty-one he'd completely disinherit me—I didn't realise then that he couldn't entirely because of the way the money had been put in trust to save his supertax, he must have kicked himself for his stinginess on that front—but much worse than that was what he did about Christopher. I don't know if I dare to tell you, it reflects so badly on him. I haven't told anyone, or only one or two people.'

'Don't tell me, if you don't want to.'

'I do want to, I think. What he did was get Christopher followed by a private detective, and he sent reports on all the things he'd been doing that I wouldn't like. Can you imagine, a mind that would think of that? We were in Salzburg, I think, when I got this report about Christopher and this other woman. There were plenty of other girls, quite enough to upset me, but this one sounded serious, he spent weeks with her, in that very same basement. I suppose my father thought that would do the trick. God, how I hate abroad, I'll never go there again as long as I live. It nearly finished me off, but then I thought that for one thing it might not be true, a man capable of setting a detective on one's lover might be equally capable of cooking the evidence, and also for another thing even if it was true all I would have to do would be to see Christopher and he'd be able to talk me out of it. He was very good at talking me out of things, suspicions and jealousies and so on, he had to be because he was very careless, but then I was good at being talked out of it too because I didn't really believe I deserved him, part of me at least knew that I was lucky to get any of him, and I used to dream about when I got home and he would talk me out of feeling jealous and betrayed, or make it anyway seem irrelevant. I used to look forward to that. I suppose it did cross my mind—no, what am I talking about, I worried endlessly that when I got back he wouldn't want me any more, and that I'd have been through it all for nothing, and that my father would have won, but at the same time there must have been something in me that knew that this wasn't so, that he'd be there waiting for me.'

'And he was?'

'Yes, he was. We arrived back in England on the day after my twenty-first birthday, and he was there at Dover, waiting for me. It was quite extraordinary. You can imagine.'

'How did he know when you were coming?'

'Well, I must confess, I fixed it. We spent the night before in Paris, it was my birthday, and by this time I'd got a bit of pressure going on my poor cousin, and she'd got a bit of an eye on her own future, with me, we'd got quite intimate, in a way, one does after eight months of enforced confinement with somebody, and I insisted we have a birthday party in the hotel, and we gave everybody champagne, and there was a journalist there from an English paper—it was an English hotel, full of English people—and he recognised me, and I told him to phone his paper and give them the story, and he did, and somebody on the paper contacted Christopher, and he arrived to meet me, and there he was, and all the journalists, and I was free, and nobody could stop me.'

'Yes,' he said. 'I've seen the photographs.'

'Touching, weren't they?'

He reflected upon the photographs, and the interviews. They had captions like 'Weeping heiress reunited with the man she loves', and 'Rose returns blooming', and the smudged pictures showed a terrified-looking Rose clutching an equally terrified Christopher, both of them white (one might imagine) with horror at what they had done and were about to do. In the interviews, when asked her plans, Rose was reported to have said things like 'we're going to get married tomorrow we've waited long enough,' and Christopher, when asked how long he would have waited for her, said, 'I would have waited not eight months but eight years for her to come back to me.' When asked what they felt about being disinherited, both had replied that they had never wanted money, all they wanted was each other.

'Yes, touching,' he said. 'And so you got married?'

'Yes, that's right, we got married. And that was that. And we came to live here, but we only had the top floor then, it was a sort of flat. It took us a long time to buy the whole house. But I've told you all that.' She paused, for a long time, while she cut up into small pieces the rind of her cheese, and then said, 'It's a pity, really, after all that trouble, and effort, that Christopher and I didn't make a bit more of an effort when we got married. Or that's what most people say. They think it was a waste.'

'Only you could say whether it was a waste or not. I would assume that if you found it necessary, it was necessary.'

'Well, yes, I think that on the whole it was.'

'You seem to have—changed a great deal, since those days.'

'So have we all, I imagine. Ten years is a long time. More than ten, it is, now. In what ways have I changed?'

'You seem to have quietened down, a little. All this—' he indicated the room, the windows, the street beyond—'all this doesn't look like an appropriate end for so much drama.'

'I was wrong about drama. I don't really like drama. I disapprove of it very strongly, don't you? I'm sure that you do. I rationalise it, by saying that I had to have the drama before I would have all this. It was what you might call a revolution, a personal revolution. It even had a little bloodshed, to prove it. But I'm determined not to make the mistake of most revolutions, I won't revert to what it was that I was fighting not to be.'

'But what is it, that you are now, that you value so much? What do you like, about what you're doing now, that you should like it so much? You must forgive me for saying so, but you must know that—well, your life must appear to many people deliberately unattractive. An unattractive district, no husband when you could surely easily acquire one, no money when you of all people could have had it—it seems strange, perhaps, that one should make a revolution, as you put it, to achieve precisely this.'

'Well, it wasn't precisely this, when I set out, it took me a long time to learn what it was about this that I so valued—it's hard to explain, people are so unsympathetic, and when I describe it it sounds so—so absurd, and dull. I like it here precisely because it is dull, and because I can—oh, I don't know, clean my own shoes and worry about the electricity bill and look after my own children and collect them from school and take an interest in Cheap Offers in the shops. Oh, I know, people think it's not real, they think it's nonsense for me to sit here like I do, they think I'm playing. They tell me that everyone else round here is miserable and all the rest of it. But they don't know, because they've never tried it. I do know. I respond to such ordinary signals in the world. Cut prices and sunshine and babies in prams and talking in the shops. Oh, I can't describe or defend it, I expect no sympathy. It sounds unnatural to you, I expect.'

'No, not unnatural, exactly. But I'm surprised you can be satisfied with so little. You used to be more active, you used to try and get things done, even after your marriage, I know you did.'

'How do you know?'

'From what other people have said about you.'

'What do other people say about me?'

'That you have withdrawn. That you might have given up.'

'That's what Nick says?'

'That's what Nick says.'

'Nick wouldn't know. It seems to me enough, now, to look after the children. Oh, I haven't cut myself off completely, I can't do that, because I can't resist any of the claims that people make on me, and one can't lose the life that one had friends in, because they are friends, and so I see them, and I do things for them, even in public from time to time. But all those activities, they're just part of being human, whereas being here, being myself, is something quite different. It's taken me so long to learn it and now I can't lose it. I'm happy in it. It seems to me right. People are so nervous about believing anything to be right. But what else in life should one ever seek for but a sense of being right? I explain myself badly, I put it very badly, I can't justify myself—but what I feel, now, is,' and she buried her face in her hands, as though embarrassed by her own declaration, 'what I feel is that the things I do now, they're part of me, they're monotonous, yes I know, but they're not boring, I like them, I do them all'— she hesitated, faintly—'I do them all with love. Getting up, drawing the curtains, shopping, going to bed. You know what I mean.'

'How could I know what you mean,' he said, startlingly, 'when nothing that I do is done with any love at all?'

She froze, with her hands there in front of her face. She opened her fingers, dropped them, stared at him. She looked at him for some time. He was staring at the table, with a look of savage melancholy.

'I don't believe you,' she said, finally. 'It's charity, at least, to sit there for so long and listen to me. And charity is a form of love.'

'How do you know?' he said, looking up at her, and smiling, harshly, a mocking unpleasant smile that delighted her, 'how do you know that I haven't been bored stiff? How do you know I haven't been resenting every moment that I've been sitting here?'

She was ready for it. 'Because,' she said, smiling back at him, quickly, sharply, triumphantly, 'because if you had been resenting it, it would be even kinder of you. Wouldn't it? Eh?'

'I thought things didn't count unless one meant them.'

'No, no, not at all.' She gazed at him with gentle superiority, with kindness. 'You've got it wrong. The clashing of the cymbals and the banging of the something or other, you were thinking of, weren't you? And not having charity. But the act counts. See? And you've sat there and listened. You could have got up and gone away. But, you've listened, you've even bothered to ask the right questions.'

'My dear girl, I have been asking the right questions of people for long enough to know how to do it, I can assure you, so that nobody could possibly tell the difference. I have a strong sense of obligation. It is on this sense of obligation that I have conducted my whole life. It is very destructive of the emotions. Had I ever trusted my emotions, I would have led a far less admirable existence, I can assure you.'

'But in what sense, then, can you say that your existence has been admirable?'

'It has been admirable in that I have fulfilled my obligations. As I said. I've spent most of my time, I think, doing what on balance it seemed that I ought to do, not what I might have wanted to do, and now there isn't much that I do want to do. So it's rather distressing to hear you so confident of the value—or virtue, maybe—of very small activities, when I can hardly work up enough energy to pursue quite large and exhausting bits of life. I am glad that you can enjoy going shopping and taking advantage of Cut Price Offers. I wish that I too could arrive at such a state of grace.'

'I am sorry if I have distressed you.'

'Yes, you probably are. You would be. To them that have it shall be given.'

'What I tried to do was to give away.'

'But it doesn't work, does it? It stays with you, you said it yourself, you can't get rid of it, grace or riches, you can't get rid of them, can you? They increase and multiply.'

'It's not as bad as that.'

'Oh yes it is. But no, don't look like that, I really truly don't want to distress you. Tell me some more, instead, please.'

'And you will listen, dutifully?'

'It's the best I can do. It's the best you can do for me. Tell me why you gave that money to that school in Africa. Not why, I mean, why you gave it at all, that's reasonably easy to imagine, but why you gave it to that particular place. You must have had some problem in choosing, once you'd decided to get rid of it in the first place.'

'You must be tired. You must be wanting to go home. You look tired, you were tired when you arrived.'

'I feel better now. I want to hear. I'm curious, you know. On a quite simple level.'

'Are you? Are you really? That's nice of you. Oh dear. I can hardly bear to tell you about it, it was so sad, and I behaved like such a fool. The school was in Ujuhudiana, I bet you don't even know where Ujuhudiana is, do you? It used to be called Juhudi-land till it got its independence. It's a terribly dull place. Nothing much goes on there at all, that's why I got interested in it, because it was so dull, if you see what I mean. Look, here it is.' And she got up and got him a book, one in the Mundy and Gross series, with a map, and photographs.

'You see? And I got interested because it seemed a small and peaceful place. I couldn't cope with the idea of big violent places like the Congo and Nigeria. The country's not very fertile, most of the people are nomadic, there's a lot of cattle, well,'—he was turning the pages of the book—'you can see for yourself. So I started to collect cuttings, and read books. And then war broke out. You probably don't even remember. It was a very little civil war—one tribe against another—but there was a lot of violence in the capital, Gbolo, and quite a lot of people were killed and buildings burned. And one day in *The Times* there was this photograph. I'll show you. Wait. I'll show you.'

And she got up again, and went over to her desk, and took an old crumpled press cutting out of a pigeon-hole. He noticed that she did not herself look at it: she handed it to him with her eyes more or less averted, her other hand fluttering nervously over it as though she didn't want to catch sight of it, as though she didn't want it to communicate with her, as though the very touch of it was enough to alarm. He opened it nervously, and looked at it. It showed a town square—not an imposing one, the buildings were low, the road surface poor. In the square lay bodies, nine or ten bodies. The quality of the photograph was poor, few details mercifully could be distinguished. A policeman stood watching. The only part of the picture which was in clear focus was a small child, sitting cross-legged by one of the corpses. Its mother, one could see that the corpse had been. The child was naked. It was sitting naked in the dust, its face lost, its eyes sagging blank with nothingness, its mouth drooping slightly open. It was a remarkable photograph. And Rose, watching Simon look at it, remembering, as he responded to it with a movement of grief, what it had been like, felt as though she were looking at it again for the first time. She could not help it.

'You see?' she said. 'I saw that, and I couldn't get over it. It's all very well, reading books. It's better, I know. But that—I don't know, I don't know what that did to me. But it was something I had to do something about. And the next week, there was an appeal, I don't know if you remember, from this man from Urumbi, that's the Northern province, who'd come over here. Nyoka, his name was. Akisoferi Nyoka. I went to a lecture he gave at the African Institute. He was appealing for funds to build a new school, his had been burned down in the riots. So I sent him the money.'

'Just like that?' he said.

'Yes,' she said. 'That's right. Just like that.'

'And then what happened?'

'Well, this is the really depressing part. They built the school, but in another year the war, which had stopped altogether, broke out again much more virulently, and there was a real bloodbath. You wouldn't believe it. In fact you probably wouldn't know about it because it was terribly badly reported here. I thought they were a peaceful lot, but there isn't a peaceful nation on earth. They chopped each other up and floated each other down the rivers. Hundreds and hundreds. Thousands. Nobody knows how many. The Northern bit, there—' and she pointed at the map—'the bit called Urumbi, wanted to cut itself off from this other bit down here, Nchikavu, it wanted to secede. But there wasn't any point in it, there was no oil, nothing, and nobody cared here, nobody at all. There's nothing much to choose between those two wretched countries. I don't know whether that makes it better or worse. Anyway, he built my school all right, did Nyoka, but he also bought himself a huge great white Mercedes. Out of my money. I saw a photo of him sitting in it. Labour must be cheap, over there. And the school was burned down, burned to the ground. A month or two after it was opened. Christopher said I should have expected it, I should have known better, I shouldn't have trusted that man— and maybe he was right. I didn't stop to think. I couldn't have thrown the money away more ineffectively, could I?'

'No, I suppose not. But one couldn't blame you for that. You couldn't have known.'

'It makes one wonder. If there is anything one can safely do. It makes me quite ill, when one opens a newspaper and sees the causes people are prepared even to die for—did you see that piece about those French schoolboys who killed themselves, burned themselves to death, as a protest against what's going on in Biafra? As a protest, for Christ's sake, as a sacrifice to the French oil wells—immolating themselves for French business interests—it's terrifying to think of them reading those French papers, and not knowing what was beneath it all, and solemnly and so horribly uselessly dying—perhaps they saw a photograph like I saw a photograph. One can't blame them. Anyway, you could take this story as an explanation of why I've given up public causes—and why I think I ought to sit here at home and keep quiet and dig my own garden. Literally dig it, actually. Now that's the kind of activity that used to seem to me sublimely useless, and now at my age seems a good thing to do. You might well say that that's all very well for me, which is more or less what you said before—'

'No, no, not exactly,' he said, protesting, but she brushed his protests aside, politely.

'Oh, I know what you meant,' she said. 'It's a privilege, to be able to learn the lessons I've learned. The lessons of the privileged. But that doesn't mean I can't learn. I refuse to believe I was damned from birth, you know. It would be rather hard, not to allow people to learn. I can't really believe all that once a lady always a lady, and unto them that have it shall be given, can you?' She smiled, suddenly cheerful. A sudden ripple of energy went through her, as she sat there: she lifted up a hand, and held it there, the fingers spread out, mocking, smiling, serious. 'All alone,' she said: 'I arrest the course of nature. I arrest it. I divert the current.'

'It's very rash of you,' he said.

'Yes,' she said, staring at her unnaturally raised hand, tense, the veins standing up in it, like a gesture, a joke. Quickly she crumpled the fingers in and dropped it to her lap, the moment of assertion over.

'You ought to be getting home,' she said, her nerve gone. 'I've kept you too long, I've talked at you too much.'

'I haven't been much use to you, I'm afraid.'

'You listened to me,' she said. 'That was kind of you.'

'Not very,' he said, getting up, preparing to go. 'It would have been, if it hadn't been interesting. But it was interesting.'

'I never even got round to telling you about the custody thing, did I, I was so busy telling you everything else. He's definitely applying for custody to the Divorce Court. So I've got to have the Welfare round, and write an affidavit, and all that. Christopher says they shouldn't be allowed to go to school in this area, you know. That's his best point, I think. But what does the country have areas like this for, if they're too bad for children to go to school in?'

'I wouldn't worry too much, if I were you.'

'Wouldn't you? The judge thinks I'm mad already, you know. You saw what he said about me in the divorce case. And lawyers and people take education terribly seriously, you knew. They simply wouldn't have the faintest conception of what I mean by leaving them where they are. And yet they have no notion whatsoever of where that—that incomprehension leaves them. They just don't know. They can't add it up. Christopher knows, he knows all too well, the trouble is he knows and doesn't like it. If he'd come from where I come from, he wouldn't have been able to put up half such a good case for himself. But he knows it all, it's what he was brought up on, it's what turned him into what he is. Where they are now. One has to admit it, his case is far more reasonable than mine. In terms of how things are, and how things work. All he has to say is, I want them to have the opportunities that I never had, and any judge in England would sympathise with him. Wouldn't they? You know they would.'

'They might have a natural sympathy in that direction, yes. A natural inclination. But they have been known to set their inclinations aside.'

'Yes, I know. But only for good reasons. Like the fact that Christopher used to beat me black and blue and lock me in the bedroom. I sometimes wonder if really he learned all that kind of behaviour from my father. Or whether I'd bring it out in anybody. But no, the point is, nobody could prove that Christopher beats the children black and blue because he doesn't, he's very good with them, he gives them all the things I won't give them.'

'But you don't beat them either.'

'No, of course I don't. I simply deprive them. Or so he'll say.'

'But you deprive them of some things in order to offer them others. Or so I imagine.'

'But do I, do I? What, after all, do I offer them but myself? And why should I of all people be able to believe that that's such a big deal?'

'You are their mother.'

'Yes, I know. And so is he their father.'

He sighed, and buttoned his coat.

'There's no easy answer, in such cases.'

'I must let you go.'

'Yes, I must go, they will be wondering where I am.' She wondered, listening, how often she had heard this delicate plural: they, meaning she. And wondered also, as she saw him off, receiving his assurances that he would look things up for her, and contact her, and give her any help he could, why he had made her so little uneasy, as some such men did. She was exposed to men, being a friendly woman, and living alone. A lot of them upset her, more because of the brutality (as it seemed to her) with which she had to treat them, than because of any offence committed by them against her. But Simon Camish, although the kind of person that ought to disseminate unease, for some reason did not. He was so angular, and thin, and jerky, that he ought to communicate restlessness. Perhaps he didn't because he was there on her invitation, and because one could confidently rely on him not to make any kind of pass.

Because the need involved was hers, not his. Or perhaps it was because he was so quick. She didn't mind people being jerky if they were also quick.

As she went into the kitchen to do the washing-up, which she always did, these days, carefully, before going to bed, in careful repudiation of those years when she and Christopher had collapsed in drink or bitterness or fury amongst a sea of crying bodies, dirty plates, and glasses, she thought over the things she had said to him. Impossible, really, not to plead one's cause, not to lie in one's own defence. One became, in any dispute, incurably partisan, and she could not help but be so now that it seemed to her that it was the whole of herself and the whole of her past that were on trial. It was a matter of all that she had believed in, so she was bound to plead for those beliefs. Perhaps there was no truth to be told. She rinsed the plates, carefully, and put them on the rack to drain.

Going to bed, undressing, brushing her hair, she thought about the loneliness in which she claimed to have been reared. It had been real enough, but nevertheless she had grossly exaggerated it. Of course she had had friends, of course her parents had been concerned for her, and had done their best to accommodate her in their rather unsuitable lives. Her early childhood had in fact been happy. She thought of it, as she had not thought for a long time. It had been an innocent time, and always summer, as one's recollections of infancy are traditionally supposed to be. When she was four, Noreen had introduced her to the village school, and there she had stayed, for years, till she was eight, until her father had decided she ought to have private tuition. She had liked the school, she had taken to it with a great simplicity. She had made a friend there. One made friends so easily, at that age. Her friend was called Joyce. She could not remember, however hard she tried to do so, their first meeting, and the way in which they had become friends: there had been no reason for it. They had just become a pair, naturally. Perhaps Joyce had said to her, let's be friends. Perhaps she had said this to Joyce. She could not remember. Joyce was the daughter of the village cobbler, and her mother was a big woman in a flowery apron. Noreen despised Joyce's mother and said she was simple, as an insult, an insult which Rose had not understood till years later. Joyce herself was a round child, with fair frizzy hair not unlike Rose's own. Perhaps that was what had brought them together. They had played the golden-haired twins in a little school play about princes and princesses. They used to re-enact this play, endlessly, in the playground. Their favourite word was *yonder*. Neither of them knew what it meant, but they used to say to each other things like,

'Where are you going, sister?' and the other one would reply, 'Yonder,' and the word would evoke a place of such mystic and visionary loveliness, a thin aspiring castle on the brow of a green hill, a tower above the raging sea, a heavenly city. Joyce had one hand without fingers. She had burned all the fingers off her right hand on the radiant of an electric fire when she was a baby, and all that remained was a little pink scarred paw, with vestigial stumps round the diminished palm. Rose had liked this stumpy little hand, and had held it with love. It was a friendly shape, nice and rounded, more welcoming than the ordinary grasping sort of hand with poking fingers. She looked back, now, lying there in bed and listening to the rain fall, and wondered at the feelings she had had about this hand, because nowadays any deformity frightened and repelled her, as a threat to her own children. But then, she had accepted it and held it with a completely unquestioning trust: and so, moreover, had everybody in the school. She could not remember a single joke about it, a single movement of revulsion, a single hostile sneer. It had been accepted, it had been how things were. And so had Joyce herself, and all the children at that school. There had been stupid ones, and naughty ones, and dirty ones, and ones who never had a handkerchief—Miss Acomb had never commented on those dripping noses, she had kept a supply of rags in her desk and wiped children when they needed it. There had been boys who stamped on fledglings when they fell out of the nest in the school roof, and boys who stuck straws up the backs of daddy-long-legses, but although Rose and Joyce hadn't liked these activities, and had avoided the boys who went in for them, they hadn't been censorious. They hadn't thought of it. She thought of the school playground, and the Elsan lavatories where the boys used to piss over the wall into the girls', and the iron railing that had fallen on Shirley Madge's foot, and the little hole in the wall where she and Joyce used to store scrapings of sand that they called gold dust. Miss Acomb had boxes of pictures. They showed tulip fields in Holland, and rice fields in India, and maize fields in America. They were beautiful, and all the children loved them, and used to beg her to get them out to show. They were deprived of pictures, partly by the war, partly by homes without books of any sort, and Miss Acomb's pictures were treasures at which nobody thought to mock. It had been a world of such primal simplicity. And it was a world that she had hoped her own children would find, here, in this brick desert, in this dense and monstrous urban wilderness. It had been a foolish hope, a ridiculous expectation, but it had been justified. They had found it, it was there. She remembered those days when Konstantin had been five, and she would nervously wait with the pushchair in the playground to collect him, and he would run out to her, and show her his bubble-gum cards, and the swops he had made, and tell her about the boy who had given him a marble in exchange for a biscuit, and about the new photographs (cut out of a colour supplement) that Mrs Gomez had stuck on the classroom wall, and about the tadpoles that had grown legs and jumped out and died under the blackboard duster. And about the blackey who called him whitey and said I'll give you a white eye, and the whitey who had taught him a very curious rhyme about Greeks and Turkeys. (She always suspected that the disseminator of this rhyme must have been a Greek or a Turk himself, but Konstantin swore he was the little boy from the pub on Elysium Road, whose name, she quite well knew, was Roberts.)

Christopher, having prized out of her in an unguarded moment some recollection about her own early schooldays, had looked at her with savagery, and said that if she thought there was anything in common between a village school in rural Norfolk and a primary school in North London, then she must be mad. He backed this up with a few horrifying anecdotes from his own past. Her only retort could be, people like you must have been out looking for trouble and what you look for you find. But she hadn't been able to assert this with much confidence. It was on faith, not on evidence that she operated, after all.

She stopped thinking about the schools. There was something else that was worrying her, but she could not remember what it was. Something she had said or not said to Simon Camish. How pleasant it was, to lie alone in bed, undisturbed, with one's children asleep, and recollect in reasonable tranquillity. Yes, that was it, it was that eight months of exile. That, she had made too little of, not too much, but there were confidences about that which could never be made, and how could anybody believe one half of the misery she had then endured? It had been the unbearable, agonising boredom of it that had nearly finished her, but how could anybody have much sympathy for the boredom of a wealthy young girl, regaled with the choicest culture of Europe (because Sonia had been conscientious about culture, one had to give her that) and with only eight months—a diminishing eight—to wait before her total freedom? But dreadful it had been. It was hard to believe it now, when every day seemed, if occasionally painful, at least endlessly fruitful, and rewarding, and full, and above all interesting. But then, she had lived with her eyes upon her watch. She could never have believed that an hour could take so long to pass. And the image of her mother, bored without any prospect of redemption, had haunted her. The only thing she had been able to enjoy—and this was humiliating, in the last degree—had been eating. She had known, during that period of time, what her worst fate would be—to live alone, quietly eating herself to death. She had put on over a stone in those months. Luckily she had been thin to begin with, so it hadn't shown disastrously, but a lifetime of it would have been more conspicuous, no doubt. She had lived for mealtimes. Waking up was such misery that it could only be assuaged by endless rolls and brioches and croissants, covered in butter and jam: by mid-morning she was pleading with Sonia for a cream cake: and her only interest in the hotels that they stayed in came from the quality of their menus. She had no interest in the view, or in the location, she could remember little of the cultural objects she had seen, but she could remember, alas, the steaks and the cassoulets and the langoustines and the knedliche and the roast goose and the puddings. Sonia had been astonished by this behaviour: it was almost funny, in retrospect, to remember Sonia's astonishment at the way her charge, officially pining away for love, had eaten course after course in expensive restaurants with obvious relish. While her jaws were moving, Rose had been able to stop worrying. It was as simple as that, though she had never explained this to Sonia. She had in fact corrupted Sonia, who had started off with the traditionally finicky, British and abstemious views of all her mother's family—a bony spinster, she was, Sonia, once a private secretary, but now too old to demean herself in however grand a job—but by the end of the holiday old Sonia had been tucking in to whatever dishes Rose took the responsibility of ordering. She too had put on a lot of weight, and looked much better for it. On her return to England she had actually got married. Rose was very relieved about that and wondered if she should take the credit. She had been more worried at the time that Sonia would relapse like herself into a middle age of comforting boxes of chocolates.

Neither of them drank much. It would have been one solution to anxiety, but Rose, determined to play Sonia's game, had been afraid to alarm her by drinking, and also drink made her hideously miserable.

126

There were other things that had made her miserable. One was a tapestry of Hero and Leander in Bratislava. The story itself was what had set her mind going—her mind, which responded not at all to objects which she could not relate to Christopher—but the thought of the land and ocean separating her from her love had attached her to those tapestries. They were in sequence, showing Leander's swimming of the Hellespont, their happy union, and his subsequent death. There was even a Sonia figure, a confidante, holding the torch as he arrived gasping on the shore. The way that the artist and the needlewoman had portrayed Leander's limbs beneath the stitched blue curling waves had afflicted her dreadfully, because the limbs were like Christopher's, solid, white and naked. She had suffered such pangs of desire, watching these cultural objects, that she could hardly move on.

The other thing that had distressed her had been the monkeys in the Bois de Boulogne. God knows why they had gone there, because it was a nice day perhaps, but they had gone, and listened to the sad squawks of the peacocks, and commented with incredible mutual trite dullness and distaste that it was strange that such elegant creatures made such ugly sounds: then they had gone to look at the monkeys. (Or apes, maybe, she wouldn't have known the difference.) They were in a kind of rocky, barren enclosure, with a moat round, a whole group of them. Sad colony. Mothers grasped babies and gazed with despair in their eyes at the blank blue sky. Adult males sighed and scratched themselves in a bitter parody of boredom. A few young ones played, listlessly, without interest, in the dust. They looked like refugees, or prisoners, or exiles. Watching them, her eyes had filled with tears, and she had wept, and Sonia had patted her shoulder awkwardly, and Rose had sniffed crossly and looked at her watch and found that it was still, amazingly, only three thirty, with another five unbelievable hours to wade through until dinner and the Jambon de Bayonne or Lobster Thermidor she had resolved to try that night.

It was amazing, remembering such incidents, that she had survived until their return. What with all those little reports on Christopher's infidelity that had arrived to amuse her. She had said to herself, perhaps he sleeps with those girls as I eat, to pass the time. She had probably been right about that, because the one thing she could never explain, to anyone, because she was too modest, was that she knew quite well that Christopher had not been pretending to want her for the money. Oh yes, it was quite reasonable to suppose that he wanted the money too, even she would admit that the course of events would fully justify anyone who thought that, but she alone could be sure that he had really wanted her. She knew it. One could not mistake such a matter, she did not understand how anyone could mistake such a matter. (People did, she had to admit, but then people were optimistic and hopeful and willing to be deluded, whereas she had been diffident, hopeless, and had needed endless persuading.) Christopher had wanted her, and he had had her. He hadn't been able to keep his hands off her. It had amazed and delighted her. They had unmistakably done all the things that people do, and felt all the things that people feel. One couldn't imagine such a thing, it had been so. And yet this was also connected with the very worst thing, the other thing that she could never admit, because it was too dreadful, too painful, too sad. And this was the fact that by the time she came back to England, it was ruined. Oh, they were faithful to one another, they were undivided, fate had not separated them, they had swum the Hellespont, she had faithfully returned, and he, summoned by the newspapers, had faithfully received her, but their absence from one another had—there was no point in denying it, she knew it now, though for years she had tried to ignore it—their absence had divided them. They had laboured and sweated to be reunited, both of them, he as well as she, and she had loved him for the effort, but that spontaneous joy and that effortless renewal had come to an end, it had died between them, it had been brutally murdered. From time to time they made it, driven by despair, or violence, or memory, or the will to have what they had had—and Christopher, Christ, she had to admit that Christopher would have got life from a stone—but it had, nevertheless, been finished, and it would never be again. Exhausted, damp, they had lain in bed and looked at one another, in that first year of marriage, and they had known that it was so. It was through no betrayal, no treachery, the crime had not been theirs, so they could share, a little, the misery, they could reach for one another in the end and fall asleep in a communion of loss. But loss it was, and they could do nothing to revoke the death of the spirit. The spirit bloweth whither it listeth. What horrible tags her mind was packed with. It was Noreen's fault, she had made her learn a few verses of the Bible every day after tea. One remembered those that one needed. And they were all cruel ones, like the camel and the needle, and to those that have it shall be given, and the spirit simply drifting away, idly, irresponsibly, abandoning those that so needed and so implored it.

On the boat, on the way back over the channel, that last time, she had foreseen something of this, so she had not been entirely faithful. If she had been entirely faithful, surely she could have subdued her fears? But she had knelt there, in the first-class bar, looking through the round window, and the sky had been a dull dove grey, and the sea had been a dull grey, and they had met, softly, dimly, the sea and the sky, with no noticeable collision, a dim pall of neither air nor water seeming to separate, join and combine them, a pallid heavy uniformity, and she had known that she was afraid, and that Christopher, waiting bravely for her, was afraid too, but that he like her was stubborn, obstinate to the last degree, that he would never admit defeat, and that he would meet her and take her and keep her, for better or worse. For worse, as it so happened.

The journalist she had met in the hotel, on her twenty-first birthday party the night before, had been on the boat too. On purpose, to see what happened. He was an amiable, amusing fellow, and he had made light, with infinite courtesy, of any of her apprehensions, by delicately assuming that she could have none. He had bought her a double brandy, and Sonia too, and she had turned from that dim prophetic pall of sky to take it from him, and drink it. Sonia had giggled and wished her luck. Everybody had wished her luck, even the barman. She had wished herself luck. And the boat had docked, creaking into the dank wall, and there was Christopher, surrounded by photographers, nervous in his dark glasses, and she had walked down the gang plank, a free woman, a mature woman, into what had once been the safety of his arms.

THERE WERE MANY KINDS of evidence that were not of much use in court. The court, for instance, would not have been much interested in the colour of that sky. Nor would Simon Camish, which is why she had not told him. This was justice.

SIMON CAMISH, returning home, tried to think of some reason why he could have been so late. He could not, as he was an inconveniently truthful man, and any fabrication seemed to him ludicrous in the extreme. He tried to think of the least ludicrous, which was that he had been so depressed by losing his case that he had stayed on to have a drink and then, unintentionally, a meal in Southampton with his opponent, an old acquaintance, and one who luckily bored Julie to tears and who would therefore never have an opportunity to betray him. This, for some reason, seemed far from plausible, though it was exactly what he would have done had he not been intending to see Rose. But in fact, by the time he got home, Julie was already in bed. He took the liberty of assuming that since the light was off, she must be asleep, and stayed downstairs to make himself a milk drink. In the kitchen there was a message for him from his delinquent son, who had been watching soccer on the television, an interest which Simon had successfully deluded the child into believing that he shared. It said, 'Great, Dad, we did it, we beat them 3-0, 4-3 on agregrate.' He was pleased by this message, not so much by its content as by its confidence and the marked improvement in spelling and writing that it displayed. He propped it up, neatly, behind the Ovaltine jar, and took his beaker of Ovaltine into the drawing-room, and sat down. He thought how agreeable it was that the house was so quiet, with everybody in it asleep. Julie had been tired since her return from New York: she had clearly been rushing around and drinking too much over there, as most people seemed to do. He had never been. He had not the slightest desire to go. It had been a very good thing for Julie to go on her own, without him there to spoil her on the whole (he supposed) quite innocent and childish fun. He had no real ethical objection to drinking, or to art galleries, or to weddings, and lush hotels and so forth, but he found them less and less interesting. And he did have a very real objection to the sheer expense of Julie's ideas of amusement. It had once delighted him, the simplicity with which she had been able to delight herself with a new coat, a new pair of shoes, a new hairstyle, but what he hadn't realised in those days was that the objects were delightful only if new, that their sole charm was in their novelty. Getting and spending we lay waste our time. She was a typical consumer, only momentarily assuaged by a purchase or a new idea or a new friend. And such a way of life was, naturally, hideously expensive. And the trouble was that he had no real right to protest, as so much of the money was by right hers.

He had never really understood his own attitude to the money, though he had spent a good deal of time thinking about it. Listening to Rose describe her own attitudes to the inheritance of wealth had shaken him more than Rose, not knowing his situation, could have suspected. He could, he supposed, see, from what she had said, where she had got her notions from, but only her own self could account for the extraordinary fidelity with which she had pursued her notions. He had been not at all faithful. The sums of money involved were not, of course, comparable, Mr Bryanston being in every way a much bigger operator than his own father-in-law, but then on that scale the difference, in tens of thousands, was not really very significant. Mr Phillips would have taken Simon into the business, had he so wanted, but he hadn't wanted, having been unable to picture a life for himself running a large mail-order firm, and anyway Julie would never have forgiven him, would probably not have married him, if he had. And Mr Phillips had probably been more pleased for his son-in-law to practise as a barrister (such a respectable, professional, life) than he would have been had he been able to buy him over. He wondered how much, if at all, Rose had been made aware of her deficiency in sex as a business asset. She had not seemed at all concerned with it. The curious thing was that Christopher Vassiliou who had, one must admit, at first sight seemed a classically undesirable son-in-law, had in fact become deeply involved with his ex-father-in-law, and was now working for him in apparently successful and energetic high-powered financial harmony. Rose was the only person who would not fit.

He wondered if he himself should have made more efforts not to fit. He had a wild vision of himself, refusing all financial backing, and insisting that Julie live with him on the proceeds of his income alone. The vision had no reality whatsoever, it would have been simply impossible. And yet he had had scruples, he had, bitterly at times, reproached himself for the pusillanimity with which he had accepted what was, in effect, a dowry and a sizeable allowance for his wife. It was all very well to say that he had done it for her, that she would not have been able to survive on what he had had to offer her: she had not survived very gracefully on parental subsidy, either. And the sources of the money itself (this is what he could never admit, except to himself, having accepted what he had accepted) were not at all pretty. Perhaps the sources of big money never were. So stinkingly depending, he sometimes said to himself, in Shakespearian phrase: and another reference that ran in the mind was that strange inheritance of Chad in the Ambassadors, which was based upon some article of domestic manufacture too base for heroic mention. (Or had James simply understood too little of money to describe it?) He himself understood all too well the sources of Mr Phillips's wealth, and he did not really like them. In fact, as a lawyer, they increasingly repelled him, he could swallow them less and less, and yet here he was, gagged and stifled (with them down his throat presumably) unable to speak out. Not that there was anything illegal about Mr Phillips's success, it was nothing as dramatic as that, it was simply in Simon's admittedly puritanical view, unethical.

He had started off, innocently enough, with a rapidly prospering furniture and hardware retail business in Darlington, which expanded rapidly between the wars: and after the second war he had moved, massively, into hire purchase and mail order, and now most of his very healthy profits were from the mail-order business. He dealt in all domestic commodities—clothes, hardware, furniture, and even, nowadays, the most recent development, package holidays. There was nothing in itself wrong in this, but the methods of salesmanship were, in Simon's view, highly suspect. The business seemed to involve an enormous amount of sales, at highly favourable terms, to the dimmest, least credit-worthy, and most easily exploited section of the community, a section which would doubtless soon be swollen by thousands and thousands of eighteen-year-olds, now able to contract debts quite safely all on their own. The number of defections and judgement summonses was quite hair-raising: the county courts were grossly over-employed trying to operate Mr Phillips's business for him, in the role of debt collector. The mail-order brochures had become increasingly fallacious in their implications, if not in their actual wording, being now liberally peppered with the words 'free', 'guarantee', 'money back if no satisfaction', 'free easy credit' and 'generous commission'. Up and down the country unfortunate women were finding themselves obliged, to their amazement, to refund money for large expensive catalogues, and to make themselves responsible for the debts of their neighbours to whom they had acted as agent—agent, a word which the majority of them could not conceivably have understood. The current brochure had a detachable coupon on it, and a lot of meaningless verbiage surrounding the proud words 'This coupon is worth five pounds, treasure it'. He was embarrassed to look at it. Luckily, most of Julie's friends (and indeed Julie herself) had no conception of what a mail-order firm was: they probably thought it was like the systems operated by smart little boutiques that specialised in selling, by post from Knightsbridge, pricey little children's dresses with names like 'Little Birds and Fledglings', or small firms that delivered papier mache chairs and dolls' houses, or nursery gardens that delivered little trimmed dwarf Japanese Bonsai trees. Or perhaps they thought Julie's father owned a business that dealt in bulk postal orders of lavatory paper, and cat food, and electric light bulbs, a wholly admirable system, and one much patronised by the wives of his thriftier colleagues, and by people like Diana, who had said to him once that she had been buying lavatory paper by post for so long now that she would faint with embarrassment, as though buying male contraceptives, if she had to ask for a roll in a shop. In a way he hoped that they did think these things, all his acquaintances, and that their eyes would never alight upon phrases like 'Your orders delivered immediately for 1/- in the £ per week—save £ £ £ £ now!' What would they have thought of paying for their Japanese trees at a shilling in the pound per week? To them, the implications of the offer would have been quite lost.

It would be interesting to know how much Rose knew about the stinking dependence of her own family business. It was hard to tell how much she knew about anything. That mention of strikes, for instance: was that meant to be a polite indication of the fact that she was quite well aware of the disastrous labour relations that had been threatening her father's business for the last few years? Not that profits, on that scale, could ever be particularly threatened, as the strikers themselves were all too aware. There was something else that she had said that had been nagging at him ever since she had said it: he got up and walked softly up and down the room, on the thick green carpet, while he tried to remember it. It had been something to do with her father, with the fact that the business was a family business, hardly in its second generation. How great a defection must his only daughter's seem, in view of that, but that was only part of what he had been thinking. He had some sympathy, misplaced maybe, with that father, resorting to law in desperation. It was, ah yes, it was to do with his sense of social inadequacy, heightened by his superior wife, at which she had delicately hinted.

Social inadequacy was an emotion he understood: he could hardly help understanding it, so hard had he worked to overcome it, so meaninglessly, such a hideous compulsive labour. He thought back to his childhood,—to his disabled father, to his driving, neurotic, refined mother, who had worked so hard for him, who had insisted so on his rights, who had pushed him and pushed him to where he now was, through Junior School and Direct Grant Grammar School and through Oxford and on, whether he liked it or not, to the Bar. He had done it for her. He had hated her for so many years, that he had had to do it for her. The two major decisions of his life, his career and his marriage, had both been made through default, through guilt, through a desire to appease and placate, brought on by a lack of spontaneous love. He loved his mother now, he had come round to loving her, or as near as he would ever come to loving so repelling a woman, but he had done what she wanted out of appeasement. To appease her for those years and years of pain and embarrassment and ingratitude. There was no point in going back over it. There was no pride that could be taken in recalling those years of misery, when he had been obliged (by her) to take home from school for tea more affluent, charming, easy-going school friends, confronting them, accustomed to their comfortable suburban houses, with the traumatic shock of his father dribbling in his wheelchair, his mother taut and anxious, his horrid little house, his luxury salmon-sandwich tea, the dreadful prospect out the back over the canal and the gas works. What dignity could he possibly find in the remembered anguish of clothes that did not fit, of parsimony over pocket money and excursions, of lists of expenditure laboriously drawn up, every evening, by his mother, to the last halfpenny, on those bits of card that separate the Weetabix in Weetabix packets? His poor, poor, clever mother, unlovely in her efforts to survive, agonised in her efforts for his survival, repaid over years by nothing but his shrinking flesh and mean reluctance and base avoidance? She had been a gifted woman, his mother, a grammar school product herself, and she had never asked for love, she had not expected love. She had done her best for him, wanting nothing but his escape. She had nourished dreams of escape herself, once: she had looked forward to a brighter dawn. A good socialist she had been, as a young woman, though it was hard to remember it now. She had met his father at Night School in a W.E.A. class, studying economics. It was impossible to imagine what they could both have been like, how they could have got together. Simon could remember nothing of his father before the accident: he tried to reconstruct him, from the evidence, from his mother's recollections, from family recollections but it was no good, it was hopeless. Had he been a working-class intellectual, grey, hard-working, undernourished? Had he been an activist, a rebel? There was no way of knowing. At the time of the accident he had been shop steward: Mrs Camish always maintained that he had been a brilliant thinker, that all Simon's brains came from him, and who could contradict her? Whatever he had been, what was certain was that she had pushed him, as she had pushed her son. She had been ambitious for him. But it had done her no good. The accident had happened, and she had been left, with a miserly (and disputed) amount of compensation, to look after him, his old father, her own parents, and Simon himself.

His old father she hated. He had been a fisherman, from down South. Down South meant Bridlington. Most of his family had been wiped out in a storm—all of them in one day, in one boat, brother, brother-in-law, elder son, friend—and so he had travelled up to Teesside with his wife, to her people. There was nothing to keep me there, nothing but bitter memory, he would say, from time to time. Simon had liked to hear him say that, as a child, but had

had to agree with his mother that most of the rest of his behaviour was repulsive. He spat, all day long. He chewed tobacco, most of the time, but even when he wasn't chewing, he spat. When his wife died and he moved in with Mrs Camish, he nearly drove his daughter-in-law mad. It was not surprising that his wife's people wouldn't take him in. He disgusted Simon not only by spitting, but also by telling lies. The monstrous lies he told about his fishing days filled Simon with contempt.

It had not been a cheerful household. Mrs Camish had had to work to support them all, through those years while he was at school and at college, and her own high standards, her own aspirations, had made things even more difficult than they need have been. He had suffered, for her labours: indeed, he had hated her for them. He had hated her contempt for more feckless housekeepers, the scorn with which she described women who lived off credit check trading,—a scorn, incidentally, which spread with fine logic to Julie's father, when the time came. She despised his business ethics: she looked down on hire-purchase: she had nothing but scorn for those who got themselves into debt, and for those who enticed others into it. But by then, of course, she had gained a right to despise: she could afford to look down on wealth: she had succeeded, triumphantly: she had pulled it off. She had gained the brighter dawn that had seemed beyond hope: she was comfortable, even by old standards affluent: she was a success, in her own way a minor celebrity. There was nothing he wanted more, at times, than to drive down to her and to say, simply, I know now what you did, and I love you for it now, though I couldn't then: but it could not be said, it was too late, she would have to wait till her deathbed for such an acknowledgment. How could he explain to her now, in the present, that he had not realised then what it had meant, to be brought up in a street where the underwear is taken to the pawn shop? Who could blame Mrs Camish for having a pre-Keynsian view of economics? He was not sure that he had not inherited one from her himself.

Her success story was, in its modest way, remarkable. He would have found it more so had she not sold it and told it and altered it and touched it up and cashed it and invested it so often. She had started off by going out to work, in the Town Hall, as a clerk: and then, in her evenings, when she got home, she had started to write. First of all she had written a piece for the local paper, and then a small piece for a regional broadcast, and then she had written a book about her childhood, and a novel about the strikes in Jarrow. She had done it, she had made it, with what cost to herself one could not say. Pin money, she had called it at first, but she had never spent it on pins, and in the end she had given up the job at the Town Hall and had written full-time. He had never known what to think of her books and her broadcasts. In a way they were ridiculous, they were sentimental to the last degree, they could not possibly be taken seriously, and their following was of middle-aged women like herself, who knew the worst and wished to have it made acceptable to them. Her broadcasts—she became a regular on regional Woman's Hour—were about hardship, done in a tone of smug palliation and petty domestic cheeriness in the face of disaster: her public persona was one of cosy, cloying, domestic fortitude. They had seemed to him, as a child and a student, to be composed of such lies that he was bitterly ashamed of her for writing them: it was only recently that he had come to recognise their relation to reality, their relationship with a true transcendence of hardship. The relation was not in the words, nor in the sentiments expressed, but in the fact of expression. Somewhere between the words she wrote, and the woman that she appeared to be, lay the sum and the being of her.

There is a song that children sing, a game they play, which he had played as a child in the concrete spiked broken-bottle-walled playground, and in the streets when she had not been watching—(she did not like him to play on the streets, it was vulgar)—and in the region where he had been brought up, they sing

Boatman, boatman, row my boat
Across the stinking dirty clarty water

In other regions, as he had since found, they sing

Boatman, boatman, row my boat
Across the golden river.

His mother had done a radio programme on this once, on regional games, and their differences. She would take anything on, and was good at this kind of thing, because she had a good regional accent, which she had learned to adopt or dismiss at will. She had known there was a golden river elsewhere, and that the yellow detergent-foaming oily canal at the bottom of the street did not manifest the natural condition of water. Brought up in such a district, she had developed a passion for the natural, for gardens, for birds, for trees. Visiting him in Oxford, she had taken such intense delight in its floral corners that he had been quite ashamed. Sitting in a cafe with him for tea, she had told him, *when we were little, we only had an outside lavatory, you know, and I used to go and sit in it for hours to read because it was the only quiet place, and there was a kind of plant on top of the wall that you could see through a crack at the top of the door. I don't know what it was. Also you could see birds, in that little bit of sky. I don't know what they were either. We used to call them grey birds. Just like that. Grey birds.* And he had been hideously embarrassed by this confession, by the thought (quite simply) of his mother sitting on a lavatory (for it was unlike her to mention such a thing, and it must have been the impact of Oxford that had shocked her into doing so) and by the thought of her horribly constricted pleasures. She had always refused to take him to the street where she used to live, she said it was too horrible, but he'd gone there alone, one day, as a child, and she was right, it was too horrible, and where they now lived, 11 Canal Street, was a polite suburb compared with 9 Violet Bank (ironically christened by some malicious council). But the point was, he had writhed with shame at her recollections, although they had been delivered, those words about the lavatory and the grey birds, without any of the sentiment that she would have surrounded them with on the radio: and afterwards he realised what a swine he had been, what a selfish thoughtless swine, to reject, so awkwardly, her confidence. He had been ashamed of her, throughout his Oxford days, because her name, to those who knew it, was a joke name, like Patience Strong or Godfrey Wynn: so he had never taken her part. And yet it was for her, in a sense, that he had become a barrister, for her that he had married Julie, for her that he had accepted that stinking dirty money. He would have done better to feel for her more and consider her less. But what was the point, at all, in such a conclusion?

Violet Bank, in fact, he later found, had not been named maliciously. It had once been a violet bank. He went back there, later, years later, while he was up at Oxford, drawn to it by a fearful interest: it was grim and sunless, and he walked up and down it miserably, knowing himself compelled to knock at the door of the house in which his mother had been born: and he did knock, sick with fear and embarrassment, and an old lady answered, a white mumbling old lady with white hairs sprouting out of her chin and her thin hair tied up in a duster, as thin as a stick she was, her legs like matches under her flowery pinny, the stockings sagging on them, her arms like articulated pins. He hadn't known what he would say, but seeing her, he said, I just wanted to look inside, my mum used to live here—and she asked him in, and made him a cup of tea so strong that he winced and shivered as he bravely drank it down, and while he looked around at the walls and the sad furniture she told him her life story, the old lady, how she had been born near a farm out beyond Barnham, she'd worked on the farm as a lass, but then she'd got restless, she'd wanted to see the world, so she'd come into town and got herself a job in the chocolate factory—she laughed, wheezily, a ghostly laugh—and she'd married a fellow and settled down, not far from Violet Bank, and his mother remembered the day when Violet Bank wasn't built, oh, it was lovely out this way, they used to come out this way on a weekend, picking flowers, you wouldn't think so to see it now, would you, son—oh yes, times had changed, the farm where she'd been born was all a big factory, now, or so she'd been told, chemicals they made there, or some such thing, though she hadn't been out that way not for thirty years or more—no, there wasn't much growing now in the way of violets, but it was a nice name, wasn't it? It cheers you up, a nice name, said the old lady. Do you ever go to the country, now, he asked: no, she said, it's too far, really, it's too much effort, really, though she thought about it a lot, now she was getting older. I often think, she said, about what my Ma—that's my ma-in-law, I called her Ma and I called me Mum Mum—often think about the things Ma used to tell me. It must've been a different world, when she was a child. I got on well with my Ma, she said, her rheumy eyes weeping a little, unemotionally leaking, against her will. It's not everyone gets on with their ma-in-law.

And, as he escaped into the street once more, and looked up its dark perspective, its pavements, its lamp-posts, its grim walls, its dirty gutters, Simon had a sudden apocalyptic vision, unsolicited, of the day when the world shall turn to grass once more, and the tender flowers will break and buckle the great paving stones. So recent they were, the days of green. Within living memory. And there would flow again the golden river, but there wouldn't be any people waiting for the boatman. They would have gone, the people. Hell is full of people, but paradise is empty, unpolluted, crystalline, golden, clear.

It had hardly been surprising, really, that he should have been so confused by his mother's ambitions for him. Nor that he should have repeated the pattern all over again, with Julie. He sometimes thought that it was less for his mother than for Julie that he had accepted the money, and the way of life. How could he ever, now, be certain? Perhaps after all it had been for himself. He had done enough things for himself, under the guise of doing them for others, and how deplorable it was of him to make others responsible for his aspirations. He had always been a climber, ever since he could remember, and if he now didn't like some of the things he had ended up with he had nobody to blame but himself. Who was it that had taught him carefully to control his accent, his references, to misrepresent his past, to take on the colouring, first of those boys at school, then of those friends at college, and finally of his colleagues at the Bar? Like Nick, he had developed a real art of misrepresentation: his mother, when he had been obliged to acknowledge her, became in his conversations not at all the woman she was, but somebody quite different, a genteel eccentric, an amusing oddity— an image she might herself have liked to perpetuate, to see perpetuated by him, but what had that to do with it? He had done it for his own ends, through shame of the real penury that had bred both him and her. And although he would never frankly lie about his origins, he certainly did not tell the truth about them, within his profession. His whole life—the clothes he wore, the car he drove, the way he spoke, the house he lived in—was an act of misrepresentation. He must have wanted it or he wouldn't, so consistently, have done it. It was all very well for Rose to live in a dump that spoke of his worst fears, because those fears had never been real to her, as they had to him: she could amuse herself with the experience of poverty because it had never seriously threatened her. She had never had to go to school in her father's cut-down suits, hanging uneasily as they had done around his scraggy adolescent body, nor had she had to present her teacher with explanations of why she could not afford to buy the prefects' uniform till after half-term. (It always amazed him that a school, like his, which had so prided itself upon its policy of providing a superior education for the gifted poor, had been able to devise so many means for making such gifted poor feel agonisingly uncomfortable. The truth was, it hadn't really provided for the gifted poor at all, but for the gifted middle class— had it fulfilled its charter, it might have been obliged to be more realistic.) He had had the worst of it all the way along, caught between reality and aspiration—he, for instance, had never been permitted by his mother, while a student, to take a vacation job, as the majority of his much more affluent friends had done, because such an action would have smelt, to her, of defeat. He hadn't been allowed to work for the price of eating his dinners—she had done it, more easily it is true as she became more successful. She had insisted on an expensive profession, because it had been the most difficult thing.

So it was not surprising that he had accepted Julie and the money, when they had become available, when they had indeed surrounded themselves with obligations to be accepted. With what a mixture of amazement and dismay had he agreed to purchase this house in which he was now sitting, for a sum that would have bought his mother's twenty times over. He had no illusions about the professional value of such a background—it had breathed of success, in days when success had needed a great deal of invitation and delicate persuasion. He had known quite well the value of that slight surprise at his surroundings, and had never, except in exceptional circumstances, felt it necessary to explain that he had not come by these things through his own labour or his own inheritance. He felt, most of the time, like a man who drives the firm's large car and pretends that it is his own and payed for: a pretence useful to both firm and employee, a useful fostering of confidence. And slowly, his own labours had taken over, to a degree: he had grown to fit his surroundings, he had become able to maintain them, though he could never initially have afforded them. Life at the Bar these days, as the Head of his Chambers never tired of telling him, was much easier than it used to be: it was easy for a clever young man like himself to make a good living. But how far, he sometimes asked himself, would he have got, without Julie and what she had brought him? There had been other accidents operating in his favour, it was true—he had been lucky in his tutor at Oxford, who had managed to place him in a Chambers where the work had interested him to such a degree that he had had an incentive to labour, and a natural sympathy with what came his way. Union Law, most of it was, and that again (except that his entry into this world had been accidental) had represented, perhaps, a debt paid to his father. But with what ironies this debt was paid. His father, he was sure, had he been in a fit state to approve of anything, would have approved of the general tendencies of his efforts, in that he usually represented what his father would have thought of (when he could think) as the right side: but how had he become able to represent it but by turning his back upon all that had made him wish to align himself, in so far as a barrister may, upon one side rather than the other?

Julie hated the nature of his work. She wished that he were doing something more interesting. She had shown the faintest glimmer of interest when he and an academic friend had started to combine to produce a book, because books were exciting, but had quickly lost enthusiasm when she discovered the intense dullness of the book, and the fact that his contributions were to remain, through professional discretion, almost anonymous. If there was one thing Julie couldn't be doing with, it was anonymity. He often thought she would have been better married to a personality of some kind. She liked personalities. Whereas law reports she could not bring herself to read. He thought about their new car. She had wanted him to buy a big car. She liked big cars. He had said that he could not afford one, and she had said, never mind, I'll pay. So he had bought one, because he too liked big cars. And now he drove it around as though it were his, and people looked at it and registered its presence as though it were his. He had bought it to humour Julie, because what right had he to deny her the very few things in life that seemed to amuse her? What fault of his was it if her aims and needs were childish? And yet, driving it, he knew that this was what he himself would call corruption. With a faint sudden recurring shock of astonishment he would recognise, in his own behaviour, an eternal human pattern of corruption. This is it, he would think to himself, this is I, doing what all men do, I am enacting those old and pre-ordained movements of the spirit, those ancient patterns of decay, I, who had thought myself different. I, who had (surely) other intentions. Corrupt, humanly corrupt if not professionally so, and humanly embittered. And his spirit would struggle feebly within the net that held it, and he would imagine some pure evasion, some massive rent through which he could emerge. But there was no action possible that would not involve destruction, violence, treachery, of those to whom he had pledged himself, and of the only useful actions of his life. And of these, there were some. There were even many. He was caught. And his spirit would hunch its feathered bony shoulders, and grip its branch, and fold itself up and shrink within itself, until it could no longer brush against the net, until it could no longer entangle itself, painfully, in that surrounding circumstantial mesh.

HAVING PURSUED THESE reflections to their usual end, having arrived, as usual, at the usual bleak perch—a perch becoming less bleak, at times he thought, through familiarity, his hunched posture less painful as his bones learned to expect it—he finished his Ovaltine, and decided that he had better go to bed. He took the cup back into the kitchen and put it on the shelf, and looked once more at his son's note.

There was some other point that he was trying to remember, a last point. Yes. The real point about the whole of Rose's case was the question of how the children were. That was what the question was. If she could be quite sure that they were better with her, that they had in no way suffered from being alone with her, then he was fairly sure that she had nothing to worry about. He thought of the two smaller ones, rolling on the floor. They had looked all right, what he had been able to bring himself to see of them. And the eldest child, Konstantin, culturally playing his oboe, had looked, from the judicial point of view, more than all right: civil, intelligent, almost a public-school product. But there might be more to it than that. He looked at his son's laborious handwriting. There was always more to it than that. But with any luck, one could always conceal evidence that ought not to be seen.

Julie was asleep when he went upstairs. With relief, he got into bed quietly, and tried to sleep himself.

ROSE, WAKING UP the following morning, had immediately the sense that there was something unpleasant that she had promised herself that she would do. While she gave the children their breakfast and drank a cup of tea, she tried to work out what it could be—unearthing accidentally, as she did so, a whole heaped cupboard-full of nasty obligations, such as shoe-buying and glazier-visiting, and of nagging guilts, about people she should have rung back and hadn't, people she should have written to and hadn't, birthday presents unbought and promises unfulfilled. But it was for none of these pointlessly exhumed anxieties that she had been looking. Finally, as she pulled up Maria's socks, found Konstantin's football boots, failed to find Marcus's soccer cards, and kicked all three, in one continuous movement, out through the front door and down the road to school, she worked out what it was. She had promised herself (waking up, restless, in the middle of the night) that she would make herself go down to the library and look it all up. She would look it all up, in one of those dreadful law books. It was no good asking her solicitor, it was no good even asking Simon Camish, because nobody would tell her the truth: they were all too anxious to placate and to soothe. If she wanted to find out what it was all about, she would have to go and do it for herself. Having come to this conclusion, she sat down, rather weakly, and poured herself another cup of tea. She had been through all this before. Twice before. The first time, when she had herself been made a ward, she had been too ignorant even to put together the little information she had been able to acquire: having been more or less incarcerated in her father's house, she had had to rely on whatever books were lying around there, and they'd been an unhelpful selection. The nearest she had got had been *Iolanthe* and *Bleak House*, neither of which had been exactly relevant, though the latter had filled her with a quite justified apprehension. But the apprehension had been shapeless, formless, completely lacking in detail, a terror of her own helplessness and confusion. When she came to the divorce, when she became aware that after all she was going to have to divorce Christopher out of self-protection, the situation had been very different. Then, she had known what she ought to find out, though she still had little idea of how to set about it. She had gone down to the public library, with Maria still under school age amusing herself by pushing all the books, thud thud, to the backs of the shelves, and she had tried to find some useful books. *Everyman's Lawyer, Law for the Layman,* a book on divorce statistics. She had tried to educate herself gently, her mind dazed by even the simplest terms, and had in the end to admit that there was nothing for it but to try the heavy stuff. She hadn't been allowed to take Rayden home with her, as it was in the reference section, so she had had to pore over it anxiously with half her attention on a bored, trouble-making Maria: while she read, with extreme pain, of matrimonial offences and maintenance problems and definitions of cruelty and desertion. It had been a horrible experience, made worse by the fact that she seemed to understand so little of what she read, that she had to convict herself, as she struggled, of real stupidity. It would have been easier for her, perhaps, to go straight to the solicitors, but that was not how she was, she wanted to know for herself, she could not trust herself to a solicitor. Solicitors had not, after all, been much on her side, and delicacy prevented her from approaching one without a certainty of the nature of her case. She could not, had never been able, to grasp the fact that a solicitor engaged by her would have her interests at heart. She expected to be judged, and harshly. Even finding a solicitor had been a major problem, as she clearly could not use Christopher's, or her family's, and had been too embarrassed, at first, to ask her friends. She had, in the end, asked Emily, who had been as vague as herself, but had managed to recommend her one nevertheless.

She would use him again, she supposed, she would have to, but she wanted to know for herself where she was. So she put on her coat and her wellington boots, and set off to the library. She'd thought at first she would go to the main library, because it was less personal and she would feel less conspicuous there, but decided as she set off that she hadn't the energy, and might as well go to the local branch. It was a branch that she disliked, as it was run by a peculiarly snappy and short-tempered woman, a woman nearly as unpleasant as the one in the post-office, who would on principle reject parcels as being ill-wrapped, and Family Allowance signatures as being illegible.

She walked down the dark streets, past the shops, and the rain dripped unpleasantly. She thought of the post-office woman. The week before she had been waiting in the queue to buy some stamps, and a girl in front of her had been trying to post a parcel. She was a nice girl, a timid girl, and she said very politely, as she stuck the stamps on, 'Do you think it will get there by the end of the week?' 'Don't ask me,' the post-office lady replied, crossly. 'Oh, I'm sorry,' said the girl, immediately apologetic, sorry to have annoyed her: whereupon the post-office lady glowered ferociously through the grill (which took on the aspect, suddenly, of a restraining cage) and said, 'Look here, you're asking me for a cast-iron guarantee, aren't you, a cast-iron guarantee about whether that parcel of yours will get there by the end of the week. Well, I'm not going to give you one, it's not my job. I don't give cast-iron guarantees to no one.' The girl looked shattered by this attack, as well she might: but a sense of pride and justice compelled her to assert, as she moved away, 'I wasn't asking for a guarantee, I only asked.' The post-office woman sniffed, and turned to the next customer: he had come to enquire about a registered letter he had sent to his family in Nigeria. What shall I do, he said, reasonably, they haven't received my letter. How do you know, said the woman. Because they haven't replied, and it was urgent, he said. Well, she said, you can't claim till I've got it in writing from them you sent it to that they didn't get it. But how can I get it in writing from them that they don't get my letters, if they don't get my letters? he said. That's your problem, she said. No claim without written confirmation from recipient that post was not received, she said.

Thinking back over this, Rose could not help laughing. It had been too awful to be true. In fact, she had laughed as she stood there in the queue, and other people had known what she was laughing at, because they had joined in. It had cheered her up, that.

She walked past the school, a huge Victorian edifice that loomed up, complete with bell and weathercock, against the dirty sky, and felt some satisfaction at the thought that all her children were safely in there, being educated. On the school windows, pasted from inside, there were cut-out butterflies, and doily patterns, and shoals of fish. The friezes of Christmas trees, and stuck-on blobs of cotton wool from last term had disappeared. She remembered how the sight of this school had alarmed her, years before, when she had first seen it, when Konstantin had been a baby: and of how it had gradually transformed itself through connection and familiarity. Like the streets she walked upon. She turned the corner, into a dingy terraced residential road, and there was the library, a modern building of spectacular ugliness, a low, inadequate building, disgraced by its surroundings as it disgraced them. In the spring, sometimes, it looked all right, when there were some flowers on the tree planted in the concrete. But now it was not yet spring.

There was nobody much inside the library. There rarely was. Two elderly ladies were looking at the Light Romance section. She disapproved of a library that actually classified books under Light Romance. A black man and an Indian were sitting at tables trying to work. The tables were clearly not designed for working on, and she had once heard the librarian point this out. And now, as she stood there waiting to return two of the children's long overdue books, she heard something even worse. In front of her there was a man—a Ghanaian, she thought, though even after some experience she was not very good at these assessments—and he was asking the librarian about a book. Reasonably enough, one might think. Rose listened to what he was saying. He was asking her if the library had a copy of *Animal Farm*. It was quite true that his accent was not as distinct as it might have been, but she had herself understood him perfectly, and she was quite astonished to hear the librarian snap back that no, of course they hadn't, the library didn't stock zoology text books, if he wanted that kind of thing he'd better try the main branch. She wondered if the man would retort, but no, he mildly raised his eyebrows, and returned to consult the catalogue once more. Handing over her children's books, and paying the fine that more enlightened libraries no longer exact from children, she wondered whether she should remonstrate, or whether she should go and try to help the man wrestle with the catalogue, but of course did neither. She wondered, as she made her way to the legal section, whether the librarian had spoken through ignorance or malice, and which would have been more deplorable. It was the man's look of polite patience that had most distressed her. What must life be like, in its daily texture, when such incidents were a daily fare? Some of these misunderstandings, as she well knew, were inevitable, because they were caused by the language problem, not even by the culture problem. It was something that people would never admit: nobody would admit that so many immigrants, inevitably, verged in speech upon the incomprehensible. She knew it herself all too well from those days when she had answered the telephone for the Anti-Discrimination Co-operative Accommodation Scheme, because the chief worry (apart from the inevitable shortage of accommodation available) had been the basic inability to communicate to most of the people who rang her up. It was worse on the telephone than in person, of course, and she had become quite frantic at times as she listened to lengthy explanations of which she could understand but one word in ten. It was, in fact, not unlike reading legal language: the details and refinements of the explanation remained totally obscure, and it was only by an immense effort of the will that one could understand the main drift. One could understand it, if one stuck at it, but the strain was dreadful, and in the end she had had to give it up. The organisers of the scheme had persisted, despite her constant denials, in the belief that she could understand Greek, being married to Christopher, and how could she explain to them that Christopher himself, on principle, could understand hardly a word, and would certainly never speak a word, of his own language? Battered by gales of Greek, she had tried to learn it herself, and had failed dismally. There was a Greek family who lived next door to her, on the other side from the Flanagans, who spoke little English, but they had been keener to learn from her than to teach her. Christopher's family despised this family, and they, for their part, hated Christopher's. After he had left her, they had tried to explain to her that the Vassilious were exploiters, that the house they lived in belonged to just such a family, who charged them an exorbitant rent. Traitors to their own kind, they would have said, had they been familiar with such a phrase. They had not needed the phrase. Rose had got the message anyway. As she had got the message that awful day last summer, when she had gone out to sit on the front steps, and had found there the black-dressed grandmother from next door, who had pointed to the sky and muttered in Greek about something or other. Looking at the blue sky, Rose had said (not knowing what to say, smiling cheerfully, pleased with the sun) Yes, it's a lovely day, isn't it. And the woman had continued to gesticulate sadly towards the heavens, and Rose had continued to praise the sun's benevolence, until Mrs Flanagan, drawn also into her front steps by the activity outside, had informed her that the old lady's husband had departed heavenwards during the night, and that her pointing finger was indicating his spiritual ascent. How Mrs Flanagan had discovered this, Rose did not know, perhaps she had a better instinct about such things. It had remained a lovely day, the sun had continued to shine, Rose and the old lady had continued to sit on their steps and nod at one another. The old lady had not taken her incomprehension amiss. Rose wondered whether she herself would have been so tolerant.

As she got out Rayden on divorce from the reference shelf, and a useful looking work by Thomas E. James called *Child Law,* she suddenly remembered a bit she had read in the paper that week about a woman who had taken home the *Gnomes of Zurich,* thinking it was a children's book, and who had been surprised to find her children reject it. Inspired, she went to the children's section, and there, sure enough, under O for Orwell, was *Animal Farm.* She got it out, and took it to the man, who was still struggling with the catalogue. He looked at it with surprise, and then with gratitude. He smiled. She smiled. 'Thank you,' he said. 'Not at all,' she said, and then she went and sat down with her law books again.

The very names of the chapters were enough to give one a headache. She persevered. She had known, anyway, that her divorce having been defended and heard in the High Court, she would have to go back to the High Court, and could therefore miss out all the bits about magistrates, but she was not sure why, because some of them looked relevant. What on earth was statutory authority? At last she found a sentence that seemed not to be disqualified, that said, quite bleakly, 'Variations of an order of the Divorce Division as to custody can therefore be made at any time, but only in very exceptional circumstances if the child is over sixteen years of age.' Apart from that strange 'therefore', the antecedents of which she could not trace, this seemed to make relevant and not very encouraging sense. It seemed to mean that Christopher had every right to apply for the custody order to be varied. She looked, anxiously, for something about the grounds on which such orders should be varied, but (through stupidity, probably) couldn't find very much except a slightly more comforting sentence which said that the discretion of the court to grant custody of a child is subject to its welfare being a paramount consideration. 'The misconduct' it said, 'of either of the parties is not the guiding principle in this respect.' So presumably she had to prove that it was in the interests of the children's welfare that they should remain with her? And Christopher would have to prove that it wasn't? It seemed, either way, a very unpleasant business, as bad as getting divorced all over again. She wondered, not for the first time, what he could possibly be doing it for. Not because he really wanted the children, surely? She did not give him such credit. One of the things that had so corrupted their marriage, while it had existed, had been his attitude to children. He had felt that they should be brought up by the mother, that they were women's work, and she had thought this fair enough at the beginning when he had been working hard to keep them alive: it had seemed not exactly just, that she should struggle endlessly to make herself get out of bed in the middle of the night, and cook meals with children hanging round her knees crying, and drag herself down to the shops with a raging temperature, through the rain, pushing a pram, simply in order that he should not have to endure the technical dismay of finding himself baby-minding, but she had done it with a reasonable grace. She used to tell herself, in those early days, he comes from a different world, he objects to the principle of the thing, it's his history, but as time had worn on and she had discovered that (inevitably) he used history to suit himself, and was able to find himself quite liberated from racial and historical prejudices when it was convenient for him, she began to lose patience, her efforts to adapt herself to the role of obliging Greek wife became less and less convincing, she began to think (in the normal course of marriage) that it was time he did a bit of adapting. He even called it 'minding the baby', if she tried to leave him alone in the house with a child sleeping in bed upstairs while she went to the launderette with his shirts and socks. (That was how she put it: there were other people's shirts and socks in the bundle as well, naturally.) He was good enough with the children when she was there also being good with them, but there was little point in that: overtaxed, overstrained, physically exhausted, she had found herself no longer able to resist the movements of violent rejection and resentment within her, and it was this, perhaps, that had led to those worst degradations, those insults to his race, to his family, to his whole being. How inconceivable they would have seemed at the beginning, and how impossible to stop them, once she had started. It was his rejection of the role of ordinary English father that had made her, forcibly, making a virtue of necessity, draw the children to herself, take them entirely upon herself, set up, even while he was still there, a solitary life with them, in which she took sole charge, sole responsibility. He had not cared, when Konstantin was five, which school Konstantin should go to: it was she that had made the enquiries, it was she that had braved, alone, that grim Victorian edifice. And how could he now permit himself the luxury of criticism and complaint? He should have started to care earlier, if he had meant to care at all. It was no wonder that she had ended up alone with the children: she had been forced to take them on alone, she had strengthened herself on those hard years, she had developed the muscle to deal with them, she had learned to love the hardship of dealing with them, she had made them a life from which he had voluntarily abstracted himself. It was a life she could not change or abandon, because it was her only one, and it had been acquired through too much labour to be relinquished. In the last year or two, when Christopher had been making money, he had started to propose alterations—a new house, a better district, a washing machine—but by then it was too late, she had become what she was, she had wanted to continue to be it, she could not have it taken from her. And the thought of his wishing to take on the children, without her, appeared to her ludicrous, she could not see it other than as an effect of malice, she could not see that it could express a real intention or even a real concern. But knowing Christopher, and the brutalities he had after all endured for her, how could she be sure that malice alone would not carry him the whole way?

The children had suffered from all this. Of that she had no doubt. She had taken them from him, because he had wanted her to have them: she had prevented him from attempting to repent. She had not allowed him to re-enter the small world she had made for them. She had (he said) poisoned their minds against him. And it was true. She had tried not to, but it was true. When he had made efforts towards the end, to reassert his authority over them, she had undermined him, she had persuaded the children to reject the interests he offered them, she had ignobly set up herself against his forfeited power. She had been ashamed of it, she had despised herself for it, but she had been incapable, totally incapable of doing otherwise. Now, when they came back from their days out with him, loaded with unsuitable gifts and subversive views and accounts of what they had done with him, she tried to keep her mouth shut, in the silence of the victor. But it was too late for justice, too late for an uneasy peace.

She shut the book on child law, and braced herself to look again at Rayden, that miserable catalogue of human misery and strife. She knew, by instinct, or perhaps by some dim sense that she had pieced together from previous bits of information, that she would find something there that would justify all her forebodings and apprehensions. It took her a long time to find it, because, again, most of what she could find on custody seemed either irrelevant or inconclusive, but in the end, there it was, as she had suspected. It was a small sub-section on education. She read it, and felt her hair rise on the back of her neck. There it was, clearly enough. It said: 'On the question of education, the Court considers the welfare of the children from the point of view of their religious education (a), or worldly career (b) and their general upbringing (c).' She sat there, and considered this statement. She knew that it meant trouble. The religious education bit one could safely dismiss, as nobody could suppose that Christopher could plausibly now develop a belated passion for the Greek Orthodox Church, but the other two factors seemed quite terrifyingly relevant. The general wellbeing of children was a vague enough concept, and she could imagine herself arguing reasonably enough that their general wellbeing might consist precisely in staying where they were, without interruption or distraction, at Harringdon Road School, but the phrase 'worldly career' was another matter. What could it possibly mean except exactly what she was not offering them, and what Christopher thought they ought to have? She looked at the small print at the bottom of the section, and found that the only case quoted was Symington *v.* Symington in 1875, whereas there was a case on upbringing as recent as April 1958. Perhaps the concept of worldly career was not invoked these days, but how could one be sure? And if it were, what judge would ever have the nerve to identify worldly careers with Harringdon Road? Times had changed a little in the world since 1875, but not in the world of judges. They would have little sympathy with the Plowden Report, and bubble-gum cards, and a nature table littered with the eloquent scourings of waste lots and Alexandra Park. And (more horribly, sitting there, her faith shaking at the prospect of attack) how much real faith had she? Oh, she had declared it, she had maintained it, she had lived by it, but she, like everybody else, had worried about it, she had had her doubts. Necessity (a forced, unnatural, voluntary necessity) had kept her at it, but God knows she had had her anxieties, her moments of real panic. She had seen herself, surely enough, and knew that others would see her, as a crazed woman, denying her children for the thin glamour of an idea, like a Jehovah's witness or a Christian Scientist denying them their life blood in the operating theatre for the sake of a delusion, a principle so vague and abstract that even she could not properly define it. She was prepared to take this, she was prepared to endure even her own doubts, but at the same time she uneasily knew quite well that her position was false, whatever it was, and that she could only maintain it through certain kinds of cheating. She could afford to leave them there because she had a house with books in it, because she herself pursued a rigorous life that she knew she must (perhaps even too much) transmit, because she had friends whose children were more like the kind of children her own would normally—

though what for her could have been normal?—have known. She had worried, in the early years, that her children would not get asked to birthday parties, nor have friends with intellectual interests, friends who would be of use in later life. (Use? In what sense of use? It did not bear too much investigation, which was her best defence against Symington *v.* Symington.) She had relied heavily, for instance, on their friendship with Emily's children, dirty, scruffy, jumble-sale-dressed little intellectuals, full of precocious views on the nature of God, the extent of the solar system, and the practicability of free public transport in Inner London. They had provided what Harringdon Road could not, therefore she was cheating, intellectually, as she had cheated financially.

About some things, on the other hand, her fears had been ludicrously misplaced, and easily dispelled. About birthday parties, for instance, which happened everywhere, throughout the social scale—everywhere, that is, except in her own remembered childhood. Her children went to more birthday parties in a school term than she had been to in a lifetime. This seemed to her particularly significant, a triumphant justification of her own approach. But then, her attitude to birthdays was neurotic. She did not like to look at it too closely. Something lurked there, in her memory, that she did not wish to see. She saw its shadow, each time she bought a gift for a child to take, each time she tried hastily to clean their shoes or find a clean shirt or dress, each time she stood in the doorway collecting, with a row of other mothers, exchanging the idle coin of mothers' conversation. Neurosis was behind all that, so perhaps she could not truly quote it as an example of the virtues of her own theory of education. She was on safer ground with the education itself. She had had, at times, elementary fears that they might not acquire even an elementary education, but they had all learned to read and write with great facility, and seemed to be progressing, through a maze of projects and binary maths, whatever they were, to some higher forms of knowledge. (Aha, her nasty friends said, that's because of their heredity, not because they're well taught, you know. What do you mean, Rose would retort, in pained and deceitful surprise, look at Christopher, he is nothing to boast about as far as heredity goes, he is one of these immigrants who hold things back so much, and as for myself, I am quite stupid, I am totally uneducated, I have never passed an examination in my life.

You know what we mean, the friends would say.

No, Rose would say with dignity. It is clear that *you* know what *I* mean.) The school was rather good on music, they learned to play a variety of musical instruments, at Harringdon Road, a fact which she had flung often enough at Christopher, until he in turn in a fit of rage had flung Konstantin's oboe out of the bedroom window. It hadn't been his really, it had been borrowed from school. There had been a terrible scene with him about it. God, how she repented of her self-righteousness, and how necessary it had seemed.

But the fact still remained that Konstantin was top of his class. Whether this was a proof of the triumph or failure of her system she did not know. He seemed equally happy, with Emily's children, or with his own school friends: he never murmured even faintly that he might prefer anything other than what he had got. She had once asked him, rashly, in a suicidal moment, which he liked best, Ben (his closest friend) or Saul (Emily's eldest) and he had looked at her cannily, sounding her, knowing her through and through, and had thought for a moment, and had then said, 'What a funny question. I like them both.' Then he had thought again, and had added, 'Though Saul is very annoying, sometimes.' One never knew where one was with Konstantin. At supper the next day he had suddenly said, 'Mummy, which do you like best, me or Emily?' and had laughed at her attempts to reply. She sometimes thought she had brainwashed the child, he was so good, so hopeful, so protective of her and all she wanted for him, so loyal to all she had given him, so undemanding about the things of which she deprived him. He was a heroic child, so lovely and good to her on the whole, after all she had inflicted on him, and she wept tears, at times, to see him be all that one could ever wish him to be.

The week after Christopher left her, Konstantin was appearing at a school concert, and he had to wear a tie. He had asked her to tie it for him, not knowing how to do it himself, and she hadn't been able to, she hadn't known how to. In tears, kneeling before him, knowing it to be her own fault that there was no man in the house to do it (for this was one task that Christopher had not considered too menial to undertake), she had waited for him to panic, as she fumbled, she had waited for him to reproach her with the fact that Daddy could have done it, but he didn't, he even protected her from thinking that he might, by saying, with such kindness, that a lot of the boys couldn't do their own either and if he took it in his pocket, Mr Bell would do it for him, he was used to it, he had to do it quite often for other boys. She had gone along to the concert, that evening: it was an ambitious little piece, an operetta, the headmaster was keen on music and organised it very well. It was about a turtle and a man who went under the sea and came back and found a hundred years had passed and that all his friends had died. Rose sat there, with Marcus by her side and Maria on her knee chewing Smarties, and had watched Konstantin playing his oboe, and the other little children singing and dancing, and the refrain was:

O dance upon the silver sand
And beat the turtle drum
That youth may last forever
And sorrow never come

and Rose had started to weep, uncontrollably, and whether moved by the thin children's voices, or the fact that there were so many of them, such different cultures and nationalities, all singing this song of which God forbid that they should have the faintest understanding, or by the fact that Christopher had left her, or simply by the dreadful sentiment expressed, she could not possibly have said. It was more likely, she later thought, that she had been weeping for the knowledge that Konstantin would protect her from herself. She did not feel that she could possibly deserve to be spared the evidence of her own tragic failures. But he spared her: he flourished: he was cheerful, polite in public and horrible, when all was going well, in private, and he was, the headmaster said (though there was another problem) good grammar school material and sure to get a good place.

The little children she didn't worry about. They had been born into a world of blows and rows and partings, they didn't know about anything else. Unlike Konstantin, they had no tender infant images to protect. A friend of hers, a psychiatrist, had said to her once that Konstantin, brought up in reasonable peace for the first three years of his life, would be secure for ever, no matter what storms thenceforward broke over his head, because the foundations of personality were immovable. She wondered about this a great deal, not quite believing it. It did indeed seem that Konstantin had a steadiness of purpose that the smaller two lacked, but it was also a steadiness, she feared, of suffering. Marcus and Maria, endlessly buffeted, had become endlessly resilient: they were emotional, quarrelsome, cheerful, and they forgot about things as soon as they were over. They were adaptable, they were born survivors. But Konstantin, although he could be difficult enough on a trivial level, had a truly alarming capacity for recognising, seizing, embracing, enduring and surmounting a real sorrow, as he had in the matter of the untied tie and the loss of his father. Perhaps this is what the psychiatrist had meant by an unshakable personality. If so, Rose was far from sure that it was a blessing. Better not to know, better, at that age, not to be able to distinguish. Time alone, doubtless, would show, which of these children had been most damaged, most affected. She would have to wait for the effect of its operations. But, as it stood, there didn't seem to be much point in worrying about Marcus and Maria. They were happy, they were all right. When she sat down and cried, as she did more rarely now, thank God, they waited patiently till she had finished, and then asked her to fix their rifles or pour them some orange squash, as though nothing had happened: just as, when Christopher had still been at home, they had listened to those appalling rows, had heard those screams of abuse and self-defence, had witnessed blows and broken glasses, and had waited, with a slight boredom, for it all to end so that they could get on with watching the television. They never seemed to be much disturbed by her troubles: they were far more interested in their own incessant disputes. Perhaps they were repressing the symptoms of their disturbance: how could one know? They did not seem repressed. But perhaps their blank and indifferent silences, their veiled waiting faces, were after all more dangerous signals than Konstantin's constant anxious surveillance: perhaps they were growing up to be split, to cut out, to refuse all experience that was not immediately acceptable to them. And yet it was not even true to say that they were always as she usually thought of them as being: Marcus was sometimes anxious, Maria would sometimes nervously tug at her skirt and clutch her knees and beseech her not to yell at Daddy down the telephone. (Not that she was about to, not that it was, ever, Daddy on the telephone these days, but Maria had remembered the days when it was, she had not forgotten them, as would have seemed more probable.)

Impossible, really, to make one's mind up about any other human person, even one's own children, whose whole life had un-rolled before one's eyes, whose every influence is known: they were so contradictory, so inconsistent, so confusing a mass of shifting characteristics, so that if one went so far as to define, to a friend, Marcus as the one who was good with his hands, he would the next instant be making an appalling bosh of some very simple sellotap-ing. And whenever she was thinking of Konstantin as being partic-ularly wise and restrained and disciplined, he would at once, as though reading her mind, start to shout, nag, abuse, and behave like the hooligan that she most of the time believed him not to be. How could one ever decide what was happening to them, what one was doing to them, when everything was so uncertain? And yet, nevertheless, she did not worry about Marcus and Maria. They would come to no harm, there was nothing in her that could harm them, she loved them so, their faces and their voices, that she could never harm them, she could transport them to the Pole or enclose them in a cellar and they would not be harmed, because of her love. With Konstantin (and this was the truth of the matter) it was different, because there had been a time when she had ceased, almost, to love him, when he had become unacceptable, in some way, to her, when his growing self (repelling kisses, suspicious, ungainly) had been impossible to indulge. They had quarrelled then, he and she (at the worst time, before she made her mind up to divorce Christopher, before the end, worn out with the two demanding babies, unable to cope with an articulate, complex, sulky growing boy)—they had bickered and quarrelled, and she had ceased, secretly, briefly, ceased, physically, to love him. She had stopped going in to his bedroom when she went to bed, to see him asleep. She had ceased to love as she had once loved. The spirit bloweth whither it listeth, with vicious negligence and malice. She had learned, now, to love him again, she loved him again passionately, yearningly, but she would never cease to worry about that gap, that space of time when she had quietly, wearily failed him. He had regained her love: she had not freely given it, he had regained it by his own lovely behaviour, by his own perceptions, his own concessions, his own grace. He had made the truce: he had ceased, of his own free six-year-old will, to pick quarrels with her, to attack her, to goad her. And for this she loved him the more, she reached out to him the more, she loved him for his generosity, as she loved the others for their baby faces and their innocence. But it was a love for ever involved, thenceforward, in anxiety: it could never regain its lost simplicity, its lost continuity. The other two had never forfeited these things, and this was why she did not worry about them. They were redeemed not in themselves, but in her feeling for them. In vain did she tell herself that such failures, as her brief failure with Konstantin, were inevitable: that they were the cross the eldest had to bear: that the failure had not been noticeable to the child but only to her own unnaturally sensitive self. She reproached herself. She did not forgive herself. She was not much good at accepting, in herself, the natural shortcomings of humanity.

There was not much point in speculating about such things. They were not, anyway, thank God, classifiable. They were not grounds for varying custody orders, after all. She shut the thick divorce book, returned it to its shelf, and set off to do her morning's shopping. On the way she went into the sweet shop on the corner of Harringdon Road to buy the children the sherbert fountains that she had promised them that morning, thinking that she might as well do it now while she was passing, while she still remembered. It was the school sweet shop, it was full of all the penny and halfpenny sweets—liquorice bootlaces, penny chews, gob stoppers, humbugs, toffee strips—that ignorant adults, who no longer frequent such shops, believe, in their arrogant adulthood, to have vanished from the face of the earth. But the sweets are still there, and Rose had promised either twopenny sherbert fountains with liquorice suckers, or sherbert dabs. To reach the counter, she had to step delicately over the washing operations of Janet from down her road, who was washing the floor, on hands and knees, with a damp rag. Rose trod with care, in order not to spread the dirt— she need not have bothered, Janet was merely spreading the dirt herself, as she never rinsed her rag—and took care also not to acknowledge Janet with more than a nod of the head. Janet, who would talk for hours on the street or sitting on her own front wall, did not like to be caught out washing floors on her hands and knees. The first time Rose had come across her in the sweet shop washing, Rose had greeted her as she would have done elsewhere, but the greeting had been returned with such faintness, such diffidence, such a simulation of not-being-there, that Rose had taken the hint. It was a fairly recent job for Janet. Before she had taken to this, she had minded a black baby called Melissa. But the Council had checked up on her and decided that she was too old and her basement too damp. So there she was on her hands and knees spreading a thin film of mud aimlessly about the lino tiles. Janet wore a faded print apron from another age, and her hair was yellowy-white and wispy, and her face trembled like a rabbit, and while she talked she would also mumble. It was quite an art, talking to Janet, because one had to pick the words out of the mumbles. It was an art that everybody in the street had acquired. One had to talk, ruthlessly, through the mumbles, if one wished to respond at all, because she could not keep silent, she could not keep the noises out of her throat. She was mumbling now, as she bent her wispy head, as Rose asked for three sherbert dabs, as Miss Lindley, Infant Teacher, followed Rose into the shop, stepping delicately from the mat to the bit of newspaper in her highheeled fashion boots, in order to buy herself a packet of fags to see her through break, which had just begun. Rose, half-turning her head, saw her courteous avoidance of the symbolically washed floor, and thought, for the hundredth time, what a nice girl she is, Miss Lindley.

Miss Lindley, seeing Rose, smiled. There was a look of unease in her smile, which at first Rose assumed must be related to a letter which would have arrived or would shortly arrive for the headmaster from her solicitor, suggesting that he and his staff might testify to the solidity of the characters of the Vassiliou children, but when Miss Lindley spoke the shadow was dispelled. (As Miss Lindley had intended that it should be.)

'I shouldn't really be here,' said Miss Lindley, 'I just slipped out for a packet of fags.'

'I was buying sherbert fountains,' said Rose.

'Much healthier,' said Miss Lindley.

'I don't know,' said Rose. 'They rot the teeth.'

'Your children's teeth look fine,' said Miss Lindley. 'A frightfully healthy lot, your children.'

'Yes, they are, I suppose,' said Rose, modestly.

'So bright, too,' pursued Miss Lindley, who was generously committed to the topic. 'Really, they're a pleasure to have in the class.'

'Don't you find Maria a bit noisy?' said Rose.

'They're all noisy,' said Miss Lindley, 'but at least Maria makes a cheerful kind of noise.'

'She talks all the time.'

'Yes, she talks all the time, but only because she's keen. She knows it all, you know, she keeps telling me, when Marcus was in Class 12 *he* didn't do The Little White Elephant, *he* did The Big Bad Rabbit. And stuff like that.'

They both laughed.

'She sounds a bit of a nuisance to me,' said Rose, who did not think so, but expected Miss Lindley to think so.

'She's not at all,' said Miss Lindley. 'It's nice to know they pay attention.'

And so, smiling too much at each other to express goodwill, on the threshold of the sweet shop, they parted. And Rose Vassiliou went away thinking, lovely Miss Lindley, she likes all those children so much, she is so energetic and kind and undiscriminating, and what she loves in those children is the returning image of her own cheerfulness, her own affection, her own faith. And Miss Lindley thought, Mrs Vassiliou is such a nice woman, she really doesn't know what a nice lot her own children are because she thinks all children are nice, and all she'll think if I tell her her own are a particular pleasure to me is that I am being particularly nice to her because she has troubles, poor woman, she'll never know I mean it. And thus, doing each other rightly more than justice (because it was not a question of justice but of goodwill and faith) they diverged. Lovely Miss Lindley, striding across the asphalt playground in her long boots and her short skirt, her long hair bouncing with the energy of her stride, her face expressing authority, amusement, conviction, tireless, vain, adored by her infants basking radiantly in the warmth of their adoration and her own virtue, reaping each day what she sowed, a whole harvest of smiles and confidences and hands tugging at her rather high hem, and voices saying Miss, Miss (or Mum when they forgot it was Miss). Guess what, Miss, you'll never guess. It was a job she was doing, and she loved it. Lovely Miss Lindley, striding across the asphalt playground to that building that looked like a prison but thanks to her and people like her was not one: let her so forever stride, ask no questions about her future or her past, her motives, her endurance, do not ask when that youthful energy will fail her, but let her walk across that playground in her sexy boots, perfect, accomplished, across and across, again and again, her hair bouncing, a cheerful commitment and dedication in her very step. Do not seek to disbelieve it, do not disturb her with disbelief, because she is, there she walks, towards that ever-waiting classroom, and as she opens the door she will smile, greeting their smiles, she will receive with love that daunting chorus of demands, claims, cries and exhortations. Do not believe that she does not, could not exist. O lovely Miss Lindley. O almost confident apostrophe.

ON THE WAY HOME Rose bought herself a piece of cheese for lunch, and various other items for supper, at the Co-op, and deplored once more that the Co-op had descended to the vulgarity of giving stamps. 'It's a real shame,' said the woman at the desk, for the tenth time, sniffing with contempt at the working classes, 'but if you can't beat them you've got to join them.'

'I used to like giving my number,' said Rose, plaintively, also for the tenth time.

'People these days, they haven't got the brain to remember their numbers,' said the lady at the desk, quite untruthfully, but perhaps truthfully expressing sorrow at the decay of commercial standards.

'Oh well,' said Rose, 'never mind,'—shoving the blue stamps into her purse. She had heard this same woman agreeing with various other customers that stamps were a good idea because then you could see what you were getting, but with a number how could you be sure your number had ever got through? It would be interesting to know which of these views she really held. Perhaps she held both views simultaneously and with equal conviction. That was how most people were.

When she got home the second post was waiting for her on the doormat. She did not like the look of it, there was one letter that looked even from a distance as though it was from her solicitors. She put her shopping away in the kitchen and came back to pick it up, and it was. She sighed and opened it. Luckily it was not very interesting: it simply said (though not in such simple language) that since Rose was so reluctant to answer her post or her telephone, perhaps she might find time to go to the office to talk her problems over. She sighed again, heavily. It was the last thing she wanted to do, but she saw that she would have to. She had an uneasy feeling that her solicitor was much keener to talk to her than she was to talk to him. He was really just a little bit too interested in her affairs. She couldn't blame him for this, it was good of him in a way, but she found it embarrassing. In fact, she didn't see how it could be anything other than an embarrassing relationship, in view of all the things that he inevitably knew about her. He was too kind, too human, too involved—and it was precisely for these qualities, of course, that he had been recommended to her. But she'd never been able to accept his kindness very easily: she had, in fact, she had to admit, felt more at ease in the divorce case with the barrister who had seemed to assume that divorce was a sophisticated mental exercise, not intended to touch too closely on the realities of conflict. Her solicitor, Mr Alford, on the other hand, had attempted sophistication (thinking her, at first sight perhaps, that kind of person) but had been unable to maintain it, he was so genuinely upset by some of the things that had happened to her. At least with the divorce he had known what to be upset *about,* poor man: he was a gentle, diffident, courteous English person who did not like the thought of a woman being knocked about or locked up in her bedroom. (He had tried, bravely and dutifully, to question her about sexual irregularities on Christopher's part, assuming an uneasy bravado, but both he and she had found it so painful that they had abandoned the investigation and had agreed to miss such matters out of the evidence completely. Not that she could have borne, anyway, in conscience and honour, to complain about things that Christopher had done that she had quite enjoyed at the time.) But with the custody of the children she was on different grounds altogether. He had been terribly upset to have to tell her that she would have to be investigated by the Welfare, much more upset than she had been—(though she had been a bit rattled, and had gone to the lengths of pulling out the sideboard to see if there were still any of those big black beetles nesting behind it)—and had hardly been able to bring himself to ask her what she thought the grounds for her husband's sudden accusations were, in case it emerged that she had been drinking herself into a stupor or sleeping with every man in the street. She had reassured him on these points, but she still hadn't been able to explain to him why it was that she lived where she did and as she did in any way that he could understand. She had got used to people not understanding her. And at least Jeremy Alford was polite about his incomprehension. Some of her friends had been positively abusive. She had been quite amazed. You're being very selfish, they used to tell her— though surely they must have meant masochistic rather than selfish, if the thought of living as she did filled them with such alarm? They had produced all kinds of arguments against her, those hard realists with their central heating and their fitted carpets and their ambitions, and how could she persuade them that her life was as pleasant to her as a fitted carpet: to walk down the street, greeting this person here and this person there, to call in the sweet shop, the chemist, the greengrocer, the launderette (especially the launderette, because she knew all about it having worked there once)— to do all these things was a pleasure to her, and a profound satisfaction. There were some disagreeable people around, it was true, like the librarian and the woman in the post-office and the old couple on the corner who went round sticking racist posters on walls and lamp-posts, but on the whole they were people, just people, that one liked because one liked people, and because they were there. And perhaps one liked them all the more because one had not at first been able to get to know them. She didn't think (as her critics, of course, hinted) that she liked them out of pride and arrogance, because of the difficulty of forcing herself to do so: on the contrary, she sometimes thought that she'd like anyone who liked her, even that couple of old racists. She didn't want to lose it all. It was where she belonged. Quite simply, like many unreasonable slum dwellers, she didn't want to be rehoused. She liked to be with people who were quiet and minded their own business and didn't try to upset one another. They had watched her carried from the house in an ambulance, that day when she had swallowed a bottle full of aspirins, and they had said nothing. They had made no difference towards her. They had watched her dripping blood down the front steps from her gashed wrist—huge red wet drops the size of pennies—and they had never mentioned the sight again, though they had watched it carefully through their lace curtains. She liked them because they were not officious. She liked them because they did not know what to do. These really were the poor in spirit, these people. She had gone out one evening last summer, to sit on her front steps, and on the front steps next door had been assembled the whole of the Greek family, its cousins from across the road, and its various children. They were sitting there, looking vaguely worried, but doing nothing much. After a few minutes, as Rose sat there reading and watching her own children play hopscotch, the father of the family addressed her, saying, what do you think, Mrs Vassiliou, do you think we should do anything, my brother's little girl has just eaten a bottle of those orange aspirins, do you think we need to do anything? What, Rose had cried, leaping to her feet, scattering her paper and cigarettes, what, tell me about it. And they had told her, again, quietly, without urgency. You must ring the hospital at once, Rose said, at once. They will think we are making a fuss, said the man, nervously. Not at all, not at all, said Rose, supplying in her manner the missing urgency. The telephone box on the corner is broken, as usual, said the man. Use mine, said Rose. Oh no, they all said, we cannot bother you, we should not trouble you. So Rose had tried to convince them it was a serious matter, and had succeeded, and had rung the hospital, and the ambulance had arrived. The whole incident had moved her profoundly. It was impossible to convict these people of negligence, or of criminal irresponsibility: they had been anxious, concerned, but they had not known what to do. It had been much the same when Mrs Flanagan had been called as witness in the divorce case. Mrs Flanagan was a solid woman, a respected person, an elderly matriarch, safe enough in her own confines: she had stood by Rose, discreetly and without much personal approval, over the years, helping her once out of a bedroom window, letting her in once when she had been locked out of the house in her nightdress, and she had overheard over the years through the thin partition walls the birth pangs of Marcus and Maria, the breaking of crockery, the screams of anguish, the solitary moans of Rose in despair. She had taken all this very calmly, and had through sexual loyalty taken Rose's part, so had been a natural witness to call: but when she arrived at the court on the morning of the event, her voice had vanished. It had quite simply vanished. Confronted by alien articulations, she had retreated into silence. She stood there in the witness box, croaking and muttering inaudibly, quite unable to answer the simplest question. Christopher remarked maliciously that this was an unprecedented development for Mrs Flanagan, who was vocal enough at home, and suggested that perhaps her curious impediment was the expression of a subconscious wish not to perjure herself. The judge was evidently inclined to take this line too, as he was very short with her. The loss of voice persisted, quite genuinely, for three days.

How could one explain that one wished to live in a house because the neighbours on one side let their small child swallow a bottle of aspirins, and because the woman on the other side lost her voice when she needed it?

There was something more than the daily pleasures of streets well trodden, faces well known, small moments of architectural madness and felicity amidst acres of monotony. There was some inexplicable grace, in living so. Useless it probably was, like living in a closed order. Irrelevant, unproductive. But, as a nun attaches significance to arbitrary vows, so she had attached it to this place that she inhabited. Like a nun, she had recklessly committed herself, expecting perhaps little, expecting doubt and even despair to persist, but the rewards of faith had been hers, the sun whose existence she had merely supposed, through faith (because if it were not there, why live?), had shone forcefully upon her, it had illumined her and the relations that she had, in theory, supposed to have existed. They were there: so bright, so lit, she could not suppose that she had invented them.

What sort of defence would this make in a court of law? And who was to set about reducing it to an affidavit?

THE REST OF HER second post was less interesting. There was one library reminder, for the books she had just returned, and two appeals from charities. The number of these appeals had reached such a point, at one stage, that she had been forced to write back, in unstamped envelopes, being unable to afford the postage. Most people had taken the hint, but on the other hand a lot of people knew that she was going to come into some more money some time soon, and they wanted to keep reminding her of the worthiness of their claims. Most of their claims were very worthy, though she had become cynical, over the years, about the ability of many of the smaller organisations to fulfil their obligations. She had known too many of them fold up, through bad management or ill-will on committee level or conflicts of aims with other bodies. Some of the collapses were tragic. There was an appeal now, to rehouse a disbanded group of disabled people who had fallen through the mesh of any other organisation: a Methodist minister had persuaded a local council to lease him a house for them, where they had been set up in cottage industries of various sorts, but now the lease had expired and would not be renewed because the local residents had complained that the disabled people were unsightly and lowered the tone of the neighbourhood and frightened the local children. The Methodist described this meanness with passion and fire, and appealed to Rose and all the other people on his mailing list to raise funds to purchase a freehold dwelling where his protégés would be free from such selfish interference. She thought of her bombed school, and wondered whether people were worse off, if helped and then abandoned, than if they had never been helped at all. The other appeal was for a new extreme left-wing splinter group magazine of anarchic tendencies: a hangover hope that she would respond to solicitations from her early years. She looked at it, and read its manifesto, with extreme distaste. Some of the friends of her non-student days had been mad enough, God knows, but none of them ever as mad as this, and they had moreover been gentle people. Perhaps these young people, who seemed to see the world through the red blood of their own eyelids, were nice and gentle too, it was just that she was too old to know them, perhaps they merely wrote like homicidal maniacs because they weren't very good at writing. She wasn't to know, she was too old. It wasn't worth finding out. Better to do no very evident good than to do harm. She threw both letters in the bin, and went upstairs to make the beds. It was the divorce judge's fault that she got these letters every day. It was entirely his fault that she had become widely known as a dispenser of large sums of money. The matter of her African donation had been raised, naturally, during the case, but the papers wouldn't have been able to report it with such glee if the judge hadn't gone on about it in his summing up. They wouldn't have been allowed to. But as it was, they could really go to town on it. She'd managed to keep it quiet till then, but once it was out it was out, and she was inundated with telephone calls, begging letters, photographers, journalists. She wondered, sometimes, if this was what the judge had intended, if this was the price she had to pay for her decree. Because the judge hadn't approved of the folly of her largesse, it had been easy to see. And if it was to be (as seemed probable) the same judge dealing with the custody case, he would be given a second chance to show his disapproval.

Part Two

As the weeks passed, and a late spring came slowly on, and the solicitors lost all sense, in endless delays, of their initial urgency, Rose Vassiliou and Simon Camish continued their communications. At first, she would ring him up to ask him things: he had a suspicion that there were many people she rang, and that she was merely adding him to a list. But he responded, nevertheless, and came to anticipate her calls. As he assumed he had been cast in the role of legal adviser, he responded, on the whole, in terms of legal advice, a convenient formula. He looked things up for her, he explained things for her, and she thanked him politely for his interest, while appearing, delicately, at the same time, to find it quite natural. He wondered himself how natural it was. It was a long time since he had concerned himself with the affairs of another person in such a way, but then it was also a long time since anyone had appealed to him in such a way. He thought about her, he was quite well aware, more than strict necessity warranted, and worked out one day (while considering this) that he had formed with her possibly the first new connection in his married life, the first new relationship in years. He had been obliged to keep, for years, his professional and social life separate, as Julie so disliked having anything to do with lawyers, and he was uncomfortably aware of the fact that his connection with Rose was entirely surreptitious. She rang him, always, at his chambers, and eventually, inconvenienced by this, he took to ringing her instead. This arrangement gave their connection a disagreeably secret and pleasantly intimate nature. He valued this, but had no means of knowing what it might signify to her. On the whole he thought that she spoke to him because he was fixed and harmless. He was aware that in her position, as a woman alone, she was exposed to attentions of which she sometimes, allusively, complained, and thought it likely that his own manner, lacking as it clearly did any sense of expectation, was a relief to her, on this most negative level. If so, he did not much mind having found a practical use for his own self-negations. He could not have coped with anything more. It was almost impossible, really, to think of her as a woman, so entirely did she manage to present herself in a neutral light. He admired this presentation. In such a way, he, too, had always presented himself not as a man, but as something less dangerous. She had, she once sighed, had quite enough of men, gallantly implying that he was acquitted of the crime of belonging to this rejected category. Perhaps it was the only way to talk to anybody. He did not regret it.

Oddly enough, wherever he went now, he heard her name. He wondered how he had avoided it for so long. As a new word, once acquired, presents itself in every piece of print, so her name arose in every social gathering. Everybody seemed to know her, or to have heard of her, and to have views about her. In a way he judged her for the evident promiscuity of her interests, for having put herself in a position where she would be talked of. She had brought it upon herself, and there was no point in defending too much the honour or privacy of somebody who had exposed herself as she had exposed herself. But at the same time, he flattered himself that he had some personal access to her private nature. Perhaps, he thought, everybody who speaks of her assumes just such a privileged knowledge, so careful is she to relate, so anxious is she not to cause offence, so anxious is she to be liked and not condemned. And yet, nevertheless, he continued to believe that she bestowed upon him an especial light, an especial favour. He liked her, he truly liked her. If he was deceived, he was willingly deceived. He did not believe that she put down the phone after speaking to him, only to lift it again to ring up another comforter, seeking the same reassurances, imparting the same woes and same amusements. He thought he understood her. He wished to understand. Such a modicum of goodwill (for so he thought it) was nothing less than a re-birth in his nature. As such he valued it, and wondered from time to time if she suspected how exclusively she claimed his interest.

She did not, in point of fact, claim much of his time: his time was consumed by work and by placating his wife. A phone call or two a week, and the odd visit, were hardly the structure of a mutual life. It was only in the surrounding barrenness that they appeared so. (He believed her life to be empty, wished it indeed to be so, wished her to sit there in that house with those children, but did not expect that that was what she did.) In fact, that spring his attention was more than usually claimed by work, as the book which he and an acquaintance had been combining to write and had nearly completed, had suddenly become subject to an unexpected amount of revision. The book was about International Labour Law, and the inconvenience of such a subject was that it did not, alas, remain static. They had been hoping to get it out before anything too dramatic happened, but unfortunately two bits of legislation, both in Western Europe, had been passed at such a point in time that their implications could not possibly be excluded, so Chapters Eight and Eleven had to be extensively rewritten. His fury at the threat of this legislation and its subsequent enactment was not lessened by the fact that it embodied principles of which he himself thoroughly approved, and which he had been gloomily prophesying that no government would ever support. They had been supported, to his personal expense to the tune of several thousand new words. It's all very well, he and his friend Antony said, sadly piling cigarette ends into the ashtray, it's all very well, very sound and all that, but they might have waited till we'd got the book off to the printers. The publishers were sympathetic, but would not let them off. Simon felt some of the despondency that John Stuart Mill felt when, having comfortably worked out the amelioration of the human lot, he began to suspect that a life so ameliorated wouldn't be worth living for him personally, for ameliorator John Stuart Mill. Rebels without a cause, that's what we're going to look like if we're not careful, he said to Antony, and they looked at each other crossly and thought of their publisher's advance. Oh, I don't know, said Antony, one government or another is going to bring in some marvellous Industrial Relations Bill in the next year or two, that'll keep you and me happy with rage for years. And they laughed, and sat down to write it all again.

Julie was furious. She had fixed up some interesting diversions, in the form of dinner-parties, theatre-parties, God knows what, extending as they always did, frivolously and tediously, well-plotted, over the six weeks in which he was going to have to rewrite. She had no intention of letting him off, she needed him. She didn't make it any better by saying, you might have known this was going to happen—which was true, in a way, though she had no possible means of knowing it was true.

For some reason (for he did not often speak of his own affairs) he told this story to Rose. He told her on one of the few occasions when he actually saw her: he had gone round there to see her after work, having finished unusually early, and had found her, as he always chose to imagine her, sitting in her sitting-room watching television, but somehow unexpectedly holding a very small baby on her knee.

'It's not my baby,' she said, 'it's Eileen's, that girl who used to sit around here, you remember.'

'And where's Eileen?' said Simon, looking at the infant with some alarm.

'Nobody knows,' said Rose. 'She cleared off. Awful, isn't it?'

'She didn't by any chance leave you in charge of it?'

'No, no, God no, nothing as ghastly as that, she left it with her mother. She'll probably be back. It was probably a bit of a shock to her, having a baby. Her mother thinks she went to look for its father. I'm just looking after it for a bit till Mrs Sharkey gets back. Here, have a look at it. What do you think?'

'What do you mean, what do I think?'

'Do you think it looks—well, do you think it looks a bit kind of *dark*?'

'Black, you mean?' he said, peering at the baby, thinking that it indeed did look rather black in colour and in feature.

'Well, what do you think?'

'Yes, it does, a bit.'

Rose sighed. 'Awful, isn't it? I'm sure that's why she cleared off.'

'It would be the father, I suppose?' said Simon.

'I suppose so,' said Rose, and sighed. 'She really is a dreadful girl, Eileen, she had real ambitions, you know, she used to dress up and daydream, she even used to borrow books off me sometimes, I don't know why, she never read them, but she had ambitions, you know, and that's why she was so awful and sulky, and her mother is really such a good woman, so terribly hard-working, five children she had, and worked awfully hard for them, and the rest of them turned out a real credit, as she said, but poor old Eileen is a real bad lot. And the thing is, one can't help rather sympathising with Eileen. Even her mother can't help sympathising with her. One can't help in some way admiring her for being a bad lot.'

'I don't see anything very admirable,' said Simon, 'in walking off and leaving you and her mother holding the baby.'

'No, I suppose not,' said Rose. 'No, you're right, of course. But it must have been rather awful for her, with all those ambitions she had.'

'Whatever sort of ambitions were they?'

'Oh, God knows, I'm sure she didn't know. She wanted to be a Spanish duchess, or a wicked woman, or a make-up girl at the

BBC. And she hadn't a hope in hell of being any of them. It's enough to make anybody sulky. She'll be back, I expect. She'll stay away a day or two, and then she'll be back.'

'Who was the father?'

'She wouldn't tell. Well, actually, she did tell, she told me, but *I* promised not to tell. But I don't suppose telling you would count, would it? She'd probably like to think of me telling someone like you. He's a boy in a garage in Stoke Newington.'

'Why don't they get married?'

'He's married already. So she says he says. He probably isn't at all. He probably just doesn't want to marry Eileen. You can't blame him, can you? Look, would you like to hold the baby for a minute, and I'll go and make you a cup of tea, or coffee, or something.'

'No thank you,' he said, sincerely. 'Please don't bother.'

The baby heaved, and spat. A glob of milk landed on Rose's shirt. She wiped at it ineffectually with its own nightdress skirt.

'Poor thing,' she said, sadly. 'Poor little thing. It's got something quite disgusting called projectile vomiting. Dreadful, isn't it?'

She bent her head over the child, wiping its face. When she looked up again, her eyes were red.

'What's the matter?' he said, feeling he had to speak.

'Nothing,' she said, sniffing. 'Nothing. Everything. It's just so sad, that's all. Life.' She blew her nose.

'What's the matter?' he said again.

'Nothing,' she repeated. 'Nothing. I'm so lonely, sometimes. It was nice of you to come and see me.'

Astonished, he stared at her, then looked the other way.

'I'm just depressed,' she said, 'that's all. You don't look so cheerful yourself. You probably know what I mean.'

'I am depressed,' he said. 'Yes, I suppose I am. But it's no good deducing it from the way I look, because I always look depressed. So I'm told.'

'What about?' she said: and, to the background of *Bonanza,* he told her about his book.

'It isn't even,' he said, having finished the story, 'as though I've any right to be depressed. Logically, I ought to be pleased.'

'Oh, Lord no,' she said, 'that would be expecting too much of yourself. Really. For goodness sake. How long is it going to take you to rewrite?'

'One can't quite be sure. The problem is that Antony and I are supposed to be collaborating on it, and there's so little time when we're both free.'

'You don't actually write it together, do you?'

'Well, yes, as a matter of fact we do. It sounds mad, as a scheme, but in fact we don't get on too badly once we get down to it. And we neither of us have the will power to sit down and do it on our own. It's not as though it's going to be a masterpiece of prose, you know.'

'Will it be readable? I mean, will people like me be able to understand it?'

'I don't know quite what you mean by people like you, but if you mean is it written for the layman—well, no, I suppose it's not, really. It's more an academic text book, I suppose. It's in a series that Jacobs and Mayer are doing, I don't know if you've seen any of the other titles, you may have done—there's one on Urban Development, I think, and one on Women's Employment, and one on Penal Reform.'

'It sounds very interesting,' she said.

'Yes,' he said. 'That's what most people say when I tell them about it, and even while they're saying it their faces stiffen with the effort not to start yawning.'

'I *mean* it sounds interesting,' she said, plaintively, possibly even slightly hurt: and proceeded to interrogate him further, to prove her good faith. He had in fact forgotten that she had some possibly genuine interest in the subject, through her father's business, and despite himself, as she questioned him, he began to warm to the topic, because after all he *was* interested himself, of course he was, he might as well admit it, that's what he was doing it for, however he might try to disguise the project as a ruse for getting out of his own house and into Antony's, or as a means of making money, or as a furthering of his career. He was writing the thing really because he was interested in it, and because he wanted it to be written by somebody like himself, whose views he agreed with. So he expounded his line, and described one or two of the points on which he and Antony had had some difference of opinion, and forgot for a while to be surprised by her appearance of enthusiasm. In fact, however unlikely, it did seem to be more than an appearance, for if she had been listening without paying any attention (as most people did) she wouldn't have been able to ask any relevant questions. And when they got to the peculiar problems of industrial growth in Africa, she actually knew what she was talking about; though all her information came from a very small area: 'You see,' she said modestly, 'the thing is, I'm sure now that I chose to become interested in Ujuhudiana precisely because it *is* such a tiny place, population-wise, I mean, it's only got one and a half million inhabitants, and I thought if I could get my mind round what one and a half million people were doing then it would help me to understand what goes on on a larger scale, if you see what I mean? But of course it doesn't really work like that, because here the problem of density is in itself the problem, and there isn't any parallel at all between the building of a factory in Gbolo and say the idea even of building a factory in Anglesey. They developed a sort of Trades Union for this new Gbolo factory, you know, but it was really most extraordinary, because most of the men had never been employed in industry before, and a lot of them thought—' but what the men of Gbolo thought about Trades Unions was lost (unfortunately, as Simon Camish had been so interested that he was in his head composing a new footnote) by the arrival of the baby's grandmother, who appeared, slightly out of breath and full of apologies, to collect the infant, whose presence both he and Rose had more or less forgotten, as it had fallen quietly asleep.

'Any news from Eileen?' said Rose, as she handed over her charge.

'Not a word,' said Mrs Sharkey, who would have liked to have stayed to chat and to relieve her feelings by abusing the absent Eileen, but who was not prepared to do so in front of a stranger, for the sake of family pride. 'She'll be back tomorrow, I don't doubt, as large as life and twice as useless.'

'I hope so,' said Rose, ushering her out into the corridor.

'And if she's not back, Mrs Vassiliou,' Simon heard her say, lowering her tone discreetly by the front door, 'if she's not back, you wouldn't be able to have Sharon again, would you? I'd be ever so grateful, it's only for an hour tomorrow, it's my day at the Home, you know, I only do an hour there on a Friday evening, I'd be back by six, but I'm that worried about this baby, and the money, I daren't stay home, you know what I mean, every little helps...'

Her voice trailed off, and he heard Rose reply, soothingly, 'No, no, don't you worry, that's quite all right, of course I'll have her, I like having her, it's nice to have a baby in the house, you know...'

She sounded quite placating as she spoke, but when she came back into the room she looked distinctly unnerved, and indeed angry: she yelled at the two little children to go to bed, which, hearing the tone in her voice (a tone which he had never heard before) they meekly did. She then walked up and down the small room once or twice, and then flung herself crossly down in a chair and said, 'Well, really, bugger that.'

'What's the matter?' he said, obligingly.

'It's that bloody baby,' said Rose. 'I can see I'm going to get lumbered with it if I'm not careful. That's what comes of being sympathetic.'

'You could have said no,' said Simon.

'Oh no I couldn't, that's where you're wrong,' said Rose. 'How could I possibly say no? It doesn't really hurt me to have a baby hanging around, though in fact I've got to go out tomorrow night and it's always tricky getting the children off to bed when I'm going out, but no, the point is, I can't possibly say no, I've put myself in a position where of course I've got to say yes, it serves me right. I really didn't want that baby this evening, you know, I really didn't want it, the poor thing, all that vomiting' (and she dabbed at her stained skirt) 'and I'd been looking forward to having a drink and reading my book, and I know a baby doesn't really get in the way, so I felt really mean not wanting to have it, in fact I think I *am* really mean, I really resent it when people ask me to do things for them. That's what I was really so cross about when you arrived, I think, my own horrible meanness. And now I've got it again tomorrow. It really is too much.'

'You must be mad,' he observed, pleasantly, 'to consider yourself mean.'

'Oh yes, I know it all looks all right, I do the right things most of the time, but it's not because I really want to you know, it's just because I don't know how to say no. Quite frankly, I haven't the face to say no, when I know that Mrs Sharkey is going to spend that hour tomorrow on her hands and knees scrubbing the cloakrooms at the Mental Home for five and sixpence, while I'll just be sitting here like a cabbage with a baby on my knee drinking a cup of tea and watching telly and waiting to go out for dinner. I mean, Christ. One would have to be really mean to say no.'

'A lot of people,' he said, 'are really mean.'

'But they wouldn't say no, in a case like that?'

'You're being very innocent,' he said. 'Of course they wouldn't say no, because nobody would ever ask them. Mean people broadcast around by secret messages that it's no good asking them to do things, they make quite sure that they never expose themselves to the embarrassment of refusal, they never let it get that far. But nice people like you are recognised a mile off. Aha, people say to themselves, she won't mind, we'll ask her.'

'I'm a fool,' said Rose. 'That's what I am. I don't even like babies any more. Now mine are grown up I don't even like babies. I just pretend to. They bore me stiff, really. And they're repulsive. I mean, one must be honest, they are repulsive, aren't they?'

'Was I repulsive, Mummy?' said Konstantin, suddenly, looking up from what looked like old-world homework, and Rose smiled at him, and said, 'No darling, you were quite beautiful, you were lovely, you were a *gloriously* beautiful baby,' and Konstantin looked at her shrewdly and said, 'That's just what you said about Eileen's baby, that's just what you say about all babies. Do you know what you are, Mummy, you're—a whited sepulchre!'

'A *what*?' said Rose.

'A whited sepulchre,' said Konstantin, firmly. 'We had them this morning. Mummy, while you're paying me a bit of attention, perhaps you might tell me what the difference between continual and continuous is, would you?'

'I haven't the foggiest notion,' said Rose, crossly. 'And don't be so rude. Go to bed.'

'Do you know, please, Simon, about continual and continuous?' said Konstantin: and as Simon tried to explain, he knew quite well that both he and Rose were attached not to the grammatical point that he was making, but to the social effort—so nearly concealed, so painfully adult—with which the child had pronounced Simon's christian name. He had hesitated at the hurdle, he had nearly shied at it, his eyes widening a little in alarm, as it approached, but he had taken it, bravely, he had cleared it, and all that one could say was that at such an age he should not be required to take such shadowy leaps. Much better, of course, that he should be crossing shadow barriers rather than real ones: but perhaps after all there were real ones, perhaps Simon himself was in the shadow of, was the shadow of, some more substantial obstacle? (He found himself remembering, ominously in this context, phrases from other people's affidavits—phrases in which children had described the false uncles that frequented their mother's houses, false uncles, undesirable influences, co-respondents, or worse still, not even co-respondents, but unknown interlopers. But then again, these interlopers, perhaps they were shadows not in the child's mind nor in the woman's life, but of the husband's jealousy? How could one know what Christopher Vassiliou said to these children when he got them alone at a weekend, how could one know what questions he asked them, what notions he fed into their innocent but suspicious hearts? Thinking of this, taking it this far, he grieved all the more for Rose, for her predicament: he acquitted her, he credited her, he preferred to blame the man he did not know, the absent father. And yet the child, in his divided loyalties, might not like such blame?)

'Make up a sentence, for me, then,' said Konstantin, having listened to the explanation of continuous and continual, 'to illustrate the difference.'

'Perhaps you should do that yourself,' said Simon, thinking himself pompous as he said it, but saying it nevertheless.

'Yes,' said Rose, 'Simon's quite right, you can't expect us to do your homework for you, you must do it for yourself. And you must go to bed now.'

How easy it is, thought Simon, watching the child go off with his exercise book, to support a woman who is not one's wife, a man who is not one's husband. How easy, to talk to a child who is not one's own. But what he said was, 'That's a very intelligent child.'

'Yes, I think he is,' said Rose, 'God help him.' And she smiled, feebly: she had run down in some way, she had all ebbed away, she was no longer making any effort, and he remembered the first time he had seen her, and the impression which she had given, at that dinner party, of overcoming an almost deadly fatigue. She seemed so tired: her life, for all that she said she liked it, must be a hard one, he thought.

'You should go to bed early,' he said. 'You look so tired.'

'Yes,' she said, 'I'm going to. I'm going to sit up and watch a documentary about Dahomey and then I'm going to bed. Why don't you stay and watch it with me?'

It sounded so attractive an evening that he was tempted to consent: but, looking at his watch, remembered with a horrible sudden misgiving that he was supposed to be home, that people were coming to dinner, that he had completely forgotten he had said he would be at home early in time to receive his wife's guests. So he said, as calmly as he could, that he wouldn't stay, that he had to be off, that he would ring again next week to see how she was, to see if there were any developments (their usual pretext) and so he took his leave. She came to the door, to see him off, and stood there on the steps as he got into his car. She was still standing there, in the falling darkness, as he drove away.

By the time he got home, he was filled with a quite genuine sense of apology, and of foreboding: he ought to know better, by now, than to be late, knowing what the consequences of his lateness usually were. It was eight fifteen already, and he had promised to try to be home by half past seven. As he drove the car into the garage, he tried to remember who the guests were supposed to be, but couldn't for the life of him recall: he was worried that he wouldn't even know their names when he saw them, he had a shocking memory for names, and however hard he tried to explain it away he knew quite well that it meant exactly what people, offended, always took it to mean: a total lack of real interest. He went in through the kitchen door, hoping to gain a few moments warning, or even to brief himself from the notes on the kitchen calendar, but the kitchen was occupied by their au pair girl, who was sitting on a chair reading a hideous teenage magazine, in total silence, watching, or rather not watching, his eldest child eat a fried egg. The damp, cold, silent atmosphere in the room filled him with rage. His heart was full of rage, for the child abandoned. The child looked up and said, 'Hello, Daddy,' then looked down again and went on eating. Not a flicker of recognition had showed in his eyes: they had been veiled by fear, by a premonition of the disapproval that flooded angrily towards him from the front of the house.

'Hello, Dan,' he said, quite unable to offer anything to replace or colour the reception he had been given. The au pair girl did not even look up at him as he entered. She went on reading about how to stick plastic flowers on her nipples under her see-through blouses. She never wore see-through blouses: she was a thin, neurotic, weepy girl, who never went out anywhere because she was afraid of going on public transport.

Bracing himself, he went through: putting his brief case on the hall table, hanging his coat where he was not intended to hang it, on the newel post at the bottom of the stairs. A hum of voices from the drawing-room met him, and he opened the door: a polite silence fell, to greet his entrance. Julie, who was sitting by the drinks table, put down her drink loudly, and said, loudly,

'Well, look who's here.'

The politeness of the silence intensified into embarrassment.

'Well,' repeated Julie, 'look who's here. Wherever have you been?'

'I was held up,' said Simon. 'I'm sorry.'

'Not at the office you weren't,' said Julie, 'because I rang Hindley and he said you'd finished at five.'

'I had to go and view a site, with a client,' said Simon. Mildly. He never rose: it was never worth rising.

'Nice of you to turn up at all,' said Julie. She couldn't help it, he said to himself, she really couldn't help it. And the silence, he felt, became no longer embarrassed, but positively sadistic. That was the effect that Julie had upon people: they were breathless, waiting hopefully to see how far she would go.

'I really am sorry,' said Simon, crossing to the table to pour himself a drink, and trying to work out who else was in the room: one of the couples he could recognise, there was a prematurely balding man called Houghton and a girl who was possibly his wife. The other couple he did not recollect that he had ever seen before: he smiled vaguely round, hoping he might be mercifully enlightened. He was.

'I don't think we've met,' said the girl, sitting there on his settee, swilling a gin and tonic round in her glass, introducing herself (he immediately recognised) in order to put Julie in the wrong for not having done it gracefully and at once. Julie was forced to respond: her rudeness never embraced anybody but himself.

'This is Caroline,' she said. 'Caroline and Hugh Simpson.' And they shook hands, and resumed conversation, as best they could after such a shock. Julie did her best to disrupt this reassumption of normal behaviour by rising abruptly to her feet, after a couple of minutes, and saying very loudly, 'Well, now that *he's* back, I'd better go and have a look at the dinner. If it isn't all burned to a cinder by now. You must forgive me,' she said, turning and smiling fearfully at her guests, 'if the dinner is quite ruined, we will all know who to blame if it is, won't we?'—and so she made her exit, leaving Simon to pour more drinks (which seemed the only thing to do) and to try and piece together what was going on. The Houghton man, he now recalled, was a gallery owner, who had recently achieved notoriety by having his gallery raided by the police on the grounds of obscenity, and this raid appeared to be the subject of the conversation. Hugh Simpson revealed himself as an art-critic or art-historian: he was a young-looking, over-healthy, worldly mannered man in his forties, considerably older than his wife, and Simon suspected that in other circumstances he might have been quite tolerable, but as it was he was being constrained by the pre-existing tone to talk in a manner that Simon found profoundly offensive. He found them all profoundly offensive. They were discussing obscenity in a way that he found (there was no other word for it) obscene. The language was not such as he expected to hear of an evening at dinner, though these days he seemed to hear little else: he was sick to death of hearing the young middle-aged discuss sex with such a mixture of self-congratulation, envy, yearning and nosy vulgar curiosity. God knows he had little sympathy with the arbitrary and undiscriminating activities of the police, and a great deal of sympathy with a few of the victims of their malice—but these were not victims, they were profiteers, they made a really shocking defence of their to him not particularly interesting cause. Perhaps they're drunk, he said to himself, trying to excuse them, perhaps they got drunk waiting for me because I was so late and because Julie was making things so difficult for them. The only one of them who wasn't participating was the Caroline Simpson woman, who was evidently, for some perverse reason of her own, biding her time to pay him a bit of attention, and he rather dreaded the quality of her attention. He didn't like the look of her. She was an exceptionally handsome woman, pale and very tall and delicately-featured, with long limp red hair, and she was wearing a long silvery dress. From her emanated such gales of dissatisfaction and destruction that he flinched, knowing that he could hardly face dealing with her if she turned on him. And turn on him she did: he knew she couldn't help it, she was the kind of person who would turn on any man, no matter how quietly he tried to sit and mind his own business. Every time her husband spoke she shivered, gently, like a tree, with dissociation: she was trying to recommend herself by these faint tremors, but it was no good, she couldn't hit the real cause of his own dissociation, she could not recommend herself to him (though he could see she wished to) by condemning the tone of the conversation, because she couldn't see what was wrong with it, he was fairly sure—or if she did object, her objections were aesthetic, she probably didn't like Julian Houghton's bald head or his wife's flouncy dress. She turned on him, when she did so, quite deliberately: she got up from her chair and came to sit by him, and said to him, as he waited for the attack,

'I think you're a friend of a friend of mine.'

'Oh, really?' said Simon, in a panic thinking irrationally and guiltily of Rose (he would reject her if her catholic tastes extended this far, and anyway the last thing he wanted was to be acknowledged in public as her friend)—but he was safe enough, for the moment, for she went on, 'A colleague of yours, I think he is, Antony Mitchell, you know him, don't you?'

'Yes, indeed I do,' he said, trying to smile in some more or less natural way, but anticipating trouble enough on this front too. Because once he heard Antony's name he knew what it was about: poor Antony, he had always a disastrous leaning towards precisely this kind of woman, he could see it all in a glance.

'You're working with him, I think,' said Caroline Simpson, and he could tell that her husband had stopped concentrating on Mrs Houghton's thrilling account of her pre-marital sexual experiences in the United States in order to overhear (as had been intended) whatever Caroline Simpson had to say. 'He told me so, when I had lunch with him the other day,' said Caroline.

'Yes,' said Simon, neutrally. 'Yes, we're working on a book together.'

'He told me,' said Caroline, 'that you'd had a little setback, that you're going to have to do some re-writing, is that so?'

And she smiled at him, sweetly, intently, desperately. Bloody fool, Simon thought to himself, telling her anything at all, but what he said was 'Yes, that's right. It's not too serious, though, we should be able to straighten it out without too many problems.'

'He seemed *quite* put out,' continued Caroline, 'but then, he's very easily put out, isn't he? I was half an hour late for lunch, you know, last week, and by the time I got there he was really in *quite* a state. I mean, half an hour is *nothing,* is it?'

'I don't know,' he said. 'I always try to be punctual myself. Though one might hardly believe it on this evening's evidence.'

She was not, however, to be deflected: she hadn't yet had enough of the subject of Antony's anxiety on her behalf.

'And then,' she went on, 'there was a time, not so long ago, when I couldn't make it at all, and he was awfully annoyed about it. He's a bit of a rigid thinker, wouldn't you say? Perhaps all lawyers are, would you say?'

'Maybe,' he said, thinking, what bloody fools women are, does she really think she can ingratiate herself with me by knocking and exposing Antony, bloody fool though he may also be? And anyway, what on earth does she want to ingratiate herself for, what on earth does she want with me, it can't simply be that she wants to take advantage of Julie, can it, or would she do it to anyone? Perhaps she was doing it to Houghton before I came in.

'I nearly married a lawyer once,' she continued, and he felt her husband stiffen: she gazed at him, preparing to tell him the story of her lawyer, her dark eyes fixing him in an almost comic effort at hypnosis, or an effort that would have been comic if it hadn't been so singularly effective, and he struggled desperately, trying to think of some means of avoiding the story of this hapless lawyer—(he bet she had nearly married one out of each profession, according to audience, did she really think that men liked this kind of approach, manifesting as it did such deplorable weakness of character?)— and was, fortunately, saved by Julie's arrival upon the scene, with a summons to dinner.

'We can go and eat, now,' said Julie, 'what is left of the meal.'

And off they went to eat: he was able to bear her commands to open the wine with equanimity and even grace, knowing he had been reprieved from worse. Not that the reprieve lasted for long: during dinner he had to endure the sight of Caroline Simpson turning her food over and over on her plate with a look of disgust (and it hadn't been ruined, thank God, it was perfectly good, as Julie's meals always were) and the knowledge that she wouldn't have dared to mess about with it in that disdainful manner if she hadn't sensed, with what was probably the only part of her intelligence, that he and Julie were hardly the most united of couples. Though there, of course, she in a sense sensed wrong: for united was precisely what he and Julie were, and this might even, he thought, as the meal continued, have got through to her, because she did lower the tone a little, she even transferred her attention a little to Houghton. But he wouldn't forgive her for the way she had smiled when asked if she would like more Quiche: a little dry knowing smile of contempt it had been, as she declined, as she pushed eloquently at her untouched pastry shell (and it was a good pastry, it was not as though Julie ever let it sog or harden)—a smile that indicated superior discrimination, the non-eating smile of the Victorian exhibitionist, a smile that embraced Julie's thickening arms and slightly overheated face (and naturally she was overheated, she'd been bending over the oven, hadn't she?) and Houghton's receding hair and his girl's frills and doubtless his own scraggy neck, and deficiencies on her elegant husband's part that were too profound to manifest themselves.

The conversation turned, mercifully, from obscenity to country cottages and Easter holidays. The Houghtons had a country cottage in the Cotswolds, the Simpsons had one in Norfolk. Good luck to them, thought Simon, chewing on his coq au vin, that lets me out. But Easter holidays as such were another matter. He and Julie and the children were going to a hotel in Cornwall for Easter, and he had to listen to Julie describing their arrangements in some detail. The reminder of this approaching excursion filled him with an indefinable unease: he couldn't locate it, he would have to return to it later. As it was, he sat there, and spoke from time to time, and tried to avoid the silvery glimmer of Caroline Simpson's bosom, and wondered whose fault it was, that he should spend so much time like this, with people he really deeply disliked, talking about things that bored him rigid. It would have been better if he could have felt that the others were enjoying themselves, but from every soul there seemed to him to rise a cry of mute anguish and lonely fear: ugly cries, like the wails and squawks of sea gulls, hovered over the surfacing wine bottles and the wreckage of cutlery and the white napkins, and on Julie's face (he watched it anxiously) there were such lines (in the roundness), engravings of a quite inappropriate suffering, marks of suffering unsuited to her physique or to her nature. She picked up, as he watched her, a chicken bone from her plate, and held it in her fingers, and started to gnaw at it with an inelegant greed, speaking, as she ate, of the reputation for good food that this Easter hotel possessed, and as she spoke she reached into her mouth with her fingers and abstracted a lump of chewed tendon, which she deposited, quite unself-consciously, upon the side of her plate. It lay there, transparent, repellent, an indictment. He loathed such habits in her, and loathed himself for loathing them; there was no way out. She was not built for dinner parties. He hated his own shrinking, and sitting there he thought of his mother, from whom he had inherited these excessive delicacies: his mother's house stank of cleanliness, it stank of bleach and disinfectant, the lavatory in her house was unusably hygienic from noxious poisonous fumes of purity, and yet he was, no doubt about it, his mother's son. He had been trained up early, by her wincings and shudderings: at every word his grandfather spoke she had instilled in him disapprobation. He recalled her, when his grandfather hawked and spat (a healthy habit, after all, and a skill he sometimes wished he had inherited)—he recalled her averting her eyes, shivering, making little noises in her own refined throat. And he had married Julie to escape these delicacies, he had tried, God help him, uselessly to cast off these deadly niceties and cruel rejections, and here he was, playing in a sense his mother's role, repelled, silent, disapproving, a superior sensibility. He disliked such an inheritance. His mother, she had aspired to evade her environment, she had purged it with Domestos and Pine Fluid, she had reached upwards—never very high upwards, it was true, tinned salmon remained for her a delicacy, her aspirations had not risen to Quiche Lorraine, and the truth was that he still rather liked tinned salmon himself, he liked the pink violent delectable chunks of it with their tinned crumbly assimilated bones, he would rather have it than smoked salmon any day.

He and Julie had over-reached themselves, they had set their sights too high, and therefore it was that they clashed and bled, and that their faces were lined with the furrows of an unsuitable strain. Julie had been made for a life so different, so much simpler (if one could have a concept of simplicity) and yet at the same time she had had in her some spark too of aspiration, a minimal artistic talent, a talent wickedly too small for the burdens her wealth and his intelligence had laid on it: she would have been happier without it, but

how could one say that happiness was what one should have, as a woman or as a man? What was one human for, but to aspire, and where had it gone wrong, what was it that had condemned them? There were no virtues, moral or aesthetic, in tinned salmon or in hawking and spitting or in denying even the most minimal gleamings of a higher intellectual or social existence: but there was something hopelessly wrong with a life where a child sat in a kitchen eating a fried egg in terror, watched by a hostile alien, while adults in the drawing-room gulped down alcohol and displayed their unlovely hypocrisies. There must have been, there might have been, a right life for them, a possible life, which might have embodied a little warmth and beauty: a natural life, for them, for people, to which it would not have been a mockery to aspire. One had to suppose a good life and a happy resolution, or was that a childish simplicity? Exhausted, embittered, he no longer knew. Perhaps there was only the point of time in which one lived, and its accompanying ills. But nevertheless, he would swear, there had hovered before Julie herself a higher image, a legitimate hope: she had miscreated and deformed it, but it had been there, and it had fatally lured her on into this chattering of monkeys.

He remembered (thinking of fish, and eating chicken bones, and his mother) a tea time, up North, in his schooldays when they had been eating bloaters, bloaters full of bones, and the lights had gone out. The lights had gone out, the electricity had failed, and his mother, furious at first, as she was at any crossing of her purpose, had stumped crossly off to find candles, muttering darkly in the dark of the malice of electricity boards—and then, when she had returned, and illuminated the tea-table with the thick white wax lights she had become suddenly, rarely, gay, cheerful, relaxed. 'What a very *unsuitable* meal,' she had said (picking the small hairlike bones from her mouth with her soft fingers), 'what a very unsuitable meal, to eat in the darkness, look at us here, swallowing all these bones in the dark! *Anything* would have been better than bloaters, anything at all.' And she giggled, and then said, laughing to herself, choking a little, discreetly, 'Anything but *kippers,* I suppose.' And he had laughed too, a growing clumsy boy, overcome with gratitude at this unusual lightening, at this gleam of joy in the face of adversity. She had used the episode later, his mother, she had incorporated it into a domestic radio chat: all these chats she enlightened with the same glow of nostalgic warmth, the same sense of the shared amusing little trials of motherhood, a sense to which she was on the whole quite alien, a tone that betrayed her material, on nearly all occasions, quite monstrously, for on other occasions things were not at all as she described them, they had been setbacks that she had met dourly and with ill-nature, and he would writhe to see them re-written, touched up, translated into what she would have liked them to have been. And yet, perhaps the bloaters had shown that she might have been capable of living in the style she chose for herself: and if she had not chosen such an image, things might have been worse, there might not have been even those rare moments? Perhaps, after all, his childhood had been in sum more nearly what she had intended than what she had achieved? She had fought herself, valiantly, she had courageously denied the truth of the bleakness which was what she truly had to offer. If she had not aspired she would have sunk or died. Oh Christ, it was exhausting, this living on the will, this denial of nature, this unnatural distortion: but if one's nature were harsh, what could one do but deny it, and repudiate it in the hope that something better might thereby be? It was for him that she had hoped, and so on, through the generations. And to what end, to what end, to what right end of life, to what gracious form of living, to what possible joy, there was nobody who had achieved it, there was no achieving and no arrival, there was merely a ghastly chain of reiterated disillusions, and each generation discovered a new impossibility, and all the more miserably because it had been given to hope for more. He thought once more of John Stuart Mill and the despair that had seized him: to conceive the right end, and then to despair, that was a fate he had feared often enough for himself, with his petty tinkerings and his niggling readjustments and his dreary slow calculations. Oh yes, he cared for the fate of mankind, he cared for the quality of the living of life, but man had been formed too low in the scale of possibility, with just enough illumination (like Julie and his mother and himself) to suffer for failure, and too little spirit to live in the light, too little strength to reach the light. Or rather, there was no light, or none that man might enter: he could create for himself an ordered darkness, an equality of misery, a justice in the sharing of the darkness, his own hole, by right, in that darkness, and his sense of light, his illuminations, were an evolutionary freak, an artificial glow that had etiolated him into hopeless pale unnatural underground yellow green deformities, a light misreflected through some unintended chink, too far away for such low creatures ever to reach it and flourish by it. He might as well lose his eyes, man. He might as well grow blind, like a fish in a cave, and maunder on through the centuries in his white plated armoury.

He cut himself a slice of Gruyère. Even such an image, nasty as it was, presupposed the existence of the light. The distortions themselves, they were not arbitrary, after all. They were ugly, but they followed a pattern. They rose, sorrowfully, like plants in a cellar, deprived, but always rising. Plants in a cellar, laid away until the spring. He buttered a biscuit, and restored his attention to Caroline Simpson, who wanted to tell him, for some reason, about another man she had nearly married, this time a ski-instructor, who had fallen passionately in love with her when she had gone at the age of seventeen to Austria on a school outing. She had rejected his overtures, but was happy to report that he had turned out well, this ski-instructor: no ordinary Austrian he, for he had gone off to the Himalayas and had dwelt there for some years in dramatic seclusion, and then had returned to civilisation to report upon his experiences (in German, alas) in the form of a best-selling book, and had subsequently become an actor, appearing in films and upon the television. The implication, too clear to avoid, was that anyone who had had the taste to admire her, even at so tender an age, could not but have resources.

'It sounds,' said Simon, 'as though, had you married him you might have had rather too exciting a life.'

'Oh, I don't mind excitement,' she said: unwisely, for he then had the satisfaction of seeing her wince at her own crudity, he saw her withdraw from her vulgarity. Because, after all, she operated on a high level, on the whole, this woman: he could see what Antony saw in her perilous overtures. He thought, suddenly, of Rose's Eileen, who aspired to be a wicked woman. Here, by his side, was a perfection of the type. He thought of Rose, her wrinkled fingers picking fretfully at the stain on her skirt. He thought of Rose. She would be in bed by now, he thought. She would be sleeping (the phrase rose in his mind unsolicited) the sleep of the just.

It was after midnight before the Houghtons and the Simpsons left. They sat it out, to prove that they were enjoying themselves, to prove that they had forgiven their host his delayed arrival. Having resented their presence during most of the evening, he found himself dreading their departure, knowing that he would have trouble before he was allowed to go to bed. And so he did, for Julie, once the door had closed upon them, turned upon him with an anger that had had four and a half hours to gather and thicken, and which had been not at all assuaged by her original hostilities when he had first entered. He had seen the storm signs during dinner, hung as clearly as a black cone by a bad sea: the violent way she had slopped his chicken onto his plate, the overforceful way with which she had put that same plate down on the table before him, the way she had pulled her chair sharply to one side when he crossed behind her to get the corkscrew, the noises she made in her throat—sighings, clickings, dismissals—whenever he opened his own mouth. She had not looked at him once during the meal, nor addressed one remark to him indirectly: she had been biding her time: and now she let him have it, all of it, trembling with rage as she denounced his cruelty, his rudeness, his inadequacies as husband and father, his dullness as companion and host and guest. She went back over the whole of their past, raking up ten-year-old offences, divining in their pattern a deliberate plot of destruction, ending up, as so often, yelling at him, her face discoloured with emotion, her hair damp and oddly flying from her face in strange directions.

'What did you marry me *for*, what *for*, what *for*?'

And, looking at her as she then appeared, what answer could possibly be offered? It seemed, indeed, a mystery. He offered no answer, on principle: he never did. He had sat there quietly and taken it, as the roll call and catalogue of crimes lengthened, the familiar motifs of abuse—(that time you forgot about collecting Kate from the hospital, that time you were late to meet me at Kings Cross, that time you had to go back for the ticket, that time we were held up for three hours at Chambers while you waited for that brief, that time your mother said Dan's hair needed cutting, that time the men came around about that parking ticket, that time your mother wouldn't eat the chicken because of the garlic, that time you made a fool of yourself by telling Hart Stanley you didn't like Hockney, that time you made a fool of yourself telling Carla you did like Magritte, that time you spilt that wine on Jessica Wainwright's leg)—and at the final question, what could he be but silent still? He sat there, running one finger round the rim of his empty glass, waiting for her to run down, and wondering, as he waited, if it would have been better, once, to greet these attacks with counter-attacks, to shout back, to deal blow for blow. It was impossible, now, to do such a thing, though it might once have been possible; but he had taken the line of no resistance, afraid to lose his temper, afraid to destroy her by losing his temper. That it seemed, now, as though he had destroyed her by keeping his temper was an irony that he had not foreseen: he had wished, perhaps, to preserve his dignity at her expense, and now had no option but to pursue the policy to the end, hoping against hope that his original faith in non-retaliation might one day be vindicated, because he had no other faith.

When she had run down, she sat down at last—(having been standing over him, her hands at times actually on her hips)—and buried her face in her hands and began to cry. Through her tears she moaned, 'I hate you, I hate you, I hate you.' He stirred, slightly, and put down his glass. It was nearly over. She wept for a couple of minutes, and then stood up and stared at him, blotched and blind, as though she did not know him, and said, 'I'm going to bed.' It had all fallen, the ground was flattened, there was nothing left. A curious empty stillness filled the room. She stood there for a moment, as though not knowing where she was, and then turned and left the room, walking as though over a beaten stubble. He sat there, and let her go.

Alone, he thought at first of nothing, blankly. Then, not wanting yet to join her, he thought about domestic violence, and Rose and Christopher Vassiliou. There were thoughts in his mind about Rose Vassiliou that now, in this lull and emptied heaven, seemed to wish to reassemble themselves, small delicate formations in a feathery washed new sky. He thought about the Easter holidays. He did not want to go away for Easter because he did not wish to leave London because he did not wish to leave Rose. This discovery, this assembly, had to him a pale, hopeless brightness: it shone like the weak light of dawn reflected from the buildings of a silent street. Confusion would fill the street, but not yet. He thought of the time he had spent with Rose that evening: the baby on her knee, the children watching the television, the book she had been looking forward to reading (*The Journal of Mungo Park*, it had been) and the programme she had been going to watch on the television, after he had left her. Why had she entrusted him with this vision of felicity? Had she known what she was doing, had she known the images that she was slowly forming? No, she had not known: he was sure of it, there had been not a shadow of intention in her. The images that gathered round and above her were emanations, simple risings and gatherings from the soft, full lake of her nature: they

were not beckonings or clamourings, they were herself, they did not concern him at all, they would dissolve back into herself as she slept and breathed and woke again and was. There was no point in remarking them, except, indeed, as one might remark the dawn, or other natural manifestations of the self-sufficient natural world.

He had a friend who was in love with a married woman. She loved him, too, or so his friend said, and he had no reason to doubt him, but that did not mean they had much of a life of it. But he remembered, now, suddenly, that his friend had said to him once, in a rare moment of confidence, 'I dread the times when she leaves London, you know. Christmas, when she goes to her parents, and the summer holidays, when she and her husband go away. It comes round so often, the years go by and she's always going away. I don't know what to do when she's away.' 'But you don't see much of her when she's there,' said Simon, unsympathetic over so vague a loss. 'Yes, I know,' his friend had said, 'but I can't tell you what a difference it makes, to know she's there, at least.' This was the recollection that had been troubling him throughout dinner, from the moment that Julie had started to describe the hotel in Cornwall. Now that he had placed it, it troubled him more than ever. Really, there was no point in evading the conclusion of so much unease. That uncomfortable revelation of himself, through Konstantin's eyes, as an intruder, that vision (contrasting with so much) of a desirable evening, that pang of anxiety at the thought of going even so far away as Cornwall; there was nothing else that they could mean. Once he acknowledged it, he was amazed that he could have mistaken or ignored the portents for so long. Only a habitually hopeless person like himself could have ignored them. 'I want her,' he said to himself. The words walked into his mind and stood about there. They shocked him. They were shocking. He wished instantly, and knew he would continue to wish, that he had never known. 'I want her,' himself said again. And then more fully, more decisively repeated, 'I want what she is.' That was all there was to it. Of course it was so. How could he not have wanted her? It was over, it was known, it was decided, there was nothing at all, ever, to be done about it. He might as well, now, go to bed.

So he stood up, put down his empty glass, looked at himself with some curiosity in the mirror, to see if he looked different for having understood, and went up to bed. Julie was lying in bed, not yet asleep: she looked up, as he came in. He could tell, from the way she looked, that it was time for conciliation. It was a duty, that despite all, he always performed with relief.

'Well,' he said, taking off his shoes, 'wherever did you find that Caroline Simpson woman? What an amazing creature.'

'Ghastly, isn't she?' said Julie. He was overcome with tenderness for her.

'A right bitch,' he said, pulling at his socks.

'Beautiful, though,' said Julie. 'Don't you think?'

'Is she?' he said, and Julie, faintly, smiled.

'It was a very good dinner,' he said. 'I like that pastry thing.' (He didn't like to pronounce the name for it.)

'I know you do. That's why I make it,' she said.

He got into bed by her.

'What kind of a day did you have?' he said.

'Oh, all right,' she said. Then, brightening, 'Quite nice, really. I went into that new shop near Joy's, you know, that one with all the long dresses in the window, and there's a terribly nice woman there running it, do you know, she used to be married to Bill Wakeham, you know' (as he clearly did not) 'the one who introduces that programme about pop, and then he left her, or perhaps she left him' (loyalty had already set in towards this new acquisition)—'and she decided she'd have to do something with herself, and first of all she had this boutique in Marylebone High Street, and then she moved up here because she said she had more friends up here, and she's got some awfully nice things there, really nice and not at all expensive, and so I bought myself a new long dress, I thought it would do for Easter, I needed something for Easter, it's a lovely colour, a

kind of reddy brown, a sort of terra cotta I suppose you could call it, I found a nice bag for Nicole, too. Crochet. It's her birthday. She was awfully nice, the woman, she said she'd look things out for me if I wanted them. She was really awfully nice.'

I bet she was, thought Simon, who would not be, to so willing a customer? But at the same time he could not help feeling thankful. He was glad she had had a nice day, and had found a new friend, however short-lived or mercenary the friendship might prove to be. Despite himself, there was still part of him that warmed, from time to time, to her ephemeral enthusiasms, to her wholesale commitment to the feminine pursuit of shopping. Fundamentally it shocked him, this acquisitiveness, this relentless pursuit of unnecessary garments, this desire to buy in order to placate nice, friendly, profiteering, obsequious boutique owners, this obligation to have new garments, new bags, new shoes, new scarves for every trivial expedition or occasion, this giving of gifts on the slightest pretexts, and yet at the same time there lingered in him the emotion that had originally been aroused by this indiscriminate generosity of purchases. He had been accused, from time to time, by intellectual women friends, of antifeminism, because he thought of women as people who spent their time buying luxury goods for the packaging, and lighting up with desire whenever they saw an attractive window display: and part of him liked (or had liked? perhaps he had, after all, changed?) to think of them so. If they behaved like that, after all, it settled them, it defined them, and (more significantly) meant that they could be kept happy, as long as there was enough flow of money for them to gratify their endless whims. What did Julie want with a new long dress? She had dozens. But he saw, he could even feel, that she was happy with a new one. It made her happy to send flowers, to give drinks, to buy gifts for herself and others. What did it matter, after all? It was nice, it was innocent, to be placated so easily.

'It might be cold at Easter, in Cornwall, I thought,' said Julie. 'You'd better take something warm yourself. Don't you think?'

'Yes. Yes, I will,' he said, and switched off his bedside light. She shouldn't have mentioned the word Easter again. She had mentioned it once too often. The thought of the hotel, and the meals, and the boredom, and the waiters, and the other guests, made him feel quite ill. He would probably enjoy it. But he didn't want to think that he might.

ROSE, ALSO, HAD FALLEN ASLEEP thinking of Easter, and with as deep apprehension. She was frightened by it, because she had agreed that Christopher could have the children, over the Easter weekend. He had written to her, saying that he wanted to take them away with him for the three days, and she had agreed. She had not found herself able to protest, because she knew that the children would like it, but once she had agreed she had begun to worry about whether she would ever get them back again. Her solicitor had actually warned her to be careful about letting Christopher see too much of them while the custody case was pending: he was as nervous as she was, by now, and with good cause, about Christopher's capacity for dramatic and unexpected action. On the other hand, to deny him access at all would have been unwise, he said: and she herself would not have been capable, even if permitted, of so outright a denial. She had taken her stand and could not, in her nature, exceed it. She had to continue to behave as though Christopher were a reasonable person, although she knew that he was not, hoping that he, with as little grounds, would treat her in the same way. Lying there awake, she allowed herself for the first time to imagine that he might actually kidnap them. She had read of such cases: there had been one, only three weeks before, when a father had taken his children out, ostensibly for the day, and had gone off with them on a small boat to France. Who could tell what violent abductions Christopher himself was contemplating? She tossed and turned. The children loved him, and with good cause. She had, at times, wickedly, desperately, shamefully, tried to unknit their love, but the thought

of the hideous unravelling, the frightful consequences, had always prevented her from saying too much, too often. And yet, while they loved him, while they were bound to him, she could never be safe. The situation was impossible, insoluble. It was a penalty, it was a judgement. She thought of all those other people, who had done the things that she had done so easily: who had left their husbands and safely remarried, whose ex-husbands had remarried safely themselves. How few fathers displayed so tormenting and dangerous a concern with their children, how many of them simply walked out, with a sigh of relief, and were rarely seen again, except for the odd obligatory Sunday. She had once thought it an indictment upon the whole sex, the ease with which men would abandon their offspring for other women, other lives, and now was forced to wonder what bad luck it was of hers, what fault of hers, that her own husband could not be thus true to type and negligent. Why didn't he remarry, thoughtlessly, why didn't he set himself up elsewhere? Was it possible (and this was her worst fear) that she should never have left him? Should she have found in herself the strength to endure their dreadful mutual life? Nobody else had thought so: she had been exonerated, by the courts, by the press, by friends. She could not have taken what she had been expected to take, and so, by leaving him, it must have been the right thing that she had done. And by doing it, she had found happiness, and a life that she could peacefully live, and usefully. But perhaps too much had gone before her to be allowed to live it. Perhaps she would be forced to abandon herself and to return to her non-self, to the self she had been with Christopher, and on his terms, this time, too.

This was something she did not often dare to think of. But the truth was that even if she won her case, even if the children were left with her undisturbed, how would she be able to build upon such a victory? It was not only the fear of loss that alarmed her—a sudden loss, through their disappearance to Switzerland over Easter, or a slow legal loss through the judge's decision—it was the fear of living with victory, after these painful, clamouring manifestations upon

Christopher's part. What had she done to him, by leaving him? It was not that she thought he would want her back, she was too modest to think such a thing, it was more the fact that she had been made to recognise that her own actions, in divorcing him, in taking the children to herself, had been brutal and cruel. She had resorted to the law, as her father had done before, and now she was a victim of its processes. There was no longer any way of settling out of court, but even a court's settlements could not end the confusion.

It was not reasonable to suppose that Christopher would disappear with the children over Easter. What would he gain by it? He would put himself in the wrong, which he had no need, yet, to do. And yet the idea of it, once fully conceived, would not leave her. It even crossed her mind, as she lay there awake, that perhaps she herself, not him, should make the children wards-of-court, so that he could not remove them. The notion was grotesque. What would happen, she wondered, if both she and Christopher simultaneously decided to apply for wardship? What would the lawyers have to say to that? They would probably be so angry with them both that they would take all three children away and put them into care, and neither parent would ever be allowed to visit them again.

She hadn't dared to tell her solicitor that Christopher was having the children for Easter. She had been afraid to arouse issues that were better left sleeping. She hadn't told Simon Camish, either. She had been afraid that he would tell her she was a fool, that she shouldn't have done it. Now she wished that she had asked his advice, because the anxiety, the uncertainty, was dreadful. Her head ached with it. Her head was splitting with anxiety and irresolution. She started to bang it backwards and forwards on the pillow, as she used to do when she was a child, unable, then, to sleep, because she was so bored and lonely and not at all tired either. And the banging, the thudding in her head, the self-inflicted blows, reminded her of those other blows, some of them inflicted, in this self-same bed, her head battered against this very bedstead, and she thought, she remembered, that she had divorced Christopher so that there would be an end to blows, because otherwise they would have gone on forever, being self-perpetuating, but was now realising that the law too and its processes, far from drawing ends and lines and boundaries, were also self-perpetuating, that they, like blows, answered nothing, they solved none of the confusions of the heart and the demands of the spirit, but instead generated their own course of new offences, new afflictions, new perversions. Even if the judge laughed at Christopher's claim for custody, as she had at first hoped, it would not be an end of it; he would find some new way of assailing her, or she would of assailing him. There was no solution, through violence or law. She had always known it; she had acted as she had thought wisely, as others acted, reasonably, obeying the world's decisions and its values, and she had got nowhere. Christopher was still married to her, still with her, the problem was still there with her, her heart was still dark with the shadow of him, she would never cast him off, she would never be single, and simple, and separate, by any processes known to courts and lawyers, by any limits that could be imposed upon her own expected powers of endurance or tolerance. It was well enough for a man to say, that is enough, you need take no more, you have suffered enough; the spirit is still awake and avid, it can take more, it refuses to be bounded, it refuses to sit within its limits, quietly, and say to itself, well, so be it, into those regions I will no longer go, because I cannot take what I see there. There are no limits, the surrounding darknesses can never be chained off. Not by such means could she find peace and an exemption from the past; there was no exemption, no cancelling of bonds, no forgetting. That dim surging and conflict within her when she thought of him and what they had been through together could not be parcelled out or judged or ended by any means but its own. In its own place it must be decided. Violently she banged her head from side to side, clenching her teeth, unwilling to recognise these endless, eternal, always known claims: caught by terror at the thought of the darknesses, the struggles, the anguished reassessments that lay ahead, and yet at the same time, beneath the terror, on some level rarely visited, exultant, full of exultation, because, after all, in the human spirit there was depth, there was power, there was a force that would not, could not accept any indulgence or any letting off. Struggle on it would, because it could not rest, it could not say, forgive me, I have had enough. She had known it, she had always known it: the divorce court had been a game played by others, custody cases were nothing but a sketch, a diagram of woe, and the full confrontation would take place on other territory. The decisions of judges, even when in her favour, were irrelevant; they chalked up no victory. The confrontation (ah, this was it) could not end in victory, because it was a fight in which there was no winning. Some other resolution would have to be made, in which victory and defeat played no part, in which the boundaries did not enclose the spoils of war, and were not drawn by neutral external treaty and convention. She did not see how it could be done, she despaired at the thought of it, she knew herself incapable of voluntary and true concessions, incapable of sitting calmly at the table, incapable of ceding a square inch of her land, and yet it consoled her, it consoled her, that there could be no other way.

IT WAS A COLD EASTER, as usual. In Cornwall, snow fell, large white flakes dropping unremarkably into the large grey sea. In the hotel, elderly couples sat in the lounge and read detective stories, middle-aged couples sighed in despair and complained comfortably to one another about the ingratitude of their moping, sour, bored, sulking teenage offspring who used to like it there so much five years ago, and younger children fed endless sixpences into fruit machines, and played endless games of table tennis, quite content, most of them, in their innocent way, with these delightful facilities. Young mothers sat in the bar drinking and competing, mildly and decorously, in the prestige stakes, and Simon sat in his bedroom, when it was not being cleaned out or turned down, and stared gloomily at his Chapter Six and his next brief, wishing he were like the *pères de famille* who led their young ones out, bravely, in boots and anoraks and large jerseys, to walk along the cliffs or along the icy beaches. He admired such energy, and knew he would enjoy it himself if he tried it, but couldn't find it in himself to face the initial shock. Nor had he the confidence to approach his own children. He feared they would reject his overtures. He felt so cut off from them, most of the time. He watched them guiltily, from a distance. The boy Dan worried him, his disturbances disturbed him, he never knew if he was receiving too much specialist attention or too little. The middle one, Helen, alarmed him: she resembled Julie uncannily. She is so like her mother, people would say, and she and Julie were for ever locked in mortal combat. He dared not interfere. But at times he caught Helen looking at him, for support, as though she felt the trap close. Once she said to him—small, anxious, eight-years-old, in a rare moment of confidence—Dad, she said, can people help what they grow up like, or does it just happen? Of course they can help it, he had said, lying bravely. Of course they can. And she had smiled at him, suspicious yet assuaged, before returning to the fray. As for Kate, she was still small. He thought she was canny. He thought she was a survivor. He had hopes, for Kate.

At least Julie liked the hotel. She was happy, and that was something, after all: she had struck up with a woman of her own age, the mother of two young boys, who, he could not help feeling, was exactly what she herself could have been, had she not been so misled by false images: warm, fat, generous, amusing, immensely pleased by every drink she was offered, every course on the menu, everyone who spoke to her. They shared a table in the evenings, she and her husband and Simon and Julie, and Julie, having no domestic anxieties, and clearly feeling herself (God knows why) an easy winner in smartness and *éclat,* was at her best. She embarrassed him, inevitably, by her insatiable name-dropping, but her friend Sally took it in such good part, and was so willing to appear impressed and interested, that even this was not the trial it might have been. The husband, a chemist with ICI, was not at all bad either: he referred to the women as 'the girls' and teased them both about their incessant gossip and their large appetites, which seemed to suit them both admirably. Simon tried to emulate his false jollity, but gave it up, after a while, as it came so unnaturally to him: and he felt, as one of his efforts petered into nothing, that Sally's husband actually gave him a look of sympathy, a look of commiseration, the look of one who knew the problem, admired his inability, and slightly deplored his own success.

On Easter Monday, after nearly three days of confinement, he decided that even he would have to face the outside world: he had been reared on Spartan holidays, a week of shivering in furnished lodgings on the Northumberland or Yorkshire coast, and the ease of sitting around waiting for the next meal while digesting the last one began to generate, as he had known it would, a sense of guilt strong enough to propel him into action. He suggested to the children that they might like to go for a walk with him, but Helen stared at him in alarm at the suggestion of leaving the ping-pong table, Dan refused to leave his two-day-old game of monopoly, and only the little one, Kate, consented to accompany him. Julie expressed horror at the very thought of going out into the cold, and he knew that it would be impossible to dislodge her, as she had the moral support of Sally, who also shrank from all exertion: the only year when he had been able to persuade Julie to go out had been one year when they had gone to Scotland, when for some reason it had been the thing to do: all the fast set in the hotel, had, freakishly, been keen walkers instead of idlers, and they had persuaded Julie to join them. She had enjoyed it: she had marched on, healthily, triumphantly, glowing, pleased by the compliments of more practised hikers, remembering her country childhood and the county set she had feared so deeply. She marched them out of her system, all those horseriding girls. He had been proud of her. She was a healthy woman, Julie. She had not even minded the rain. But now, without so strong a social force to motivate her, inertia conquered, so he set off, in the morning, with Kate and a packed lunch.

It was raining, but not heavily: a fine, damp, cold, not uncomfortable drizzle. The hotel was on the cliff tops, and they set off along a walk that led along the top, and gradually down to the sea. The grass underfoot was short and springy, and small alarmed birds flew up from time to time at their approach: in the grey sky sea gulls swooped and yelped. Kate ran ahead at first, examining evidence of rabbits, looking, as children should, for flowers and stones, but after a mile or so she tired, and returned to Simon, and took his hand, and started to talk to him, a long monologue, completely vague and unedited, about school, and a friend of hers who had gone to France, and why her mother would never let her look after the school guinea pig in the holidays, and what was a barrister, was it anything to do with bannisters, and if not why not, and did he remember that time they had gone to Scotland and gone to that little old tower and there was that little old lady who kept cod fish in a pool that was really part of the sea, and when the lady went to feed the cod fish they came and poked their heads out of the water and the lady stroked them, and she, Kate, had stroked them too, and they had liked it, they were very friendly creatures, and could she keep cod fish, no, she supposed not, there wasn't any sea in Hampstead, but could she have a goldfish, they had goldfish at school, and how she had dreamed a terrible dream that Clare wouldn't let her play monopoly with her and her friend and when she woke up it was true, and why couldn't she have dinner in the restaurant, she was fed up with having fish and chips and horrible melty jelly in her bedroom. Simon listened to this, enchanted, flattered by her confidences, wishing he listened to her more often, and all the time the sea thundered and clapped and slapped at the bottom of the cliffs, and the track got narrower and narrower, and nearer the edge of the cliff, and he moved Kate on to his inland hand, and looked nervously downwards, and had visions of them both slipping and going over, and wondered what the hell he had brought a small child up here for at all, and just as he was about to give up and go back (though going back would have been nasty enough, like climbing down a ladder when one had only just had the nerve to climb up) the track started to descend, and at every foot he thought, well, that's better, at least if we fall now it'll only be forty feet, not fifty. But they didn't fall, they got down there on to the beach quite safely, after crossing a little wooden bridge over a stream full of watercress—he knew it was watercress, it was quite obviously watercress, but all the same he wouldn't let Kate eat any, because he was afraid it might be a kind of trick poisonous watercress, specially grown for tempting ignorant townsmen like himself, and he remembered something his mother had told him about how one should never eat watercress that hadn't been artificially cultured as it absorbed through its stems all the badness in the water—(what badness? what watercress flourished, lethally, on those Lethean canals on Teesside?)—and he thought also of his mother and those grey birds glimpsed through the water-closet window, those grey birds whose name she did not know, and he looked round at all the sea gulls, not one species of which he could identify, and remembered that once, as a child, he had written off to Children's Hour on the radio for a free chart of the names and means of identifying sea birds, and not one of them could he remember, not one, not one. What his mother had said about the watercress was probably true: she was not an ignorant woman, she was always right.

The beach was a pebbly small bay, with caves and rocks projecting into the water, and large waves crashed threateningly. It was not unoccupied: there were two other families there, hardy families: one father saluted him with a comradely self-congratulation. Simon sat down on a rock, to watch the water come and go, while Kate scrabbled around, looking for stones with their delusive watery colours and astonishing ephemeral gleams. Mussels and limpets clung to the base of the rock on which he sat. He watched

Kate, small against the large scenery, in her Austrian braided anorak, with her black hair in rats-tails and her cheeks red with the wind. He did not really know his children at all. He had gone too far in non-intervention, he had abandoned them to their fate, and it was too late now to take their part. He had thought once that they would return to him, in adolescence, trustingly, recognising the reasons for which he had kept himself apart: but why should they, why should they ever? What had he ever done for them but exist? Perhaps, he said to himself, sitting there on a rock and watching the Atlantic and wondering what was in his picnic lunch, perhaps I am so bad a father because I had no father, because I considered fathers dispensable, because I had no image to pursue, no pattern for the life I should create around me. But there was a difference, because my mother, say what one might of her, reject her as one might, she was at least a serious person, she made a life, she set herself problems, she took life earnestly: whereas Julie spreads nothing but uncertainty, she wants nothing but that they should play ping-pong and not trouble her, at no matter what price. She does not really like them. She looks maternal, but she does not like children. They are useful adjuncts at times, she would be embarrassed not to have them, but what she really wants is fun, is youth, the friends I could not keep for her, the confidence I have taken from her, and she will never make up for these losses, never, and there is nothing left over from such a person for children. Nothing, because she herself is so unsatisfied.

He wronged her in his mind, wilfully. It gave him some malicious satisfaction.

He called Kate to him, and sitting uncomfortably on the rock, on its wet gritty edges, they ate their sandwiches and their piece of chicken, and their tomato and their banana. When they had finished, remembering another of the delights of the North Yorkshire coast, they went to look for sea anemones, and found some, clinging and wavering under the water, below the jellied hard censorious blobs of their stranded relatives, and they fed them with bits of left-over ham. The anemones embraced the scraps avidly, and avidly engulfed them. Kate was utterly delighted. He had never seen her so entranced. She had never seen anything so exciting in her life, she said, and he knew what she meant: the way the dark red muscular flower-like fronds seized and closed in upon the threads of meat was a treat, a spectacle. She would not leave them: she hung around, trying them, when the ham was finished, with bits of bread, but the bread they spat out, crossly, spurning it, and it was spewed forth, along with grit and sand, to disintegrate, soggily, clouding the clear sucking water. 'They don't *like* it, they don't *like* it,' she cried, enchanted by their discrimination, and then, quickly, wishing to perpetuate for ever the delight, 'can we come here tomorrow, we could buy them some shrimps, can we come here tomorrow and bring them a tin of sardines?' He knew what she meant: how could one relinquish such a pleasure, once discovered, yet how explain that it might not be so amusing the next day? He diverted the conversation to oysters and pearls.

After a while they began to get cold, and Simon suggested that they should move on: they could continue onwards, without retracing their steps, up the cliff and on to the next village, and then back to the hotel along the road. Kate was reluctant to move: shivering, damp, her face by now mottled and her lips blue, she was unwilling to leave so rich a treasury, unwilling to abandon the scene of so much emotion, even though the emotion was spent and destroyed by the cold. 'We'll come again, one day,' he said: and she hovered on the verge of accepting the promise, knowing that it was not firm, and that even if it were, another day might find her changed or the scene dried and colourless. In the end she pretended to accept, and followed him. The path upwards was steep and slippery, from so much recent rain: after a while he made her go first, in case she slipped. They were out of breath by the time they reached the top, and he could feel that Kate was about to start whining, but luckily they could see the village ahead: it offered them an objective, and they picked up. Kate started to sing, tunelessly, a French song which she had learned at school, of which she understood not a word: it was an incantation, to her, meaningful because incomprehensible. He was full of hope for her. He ought to have known that it could be like this. They passed one couple, coming towards them, on the way: the man smiled, and raised his hat to Kate, and said good afternoon. The village was further off than it had looked, and for the last quarter of an hour he had to cajole her with promises of sweets: she said that she wanted an ice-cream, and he said that he couldn't believe that she really wanted one, on so cold a day, and she stared at him in amazement, unable to understand that the weather could in any way affect so absolute a desire. The first building that they reached, on the cliff top, was a small chapel: they paused by its gate, and Simon, under the influence of those past years of arduous instructional sight-seeing, thought that he would go in. She had been a great one for visiting such places, his mother: churches, castles, stately homes, Roman walls, she had taken them all in, leaving his father parked in the small Ford, immobile, gaping at the changeless car-parks of England, like an old grandmother taken for an airing. Kate followed him, nervously, through the arched doorway, and hovered by the postcards and visitor's book, hoping to be bought a postcard, while he walked slowly round. There was not much to see: it was bleak and empty, and the glass was white. There were plaques to drowned seamen on the walls, and a model of a lifeboat, and a tattered flag, rescued from a wreck two hundred years before. Tattered and threadbare it was, as though a breath would have crumbled it: dark and spined, like a dry leaf or a bat's wing. There was an eighteenth-century plaque to the squire's daughter, who had died at the age of twenty-five, unparalleled for her elegant accomplishments, and gentle virtue: discreet marble scrolls and thin sloping gently curled script bore witness to her departure from this life. Beneath the inscription, there was a quotation, in quotation marks, but unacknowledged: it said, 'They sorrow not as those that have no hope.' Simon read this, and stopped still, and read it again. It seemed to echo in him, but why he could not say. 'They sorrow not as those that have no hope.' What hope had they had, those that had lost her? And what sorrow had they suffered, then, so delicately distinguished from his own? He aligned himself with the hopeless. It was blank verse, the line, iambic pentameter, and perhaps it was from that alone that it drew its authority and its strange reverberations. He thought not. There was more to it than that. He would remember it.

On the way out, he bought Kate a postcard, a crudely tinted job with a falsely smiling sky and a floral graveyard. She liked it, clung to it, and expressed astonishment that one was trusted to pay: 'But we could take them *all* and nobody'd *know*,' she said, whispering breathily, amazed at the church's faith, as he gave her sixpence to slip into the ornamental tin box. 'Who would want them *all*?' he said, as they emerged into the light, and then was sorry he had said it, as he saw her clutch her booty and wince at the suggestion that it was not universally desirable and worthy of theft. He was delighted by her timidity, her sense of honour, her pleasure at so small a price: but his delight suffered slightly when she stopped in front of the first village shop, which was a gift shop, and tried to persuade him to buy her an owl made out of shells or a horrid little sailor boy with joints made out of springs. 'But they're horrid,' he said, without hesitation: and then, seeing her lip tremble and her brows darken, he added hastily, 'and anyway, it's Easter Monday, the shop's shut. Come on, I'll buy you some sweets.'

'I want an icecream, I want an icecream,' she wailed, crossly, tired and wet, trailing behind him, luckily not seeing that the shop was in fact, of course, open, in a vain attempt to catch the nonexistent Easter tourist trade: she wailed this incessantly till they arrived at the village grocer's, and he said to her several times that she couldn't have an icecream but could have sweets, but when they got there she had irritated him to such a degree that he bought her what she wanted, saying, 'It serves you right if it freezes you to death.' He then had to stand there watching her eat it, on the pavement, turning bluer at every mouthful, her ungloved hands (she had lost her gloves) turning a shocking shade, her lips a pallid violet, her whole body starting to tremble with chill, and icecream dripping down the front of her anorak. As soon as she had finished it, she started to whimper, afraid to voice the idea but unable to conceal it, 'I'm cold, I'm cold, I'm cold.'

'There, what did I tell you, I told you so,' said Simon, crossly: and then as suddenly softened, because the poor creature looked so pathetic standing there, ashamed and defiant, having known all along that an icecream would finish her off, and yet quite unable to resist it: and he took her hands, and rubbed them, and knelt down and folded her inside his coat and tried to warm her up. She cheered up as soon as he relented, and hid her face inside his jacket and breathed warm air round herself. She felt small and wet and bony: she had been quite fat, once, this one, but since starting school the year before had grown long legs and had thinned off into a childish skinniness. He liked her thin: thin, she was more his own.

'We ought to set off back, now,' he said, when she had warmed herself a little. 'We'll both get cold, if we stay here much longer. Shall we go?'

'Yes, let's go,' she said, and took his hand. They walked back along the road, a much shorter route than the way they had gone, and from the road, for part of the way, they could see the cliff track below them that they had walked along, and the tiny figures of people walking, bent in the wind that was now gathering force: he thought that snow would soon fall. He pointed out to her the woman and the man who had taken his hat off to her, small and far away: '*They* haven't got far,' said Kate, bravely, fighting the numbness in her boots, and wishing she hadn't got water in them in the rockpool. After a while they came to another footpath down to the cliff track: a large car was parked at the top of it, on the grass, a large expensive car, a Mercedes, not the kind of car for such excursions, and Simon looked to see if he could see who had been in it, and whether they were indeed walking in such weather, abandoning such luxury: and there, half a mile down the footpath, he could see a man and three children. The man was carrying the smallest child, and the two larger children were running ahead, and shouting in excitement. The thin calls of their excitement just reached him, like gull's cries, on the wind. He thought that he recognised Konstantin Vassiliou: it was the same blonde hair, the same stature, the same movements. He stood still and stared. He was sure it was them. And there was Christopher Vassiliou, walking into the wind with a child on his back. He stared and watched, but the distance was so great that it was impossible to be sure. He had missed them by perhaps a quarter of an hour. It was impossible to be sure: it could have been any blonde-headed child running there towards the sea, it was impossible to say why the idea had flashed into his mind that it could be them. He looked back at the large car, parked at the road side, already ten yards away: he could have gone back, he nearly went back to look through its windows, to identify possessions, he would have gone back had he been on his own, but because his daughter was there he could not. He stood there, and shouted: 'Konstantin,' he shouted, and the wind, as he had known it would, took the voice from his lips and carried it far inland. Had the wind been blowing the other way, he would not have called: and had the children turned, they would not have known him. They did not turn. They continued to run towards the sea. The man that might have been Christopher stopped, and the child that might have been Maria climbed down off his shoulders and ran after the others. The first flakes of snow fell, obliquely, blown on the wind, eddying. The car still stood there: new, but covered in mud. His eyes were not good, he could not read the number plate, he had taken off his glasses, they were no use in such weather.

'Who was it, Daddy?' asked Kate, who had stopped with him, obediently, like a dog, subdued by fatigue.

'It's nobody,' said Simon, 'I thought it was somebody I knew. But it wasn't.'

'It's starting to snow,' said Kate.

'Yes, it is,' he said. 'We'd better get home quick.' And he set off at a brisk walk, Kate lagging behind: after a hundred yards she started to whine again, about her wet feet, so he carried her, in imitation of the imaginary Christopher, who had disappeared into the bleak landscape. She was heavy: like the imaginary Christopher, he did not keep the gesture up for long.

When they got back to the hotel, they found Julie sitting where they had left her, with Sally, in the lounge: they were having tea. He half expected the welcome due to a returning astronaut, after so bracing an excursion, and he could see on Julie's face the shadow of an impulse to rise, to fuss, to exclaim, to commiserate and complain about wet clothing, the weather, the cold, but indolence conquered it. She had been sitting down for so long that she hadn't the energy to get up. 'Hello,' she said, puffing cigarette smoke. 'You're back, are you? Was it nice? Have a cup of tea, I'll get some more cups. The cakes are awful, I was just saying to Sally, the rest of the food's so good, it's amazing they can't get better cakes.'

'I think we'd better go and get dry,' he said, unable to resist a faint echo of reproof: she received it, but chose to ignore it.

'Shall I come and find you some dry things, Katey?' she said, without conviction, not intending to move.

'No, no, I'll go,' said Simon, fishing in his pocket for his steamy wet glasses. 'I'll have to go up anyway.'

'All right,' said Julie, relapsing from her slightly inclined position of attention: the armchair received her, she was rooted to it.

'Come on,' he said to Kate, and they went up in the lift. He remembered to let her push the button. They went into her room first: she was thawing out now, her nose was running, and she complained that her hands were all tingly. She sat down on the bed, and he knelt down to pull her boots off, as she reached for her book: she had got it out of the library downstairs, it was called *The Ship of Adventure*. She was a keen reader, unlike the other two. He pulled off her boots, and her wet woollen socks, and stared in dismay at her white bloodless feet: they were icy, and solid, and a pale waxy yellowey white. She smelt of wet wool: she had no body smell at all yet, her flesh still had the firm self-contained ungiving purity of infancy. Her toe nails needed cutting. He held her feet in his warm hands: he felt sorry that he had made her walk so far, that he had been so irritated by her whining. Her feet lay in his hands like separate creatures. She turned a page of her book.

'Shall I run a warm bath for you?' he asked her, penitent, but she wasn't listening. He wriggled her toes, trying to soften her up a bit: her feet looked frail and pathetic, like (he could not help the comparison) the feet so often painted on crucifixions. 'Kate,' he repeated, 'aren't you cold, don't you want to warm yourself up?'

'I'm all right,' she said, closing her book with a sigh of tolerance. 'I'm all right, really.'

He got a warm towel, from the heated towel-rail in the bathroom, and rubbed her hair, and her feet, and got her a dry jersey and pinafore dress. She was beginning to revive. She smiled at him. 'My verruca tickles,' she said. She was proud of her verruca: she had picked it up at school, in the swimming bath, it was a badge of honour, a true school-age affliction, an initiation into the six-year-old world. He inspected it, dutifully: there it sat, a little round rather dirty wart, growing and flourishing in the middle of her heel.

'How's it coming on?' he said, and she smiled, sharing his amusement at her pride in it. 'It's very well, thank you,' she said.

'I had one, when I was at school,' he said, 'and I cut it out myself, with a razor.'

He recalled, as he spoke, its stubborn roots, and the perseverance with which he had hacked at it, night after night, and the satisfaction he had felt when, one night, it had dropped out, leaving a neat little hole in the middle of his messy excavations. He had since recognised that it had probably died in the course of nature, as they usually do, and that his self-inflicted surgery had done nothing to aid its final loss of grip. But he continued to remember his efforts with some pleasure.

'I don't want mine cut out,' she said. 'I like it.'

'You're a silly girl,' he said.

'No, I'm not,' she said, and reached for her book, looking up, just before she started reading, to remark, 'There's a book of Grandma's, you know, in the bookcase downstairs. I noticed it.'

'Is there really?' he said, but she was away, her thumb in her mouth, her neck sunk in her blue poloneck jersey, her bare feet dangling.

'I'm going to get dry myself,' he said. 'Put some dry socks on before you go down, won't you?'

She didn't answer, so he left her, and went to his own room next door. Somebody had tidied away his papers: he had left them out on the table. They sorrow not as those that have no hope, he said to himself, and had a shower. He wondered if other fathers, like himself, were making a brief obligatory delightful holiday contact with their children, in this very building, here, and all over the country. He thought of Christopher Vassiliou, and Rose, and their dreadful divisions. He had thought, at one point, that he might ring Rose, to see how she was, to see if there was any news: it had seemed a possible, even a probable and expected thing to do, before he set off, he had looked forward to it, but now he felt uneasy about it, he felt it would be unnatural, a breach of an arrangement, an error of propriety. He knew quite well that he wanted to ring her not at all for her sake, but for his own: that he had been using her anxiety as an excuse for maintaining contact, much as one might use a financial debt or a forgotten brief case or a family connexion. There was no particular reason why he should ring her: in fact there was less reason than ever, for lawyers, like other people, do not operate over Easter weekend, so there was no possibility of any action having taken place. It would be thoughtless, on his part, to enquire. And yet she never seemed to mind his enquiring: she seemed to need it, to like it, to want it. As perhaps, she needed, liked and wanted everyone. Perhaps she had recognised his need: perhaps she, kindly, had used her own troubles as a convenient pretext for alleviating his. Perhaps it was simply all the same to her:

perhaps she dismissed no callers on the phone or at her house, as she dismissed no neighbour babies from her knee. Maybe he was, to her, but another obligation, along with other people's children and unmarried mothers and emergent Africa and Methodist homes for disabled workmen. She had added him, adroitly and knowingly, to such a list, with kindness and undistinguished sympathy. With her, how could one ever tell the difference?

He put his clothes on, and sat down at the table, and opened his brief case, and stared at his next brief. He did not much like the look of it: he did not much relish re-reading for the thousandth time the Redundancy Payments Act. It was not a particularly interesting brief, he suspected, though inevitably he would get interested in it, once he had started on it. That was how it always was. Instead of this case, he had nearly come away with a case involving one of the subsidiaries of Rose's father's company: a claim about some heavy lorries, and whether they had been employed or subcontracted. It had looked quite intriguing, but through some vague sensibility he had refused to handle it, saying that he would prefer not to, for personal reasons. The use of that phrase, personal reasons, had given him great satisfaction. Perhaps it was in order to use it that he had declined the case. The Head of his Chambers, Jefferson, had got to hear of this, and had been very impertinent about it, in Simon's view. Simon thought about Jefferson. He was getting distinctly odd these days: having started off with Simon in a flood of bonhomie and familiarity, comparing, whenever they met, notes on their not too dissimilar backgrounds, full of encouragement and praise, he had gradually become more and more difficult, quibbling about minor points, taking Simon up on trivial incidents, even taking exception, on one occasion, to the colour of his shirt. They had met, one day that winter, as they crossed the courtyard: Jefferson had stopped in his tracks, stared at Simon, pulled several very strange facial expressions, and had finally delivered himself of the sentence, 'You know, times may have changed, but what if you met somebody important while you were wearing a *pink* shirt?' And he had frowned, scratched his ear vigorously, and marched off, without waiting for a reply. Simon had been unable to tell whether the remark had been a joke or not, and had given up wearing his only pink shirt. He would not have liked a repetition of the incident, had the remark been either jocular or critical. Other colleagues had complained of similar attacks, so on the whole one could put them down to a general, not a personal state of susceptibility and irritability, but Simon had so long been used to consider himself as the favourite son and honoured heir that he was particularly alarmed by these new eccentricities, and felt particularly obliged to placate or circumvent them. It had got back to him one day that spring, through eager reportage, that Jefferson had said to Baker something to the effect that, 'It's no good asking Camish about it, he can't see the trees for the wood.' He had puzzled over this endlessly, wondering what it could possibly mean: was it a reference to his method of working, or his intellectual capacity, or his political bias? Jefferson had on various occasions made remarks about the possibility of Simon's standing for Parliament: 'You've got it all,' he used to say, 'you're a graduate working-class Fabian, what more do you want?'—and again, Simon had been unable to understand whether these suggestions were made seriously or ironically. It was well known that Jefferson himself had stood, but failed to be elected, in 1946, and had never forgiven the backbiting amongst his own party workers, which, in his view, had ruined his campaign: and since then his attitude to politics had been so heavily ironic that it was almost impossible to tell where his true affiliations lay. The whole tenor of his work was socialist in principle, and indeed that was why Simon, via his Director of Studies, had found himself in his Chambers in the first place: but despite this his attitude to 'the workers', as he described them, was far from benevolent, and he always spoke of them, even while ostensibly defending their interests, with a profound dismissive hostility, and when there were any particularly unsympathetic demonstrations of working-class prejudice, such as the dockers' parade of support of Enoch Powell, his comments were positively triumphant.

It was almost as though a legitimate desire to be circumspect and not to expect too much of people had fed itself so much on justification that it had become a positive conviction, and had so settled itself into a habit of mind that any evidence contradicting such a low assessment was now regarded as positively unwelcome. And Jefferson now defended himself by irony, by cynicism, by mockery, from the progressive policies and arguments he in fact pursued. He even took pleasure in taking on cases, every now and then, that were fought, as it were, against himself, and against his own previous pleadings, maintaining that by doing so he was demonstrating the inviolable impartiality of the law: a fine enough principle, and one that one could not but approve, but it remained evident that Jefferson's pleasure in such cases had become far from impartial. Anyway, Simon said to himself as he re-read for the tenth time a sentence about place and capacities of employment, everybody knew that the law was far from impartial, it was one of the most biased professions in the country, and Jefferson ought to know that if ever anyone did. What he had been able to achieve, personally, had been a mere feather on the opposite scales: and it was ridiculous of him to leap from time to time, as he now did, grinning gnomishly and virtuously, into the heavier measure, sitting there cockily amongst the heaps of gold, pretending he had made the leap for the sake of balance. Perhaps, thought Simon, I will write another book, about the class structure of the British legal system, which will put me out of business for life. It would do no good, less good even than a book on comparative trade union practices, but at least it would be interesting.

He was just about to make the effort of lifting a biro to make a note when the telephone rang. He assumed it would be Julie, asking him to bring down her cigarettes or her book, but it wasn't, it was the girl on reception, telling him she had a London call for him, and when the call was put through, it was Rose.

'Hello,' she said. 'I thought I'd give you a ring. I hope you don't mind.'

'Of course I don't mind,' he said.

'How are you?' she said. 'Is it nice there?'

'It's all right,' he said. 'In fact, it's quite good.' And, as she did not immediately continue, he told her that he had been for a walk with Kate, and how he had enjoyed it, and how bad the weather was.

'What are you doing with yourself, for Easter?' he asked, then, when she still did not speak.

'Oh, I've been out quite a lot,' she said. 'Out to dinner, and things. I'm just going out now. I thought I'd ring you before I went. I didn't have anything to say, really. I just wanted to talk. What's the hotel like?'

And he told her about the hotel, and how the less one did the less one became capable of doing, and how odd it was to sit around eating so much. 'Grotesque, really,' he finished, on a note of apology.

'It's quite nice,' she said, 'for a change, though,' and he agreed that it was quite nice. He couldn't make out why she had rung him, though when she then said, 'The children aren't here, they've gone off with Christopher for a day or two,' he sensed that she was seeking some kind of reassurance: but could not guess at her true anxiety, which was that he would not bring them back, so all he could say was, 'Is it good, then, to have them off your hands for a day or two?'

'Yes, in a way,' she said, and sighed.

'Where did he take them to?' he asked, wondering if it could have been them that he had seen, and if so, whether he should say so, and he heard the anxiety content of her voice rise considerably as she replied, 'Well, that's it, that's what I don't quite like, I'm not quite sure where they are, you see.'

'He didn't tell you where he was going?'

'No,' she said. 'And it didn't seem right to ask.'

'When will they be back?'

'In the morning, he said,' she said.

'Well, they'll be back soon,' he said.

'Yes, I suppose so. I wish now that I'd asked him. I don't like not knowing where they are. He might have taken them to my parents. But I don't know. He sometimes does.'

'They'll be back soon,' he repeated.

'And when will you be back?' she said, brightening: her fear, even so obliquely voiced, had been dissipated by being shared. 'At the end of the week?'

'On Friday,' he said. 'I'll give you a ring when I get back. I'll come and see you, if I may.'

'I'd like that,' she said. 'I hope you don't mind my ringing. I wanted to speak to somebody. And the house seemed so empty.'

'You know,' he said, 'that I'm pleased that you did. I was thinking of ringing you myself.'

'Were you really?' she said, obviously pleased. 'That would have been nice of you.'

'I'll ring you tomorrow evening, shall I, and make sure you're all safely reassembled?'

'Yes, please,' she said, 'that would be nice, if that's not too much trouble,' and he could tell from her voice that he had got it right, that this was what she wanted.

'I'll do that, then,' he said, and they said goodbye, and she rang off, and he was left wondering whether he had acquitted himself adequately, whether there was something else he should have guessed or said, or whether she had rung him after all because she wanted to speak to him. He remembered, now, before Easter, complaining to her rather treacherously about what a drag it was having to go off to a hotel, and how much he disliked sitting around doing nothing when there were so many things he ought to be getting on with: perhaps she had rung to cheer him up. He quite liked the idea. He did not recall that he had given her the name of the hotel: he certainly hadn't written it down, the most he could have done would have been to mention it in passing, and he wondered what it meant that she had remembered it. Though she could have found it out, of course, from the au pair girl, left behind to feed the cat. Even so, either way, he was pleased. It was luck that she had been put straight through to him. But perhaps she hadn't been put straight through to him. Perhaps the receptionist had sent somebody to the lounge to tell Julie there was a woman on the line for her husband. He had better go down and find out.

Julie was waiting to interrogate him, when he got downstairs. 'Who was that on the phone?' she said. Taking a chance on the extreme unlikelihood of the receptionist having specified the caller's sex, he said, mentioning the most boring and likely person he could think of: 'Hindley.' Hindley was the Clerk of his Chambers: his name, to Julie, spelled such profound dullness that she would never pick up such a gauntlet.

'They never leave him alone, even on holidays,' she said to Sally, with a sigh of curiously mingled contempt and pride.

'Awful, isn't it,' said Sally, not listening. She had begun not to listen to everything that Julie said. How very wise, thought Simon, looked at his watch, and decided it was time to ask everybody if they would like a drink. They did like, of course, and that was the end of another fourteen shillings and sixpence.

Later, after dinner, over coffee, he made a connexion he had been trying to make for hours. Ever since he had remembered Jefferson's remark about not being able to see the trees for the wood, it had plagued him, as it had done when it had first been recounted to him: he'd never known what it meant, and on any level it seemed, when applied to himself, grossly untrue. What he did precisely do was to see trees, not woods: he tackled each bit of life as it came up, he was a devoted believer in empiricism, he was so far from having any final vision or aim in view that he had, perforce, to believe in the necessity of taking each step as it came. Anyone involved in the amazingly complex historical tangle of trades unions and labour legislation would be very foolish to have any other attitude. There was no way of putting the whole thing right, even if one knew what right was, in a capitalist society: there was only the possibility of defending individual and minor points, redundancy payments, hours and compensations, laws of contract, conditions of work, rights to bargain: there wasn't such a thing as a wood that one could see, there were trees only, and some of those were no more than little thorny scrubs. All that he and people like himself could do was to defend those trees and scrubs: and even that defence might well be undone by ill-disposed judges or governments driving their bulldozers (or, to use a more classic archaic legal metaphor, their coach and horses) through the plantation. So how could he be accused, politically, of not seeing the trees? He was no idealist, no visionary, no revolutionary. How irritating it was, this habit lawyers had of using clichés, inverted or simple, to illustrate their points: as though the introduction of a metaphor were in itself the signal for applause for ready wit. It was a habit he had himself. How often, in court, had he heard the sycophantic laughter that would follow a turn of phrase so unoriginal, so pedantically unfunny, that it would have been sighed or smiled out of existence in ordinary conversation between friends.

And yet, perhaps it was true that he was biased. There was a connexion, a comparison, somewhere, that he was on the verge of grasping. It was true that he aligned himself often irrationally on the side of the employee, even in such absurd cases as this ridiculous twenty-four-hour strike that was going on at the moment at Caxton's: a strike against the management, it was, but motivated by the fact that other firms, through strikes, were likely to fail to produce the necessary parts. What possible blame attached to Caxton's management at that point in time it was impossible to see, and he had seen all the workers on the television in the hotel lounge the night before, standing baffled in front of the interviewer, unable to justify their line, mumbling embarrassed and shuffling off, and had heard the rustle of understandable indignation amongst the other hotel viewers. Those inarticulate men in their overalls. They protested against the wrong things, sometimes, and sometimes protested maliciously, he knew all that. Not one of them had even thought of making a case: not one of them mentioned the problem of lay-off pay. One phrase of comprehension of the real meaning of their prospective plight would have been enough, and it had not been forthcoming. What was the point of defending those so stubbornly unwilling to defend themselves? But perhaps they were not unwilling, perhaps they were incapable, and ah yes, that was it, he had it now, the connexion he had been after, and it was the question of his own alignment, his own bias, that it concerned. It was Rose he had been thinking of, yet again, Rose, with the next-door baby on her knee, stating quite simply that it was not possible to refuse such a service because the baby's grandmother (he had forgotten the details) worked for such and such a small sum, on her knees, scrubbing floors, whereas Rose was sitting safely in her chair and what did one baby more or less upon her knee signify? The issue was of such simplicity. Those that have may not reject those that have not: they may not in any way accuse of greed those that have less than themselves: they may not talk of profits declining while still in their large houses: they may not sit in front of television sets in expensive hotels which cost one man's weekly wage per person per day and criticise men in overalls who do not understand why they should be laid-off next week, through no fault of their own. When profits have so declined that the owners too stand on street corners in their overalls, and sell up their second car and their large house, then they may complain. The naiveté of such a view was as bad as Rose's, ignoring as it did the demands of the nation and the economy, ignoring, as hers did, her total lack of personal obligation to that particular baby, but it was fundamental, it was a view from which he could never train himself: it was the wood in which the trees grew. May the forests of it cover the earth, he oh so hopelessly desired. Shake down the superfluity. There was nothing else to hope for, any other hope was intolerable, and yet it was so hopeless, it was as though one were to desire the kingdom of heaven. Where the rich may not enter, where greed may perish. Not of this world is the kingdom, but there is no other world. Oh God, he said (staring into his coffee cup, a non-believer), Oh God help us to help each other, for if we do not, what are we, and what shall we become?

'*You're* very quiet,' said Julie, suddenly. 'What are *you* thinking about?'

She broke off her conversation with Sally and her husband to say this, turning to him slightly: there was a menace in her tone, he drearily noted, she spoke to him with a hostility that boded no good. It was his own fault: he should never have asserted himself by going out for a walk.

'What are you thinking about?' she continued, as he smiled weakly and apologetically at them.

'I was thinking about the strike at Caxton's,' he said. He could not think of anything else to say. It was not a politic answer.

'Whatever for?' she said. 'You're not mixed up in it, are you?'

'Of course I'm not,' he said. 'There's nothing to be mixed up in, from my point of view. I was just thinking about it.'

'And what fascinating conclusions did you reach?' she said, with a heavy childish irony.

'None in particular,' he said. 'I suppose I was thinking that it was a pity that public relations are so bad, and that nobody ever explains what's going on in simple enough terms. That's all.'

'Well, please don't start explaining to *us*,' said Julie. 'I'm sure Sally and Howard don't want to hear about your speculations on the state of the nation. And I've heard enough about it to last me a lifetime—you wouldn't believe what I have to listen to,' she said, turning back to the others, who smiled and bristled with incipient embarrassment.

'Oh, I don't know,' said Simon, trying to lighten the tone, but quite well aware that it was too late. 'I don't know. I keep most of it to myself, you know. I don't think I've given you a lecture about it since the last Ford package deal, have I?'

'Well, you just started off on it again now,' said Julie.

'No, not really,' said Simon. 'I was just thinking. And I only told you what I was thinking about because you asked me. You took me by surprise, I didn't have time to invent an exciting enough alternative. But I will, if you like. Or you could tell me what you were talking about, and I could talk about it too.'

'You should have been listening,' said Julie. 'You can't just sit there thinking.'

The contempt in her voice was so painful to hear that Sally started to pour out second cups of stone-cold coffee, and her husband reached for a newspaper.

'There, you see what you've done,' said Julie, her anger heightening dangerously. 'You've ruined everything, Howard's going to start reading the newspaper because you won't talk about anything interesting, I know I'm boring but I don't like sitting around thinking, I do enough of that at home, and anyway, you've been out on your own all day, haven't you, you might at least try to be sociable when you get back.'

'I wasn't alone,' said Simon. 'I took Kate, if you remember. And you could have come too if you'd wanted.'

'What, in this weather? You'd have to be mad to go out in this weather. What a dump, it's appalling.'

'I thought you liked it here,' said Simon, resisting the temptation to point out that it was she that had insisted upon it.

'Why ever should I like it?' said Julie. 'I don't come on holiday to sit alone all day.'

Simon did not want to involve Sally by pointing out that she had been not alone, but with Sally. So he said nothing. She was not appeased. He could tell that she was planning a final blow, and out it came.

'Though why,' she said, 'I'm complaining about you going out I don't really know. Your company isn't all that exciting, is it?'

Simon lit a cigarette. It was over, now. It could not get worse so it was sure to get better. Sally smiled nervously. Howard read his paper. Julie sat there, her face flushed with contention. At such moments, and God knows they came round regularly enough, Simon sometimes wondered how far things would go, if he let them. But the truth was that there was no further. This was the limit. And he could live with it, after all.

'Perhaps the weather will be better, tomorrow,' said Howard, finally, looking up from his paper and looking round as though he had heard nothing of what had passed.

'I hope so,' said Sally, with relief.

'Then we could all go out,' said Simon. He jumped in, recklessly. 'You'd quite like it, you know, Julie, once you got going. You remember that walk we had in Scotland?'

He looked at her: she was sitting there, breathing rather quickly, leaning slightly forward. Her eyes were unseeing. He waited, anxiously, and suddenly something went out of her, it was almost as though a spirit passed out of her, and she crumbled a little into the chair, and smiled in a disorganised fashion, and said, 'Yes, yes, that's true, that was very nice.' And as though she were putting on a coat, or lipstick, she put on her manner, and leant over to Sally and said, 'That was a *very* good holiday we had, and guess who was staying in the hotel . . .' and Simon listened, and offered confirmation of their past adventures. It was all he was expected to do. Howard also listened, politely. Poor bugger, thought Simon, I bet he's too nervous to read his paper in case she turns on him next, and asks him what he's thinking about. The thought gave him some satisfaction. He enjoyed it. Serve him right, he thought, though for what he didn't know.

THE NEXT DAY the weather was better: there was a little snow on the ground, but the sun shone, and it soon thawed. They all went out for a walk in the afternoon, dragging themselves off after their excessive lunch—at picnics the women drew the line, they said they couldn't risk eating all the starch in the sandwiches, but they ate so much of what wasn't sandwiched that it couldn't have made much difference, Simon thought. Howard walked with Simon and told him about ICI. Simon wouldn't have admitted it to himself, but he had actually been somewhat deterred by his wife's indictment of the subject matter of his conversation, so he did not respond in kind, but allowed himself to be gently and informatively bored instead. 'How interesting,' he kept saying, with an effort, meaning how dull, the tables turned. In the evening, when he got back, he went straight to the telephone, saying he was going to ring his clerk, and rang Rose. She answered with relief, apologetic for having put him to the trouble: the children were safely back, they had had a good time, they had been to Norfolk, Christopher had got a new car and they had been very excited about it. She said this with a desolate goodwill. Now they were back, of course, she was wishing they weren't, because they were making such a hideous noise, which he could probably hear over the line, but that was life, was it not. The headmaster had spent his Easter composing an affidavit, perhaps he would like to have a look at it when he got back. How had he been, had he been for another walk? She envied him being in the country, she missed it, and it was impossible to get there, not having a car. She had been on trains, and green line buses, but it was a drag, with the little ones. I'll take you out one day, he said, we could go out for a day when the weather's better, if I get some time off—and when he had said this (and it had seemed a natural thing to say) a small silence fell, while they both thought how they would like it, and she said yes, yes, I'd like that very much, let's do that.

When he had put down the phone, he thought, so it was not Christopher Vassiliou and the children that I saw. But it made no difference for it was the same as if he had seen them. It had had the same as yet dim effect.

And oddly enough, almost the first person that he saw, on returning to London the next weekend, was Christopher Vassiliou himself. In a way it was not odd, as he knew from Rose that he lived near: and indeed, when he saw him, he realised that he had seen him before without recognising him, so changed was he from the haggard anxious press cuttings which were all that he had had to go on. And on this occasion, he identified him from the children: there they were, Konstantin, Marcus and Maria, sitting in a large Jaguar, driving past his very front door, where he was standing, about to unpack the luggage from his own car. They saw him, they waved and shouted, the little ones, who were in the back: 'Simon,' they yelled, 'Hey, Simon,'—and he called and waved back, at their smiling excited faces. Konstantin, sitting in front with his father, did not call, and waved only when there was no option, the expression on his face denoting, even in so brief a passing, a regret that he, unlike the little ones, could not wave and shout without circumspection, and a personal message that it was not through reluctance to greet Simon that he had failed to do so. He learns in a hard school, Simon thought. Christopher, at the sound of the shouting, halting at the adjacent cross roads, had turned to look in his direction, and their eyes had met, without recognition, it would have seemed. He had changed, Christopher Vassiliou, from those early days in Camden Town: gone was the skinny famished dangerous glamour, the long hair, the untidy cheap flash clothes. He had put on weight, he had solidified, he had occupied space. His hair was short, as short as Simon's own, and he wore a suit: his face had squared up, his shoulders under his jacket looked substantial, his skin had a white certainty, as though that which had been added, over the past few years, was the weight of England, covering up the dark exposed street-living of his childhood. His only concession to the flash which he had once so affected was a pair of dark glasses, which emphasised his air of well-being. He was a good-looking man, a finished and serious person: it suited him, this new style, the transition had not been at the expense of his presence, he had not faded into any ranks, he had done it in style, he had not cut himself after a commonplace model. Simon, standing there with a suitcase in his hand, as the Jaguar receded, felt such instant and confusing pangs that he remained there for a moment before he could bring himself to move. It was shocking, to see those children, children so firmly placed in his mind, in so different a context— and laughing there, enjoying themselves—and it was shocking, too, to see the man manifested, to see him in the flesh. He had known that it was coming: the false shadow in Cornwall had been a portent. It would have to be dealt with, this new dimension, and there would be worse to come. He felt it, on Rose's behalf: he was entering into her own land, her realities would become real for him, he too would have to stand there.

He rang her, the next week, as soon as he had time, and arranged to go and see her. He arrived in the early afternoon, and could see the children playing in the street, as soon as he turned the corner: it was still the school holidays. It was a sunny day, freakishly warm for the time of year: front doors stood open, and women stood chatting on doorsteps, and prams with babies in were taking the air. He could see that such a street, profoundly depressing as it still appeared to him, might take on a more loved aspect, particularly in such weather. As he drew up against the kerb, Marcus and Maria noticed him, and came running over, followed by a troop of other children, one on a tricycle, one pushing another in a derelict pushchair, one on a scooter. 'Hello, you lot,' he said, uneasily, as he got out of the car: he hated the tone of his voice when he spoke to children. But they didn't seem to take offence. 'Hello, hello Simon,' they said, pleased to have a visitor, and followed him to the front door of their house. Konstantin was sitting on the steps there, reading. 'Hello,' he said, and Simon paused. 'Your mother's in, isn't she?' he said: he knew she was, having telephoned before setting off. 'She's doing the ironing,' said Konstantin. And then, making an imperceptible effort, he added, smiling, 'We saw you, the other day. Driving down your street.'

'Yes, I saw you,' said Simon.

'Our Dad's got a new car,' said Marcus.

'Yes, I saw it,' said Simon. 'Great, isn't it?'

'It's *fantastic*,' said Marcus, and the two little ones started to enthuse, boasting before the silent audience of their listening neighbours: it was full of gadgets, you could do this and you could do that, you could go at so many miles an hour if you were allowed to but you're not, and its numberplate was WOW 717 which was a specially lucky number. While this was going on, Simon watched Konstantin: he could see him, physically struggling with his loyalty, and in the end he lost, because he too started to chatter, excited, impressed: there were two tanks for petrol, did Simon know, and this new model had a new special way for opening the windows, they didn't just open, you pressed a button, and Daddy liked it, he said it was a terrible effort opening windows, but with this electric button you could just press and it slid up and down. He must have bought it to amuse them, thought Simon: and he had certainly succeeded.

They followed him down, when he went to look for Rose: the door being open, he walked straight in. She was doing the ironing: she looked up as he entered, and smiled, but before he could speak, Konstantin said, 'Here's Simon, Mum, we were just telling him about Dad's new car.' Simon watched them both, mother and child, as he said this, and it seemed to him that he could see them both wince at the injury, wince, repent, forgive, and draw together, all in the instant.

'Yes,' said Rose. 'They're very excited about it. It's very nice, I hear.'

'I saw it,' said Simon.

'So I heard,' said Rose.

'You hear everything,' said Simon.

'Yes,' said Rose.

He sat down. 'You don't mind if I finish the ironing, do you?' she said. 'We could go out for a walk, later. It's such a nice day. If you've time. I hope you don't mind, Emily said she might come round this afternoon, too. I didn't like to say no. She was away for Easter and I haven't seen her.'

'Of course I don't mind,' he said.

'How's your book?' she asked, and he told her: they were getting on with it quite well, quicker than they had thought they would, and it would take them only another few sessions to finish it.

'And what about you?' he said.

'Oh me, I'm fine,' she said. 'I went to the launderette this morning, and there was quite a scene there, it was awful really, but quite funny I suppose, there was this poor woman who dropped a packet of mince in with her washing, and she didn't notice at first, and when she'd found what she'd done, well, what could one do, really? There it was, all swirling round, looking all grey and bloodless, you know what meat goes like in water, and it was stuck all over everything, poor woman, we all had to help her pick it off, you've never seen such a sight. Poor woman, she had to wash them all over again, and she lost her mince. You'd be amazed, the things that happen in the launderette. I used to work there, you know. There was a drama a day. Once somebody put a mouse in, in her little boy's trouser pocket. He came belting along when he realised she'd taken the trousers, yelling Mum, Mum, where's my mouse. It was dead, poor thing.'

'What did you used to do there?'

'I was the supervisor. What a job. The machines were always going wrong and I could never get hold of the man who fixes them. A first I used to refund people their money, I felt so sorry for them, but Mr Mackay who owns it would never give it me back, so I organised a complaints and refund system. But people tell me it doesn't work very well, you're lucky if you ever see your money again. They're so fatalistic, they don't even bother to fill in the Refund Card. There was one woman who came with all the loose covers off her suite, terribly heavy blue stuff, and she put it in and it all started going round nicely—unbelievably dirty they were, the water looked like brown soup, and she and I stared at it thinking what a good job she was doing and about time too, but the thing was that the machine wouldn't stop going, it just went on and on, for about an hour, and never got to the spinning part. I really didn't know what to do, she was awfully upset about it, and in the end we just had to drag them out, they were so wet and heavy, and I told her to put them in another machine to spin, but she wouldn't, she said she couldn't afford it, she didn't trust them any more, and there they lay, all over the floor, getting dirtier and dirtier. Then she burst into tears, I don't blame her, and said how ever was she going to get them home, and I had to lend her Marcus's pushchair, and we heaved all this sodden great heap of stuff into it and off she went. God knows how she ever got them dry. Oh, there was never a dull moment. This woman with her mince, today, that was really quite something. I was glad I wasn't in charge. She couldn't bear to give it up, you know. She kept saying, perhaps if I stick it all together it'll fry all right.'

She folded a grey school shirt, carefully. The children had filtered off.

'Perhaps you could look at that draft affidavit,' she said. 'Before Emily arrives. It's on the mantelpiece there, behind the clock.'

He read it, carefully. It was official, dry, unexceptionable. I, Peter Harold Stone make oath and say, it said, that these three children are achieving the required educational standards for their age groups: their reading ages are above (figures quoted) the average: they attend school regularly, have no discipline problems, are co-operative members of their class and of the school. There was nothing much wrong with it, as a statement.

'What do you think of it?' he said.

'I don't know,' she said. 'What do you? It seems all right, I suppose. It's just that he sounds so unenthusiastic.'

'What kind of a man is he?'

'He's so nice, really, he's a very good headmaster, the children like him a lot, but it's always the same, whenever he has anything official to do or say, he comes out sounding like that.' She thought about Mr Stone: grey-haired, industrious, devoted. 'You know, when he introduces the school concert, he makes this little speech, and it's always the same, as boring as hell, about communal effort and being members of a community and stuff, all words the children don't understand too well nor the parents either, and then you get him alone afterwards, and he's so nice, and interested—I think he's just shy, really. This awful language kind of comes over him, when he has to speak in public. The same in interviews, and on his school reports. I hope it won't matter. He really is nice, as a person. I never forget, one day when Konstantin was six, and I let him come home on his own because it was so exhausting getting the others into their coats and hats and boots and things, I suppose I was wrong really, but all the other kids came home alone, you know—anyway, this day Konstantin didn't turn up, and I waited and waited, and then at about half four I set off to look for him, I was quite distraught by this time, and I'd got the pram and Marcus whining along after me, and I met Mr Stone on the way to school, and he said how was I, and I said I was looking for Konstantin, and he went all the way back to school with me to look, and he wasn't there, and then he said don't worry, he'll have gone to see a friend, and I was in such a panic by this time, and couldn't think which friend, and he took me into school and he knew all his friends' names, and looked up their addresses, and said, I bet he's with John on Albemarle Road, and he took me round, and there he was. And he said such a nice thing, when Konstantin came to the door with John, he said to him—and there was me, all overcome with relief and so pleased to see the child again—he said, "Well, Konstantin, give her two minutes, and she'll be shouting at you, and she'll be quite right, too." No, he really is a nice man. It's just that he can't manage to sound it. You don't think it matters, do you?'

'No, I don't suppose so. Lawyers are used to this kind of statement. They read between the lines. In fact, people often get suspicious, I'm glad to say, of the too expert witness. There are some doctors and psychiatrists, you know, who make a business out of it—the nicely-turned phrase, the helpful evidence. They do it too often, some of them. People get to know them. A rotten psychiatrist, they say, but a useful witness. No, at least your Mr Stone sounds as though he means what he says, even though he doesn't say very much.'

'Is there anything else he ought to say, do you think?'

'I don't know, I was just wondering. Perhaps—perhaps you could get him to put something in about the children's music. Konstantin's very good at the oboe, after all, and it's exactly the kind of extra that one might not expect a school like that to encourage...'

'I don't see *why* one should not expect—' she started, defensively, about to launch, he could tell, into her defence speech: and then paused, and caught herself at it, and smiled, and said, 'Yes, yes, of course you're right, one ought to put it all in. Yes. Thank you. That's a very good idea.'

'You see,' he said, defensive himself now, 'you ought to try to think of the kinds of complaint that are likely to be made, and one of them is sure to be that the children aren't given enough of the kind of extra opportunity that they might get at a different kind of school...'

He was on bad ground, he didn't like it, but she began to laugh, and said, 'Extra opportunities, extra opportunities. Perhaps I should start Maria off on ballet. It makes me feel quite ill, small children doing ballet, I don't know why. Perhaps I should take the judge off to see their favourite spare-time activity, which is larking about on Thursday evenings at the Club. You should see the Club, what a dump, it's in the downstairs bit of the Clinic, which is horrid enough by any standards, and this Club, they get an hour and a half and some biscuits for twopence a time, and you should see the kids, no socks, no pants, what a sight, and there's a horrible bully of a man who organises it, and yells at them all the time. Mine love it, God knows why. It's like a monkey house, I'd feel really guilty, I really would feel guilty if I *made* them go to that, but they love it. Children are very odd. Don't you think?'

'I suppose they are.' He folded the affidavit up neatly and put it back behind the clock. He thought of Kate in the church.

'I had an invitation,' he said, 'to an event where you are supposed to be speaking. Do you do much of that kind of thing?'

She put the iron down, brushed away her hair from her forehead, and looked at him. She was blushing: the blood had crept faintly into her pale uncoloured faded face.

'No,' she said, 'I don't. I try not to. What was it for?'

'It was something to do with raising funds for a home for disabled workmen, I think.'

'Oh God,' she said. 'Yes. How awful. I am sorry. It wasn't me that put you on the mailing list, you know. I wouldn't do a thing like that to anyone I knew.'

'No,' he said, quickly, this aspect of the case not having occurred to him, anxious to reassure her that he had not been suspicious, 'No, I know it wasn't you, it came through my wife, really, a neighbour got her to buy a ticket, perhaps you know the neighbour, Mrs Cookson her name is, she's the wife of Herbert Cookson.'

'I don't know her, no. I know who you mean, though. Oh dear. I hate that kind of thing. And it's my fault, really. He wrote to me, the man that runs the place, and asked me what to do about raising money, and I said why didn't he have an evening—no, really, I hate that kind of charity, six guinea tickets to hear a really lousy programme, but I couldn't think what else to say, and it would be a pity if he lost his place, because he's done a good job with it, he really got it going, so I told him to get in touch with Lady Bresson, and so it all went on from there. And then I could hardly say I wouldn't turn up myself, could I? I didn't realise they were selling the tickets already. They haven't got my name on them, have they?'

'I'm afraid they have,' he said. He thought of the ticket, standing on his mantelshelf: Julie liked to have it there, because it said in Lady Bresson's handwriting, 'So glad you are coming, look forward to seeing you there, many thanks, Margaret.' And he liked to have it there because Rose's name was upon it, and it was almost as though it brought her presence into his house, and he liked the thought that nobody knew that when he looked in its direction, he looked with emotion.

'Shall you go?' she said, unplugging the iron.

'I don't know,' he said. 'I was going to ask you.'

'It's not for another month,' she said. 'Is it?'

'It would be quite nice,' he said, 'to see you socially.'

'It's quite nice here,' she said.

She stood there, the iron in her hand. He sat, and looked at the iron.

'No, I'd like you to go,' she said. 'Though I speak so badly, I'm inaudible. And I hate that kind of function. But what else can one do?'

'I could buy you a drink, for the good of the cause,' he said. 'In the interval.'

'Oh dear me, how embarrassing,' she said. 'But never mind. Never mind. They were going to have folk singing or something, or have they changed their minds?'

'No,' he said. 'Folk singing.'

'Ah well,' she said. 'It doesn't matter, I suppose. I wish Emily would come, it's such a nice day, and we're missing it in here.'

And, as she spoke, they heard the sounds of Emily's arrival: children shouting, feet on the stairs, and the clop clop of shoes as Emily descended. She entered in full speech, a child dragging on her skirt, a shopping basket in her hand—'Just *wait*, just *wait*,' she was saying, 'I brought one for *everyone*, you don't think I can't count, do you, just give me half a *chance*, if you tear me to pieces how can I possibly find it?'—and she dropped her basket into a chair, and rummaged in her pocket, and found it, the last gobstopper, and shoved it into Maria's mouth as though putting a coin into a slot. 'Aha, silence,' she said. 'Wonderful. Silence.'—and sank into a chair.

'Don't sit down,' said Rose. 'I thought we'd go out for a walk. Emily, this is Simon Camish.'

'Hello,' said Emily. 'Give me a chance. Let me get my breath back. What a marvellous day, they're all running around in their vests up there, you know, they've shoved all their shirts through the letter box. It's beautiful out. It's like spring.'

'It is spring,' said Simon.

'Yes, I suppose it is. But one doesn't expect it, somehow. It's cold in here, it's much nicer out.'

'That's what I said,' said Rose. 'It's damp, down here. It's lovely, in the summer. It smells like a cellar. But it's nicer out, at this time of year.'

'All right, all right, in a minute,' said Emily. 'I'll just have a fag. How are you, anyway? What about Easter? What was it like at the Sendacks?'

And Simon sat there, and listened, while the two women exchanged information: it poured out of them both, news of any description, books they had read, things they had seen, people they had heard from, things the children had said, twinges in ankles and premonitions of sudden death, dreams about cabbage plantations, what they had had in the morning's post, and all of this punctuated with absurdly perfunctory remarks thrown in Simon's direction— 'Oh God, how boring for you,' or 'We've nearly finished, we'll have finished in a minute,' they cried from time to time, without the slightest conviction. Simon listened with indulgence, noted that he was doing so, and took this for a serious sign. Thereafter he listened more carefully, and watched also, wondering what it was in the conversation that he did not dislike. Other people's conversations often annoyed him quite disproportionately, particularly if they betrayed signs of intimacy: women especially had a habit of making short-cuts to intimacy, of displaying the manner without the content, of discussing personal triviality at a first encounter, that never failed to irritate. Emily and Rose he could at least absolve from that. A vainer man would have assumed that their animation was in part at least assumed for his benefit, that their jokes were directed largely at him: but a vainer man would have been wrong. For once Simon had got it right.

Rose had told him a good deal about Emily, in an intermittent desultory fashion: an old schoolfriend she was, a schoolmaster's daughter, who had been sent to Rose's not very good and expensive school on a scholarship, and had there proved to be something of a trial to the authorities, through her too great profit from the largesse so kindly extended to her. She had done too well, she had shown people up, she had been rather bad for the system, she had latched on to it a little too well. She was married now, to a man who taught in an art school: or rather he had done so, until he had lost his job through a vague fit of militancy, which had swept across him disastrously and fashionably, as such things do, without enough conviction on his part to make the subsequent unemployment tolerable. Simon seemed to remember that Rose had said that Emily did not much approve of his stand. With three children, one not yet of school age, no particular money-earning capacity, and no money, she could not afford to earn, so she spent her time making ends meet, looking after a man who had chosen not to look after himself, and wondering what she could do about it. When the little one's at school, she would threaten: but what would she do then? She had lost the relevant years of her life: the idea of a second-best, inevitably part-time job did not appeal to her. From this account, Simon had expected to see discontent and resentment flourishing in her face, but there were no signs of them. On the contrary, if anything blossomed there, it was goodwill. She was dark, very dark, with long black hair tied up inadequately, escaping round her face: her clothes were so dull and frayed as to present the idea of an old, never-quitted uniform. Her features were pronounced and animated, her face thin, the kind of face that aged well, and the deep lines round her mouth and eyes which might have looked like the marks of sorrow, in repose, were quite clearly the lines of laughter. It was her smile that they fitted. There was about her something scrappy, tough and restless. She was not what one might call attractive: and yet, thought Simon, looking at her and at Rose, how agreeable, how extremely agreeable the two women looked. They looked—he found it hard to explain it to himself—they looked complete, they looked like people. So many women, he found, did not look like people at all: they aspired after some image other than the personal. These were the women, though he did not like to think of it, that peopled his fantasies—smooth, shiny, made-up sexy women, wearing underwear under their clothes, provocative, female, other. He dreamed of such women, and what they would do to him, and he to them, and he disliked them for it, and himself. There is nothing he would have more disliked than the realisation of his fantasies. The very thought of it made him feel quite ill. It was all very well for his mind to project for him an image of himself and a woman in black lacy underclothes, and for his intellect to tell him that this was what his subconscious desired: his subconscious might well desire it, perhaps one had to concede that it did, but all he could say was that the rest of him rejected it utterly, and knew quite well that in reality he would find such a situation, such con-tact, as disagreeable as being forced to eat avocado pears (his least favourite food), and as tediously embarrassing as a three-hour tête-à-tête with his father-in-law. Perhaps he found Rose and Emily so agreeable, as a spectacle, because, precisely, he did not find them attractive. It seemed an odd conclusion, especially as he had de-cided that he loved Rose, in so far as he considered himself capable of love, and that her company was what he most desired. 'I love her,' he said to himself, to try it out, but the words sounded very strange in his head: not untrue, but strange. He looked at her, to see how she responded to the formulation, and there she sat, her pale, anxious, nervous face smiling, her hands behind her head as she leant back in the chair, her dry frizzy greeny-yellow hair, her grey-checked Viyella shirt, her flat chest lifting only very slightly, as there was so little of it, and it struck him suddenly, painfully, that it was a dreadful audacity to think of loving a whole person like that, a whole person so entirely there and so fully existing, a person with a history survived, a person who had made herself so carefully. It was astonishing, it was remarkable. It had amazing and interesting possibilities.

'Come on,' said Rose. 'Let's go out, before it's time to come back again. Let's go to the Pally.'

'Oh no, for God's sake,' said Emily, 'not the Pally. I'm bored with the Pally.'

'There's nowhere else to go,' said Rose.

'Let's just go for a walk,' said Emily.

'We could go somewhere in the car,' said Simon, but they didn't want to go in the car.

'I know,' said Emily. 'Let's go and see the chickens and the armchair. It's a nice walk, to the chickens and the armchair. Simon would like it.'

And both women started to laugh, again.

'All right,' said Rose. 'I haven't been that way this year. They might not still be there, the poor chickens.'

'Well, in *that* case,' said Emily, 'it's our duty to check up on them. They'll feel neglected. I'll round the children up.'

And she shouted, suddenly, with startling volume. '*Jimmy*' she yelled. '*Jimmy*. Get the little ones, we're going out.'

There was no response.

'They can't hear you,' said Rose. 'Never mind, we'll collect them as we go out.'

And so they set off, and there were all the children out on the street, running around, as Emily had said, without their shirts on, in their vests: Maria's vest, a hand-on, had huge holes under the armpits.

'Look at them, look at them,' said Emily, pausing on the steps, 'Our little vested interests,'—and up they came, with all their followers. 'No, no,' said Emily, shooing all the others away, waving her arms, 'Not you lot, we're not taking any extras, we've quite enough of our own, go on, buzz off, all of you—' and the strange children meekly disappeared, slouching off to watch from somebody else's doorway, as they set off. On the way, Rose explained to Simon about the chicken and the armchair: it had been a favourite walk the summer before, it was only a few blocks away, she was sure he would like it, it was quite lovely there. And he nodded and agreed, wondering if they were teasing him, not caring if they were. It was hardly what one might have described as a pretty walk: they passed rows of houses, dingy little street-corner shops, a little warehouse or two, a small factory, a railway siding. He tried to look at it with her eyes, to see in odd little efforts at decoration—carved leaves and grapes, scrolls, silly little gables—the charm and endeavour that she said she saw there, but it was hard to discern anything but an impoverished, placating, mean mass-production, a perfunctory and insulting short-changing by the jerry-building profiteers of the last century. Once more, he found himself thinking, she wouldn't like it so much if she'd seen what I've seen. And yet, despite this, the walk did have charm: the buildings shone, gloriously washed by the heavy rain of the week before, plants were growing in the gutters, the six children were happy and excited, people were cleaning their windows as though inspired by the sudden sunshine, old men were repairing their front gates, young mothers chatted on street corners with prams full of babies. The road they were walking along rose steeply: it was a hilly district.

'I always think,' said Rose, 'I don't know why, on days like this, that this road's like the seaside, do you know what I mean? I'm sure that the sea will be over the top. You know what I mean?'

And they did know, and discussed the phenomenon of *déjà-vu,* and the way that, in a strange place, from the configuration of the landscape, one can know what is there, what is beyond the horizon or round the corner: and then they had arrived at their destination, for there were the chickens. They were in a waste lot, a steep bombed site: the house that adjoined the bombsite had appropriated a small plot of land, doubtless unofficially, and had fenced it off with wire, and in it were these hens. The wall that fronted on to the site still showed vestiges of the bombed building that had stood there: the remains of a fireplace one storey up, a few scraps of wallpaper. In the fenced-off plot stood an armchair. In the armchair sat a feathery dusty old hen.

'There, you see,' said Emily, sitting herself down on the low wall, turning to Simon as though in triumphant possession of the scene. 'Isn't it nice, isn't it lovely?'

Rose and Simon sat too, and watched the chickens scavenging and scrabbling. The armchair was rotting and mouldy; grass and weeds grew out of its guts. The sun was warm. Rose leant her head back against the wire and shut her eyes. The children ran up and down, poking in the gutter, climbing along the walls, picking up bits and pieces.

'I don't know *why* it's so nice here,' said Rose, as though paying tribute to the eccentricity of the outing, 'but it is nice, don't you think?'

'Yes,' said Simon, 'it is.'

And it was. So great and innocent a peace possessed him that it seemed like a new contract, like the rainbow after the flood. He could feel it, on his bare hands and face. It lay upon him. It was like happiness.

They sat there, and chatted, idly: after a while, the children, who had run off down the street, returned, with their collection of findings. They had got two lolly-pop sticks, an old Nescafé tin, a milk bottle top, a scrap of blue velvet, a hunk of red rusty metal, a train ticket, a little toy plastic car without wheels, a sad flanged little thing like a dead beetle, a few bits of weed, an old paint tin still half full, but sealed over with a thick impregnable skin, and a french letter. Rose threw the french letter hastily to the chickens, who did not much care for it either, and they all laughed feebly while the children insisted that they be told what it was, without success.

'It's all our fault,' said Emily, when she had stopped laughing, 'it's all our fault, that they go round picking things up like that. We used to tell them to go on treasure hunts, didn't we, Rose, when we wanted to talk and they wouldn't let us, and now they've got into the habit of it, you should *see* some of the stuff they pick up.'

'This is quite a nice little collection,' said Rose, looking down at the row of objects on the wall. 'I like the paint tin. Quite a find, that is. No, don't stir it up, Marcus, you'll get it all over yourself—and look, that's spurge, that is.' She turned over a bit of greenery, a pale yellow brilliant green, with round leaves. 'Spurge. There's a poem about spurge, by Rossetti. It says something like,

> The woodspurge has a cup of three.
> After long grief and misery
> This is all that is left to me
> The woodspurge has a cup of three.

No, that can't be right, I must have remembered it wrong, because it's a nice poem, and my version's awful, but it's something like that, isn't it interesting the memory, that one can remember something is good, a poem or a painting, but not remember it at all, in detail?'

'How do you know about such things?' said Simon. 'About the names of things?' He was thinking about the sea gulls in Cornwall.

'I don't know,' said Rose. 'It's interesting, that's why. And I used to learn it, in the country. When there was nothing else to do. You should see my pressed-flower collection. Actually, to tell you the truth I thought it was bloody boring at the time, when I was a child, but it staved off the even worse boredom of doing nothing at all. And now I find it absolutely fascinating. So you see. Everything pays off.'

'We don't all find it as riveting as you do,' said Emily. 'I tried to get worked up about it once, but it didn't work. Do you remember that dreadful craze you went through, about the London rocket?'

And both women laughed, again, easily: their recollections amused them.

'Oh God, the London rocket,' said Rose. 'It's all very well, but it's a very rare plant, the London rocket, it's got three stars in the book, and as it grows on waste patches I thought we were ideally placed to find it, but we've never managed yet.'

'It's not surprising,' said Emily. 'You should just see what it looks like. Even the book describes it as a modest and unattractive little plant. And moreover it's virtually indistinguishable from the something or other rocket—the common rocket, probably—so we kept having these false alarms, when we found the dull old modest common rocket, and carried it off home, and I thought, Aha, that'll have cured her, even she will have to admit that even though it's the real thing it might as well not be, it looks so boring. But it never was.'

'Oh, come on,' said Rose. 'You know you got quite keen yourself. You'd have been just as excited as me if we'd managed it.'

'Well, more fool me,' said Emily. 'But you should make her show you the pressed flowers, Simon. They're quite good, really. A pathetic little catalogue of her empty life. I burst into tears the first time I saw them. She brought them to school with her. I told her she'd better hide them quick, if she didn't want to make herself a laughing-stock. But she stuck it out, she kept showing them to people, and you'd be amazed, how indulgent they were.'

'On page ten,' said Konstantin, who had been listening, bored with the younger ones, 'on page ten, there's a pressed caterpillar.'

'Oh, don't remind me, don't remind me,' said Rose. 'I didn't mean it, I really didn't. It got in by mistake. I was terribly sorry about it.'

'It put her off for a whole year,' said Konstantin. 'You can see, from the dates.'

'It's quite true,' said Rose. 'I was so upset I didn't collect for a year. But then I found this very nice corncockle one day, and it was too good to miss. So I braved the squashed caterpillar, and started again.'

'Mr Rampley says there are birds nest orchids, in the woods at Branston,' said Konstantin. 'But I've never found any.'

'No,' said Rose, hesitating, struggling as the shadow fell across her. 'No, neither have I. Anyway, they wouldn't press very well. They're too wet.'

'It would be nice to find them, though,' said Konstantin.

'Yes,' said Rose. 'Yes. Well, you must look for me.'

'There's a dumped car in Primrose Avenue,' said Konstantin, suddenly, eager now to undo what he had done—or perhaps, maybe, losing interest, having done enough, having no impulse to pursue, sadistically, the point he had been making. 'Garry told me.'

'Oh God, not another,' said Emily.

'Well, you're *not* to go *near* it,' said Rose, simultaneously: and on such a note they rose to their feet, and set off home, discussing as they went the danger of dumped cars, and the Council's reluctance to remove them, and the plans for the Alexandra Palace, and roller skating. 'You must come to the dog show with us one day,' said Rose, to Simon. 'They're really good, the dog shows at the Palace.'

'I'd like to,' he said: and before him stretched a vista of shabby amusements and moth-eaten modest satisfactions. It would be quite enough for him, if by any chance she really meant it.

IN THE EVENING, Rose sat with Konstantin: he was watching the television, and she was trying to sew a new zip on to an old leather purse. Sometimes it occurred to her that she was growing pathologically mean. She had had the purse for at least four years, she could remember buying it, and it had cost her eight and sixpence. The new zip had cost her two shillings. She pricked her fingers as she sewed, and made holes in her thumb through trying to push the needle through the stiff leather: her thimble had been mislaid the year before, during Maria's birthday party. Hunt the thimble, the children had played, and one of them had hidden it so well that no hunting would ever reveal it. What objects, she thought, must lie beneath the floorboards of a house like this: where do they go to, all the things that get lost, the needles, the buttons, the nail scissors, the tea spoons? When they had moved in, she and Christopher, they had taken up the old linoleum, and underneath it were newspapers, dated September 1939, covered with yellowing photographs of evacuees, huddled together on railway stations. They had read the newspapers, huddled together themselves for warmth, in the sad despairing communion of dismay that had marked the first years of their marriage, feeling a kinship with those small exiles. Then they had burned the papers, and replaced them with new ones, and replaced the better bits of linoleum. They had wanted to throw it away, but decided (as they grew used to it) that it wasn't so bad after all, that one could live with it. It was still there, but covered now by an old flowered carpet which Christopher's mother had given them when she moved from Camden Town.

She thought about her childhood, and about the pressed flowers, and Emily. She had not thought for some time about her first meetings with Emily: the flowers had brought it back to her. She had loved Emily, because by some amazing stroke she had recognised in those flowers her true history. She remembered the evening of their first conversation, and its happiness, which was still with her. She had been sitting on her bed in the dormitory, alone, a freakish late arrival, faint after only two days with the strain of lessons which she could not follow, rules she did not understand, faces which meant nothing to her, the dank smell of stale wet bread that filled the air: she felt herself both ignorant and elect, being as she was appallingly ill-instructed in any formal sense, and yet having read more, in her solitude, than any other girl in the school. The staff had been unable or unwilling to conceal their surprise at the gaps in her knowledge, and she had just left a dismal session with the headmistress, in which she had been told that if she found it too difficult to remain with her own age group, she should perhaps be moved down a year, or even two years, until she caught up. The threatened disgrace had depressed her, and she had crept up to her bedroom to hide it, and there she sat, on her bed, on the verge of tears, looking at her collection of flowers and recalling (then as now) the mixture of anguish and delight with which she had assembled them: and then Emily came in. She was frightened of Emily, whose reputation had reached her even in so short a space of time: abrupt, eccentric, imitated, and popular, her status was easy to perceive.

'Ah,' said Emily, entering the room, and throwing her books on to her bed, and herself after them. 'Ah, it's you. I was wanting to talk to you.'

'What about?' said Rose, in alarm.

'Oh, I don't know what *about,*' said Emily. 'I hadn't thought. Anything. I just thought we might talk. After all, you are a new person. I've talked to all the others for years and years and years. What's that you've got there?'

'These are my pressed flowers,' said Rose, less alarmed.

'Let's have a look,' said Emily, leaping to her feet, with the restless violence that afflicts girls in boarding schools. And she came over, and looked.

'Jesus,' she said, when she had turned a few pages. 'You must have put a few years of your life into assembling this lot. Whatever for?'

'Well,' said Rose, modestly and truthfully, quite unaware that the pathos could possibly communicate to anyone other than herself, 'I suppose because I didn't have much clsc to do.'

'Good God,' said Emily. 'Good God.' And her eyes filled, promptly, with tears. She sat there, rigid and attentive, her eyes welling.

'What do you mean, what is it?' said Rose.

'What do *you* mean?' said Emily. 'Not much else to do? Whatever do you mean? What a terrible thing to say, do you realise what a terrible thing you've just said?'

'I don't know,' said Rose, confused. 'I don't know. It's not so terrible, is it?'

'You don't even *know* what you've said,' said Emily, who was cheering up now, enjoying her own sensibility. She looked down at the book again, and turned a few more pages, and said, with interest,

'Your techniques improved a bit, I must say. The first pages look a bit weedy, you must admit.'

'I suppose they do,' said Rose. 'I wasn't as good at it then or perhaps they are a bit old, after all. I started when I was about six, you know.'

'At *six?* Are you telling me you've had nothing better to do since the age of *six?*'

'Well, not quite,' said Rose. 'What I mean is, I did it for fun when I was six. I was quite happy then, I think. I think. It got worse later.'

'Ah yes,' said Emily, 'it does.' And then, as though bracing herself for a dissertation, she got up, and started to pace up and down on the wooden floor. 'Yes, it does,' she said. 'It gets worse and worse and worse. You're quite right. You're the first person I've ever met who actually *admitted* it. But shall I tell you something? Shall I tell you something? It doesn't go on getting worse for ever, there comes a point when it gets better and better. What about that? Eh? What about that?'

'I don't believe it,' said Rose.

'Well, that's pathetic,' said Emily. 'Not to believe it. I believe it. Why shouldn't you believe it? You just wait and see. You'll be amazed.'

'How do you know?' said Rose, bewildered; for the conversation seemed to her like a conversation in dreams, a made-up daytime reverie, the kind of talk with which she had filled hours of her days, in which herself responded to herself, faithfully, on cue.

'I know,' said Emily, 'because I've made my mind up. I'm not going to put up with it. You wait and see. And you won't put up with it either.'

'How do you know?' said Rose, expecting the answer.

Emily paused, dramatically, in her pacing.

'Because I won't allow it,' she said. 'That's why. I won't allow it. See?'

'Ah, well then,' said Rose, shutting up her book. 'Ah well. That's all right, then. That's fine.'

And so it was, fine. Emily admitted later, in their endless subsequent midnight discussions in the bathroom, that she had tried the same thing on other people, but had never managed to make it, because she never got a flicker of response. 'I got sick to death,' said Emily, 'of trying it on, and getting nothing.' 'I think it was mean of you,' Rose would say, 'to try it on, and not to wait for me,'—and Emily would repent, and admit that she hadn't got even as far as trying it, so pointless had it seemed after the opening phrase. 'But with you,' she would say, 'with you, it was another matter.' They had joked enough, bitterly, in the following years, about Emily's heroic confidence: 'Christ,' they would say to each other, clutching small wailing babies, stewing scrag end, wandering dully round the park. 'Christ, if only we'd *known* what we had to *go* through, if only we'd known—' but in the very saying of it, betrayed (in Emily's case) bruised (in Rose's case) and impoverished (in both cases) they had smiled at each other, and laughed, and had experienced happiness. Life had been so much better, and so much worse, than they had expected: what they had not expected was that they were both happy people, incapable of resisting, incapable of failing to discover the gleams of joy. It was no wonder that Christopher had cited infidelity with Emily in his divorce case, and all the more bitterly because there was no sexual element to create offence. How could one not resent the natural flowing of a resilient, indestructible personal joy? Such things must not be spoken of, they must not be admitted. But why are we alive, at all?

Rose smiled to herself, the zip completed.

'A brilliant invention, the zip, don't you think?' she said to Konstantin, whose programme was ending, whose bedtime drew near.

'I don't know about that,' he said. 'They get stuck, don't they?'

'Only if you're brutal with them,' said Rose.

And she chased him off to bed, so that she could watch the news in peace. When she had watched it, she read her book for a while, and then went to bed. She had just got into bed when the telephone rang, downstairs: she was so annoyed at the thought of getting up again that she nearly left it, but of course did not. But when she lifted it to answer, there was no reply. Instead, there was the sound of breathing.

'Who's that?' said Rose, but nobody answered.

'Who *is* it?' she said, again. The person was still there. She knew that it was Christopher; he had done it before. She would not give him the satisfaction of guessing that she knew, and quietly replaced the receiver. It promptly rang again, and this time she picked it up and put it down again without listening. It rang again, so she broke the connection and left the receiver off. Then she sat there, for a moment: her knees were trembling. It had frightened her, it seemed like a punishment for having thought that she could be happy. As now indeed she no longer was.

She went up to bed, still shaken. There were times when she thought he would come back, and attack her, as he had done in the old days, and at such times the thought of living without his attacks seemed an unreality, an impossibility. She dreamed often that he was threatening her, attacking her with a knife, murdering her, crushing her, trampling on her. She dreamed once that he had set wild animals on her and was watching quietly while they munched her legs, and felt little comforted when she woke to find that she had merely fallen asleep under a pile of heavy books. Once, just after the divorce, she had woken to find a strange man in her bedroom, and had been so relieved to recognise that it was not Christopher that the event, alarming enough in itself, had hardly worried her: the man, who had broken in through a downstairs window, ran off as soon as she awoke, and the police proved as little interested as she was in finding out who had it been, and what he had been after. Now, she remembered these things, and her knees were still trembling under the sheets. It served her right, it served her right, but why she did not know.

SIMON CAMISH MET Christopher Vassiliou at a party. He had known it was coming, so he was not surprised to see him, at the other end of the long room. It was a local party, given by a neighbour whose profession and status had for once managed to interest both Simon and his wife: he was a Junior Minister, and his wife and Julie had become acquainted through sending their children, in years now past, to the same nursery school. One of their children had a paralysed leg, in an iron brace, the result of a spinal injury in infancy; this child had been befriended by his own second child, and so the relationship between the two families had necessarily flourished, though on a slightly uneasy basis, for the other parents tended to be embarrassingly grateful for invitations and attentions that seemed to the children concerned entirely natural. It could not be good for a handicapped child, he often thought, to be the object of so much deprecation, and the fact was that Julie could take the situation no more naturally than the child's own mother: there was always constraint, and an atmosphere of excessive delicacy, which overflowed even into adult contacts, so that Simon, now, at this party, felt himself for no good reason especially responsible, especially admitted, cast in the role of protector and support. He had fulfilled this role initially by hovering around helping his host to help the waiter to administer drinks, and had then moved on to chatting to a deaf old man who shouted at him rudely, and a middle-aged lady from the Ministry who proved quite inaudible amidst the noise of other conversations.

While he tried to guess what she might be talking about, and find suitable expressions to demonstrate his attention, he was thinking of Rose, and of a story she had told him (brought to mind no doubt by his consciousness of the iron brace) about a child she had seen on a bus once, a little boy with a huge birth mark all over his face, and cheap glasses and short hair, sitting with his mother in silence—a cross, dumpy woman the mother was, a French-woman, it had taken place in Paris, this episode, during Rose's Grand Tour—and Rose had thought to herself poor boy, poor boy, and then the boy had got off at the bus stop outside the Hospital for the Enfants Malades, leaving his mother on the bus, and he had kissed her goodbye, and she had kissed him so tenderly, and he had run off, waving, smiling, radiant, illumined, his mother waving with a tender pride, the boy gawky thin and sparrow-like and marked, the mother no longer cross but smiling quietly to herself, reflec-tively, and Rose had remembered that sudden change of counte-nance, that sudden transformation of what she had understood to be a grim relation, and could never think of it without a lifting of the spirit. He had kissed his mother with such affectionate trust, she had waved and smiled with such delight in him. And oddly enough, the day after Rose had told him this story, he had himself been standing in a queue in his local greengrocers doing some weekend shopping for Julie, when he had noticed a boy—quite a large boy, about ten—who was just before him in the queue. The boy was with his father, a sober professional-looking man like Simon himself, his mind intent on his wife's shopping list—(avo-cado, melon, French beans, have you any Cos lettuce, it must be Cos, he knew the kind of list)—and the boy was talking, inces-santly, in an unnatural, strange, high-pitched voice, asking ques-tions, commenting, chatting away. At first he sounded normal enough, apart from the pitch of the voice, which was too distinct and high, but after a while Simon began to notice that the content of the chat was strange: what are those bananas, is that an orange, is this the grocer or the greengrocer, what is that box for, I've been in a shop before, have you—and things like this, the boy was say-ing. The father tried to hush him, aware that others as well as Simon were gradually becoming aware of the child's peculiarities: hush, Michael, hush, I'm busy, I can't concentrate, he kept saying, his eyes on his list, meaning not that he could not concentrate but that he did not wish to be betrayed. Simon wanted to speak to the child, he wanted to answer these melancholy bright questions, but he too, like the child's own father, lacked the natural touch, he did not know how to speak, and it was with a mixture of shame and gratitude that he heard the woman next to him take over the task. A homely woman, she was, and at first she started to talk to the child out of pure chatty gossipy goodwill, saying yes, those were bananas, but gradually her tone changed as she realised what was up, her voice became more tender, more kind, less mechanically jolly: she asked the boy questions, whether he often went shopping, did he like shopping, did he live nearby, questions to which he replied with what was clearly his characteristic note of inconsequence, sometimes hitting a relevant answer, sometimes, wildly off the mark. Then the woman, her purchase completed, left the shop, saying to the boy, Goodbye, perhaps I'll see you next Saturday, I'm always here. Good bye, good bye, said the small fat boy, beaming with enthusiasm. Then he turned to his father, who was still struggling with the purchase of endives, and said, in piercing tones, 'Did you hear that, Daddy? She talked to me, that lady. What a very *nice* lady, to talk to me.' And in a flash the father, saying hush, met Simon's eye and blushed darkly, Simon looked away in pain, and realised what it was that the child's odd tone meant: it was the odd mimicked cheerfulness of institutions, he had hit off perfectly, poor parrot, the horrid brightness of Matron, the optimistic parody, the impersonal forced friendliness. Perhaps he would talk like that for ever. He had no other speech.

Thinking of these things, and trying hard to look as though he was catching the muffled monologue of the lady who was talking to him, he suddenly caught sight of Christopher Vassiliou. He was interested to note that his first illogical reaction was to think that he should go and introduce himself, which, in fact, he shortly did, for he also noticed that Vassiliou was talking to a man whom he knew quite well, an extremely aggressive and frequently disagreeable academic. So, handing the lady from the Ministry back to those from whom he had received her, he made his way across the room, and greeted his acquaintance. He was congratulating himself, as he did so, on having effected the introduction thus naturally, without any evident intention on his own part, but Meyer's first words were, 'Why, hello, Simon, I was talking about you only the other day.'

'Who to?' said Simon, already nervous, recalling to himself that he had been a fool to approach Meyer so casually: Meyer looked back at him, with his offensive black beaky knowingness, glinting with some private satisfaction, and said, 'To Emily Offenbach. Simon, do you know Christopher Vassiliou? Christopher, this is Simon Camish.'

And he took, as it were, a step back, smiling, attending the results of what he clearly knew to be a deliberate offence. Simon and Christopher Vassiliou looked at each other, nodded, mumbled a greeting, Simon acutely aware of the fact that he felt as though he looked shifty, whereas the other man looked, as well he might, cool, curious, sardonic. There is a chance, said Simon to himself, that he has no idea that I have any connexion with him other than a casual connexion with Emily, which Meyer might well suppose sufficient to get things off on an interestingly bad footing: but on the other hand Meyer himself clearly knew more, and was not likely to conceal it. In the moment before speech became necessary, Simon found himself looking at Christopher, at his wide, heavy, elegant head, his brown slightly greasy hair, his dark glasses, his pallid skin, and thinking yes, that's it, he looks Greek, he looks like those wide-faced statues, insolent and blind and bland, an antique model after all, and a person, a person who will shortly speak. To forestall him, he spoke himself. I'd rather mix it myself than have it mixed for me, he thought, and what he said, to Christopher, was, 'Oh yes, Emily Offenbach. I met her for the first time a week or two ago. Do you know her?'

Christopher knocked some ash off the end of his cigarette. He opened his mouth, though not very significantly: he always spoke with his mouth half shut, as though to move the lips were an indiscretion, inviting betrayal or attack.

'Yes,' he said. 'Yes, I know Emily.'

And he waited, for the next round. Simon also waited, feeling he had done well so far. Meyer, not too pleased with this reticence, decided to give them another prod.

'An interesting girl, Emily,' he said, experimentally. 'A very clever woman. Completely wastes it. Hasn't done a thing with herself for years. Too late now, I'd say. I tried to get her a job once but she wouldn't touch it. Though you never quite saw the point of her, did you, Christopher?'

'Was there a point?' said Christopher.

Meyer laughed, enigmatically or meaninglessly; it was hard to tell which. Oh Jesus, thought Simon, and with a slight coldness on his skin he said, thinking that he might as well, 'As a matter of fact, I met her at your wife's.'

Meyer continued to laugh, in a silent, eccentric way that really did not sound at all probable. Christopher looked at Simon, and sighed, on an exhalation of smoke, as though with relief, a relief which Simon felt himself to share.

'Yes,' said Christopher. 'I thought you might have done. I thought I recognised the name. The children talk of you, sometimes.'

'That's kind of them,' said Simon.

And there was a slight silence, which was certainly not of hostility: recognising, perhaps, exactly this feature of it, Meyer, with perceptible effort, said, 'I met you two through Emily. If you remember. It was a long time ago.'

But the other two men had lost interest in him: they had done it without him, they did not want to know, they were not listening.

'I think I saw you once,' said Christopher to Simon. 'I'd got the kids in the car, and they shouted at you. They didn't think you'd seen them. You live round here?'

'Just round the corner,' said Simon.

'Yes, so do I,' said Christopher.

'I'm going to get myself another drink,' said Meyer. They ignored his statement. He left. Simultaneously they turned away, together, away from the room, to look out of the window, as though excluding the rest of the room: Christopher put out his cigarette, took out a packet, offered one to Simon, lit it for him when he accepted.

'It's a small world,' said Christopher, after some time, as they looked out of the window at the lawn and the daffodils.

'It's small because we make it so,' said Simon.

'Meyer, you know,' said Christopher, 'has been after Emily for years. God knows if he ever made it. He's a real bastard, is Meyer.'

'I've often thought so,' said Simon.

'Now look,' said Christopher, quietly, heavily, confidentially, full of a lassitude that Simon had felt coming upon himself for some time, 'now look. About those children.'

And he paused.

'They're nice children. Exceptionally nice children,' said Simon hopelessly and truly.

'That's what I've always thought,' said Christopher. 'Now look. I don't know what you know and what you don't know. You know it all, don't you?'

'Not all. I know some of it.'

'Well, you should know. What do you think about it?'

'About the case?'

'About the case.'

'I'd have thought,' said Simon, 'that you were wasting your time. And that's the truth. You must know it. You're a reasonable person, you must know it.'

'Who told you I was a reasonable person?' said Christopher, smiling. Simon smiled in response, recalling the same facts.

'You might as well tell me what you think,' said Christopher. 'It can't hurt anyone, can it?'

'I don't know. I don't know why you're doing it. That's what I don't understand at all, I don't understand why you're doing it—'

said Simon, even though, as he spoke, this became no longer the truth, for the answer, so obvious, so simple, struck him suddenly in the presence of this man with such force that he wondered how he could not have known it earlier.

'It's obvious why I'm doing it,' said Christopher. 'I'm doing it because I want them. I want them back. They're mine, I'm their father, I want them. I don't like living without them. I want them back.'

While he said these words, he stared at the carpet.

'Yes, but even so,' said Simon, 'it's pointless to set out by a method that won't achieve anything. You won't achieve anything this way, you'll only make it worse.'

'What other way am I supposed to employ? There is no other way. The only thing left for me to do is to sit around and keep my mouth shut. You should try that as a way of life.'

'I rather think I do, for different reasons,' said Simon.

'That's your affair,' said Christopher, but amicably, indeed with appreciation. 'That's your affair. But in my position, I've got to show something. I can't just take it. What would they think of me, if I just took it? The children, I mean. What would they think of me?'

'They can't much like what's going on now,' said Simon.

'Why should they like it? That's not the point. It's not their happiness I'm interested in.'

'What are you interested in, then?'

'I'm interested in them.'

'I doubt if the law will think so. I doubt if the law will consider your—activities express the right kind of interest.'

'That's because the law's got a bloody funny notion of human relations,' said Christopher.

'Some people might think it was you that had,' said Simon.

'But you don't think so, do you? I can tell that you don't think so.'

'I don't know what I think,' said Simon, truthfully.

'That's because she's got hold of you. She's brainwashed you,' he said, smiling pleasantly. 'She can put up a pretty good case for herself, that woman. She learned a few things from me, before she left me.'

'I thought you left her.'

'Ha. You see what I mean.'

'I'm not at all sure that I want to hear your side of the story.'

'You may not want to,' said Christopher, 'but you're going to have to. Because I'm going to tell it to you. Come on, let's get out of here. We'll go round to my place.'

'I can't,' said Simon.

'Why not?' said Christopher.

'There's my wife somewhere around, I can't leave her.'

'I don't see why not,' said Christopher. 'She's perfectly safe here, she'll come to no harm here.'

'No, I suppose you're right. Yes, of course you're right. I'll go and tell her I'm leaving,' said Simon: and indeed went and did exactly that. She did not seem perturbed: slightly drunk, very gay, she was too deeply engrossed in conversation to pay much attention to his departure. And so he set off with Christopher Vassiliou, through the spring dusk. They walked in silence, down the road and round the corner. Christopher had a top floor flat in a large family house. Simon had not known what to expect from it, and from Rose's comments about her husband's aspirations he had perhaps composed in his mind a glossy penthouse, full of the corrupt luxury articles that Rose herself so scornfully avoided, with copies of *Playboy* and motoring magazines lying on glass-topped tables. It was not like that at all. It was rather bare, as though little attention had been payed to it, and the furniture looked as though it had been provided by the parents of the family downstairs: there was a large carved mahogany sideboard with a mirror, a settee and chairs with wicker backs and claw feet, a glass-fronted inlaid cupboard with china in it, a couple of small odd useless tables, with twisty barley-sugar legs. The carpet alone, a long-haired thick white stringy woolly object, looked as though it might have been purchased expressly in a fit of deep depression. Simon, settling himself down with a glass of whisky, looked round, and could not at first place what it was that the room exhaled, so surprising was it. For it was unexpected: it was like Rose's: it was intimate. It was a brown and shadowy room, comfortable and curiously homely. Two long-finned, long-tailed goldfish swam in a large tank, confirming the domestic note. Rows of books stood on an arrangement of bricks and planks, an arrangement such as he had not seen since his student days. Evidently Christopher's aspirations, whatever they might be, were not as simple as he had hoped.

Nor, of course (though he had known this would be so, from the first moment of encounter) was his account of his marriage and its subsequent problems. Christopher did not embark upon discussion until he had provided them both with a plateful of food: they sat there, each eating bacon and baked beans and fried eggs and slices of bread, and then Christopher began. The tone of his voice, like the tone of the room, was low, and unlike the tone of most men it was obsessively personal: mumbling, low, monotonous, Christopher offered no explanations of externals, he behaved as though they did not exist, it seemed to be the underlying connexions that he was after, it seemed to be the truth that he was after. And listening to him, listening to his endless rambling dissertation on Rose's iniquity, on her selfishness, on her histrionics, on her desire to degrade Christopher by proving to him her own estimate of his own motives, it became clear to Simon that he would have to abandon, for ever, his hope, which had once been as strong as a certainty: his hope, that Christopher had married Rose for her money, simply, and would as simply, one day, forfeit her. Christopher, evidently, had no interest in the money at all. He had no guilt about it, either. It meant nothing to him. What he was interested in was power, and motivation, and emotion, and love. Listening to him was like listening to

Rose. It was as crazed, as unworldly, as immediately comprehensible. Simon had known it for some time. He had known it for certain, when he had seen the false Christopher with the child on his shoulders, in Cornwall. How could he have supposed such an image to represent Christopher, if he had not been afraid of the very truth? And later, on his return, seeing the real Christopher with the children in his car, he had known it all, in his heart.

'She undermined me,' Christopher was saying, staring intently at the rows of books, 'she undermined me, she has done from the beginning, she had no trust in me, she panicked as soon as she married me, she only did it to give herself a real fright, and then she couldn't face it when I turned out all right, when I was loyal to her, I'm telling you, she could have taken anything in me except my efforts at good behaviour, and I did try, I nearly killed myself trying, I ruined myself for her . . .'

And Simon watched the fish go round and round, and some flowers in a vase, and drank his drink, and his head turned like the fish in the bowl. After a while Christopher got on to the subject of the children: Rose's obstinacy, the dreadful school they went to, her childish obstinacy in keeping them there, her ignorance of what really went on in schools like that, her ignorance of what it was like to have suffered, the way she had taken the children from him, and tried to stop him teaching them to roller-skate, her unrealistic attitudes, her stubborn perverse wicked refusal to give them a chance in life. She's demented, he said, she's demented, I don't mind what she does with herself, she can sit in a bus shelter for the rest of her life if she wants to, but I'm damned if I'll leave those children to sit there with her. And anyway, I know her, she'll not be satisfied with sitting in that dump for another ten years, she's brewing something else up, I know she is, she'll get used to it there and she'll want something worse, she'll be dragging them off to a leper hospital with her before the year's out, just you wait and see, if I don't do something about it to stop her. You've no idea, said Christopher, how absolutely wicked and selfish people are when they get hold of this idea of being good. They destroy everything about them. They end up in a burning desert. You know what I mean.

Yes, I know what you mean, said Simon, too depressed for words.

So you see, said Christopher. I want to rescue the children. That's all. What do you think will happen to them, if I don't? When they reach the age of twenty-one. What do you think they'll do, with all the money they come in to? Give it all away, to black Africa?

I don't know, said Simon.

They'll go to pieces, said Christopher. You know they will.

Miserably, Simon shifted in his chair. He had to speak up for her, but did not dare, he had not the confidence, he did not know how to phrase his faith in her, he wondered if it had not been destroyed.

'I don't know,' he said, finally. Christopher had run down into silence. 'I don't know,' he repeated, a little more firmly. 'I don't think they will necessarily go to pieces. I think you underestimate what she is doing for them. I think it will mean something to them. Even when things are very different.'

He wanted to explain that he had never had much respect for the view that one's children will not thank one for sacrificing them to a principle. He had begun to think, on the contrary, that children will not forgive one for sacrificing principles to them. But it was too late in the evening, he could not work it out. What he did say was, in support of Rose, 'And I don't think,' he said, 'that Rose had any intention of going off to a leper colony. She seems very well settled where she is,' he said, with more confidence.

'Don't you believe it,' said Christopher. 'She's just biding her time. Once every five years or so, she breaks out.'

'Perhaps she's changed,' said Simon.

'Don't you believe it,' said Christopher. 'People don't change. I don't believe that people change.'

'You have changed,' said Simon. 'From your own account, one would imagine that you had changed.'

'No, I haven't changed,' said Christopher. 'I've just put on a bit of weight and had my hair cut. I haven't changed.'

'If people don't change,' said Simon, finishing his second glass of whisky, 'then why is it that they cease to care for each other?'

'They don't,' said Christopher. He paused, lit himself his tenth cigarette, and said, 'they don't. Sometimes they get each other wrong and find out about it. But they don't stop caring.'

There was a long silence.

'She shouldn't have divorced me,' said Christopher. 'She had no right to divorce me. And she knows it. And if she's happy now, as you say she is, she has no right to be. That's why I'm going to go on making trouble for her. Because she has no right to be happy. And I won't let her be so. You can't make happiness out of destroying the lives of other people.'

'Unfortunately,' said Simon, 'that's exactly what a lot of people seem to do.'

'They may seem to,' said Christopher, 'but they don't.'

WALKING HOME, Simon realised that what had disturbed him so much was not so much what had been said—he had expected an attack, and the other side of any story is always disquieting—as the attitude behind it. The last thing he had expected had been a morality, a set of judgements, a structure as unrealistic and unworldly as Rose's own. All the accusations which he could, upon Rose's behalf, have levelled against Christopher, had been undone by the level of the attack. Of course she should not have divorced him. It was evident, both from what she had said of him, and he of her. It was as simple as that. If she had not done so, if she had not committed such an offence, there would have been no case. It was obvious. One should have known that intolerable effects, such as custody cases, were not likely to be thrown up by tolerable situations. The recognition excluded him totally. Meyer had pulled off more than he had intended. Simon, who had contemplated with some pleasure the prospect of an unrequited and undeclared affection, found himself denied even such an indulgence.

MEYER HAD IN FACT intended nothing very much. He never did. Reporting by phone, to Emily, later that night, the meeting of Christopher Vassiliou and Simon Camish, he had no sense whatsoever of making trouble, of taking the offensive. This was because he could in no way conceive of himself as an offender. The role, he firmly believed, was beyond his capacity. He considered himself a victim, having been brought up in circumstances that had indeed made of his weapon, the intellect, a dangerous weakness. Although the circumstances had changed, although he was no longer the crumpled, battered victim of his own talents, hiding in a corner from brutal scorn and malice and miserable taunts, he had become incapable of considering himself in any other light: as a boy he had been ineffective, so ineffective he must remain, and all his attempts to wound others were no more than an effort to redress an impossible balance. Himself bleeding, himself wounded incurably, savagely maimed from infancy, bayed by dogs and baited like a bear, he attempted (as he saw it) feebly, to scratch the invulnerable, to pinch and tease them a little, just to reassure himself, to comfort himself a little that if pricked, they too would bleed, never intending to cause anything other than the most minor irritation, and believing himself impotent even to do so little. He was incapable of apology, even when the evidence of offence was plain to all: he considered himself harmless. Not knowing his own strength, he did not know when to stop, he had no conception of victory, and it was not uncommon to see him, crowlike, standing on the battlefield on the corpses of dead victims, black, murderous, croaking angrily, pecking and tearing, with no notion that it was the slain that he fed upon, with no notion that he was doing other than fighting, still, for his life. People were terrified of him, and when he caught glimpses of this terror he took it as an insult, a mockery, for was it not evident, he thought, that any silly little student, any dumb wife or foolish old man, was better armed than he?

Emily had suffered from him for years, but she knew what he was up to. She knew, because she did it herself. She refused to bleed, she refused to become a sacrifice: instead, she returned blow for blow. He did not mind: from her he got what he expected, she justified uniquely, his picture of the world and of himself. It was the only form of love which reached him. She had not loved him at first; for years she had thought such a thing impossible; and then one day she had said to herself, well, this is something, this exists, and love might as well be the name that I give to it. So she had said that she loved him—to herself, not to him—and had felt much better thereafter. There is a lot in a word, she would say to herself. And in the name of love she slandered him behind his back, attacked him to his face, tormented him with her affection for others, and reported to him, maliciously, the ill-natured descriptions of him that she provoked wherever she went. In the name of love, these acts took on some grace.

'It's no use asking *me* what I think of Simon Camish,' she said now, crossly, late at night, pulling Oh-God-it's-Meyer faces at her husband, who was pulling inquisitorial, disapproving, bedtime faces at her. 'I don't know the man, I've only met him once in my life, what should I think about him? I don't think anything about him. What do you think about him?'

'He's got a ghastly wife,' said Meyer.

'He looked rather as though he had a ghastly wife, but then who hasn't? What's she like, then?'

'A blowsy nagging cow,' said Meyer, with satisfaction.

'Oh dear me,' said Emily. 'How very sad. Whatever did he marry her for, then? He looked quite a sensible person, I thought.'

'He married her for her money,' said Meyer. 'She's a wealthy woman, or so I'm told. Like your friend Rose. He must have an eye for it.'

'You keep Rose out of it. Anyway, what do you mean, he must have an eye for it? He's got nothing to do with Rose.'

'You should have seen him when he met Christopher. He looked as though he were meeting Jack the Ripper.'

'Oh, don't be childish, I don't believe it. He's just a friend, that's all. A perfectly innocent sort of person, I thought he was, and quite nice, too.'

'All Rose's friends look innocent. It's a trick of hers.'

'Now look, I've warned you, lay off Rose. You don't know her, you don't know the first thing about her.'

'On the contrary, I've had some very long and intimate discussions with Rose in my time.'

'Well, that just shows what a nice tolerant person she is. She has long and intimate discussions with all sorts of people because she doesn't want to hurt their feelings. It doesn't mean anything, with her.'

'Perhaps that's why I object to her so strongly.'

'Perhaps it is. You prefer nasty people like yourself.' She nearly said, nasty people like me, and would have done, had her husband not been listening. 'Anyway,' she went on, 'tell me about Christopher. He's nasty enough for anybody. How is he?'

'He seems well. He and Simon Camish went off together.'

'Oh, really.' Despite herself, she betrayed interest. 'Did they really? How very odd. People *are* odd.'

'They seemed quite to take to each other.'

'It's very easy to take to Christopher. I rather take to him myself. I rather fancy Christopher.'

'I thought you thought he was a nasty bit of work.'

'Yes, I do, but that doesn't stop me fancying him, does it? If one only fancied nice people, where would one be?' At this point Emily's husband got up and left the room, and so she continued, 'If one only fancied nice people, where would *you* be?'

'He's gone, has he?' said Meyer, used to these changes of tone.

'Yes,' said Emily.

And so the conversation degenerated, from gossip to a more mutual and personal form of abuse. Nevertheless, when Emily finally rang off, it was Christopher she was thinking of, and not Meyer, and Meyer knew it. She was thinking that she had indeed, for years, fancied Christopher, despite—or possibly because?—she had heard the worst version of him, the worst indictments made by the best qualified authority, his wife. She had known all too well that it was a combination of boredom and masochism that had attracted her to Christopher, but the knowledge had been of little use to her: she had suffered just the same. She had, in total concealment, watched him, and waited for his comings and goings, and listened to accounts of his misdemeanours: she had treated him with the off-hand contempt with which she treated most men, and listened with sympathy and love to Rose's misery, and all the time she had been thinking that she could herself have asked for no greater happiness than to be hit on the head by one of his vicious blows, the effects of which caused her so much genuine sorrow when manifested, in bruises and black eyes, upon Rose's body. She would have died happily from his violence, she would have lain down and asked for it. And all this she had hidden, of necessity, until it had quietly perished from suffocation, of its own accord. It was gone now, she felt nothing of it, except a nostalgic amazement that she ever had felt so much in so poor a cause, against her better judgements. She should feel pleased, she told herself, that she had successfully persuaded both Rose and Christopher that she regarded Christopher with nothing but disapproval and loyal, transferred indignation: she should feel even more pleased that she did now indeed regard him with little more. She had behaved well, she had kept quiet, she had silently murdered her own inappropriate emotions, so that now they were indeed dead, beyond revival: attention from Christopher now she would have found merely embarrassing, a humiliating reminder of what a fool she had once been. But it was sad, it was sad, that people should be like this. She stood up, and smoothed out her black woollen skirt, and sighed, and took off her glasses, and rubbed her eyes. It was too difficult, she was tired, she was getting older. She knew herself too well. There was no longer any excuse for behaving badly, and it was no longer a struggle to behave well. She had won some dreary victory. Even Meyer she had transformed from a threat into a family jester, a licensed irritant. One could not even regret the victory, for there could have been nothing better. She sighed again, and stretched, and went to bed.

SIMON HEARD NOTHING from Rose for weeks, and did not contact her. He felt as though he had lost her. At first he thought that he had resigned her, to Christopher's greater claim—he could not get Christopher out of his mind, his muttered, monotonous complaint, his tale of woe, his plateful of fried eggs, his wretched goldfish, his air of desertion—and then he began to fear that he had too well taken in what Christopher had said of her, that he had been convinced, as might a judge or jury, that Rose was not what she appeared, that her apparent virtue was truly a dim reflex of the voracious self, that she had been corrupting, not abused. Fortunately he was able to deflect himself by work: a case which he had been promised at Easter had come up, a case of such interest that it absorbed him completely. It was a closed shop case, in which he found himself representing the Union. The Union had behaved extremely badly, having refused renewal of membership to the plaintiff for highly dubious reasons. He had never had any dealings with this particular union before: it was a small, tightly knit, not particularly powerful one, and the more he inspected it the less democratic its methods appeared. Its shop stewards were, it turned out, more or less in the pockets of the management. They told their members what to do and what not to do, according to the shifts of managerial favour. Simon was amazed that they had not been challenged before. The man who had now challenged them was one

Herbert Alfred Jowitt, who had tried to organise some rival break-away group of representation: he had unfortunately, while doing this, allowed his membership of the original union to lapse, and had thus lost his job, without having been able to set up any viable alternative. The Union was refusing to allow him to rejoin. Simon, investigating the ostensible reasons for their refusal, found them to be unfortunately perfectly valid. It was very difficult to argue that they were not, as Mr Jowitt soon discovered. Simon, studying various other recent breakaways, such as the Ambulance one, found that on every count poor Mr Jowitt had the virtue of having acted with perfect good faith and under some provocation. There were no skeletons in his cupboard. But alas, his case had been taken up by members of Parliament, by the press, by television pundits, and it was being treated not as an internal affair, concerning the running of the Union itself, but as a matter of principle. The closed shop was under bitter attack. Why should a man not be free to work where he wants, clamoured certain sections of the Press. The Tyranny of the Unions, shouted others. FREEDOM TO WORK, MAN'S BASIC RIGHT, one hypocritically declared. A real Union hunt was on. And that was not the point at all. Mr Jowitt had wanted not no Union—he was a keen Union man—but a better one. He had mis-timed his operations, that was all. It was because he hadn't a proper Union that he now found himself where he was. And Simon, representing the Union, in fact found himself representing the management, who were delighted at the dismissal of the troublesome Mr Jowitt. On the other hand, it was a case that could not be lost. Simon could not afford to lose it. Because this is how it is in this case, he patiently explained to angry ill-informed friends, is of no relevance whatsoever. It is the principle which we must support.

The principle is doing an innocent man out of a job, he was told.

That's not my affair, said Simon.

You're defending the wrong cause for the right reason, he was told.

That's right, he would say. That's how it is.

And of course, the bigger the clamour, the more important it became not to lose. The reinstatement of Mr Jowitt would have been a disaster. The triumph of the Union-bashers would have been as great as the chagrin of his employers, who had no desire whatsoever to employ any non-union labour. It would have been far too expensive for them. They kept very quiet, the employers. Not so employers in other fields, where unions had made more successful attempts at representing their membership. It was a glorious collision. Simon applied himself vigorously. His industry and his eloquence payed off. He won his case, and Herbert Alfred Jowitt had to leave the scene. Later, looking back more calmly, Simon saw that he could hardly have lost it, unless he had played his cards very badly. Whatever the pressure of public opinion, whatever the true facts of the case, the union had had a perfect legal right to get rid of Jowitt. It had exercised its right, quite correctly. Its right to do so was vindicated. Everything had worked out satisfactorily. The Union remained corrupt and Simon pocketed his fee. He hoped that the publicity would have created a few more Jowitts, who would set about the union with more circumspection. He resolved never to work for the Union again. And that, as far as he was concerned, was that. But he emerged from the case a little battered. It had not been easy, trying to hold on to the thread in such a maze. At times, indeed, he had wondered if there was a thread at all. But looking back, from the daylight on the other side, he could see that without it he might well have lost, and been lost. The wood and the trees, as Jefferson had said. Jefferson congratulated him, warmly, upon his handling of the matter. I couldn't have done it myself, he said, grinning ambiguously.

One of the by-products of the case was that Julie, for the first time, recognised that there might be something in being a lawyer after all. It had been so widely reported that it was familiar even to those who do not read law reports, and Simon was quite touched to see Julie's limited imagination blossom under the sun of publicity.

Belatedly, she began to work out the possibilities before her husband, possibilities which had exercised him surreptitiously for years: she shamefully saw him on the Bench, she saw him as Lord Chancellor, she saw him robed and celebrated, she saw herself dining out with Prime Ministers, whose social cachet would compensate for the tedium and lack of style of their conversation. She became quite friendly, and he had the unfamiliar satisfaction of hearing her discuss his interests and attitudes with friends and acquaintances, as though she were proud of them, instead of bored by and indifferent to them. He had come to expect so little from her that he was pleased by this small relief. Coming into the house one night, he heard her on the phone, saying, 'Yes, of course we'll be there—I'm sorry I haven't been in touch for so long, Simon's been so busy, you know, with this USTK case—' (she had even got the initials off, she dropped them casually, as though dropping a title)—'that we really haven't been able to get out much. But of course we'll be there, yes, we're looking forward to it—' And she rang off, and turned to him, smiling, almost welcoming.

'That was Clare Cookson, reminding us we're supposed to be going to this concert at the Town Hall tomorrow night,' she said. 'You hadn't forgotten, had you?'

'No, no, of course not,' he said: though, amazingly, he had. It was the meeting at which Rose was due to speak, and he had dropped it from his mind as he had dropped her. The recollection, and the fact that he had had to be reminded, disturbed him: but nevertheless, he found himself there the following night, having made no effort to get out of it. It was the kind of event that inspires more tolerant hearts than Simon Camish's with a violent disgust for the human race: there could be few there, he thought, complacent enough to endure it without a touch of mortification, though some, perhaps, were hardened in charity. There they sat, the affluent, in six-guinea seats: perhaps, Christ knows, he thought, they are actually patting themselves on the back for being there, perhaps they do not realise what a condemnation it is to be on such a mailing list. Come the Revolution, he thought, looking up and down the glittering rows and nodding and smiling at friends—he spotted Nick and Diana, amongst others—come the Revolution, here are a few heads that will roll. It was quite comforting, to be able to dislike so many people all at once, after the confusing loyalties of the past few weeks' work. We will all be strung up from lamp-posts, he thought, amused by the very idea of it: though he couldn't see the USTK doing much in the way of stringing.

He inspected his programme. It informed him that there would be one interval: before it there would be folk songs by the well-known socially-conscious singer Jenny Page, a recitation by the well-known TV personality Edgar Edwards, and an address by Mrs Rose Vassiliou: during the interval there would be drinks at the Bar: and afterwards there would be Old Time Music Hall songs in which it was hoped the distinguished audience would participate. He read this, carefully, then turned to his neighbour, who was the wife of a well-known socially-conscious TV commentator, and said, 'Pretty decadent, I'd say, wouldn't you?' She snorted crossly, and offered him some peanuts out of a bag.

'It's *awful*,' she said. '*Awful*. Never mind, though. Have some nuts. I'm starving. It'll be over soon. Or one can always sneak out halfway.'

He munched some nuts, gratefully. The lights went out, the curtains opened, and a man came on and started making introductory noises. He was quite dreadful. Then the singer came on, and was even worse. She sang protest songs, thinking to honour the spirit of the occasion, and became visibly irritated by the tepid applause that greeted her efforts. She was used to better, from the gullible young, and flounced off the stage with an air of pique. The recitation was not too bad: it was meant to be funny, and nearly was. And then it was time for Rose. The link-man came on again and cracked a few irrelevant and tasteless jokes, and then said a little helplessly, 'And now I have the pleasure of presenting to you Mrs Rose Vassiliou, a name which is I am sure familiar to you all, who is going to explain to us what we are all doing here.' And with a wave of the arm towards the wings, he ushered Rose in. At the sight of her, Simon felt a pang of such anguish, remorse and love that he had to look away in pain: because there she was, herself, misjudged, maligned, utterly uncontaminated, agonisingly embarrassed, wandering nervously towards the microphone, as pale as a ghost, as uncomfortable in her role as a small child offering a bouquet, totally lacking in complicity, in address, in the wicked knowingness that informed the whole scene. Histrionics, he said to himself, histrionics, she's incapable of such a thing: and so she was, for she was inaudible. She spoke, but what she said could hardly be caught. She presented a spectacle, it was true: in the long white dress and flat red shoes in which he had first met her, she stood there, twisting her hands, clearing her throat between each phrase, unable to pursue her sentences through terror. It was a sight, but she was the victim of it, not its engineer. It was not herself that had organised this lamentable appearance: she endured it, rather, in modesty, she submitted herself, with no sideways winks, no deprecating smiles, no effort to ingratiate herself, apologetically, with her audience. She hardly looked at her audience. She forced herself to look ahead, some of the time, but the effort was visible. The audience coughed and rustled, quietly, wanting it to be over.

She cannot like it, thought Simon. Whatever has been said of her, this kind of thing she cannot like.

On her way off the stage she tripped over the flex of the microphone and nearly fell: the link-man caught her. The pain in his chest was such that he too had the sensation of having fallen.

In the bar, five minutes later, he found her. She was talking to Lady Bresson and one or two other people, smiling, trying hard to put at ease those made uneasy on her behalf, and when she saw Simon she moved across to him, as though she had been looking for him, and took the hand which he offered. She caught at him nervously, as though requesting forgiveness. Fortunately he had had the foresight to tell Julie, though belatedly, that he had already

met Rose at Nick and Diana's, in the expectation of such an encounter: but nevertheless he felt uneasy, as he introduced the two
women: he felt puzzled and confused, as he saw Rose and Julie
shake hands. It was not that he feared indiscretion, on either part,
for Rose he trusted, and Julie had nothing to tell. Nor had he ever
discussed Julie with Rose: he had even, honourably, for the most
part, resisted implications, which had been difficult enough, in
view of Rose's reckless confidences, and in view of the compromising fact that he had been there listening to them at all. So really he
had nothing to be uneasy about, he thought, except the treachery
of his own emotions, which he could quite well keep to himself.

But a few minutes later he had to think again. Because, alas,
Rose and Julie did not stop talking to each other. They seemed to
be getting on far too well. Talking, himself, laboriously, to Lady
Bresson, he could hear them at his elbow, chattering away. Too late
he remembered Rose's insatiable friendliness, her quite excessive
tolerance. He hadn't seen her in company since their first meeting,
months earlier, and had forgotten her absurd mixture of nervous-
ness and sociability. She was discussing with Julie her horror of
appearing on platforms, her panic whenever she found herself
doing a radio programme, her clumsiness in tripping over the microphone, and Julie was listening with fascination, offering past
embarrassments of her own as consolation. What if they become
friends, he suddenly thought. It would be impossible, awful. But
why not, after all? He recollected his own meeting with Christopher, which had taken such an unexpected turn. It was too complicated, it was really too dreadful, and it had begun with such
simplicity.

For the second half of the programme, Rose asked if she could
come and sit with them: she had been behind the wings for the first
half, and now, she said, she could sit out front and relax and enjoy
herself. So, when they returned to their seats, he found himself sitting between them, without having had an opportunity to exchange one personal word with Rose. He was annoyed with her for

concealing her knowledge of him quite so well, though how could he complain, when he himself presented nothing but indifference? But just after the curtain went up, this time on a woman singing, 'There was I waiting at the Church', he saw her take out her packet of Woodbine and start scribbling on it: he waited, and she handed it to him. She had written: what did C. say to you? I must see you tomorrow, it's urgent. He read it, put it in his pocket, but did not look towards her. She was looking at the stage: he did the same. The songs went on and on, some jolly, some morbid. Some of the audience joined in the choruses: Simon did not. A man recited a Victorian ballad about two children dying in an attic: it was powerful stuff, and under its cover he glanced at Rose, and was not at all surprised to see that her eyes were full of tears. During the next piece, which was a rendering of 'Ye Banks and braes of bonny Doon', she began to weep quite copiously, sniffing hard, the tears rolling down her cheeks.

Ye mind me of departed joys,
Departed never to return,

the singer sang, and Rose had to get out her handkerchief. At the end of the song, she looked at him, and he at her, and she whispered, 'Oh goodness me, what an absolute *fool* I am.' He agreed, but he liked it.

At the end of the evening, the Cooksons had invited them back for a drink: he would have had to go anyway, as Julie wanted to, but when he had discovered that Rose was going too, the possibility of driving Rose home had sprung instantly into his mind: he offered her a lift to the Cooksons, as soon as the programme ended, and she accepted it. She and Julie sat in the back of the car together, talking, until they arrived. He could not get a word in. They were talking about their children, discovering common attitudes that he knew for a fact not to exist: at each point, one or the other of them was lying.

At the Cooksons, they were divided, settled at opposite ends of the room, with two large chairs with people in between them, and he thought he might be able to have a word with Rose, but was again prevented by Herbert Cookson, who advanced upon Simon and started to interrogate him about his last case. They talked about closed shops, and anti-union legislation, and the division of loyalties which Simon had clearly suffered: in a way he was pleased, because the conversation became general, and as Rose was listening, he thought she might excuse his recent neglect of her on the grounds that he had been exceptionally preoccupied. He found himself, finally, defending the role of paternalism in politics, a position so illogical that it made him miserable even to think about it, and yet at the same time inevitable: Herbert Cookson, himself a middle-aged middle-class civil servant, had accused him of class treachery in becoming a lawyer at all, and in daring to talk of the Unions with the disrespect with which he had just treated them: 'It's all very well for you to criticize,' he said. 'You're exactly the sort of person who ought to be on the inside, if you care as you say you do. The 1944 Education Act ruined the country by removing people like you from the role they ought to have been playing, by creaming them off, by making them spend their lives getting degrees and good jobs...'

'Yes, yes, yes,' said Simon, 'I know all that, I know it'—and he went on to try to explain his confused feelings about representation, and the fact that one can never represent what one is part of without becoming something other, and the fact that some people are congenitally so stupid that they cannot possibly be represented by their own kind—mentally defectives, children—and the way in which democracy had to assume that all are equal, in degree of responsibility, whereas in reality some are wicked and some are gullible, some exploiters and some exploited, and mediation must take place between the two. 'The law as an institution,' he ended up saying, 'as an institution, is admirable, they've got it all wrong, it's the uses to which it is put that are wrong. It isn't the letter that kills and the spirit that giveth life at all, it's the other way round. The spirit kills and the letter gives life.'

'Ha,' said Herbert Cookson, his fat soft fingers closed comfortingly round a squat glass. 'Ha. You believe in an ideal of public service, Simon. How very unusual, at your age.'

'I see no option but to believe in it.'

'Yes. But public service is a spirit. And people don't do it in the right spirit, believe you me. The letter survives but not much else. What do you think we all go into it for? For the security. And once we're in we spend all our time trying to stop other people getting our jobs and our promotions. Where's the use in that? We don't get things done because we don't want them done.'

'Yes, I know,' said Simon. 'We may not want them done, for our own reasons. But still, there's a machinery for doing them. And that's what matters. That there should be a machinery, for doing the things, so that they get done, by those who can, for those who can't. It doesn't matter about the spirit, it doesn't matter if one believes in the case, so long as the case is represented.'

And Rose, who had been listening intently, suddenly said, 'You don't believe that, Simon. It's ridiculous, your saying that. You only say it because you care so much that you simply can't believe that other people don't. You simply can't believe that other people don't do things in the right spirit, you can't believe they don't care. You never think of yourself, you don't know how much other people are always thinking of themselves. If it weren't for people like you taking an interest in making the machinery there wouldn't be any. It's ridiculous to pretend that you don't care and that it would all work all right if you didn't. Ridiculous.'

And she stopped, as abruptly as she had begun. There was a short, giveaway silence. She blushed. She had spoken personally, irritated, with love: a tone that could not have been taken by a stranger to a stranger. It was as certain a betrayal as lipstick, lies, love letters, unexplained telephone calls. It was noticed by everybody but Julie, who, bored by abstraction, had started another conversation with Mrs Cookson about the protest singer. Simon was confused, he did not know what to say. Because after all, there was nothing to betray, except a few illicit conversations. And the satisfaction that she had just given him was more than he had ever expected, more than he had ever had.

Rose looked down at her knee, and started to fiddle with her bag, a fraying knitted object.

It was Herbert Cookson that took up the damaged topic, kindly, expertly converting Rose's attack into a general theme, speaking, as Simon had done, of the exploiters and exploited, and of men of goodwill who cannot believe that men of ill-will could positively, vindictively, out of self-interest, pursue such a policy as one which results, for instance, in unemployment. 'They don't miscalculate,' said Cookson, 'you do them too much credit if you think they miscalculate. They mean it to happen, exactly so.'

Simon, still confused, watched him speaking, saying nothing.

He was a short, fat, broad-faced mild man, Herbert Cookson, rather ugly, with a heavily mottled skin and wispy grey hair, prematurely ageing. He had a weathered look, as well he might have: his life was a succession of honourable and successful disasters, which had given him promotion after promotion, without the satisfaction of seeing much result for his labours. He had spent years composing and drafting a Bill to control the sale of land in rural areas, a subject very near his heart, only to find it killed at birth by a change of government: he had then been deflected to the promotion of industrial development on Anglesey, which had been undercut by a new version of his own original Bill. Finally he had had a little more to show for himself with a New Town or two, but they had begun to depress him: having started in faith, he had found the cheese-paring and commercialism of the reality so gloomy that he had almost lost interest in ameliorating what was left in his realm. Still, he was not a gloomy man: the dashing of projects, far from depressing him, had given him a good-humoured benevolent Olympian irony. He expected little, and was pleased with what he got. His wife was a large, quiet, efficient woman, gentle and ruthless: she spent much of her time going round making people pay up their subscriptions for the various committees and bodies which she represented. People paid up quite cheerfully, because she was so nice to them, and managed to make them feel especially favoured by her calls and solicitations. She also wrote detective stories, in her spare time, under a pseudonym. They had two children, one of them still at school, the other in her first year at university: and Mrs Cookson, who had overheard the end of the conversation about closed shops, now drifted over to Simon in her soft flat shoes, settled herself on the arm of a chair, and said,

'You know, Simon, I've been meaning to ask you for a long time about Victoria, who seems to have got herself into an awful mess at Northam—she's at the university there, reading sociology, you know—and one can hardly believe it, but she's refusing to belong to the Union and there's been the most frightful row about it. She's very upset, or at least she sounds as though she is, but then young people exaggerate so much, don't you think?'

'On what grounds has she refused to belong?'

'I don't really know. She's so vague about it. Why did she say it was, Herbert?'

'Wasn't it because she and some of her friends disapproved of the Union trying to dictate terms about the size of the portions of mashed potato?'

'No, no, don't be absurd, that was months ago, she didn't resign over that, I think it was something to do with the Union locking her Director of Studies into his study because he said they couldn't refuse to submit at least one piece of written work per term. And then they let him out again because he burst into tears and said he had to get home, it was his wedding anniversary. I couldn't quite make out which Victoria objected to more strongly, the fact that he'd been locked up in the first place, or the fact that they'd let him out again for such a non-political reason. Anyway, she said she didn't want to be represented by people who did that sort of thing, and resigned. But of course she couldn't really resign because she'd already paid up for a year, so she went to the Union office and demanded a refund, and they wouldn't give it her, and so she and some of her friends locked the Union officials into the Union office, and continued to demand their refund with menaces. I always knew she shouldn't have gone to that place, one could tell there'd be trouble, but I suppose I thought she'd like it.'

'Perhaps she does like it?'

'Perhaps she does. I suppose she could hardly *sound* as though she were enjoying it, could she? I do really find it all quite deplorable, don't you?'

'Did she get her money back?'

'No, of course she didn't, on the contrary, she was threatened with expulsion by her director of studies if she went on making a nuisance of herself.'

'Her director of studies sounds a curious character.'

'Oh, I don't know, she thinks he's very good, she thought it was quite reasonable to do one piece of written work a term. But it is a bit worrying. Perhaps you could give her a little lecture on Union Security when she gets home.'

'I must admit I'm as disaffected as she is by the idea of Union Security at the moment. And also one must admit that she had a point, in not wanting to associate with a Union who acted so unconstitutionally.'

'But they don't believe in constitutions. They believe in direct action.'

'Then they can hardly have much feeling about Union Security can they?'

'I rather gathered that the Union is taking the line that it needn't offer to protect her, as she had already proffered her resignation. So she said that as they had refused to accept it, they had either to stand up for her or give her her money back. So she was back to square one.'

'You seem remarkably unconcerned.'

'Well, it is all rather comic, don't you think?'

'I suppose it might even prove educational? And there's no real question of expulsion, is there?'

'No, of course there isn't,' said Herbert Cookson, who had been listening to this interchange with amusement. 'Certainly not. I wrote to Bert Hammond, who's up there, and he said it was all absolute nonsense, nobody took it seriously at all. They just play games, that's all.'

'She could set up a breakaway union, if she's got enough support. Send her along to me when she gets back and I'll tell her how to do it.'

'I don't know if it'll even be necessary next year, because the present lot of representatives will be leaving, and the next year isn't so militant. They've all quietened down recently, because they're doing their finals.'

'You don't mean to say they still consent to do exams?'

'Amazing, isn't it? They're such an inconsistent lot, young people. They tell us we're hypocrites, and so we are, but I'd rather be a hypocrite than a fool.'

'I don't know,' said Rose, who had been listening quietly, recovered. 'I think they're hypocrites too. There's this girl I know, she's about nineteen I suppose, and she comes round to see me sometimes, God knows why, I met her at some meeting or other last year and she sort of latched on to me, and I must say I did suspect it was because I would always cook her a nice meal and let her sleep in one of the children's beds if things went wrong, and I didn't really mind, because she's quite appealing in a way—she sort of drifts around, and doesn't do anything much, and believes in the abolition of property and money and all the rest of it, and the pointlessness of work, and I thought, that's fine, there's even something rather touching about it, and I didn't really mind her lecturing me on my bourgeois mentality while she gobbled up my bacon and eggs. And then a few weeks ago she went off on a holiday to Scotland with some friends, and I thought good, that's got rid of her for a bit, but no such thing, because in a couple of days she was back again, with her arm in plaster, because they'd had a car accident on the way up. And guess what she wanted me to do.'

'Pay her hospital bills?'

'No, no, that I wouldn't have minded, it was worse than that. She wanted me to recommend her a solicitor and lend her the money to sue the girl who'd been driving the car. I couldn't believe my ears. She told me some rigmarole about the insurance, and about how they'd only been covered for third parties, and I said, well, she must have known that, and if she didn't she ought to have found out, and that if she didn't bother about things like that and went around with people who didn't bother then it was no good complaining later. And then I said, what do you want to sue her *for*, and she said damages, and I said what damages, and the truth was that there had been no expense involved at all, and she could hardly have said that she was suffering loss of wages because she'd never earned a penny in her life. I just couldn't believe it. That anyone could be so vindictive. The girl was her friend, after all. How could one sue a friend?'

'Some people would.'

'Yes. But she wasn't some people. She didn't believe in insurance and litigation and lawyers and money.'

'I suppose if she'd been seriously injured, she might have had a point?'

'But she wasn't seriously injured. She's sprained her arm, that's all. It hadn't cost her a penny, so why should she want money for it?'

'Did you lend her the money for the solicitor?'

'No, I didn't. I refused. I even tried to ask her what she wanted the damages for, and she couldn't think of a very good reason, and finally said, well, she had lost her holiday in Scotland, hadn't she. So I pointed out that some people insure against that kind of thing, the kind of people she despises so much, and those that don't can hardly complain. It was her attitude that upset me. It was so vindictive. She wanted something for nothing, and was annoyed when she couldn't get it. And she expected me to sympathise with her. That's what upset me most of all.'

'Did she take it to a solicitor?'

'I don't know. I haven't seen her since. I don't think that the girl who was driving could have been held responsible for the accident anyway, Charlotte said there wasn't another car involved, she swerved to avoid a child and went into a wall. I expected at any moment to hear her say she was going to sue the child. She did mutter something about its parents. Don't you think it's shocking?'

Yes, shocking, everyone agreed, and sighed, and then began to laugh, as they took note of the attitudes into which they had fallen: comfortable middle-aged people, sitting around in easy chairs drinking alcohol, deploring the wickedness of youth. But it was too late to stop, even though they had become aware of what they were doing: indulgently, recklessly, they went on with it, capping anecdote with anecdote, comparing the folly of one young person with the laziness of another, the venality of one with another's parasitic idealism. Herbert Cookson had a good story about the son of a friend who had pawned the family silver: another man, whose presence Simon had hardly noticed until that moment, produced an account of a militant student of his who had sold out on all his following upon the offer of a job in a thinly-disguised advertising agency, and Clare Cookson described a girl who had warmly advocated the liberation of women and the free-for-all sexual permissive society until she became pregnant, and had then, with equal self-righteousness, insisted that the man involved should marry her, because if he didn't he would be an exploiter and a profiteer. They laughed at these stories, aware that they shouldn't really be allowing themselves to tell them: 'But after all,' said Clare Cookson, 'we must get it off our chests once in a while, mustn't we?' And indeed, that is what they did: they exorcised, for the moment, the ghost of righteous youth, and ended up feeling much better for it, defending even Victoria's ridiculous involvement—because she will, after all, said Simon, learn something from it, at least she cares, at least she tries to make sense of things.

Only Rose seemed unappeased. Rose thought about the camel and the needle's eye. What was the point of knowing what was right, if one didn't then do it?

'I must go home,' said Rose, rising to her feet. 'I really must get back to my baby-sitter.'

Simon rose to his feet immediately, to offer her a lift, but he was too late: the other man, whose name he had never caught, forestalled him. He had not the confidence to insist, even though he thought that he saw Rose give him a look of dismay. A little encouraged by it, he followed her out into the hall, and under the cover of looking for Julie's coat he managed to say that he would ring her in the morning. 'Ringing won't do,' she said, 'I must come and see you, I must come and see you.'

'You'll have to come to Chambers then,' he said: and that was all they had time for, before Julie joined them.

WHEN ROSE GOT HOME, she found her baby-sitter Eileen had fallen asleep. Eileen had returned home: she had found her garage man and had been rejected by him. And there she sat, in Rose's armchair, the baby in a carry-cot by her, snoring slightly, her heavy dark face slumped into misery. Rose could hardly face waking her, she so much dreaded her complaints: she had had to listen to her mother's version endlessly. Mrs Sharkey was in despair about Eileen: she wouldn't do a thing for herself or the baby, she wouldn't even get up to feed it, she let it cry all night, when she changed it she dropped its nappies on the floor and left her mother to wash them. 'What can I do?' said Mrs Sharkey, 'I can't just leave them lying there, can I?' 'She'll pick them up, surely,' Rose had said, without much faith. Because the truth was, whyever should she pick up, what for, ever? There she sat, nineteen, finished, excluded for ever from what she might want to be. She would never try to make the best of things, the gulf between her reality and her aspirations was total, and would remain so. They would drag on for ever, she and her mother: her mother making the best of things, because that was her nature, the daughter letting things go, because that was hers. She couldn't even go to the bad, now, with a baby around: she'd done that already, and it hadn't proved much fun. Her face was heavy, like the face of a middle-aged woman. Some people, thought Rose, thinking of Charlotte, aren't even given a chance to betray themselves.

She bustled around a bit, not wanting to wake Eileen more directly and after a moment or two Eileen jerked and came round. Rose was tired, she had enough of her own on her mind, but she had to listen for half an hour to Eileen's complaints about her mother. She'd begun to think she'd have to get a job, just to get out of the house. That sounds a good idea, said Rose: but apparently it wasn't, because her mother had refused to mind the baby during the day, and she couldn't get it a place in a nursery. Anyway, said Eileen, she didn't fancy any of the rotten jobs she could get: there was one serving in the Greek shop, but the shop stank and she couldn't work there, and there was another one in the bedding factory but the hours were so long, and there really wasn't anything else she could do. There must be something, said Rose. Oh, I suppose it'll have to be the bedding factory, said Eileen: the nursery said it would take the baby when it was six months, but it would mean getting up at six thirty to walk it down there, because it was a long way.

Rose could see that she had, in fact, faced the bedding factory. No wonder she looked depressed. What a terrible moment it is, the moment at which one abandons possibility. Gone was Eileen the wicked lady, driving around in taxis, wearing fur coats, drinking cocktails: gone was Eileen the make-up girl with false eyelashes and a pink overall: gone was Eileen the garage man's girl, taking trips up the motorway in a fast car. Eileen picked up her baby, and sighed, and accepted a pound note. Her eyes were dark brown, soft, voluptuous: she looked at Rose with a profound reproach. Oh hell, thought Rose, get out of here, you lazy cow, before I offer to adopt that creature for you. For she accepted the reproach: there was no doubt about it, the glamour of her own example had done Eileen no good. The neighbouring thrill of publicity, the drama of violence, the excitement of divorce, all had helped to corrupt her. In the old days she had collected Rose's press cuttings, had borrowed her clothes, had come to take baths in her bath. (The Sharkeys had no bath: their house was on a controlled rent, and the landlord refused to spend a penny on it.) Christopher too had encouraged her, when she was fifteen: he had offered her cigarettes, drinks, rides in the car. I refuse to accept any responsibility, thought Rose, thereby accepting it. Get out, get out, get out, she thought. And Eileen went.

THE NEXT MORNING, Simon sat and waited for Rose. There were other things he was doing as well, but principally he was waiting. She had rung his clerk at nine, to say she would be in later in the morning, and had been given an appointment for eleven thirty.

She arrived upon the dot, and was shown in: she stood there in the doorway, looking round, clutching a folder of papers. She was trying to be sociable. What strange tasks she set herself.

'So this is where you work,' she said, gazing, at the desk, at the leather chairs, the oblong shapes of briefs and files and boxes, the red tape tied neatly round the white papers, the brown and red austere masculine outlines. She sat down, edgily. 'What a nice room,' she said.

'Do you think so?'

'Well, yes, don't you? What are those notices you have on the walls?'

'Oh, this and that,' he said, looking at the framed cuttings and handwritten messages. He did not like pictures. 'Things that struck me,' he said.

She put her folder down on the desk, got up, and wandered over to the wall, and started to read one of the framed notices: it was an extract from a judgement by Lord Justice Scrutton, written in 1920, which Simon had copied out while at Oxford, and kept on his wall ever since. It said

'. . . The habits you are trained in, the people with whom you mix, lead to your having a certain class of ideas of such a nature that, when you have to deal with other ideas, you do not give as sound and accurate judgements as you would wish. This is one of the great difficulties at present with Labour. Labour says, "Where are your impartial Judges? They all move in the same circle as the employers, and they are all educated and nursed in the same idiom as the employers. How can a Labour man or a trade unionist get impartial justice?" It is very difficult sometimes to be sure that you have put yourself into a thoroughly impartial position between two disputants, one of your own class and one not of your class.'

Rose read it with attention. He was used to these delaying tactics in clients.

'That's good,' she said, sitting down again. 'That's a good piece.'

'That's why I put it up.'

'Who was Scrutton?'

'A judge. A good judge.'

'Yes.'

He looked at her: she looked very worn. For some reason it seemed entirely natural for them to be sitting on opposite sides of his desk: it was as though the desk had always been there. It was his turn to speak, his initiative.

'Now then,' he said, 'what's the matter?'

'I don't know what to say.'

'Come on, now. It must be something.'

She had extreme difficulty in speaking.

'It's this case,' she said. 'I can't go on. I've had enough. I want to give up.'

'What do you mean, you want to give up?'

'I mean exactly that. I can't go on with it.'

He reflected.

'But it's not your case. It's his. *You* can't give it up. *He* would have to.'

'But he won't. That's why I've got to.'

'You can't.'

'Yes, I can. I thought of a way. I could give him the children. That wouldn't be illegal, would it? I could just say he could have them, and then he'd drop it, wouldn't he, because there'd be no point in going on, would there? And if he had the children, and I didn't claim them, then it would all be settled, wouldn't it?'

He was so startled by this extraordinary statement that he started to draw patterns on his blotting paper.

'Well, it would, wouldn't it?' she repeated.

Such possibilities crowded his head that he did not dare to look up: that she had gone mad, that she had never cared for the children anyway, that she had been plotting to get rid of them, that she was in collusion with Christopher for financial reasons. Finally, her silence forced him to speak.

'But why ever should you do that?' he said, at last.

'Because I can't bear to go on, I can't bear it. I've been thinking of ways out of it. I've been thinking till my brain splits, and it's the only answer. Don't look like that at me, it's the only answer. They'll be all right with him, he is their father, and I could see them sometimes, maybe, he'd let me see them.'

'But why on earth,' he said, collecting himself, 'why on earth have you decided this so suddenly? It's impossible, you know, it's quite out of the question, but it's such an amazing thing even to *think* of.'

'Oh, I don't know, it's everything altogether, it's not sudden really, I've been trying to train myself to face it, but I couldn't, I just couldn't—and then yesterday the solicitors sent me a copy of Christopher's affidavit, and it's so horrible, it's so horrible . . .'

She pushed it over the desk, and covered her face with her hands. Through her hands she muttered,

'I know you saw Christopher, Emily told me, I know what he must have said to you, I know why you didn't ring me. I've made my mind up, I've written myself off. I must learn to give up, I must learn to give up. It's so hard, it's so hard, but there's no other way. He is their father, after all, and I know it, I know that he's sane and I'm mad, so what else can I say, what else can I do? I'm leaving, I'm leaving the country.'

'You can't, you can't,' he said.

'Why can't I?'

'Because of the children, you must think of them.'

'Look,' she said, suddenly, sitting upright, taking her hands away from her face, staring at him wildly, 'look, it's no good, I'm not going on with that case. I renounce it. I refuse. I've committed enough crimes. I can't go through with this one.'

'But Rose, my dear girl, Rose, you're in the *right*, you silly woman, it's not you that's committing a crime, it's him if it's anyone, you're simply defending yourself, it's not a crime to defend yourself.'

'It is, it is,' she said, her voice unpitched, screeching, 'it is a crime, I can't do it.' She rose to her feet, and started to walk up and down. 'I can't do it. I must give in, I must give in or die, I know it. There is no right and wrong. Go on, read his affidavit, read it.'

'I don't want to,' he said.

'Look, Rose, calm down,' he said.

'I can't, I can't, I can't,' she said, still pacing.

'I don't want to read it,' he said, 'because I trust you. Look, I may not know you well, but I know you well enough. Of course there are two sides to every question, and I'm quite well aware that your husband's solicitors will have made out a good case for him, that's their job, after all, but there's no need for me to believe it, or for anyone.'

'But *I* believe it,' she said, pausing, turning on him. '*I* believe it, that's the point, he's right, he's right. I'm a hopeless mother, I know I am, I'm mean and mad and selfish, he's *right* about me, how can I defend myself when he's right?'

'Now look, Rose. Sit down. Please sit down. There, that's right. Now listen. I know enough about you to know that you are a perfectly adequate mother. And also I know enough about Christopher to know that he's a dangerous man, he's got it all worked out, he knows how to get you, I can see that—but you mustn't listen to him. No judge would listen to him. It doesn't exist, this case. It's ridiculous, I can't bear to see you in such a state about a case that doesn't exist. When I think of the cases that some people have to answer, and they do it, you can believe me, without turning a hair—it's nonsense, the whole thing is nonsense.'

'But even if the case went on, and I won it, what would I do then?'

'You would carry on as you do now. Exactly.'

'But don't you see that I can't? I couldn't live, if I'd done that to him.'

'You're not doing anything to him.'

'But I am. But I am. I've ruined his life, I know I have. I ruin everything. I can't go on. I shall take myself away.'

He did not see how she could possibly be serious, however much she might look it. But he did not know how to handle her either. He had seen her in distress before, he had seen her in tears even monotonously often, but now she was not crying, she was gone far away, she was no longer regarding herself with a detached amusement: her eyes were staring, her hands clutching involuntarily, her face was white and working with an accumulation of conflicting emotion, her whole being caught up, clumsily. So he did not try to handle her: instead, he stated the obvious.

'But you can't leave the children,' he said. 'It's an impossibility. You can't do it.'

'That's what I used to think,' she said, flinging herself once more to her feet. 'I thought that was it, that was the one thing that was a fact. I can't tell you the agony I've been through, knowing that there was no way out, because I couldn't move. It was like before the divorce, but worse. Like being in a trap, in a hole, on a tightrope, and every way I moved would be death. But not every way. Because if I give him the children,—*if* I did, *if* I did, then there would be a way out. I could move, it would be different, it wouldn't be the same trap. It's *all* I can do. It's the only move. And I can't bear not to move any more.'

'There must be other things you could do.'

'I could go back to Christopher. I could move house. It would come to the same thing. But that's all. That's the only other thing I could do. It's simple. Either he has the children, or I have them, or we both have them. It's unendurable for me to keep them. He's made it impossible. It would be impossible to go back to him. So there is only one answer.'

'You wouldn't consider,' he said (surreptitiously consulting the affidavit) 'compromising? By moving house?'

'How can I move house? It's my whole being that's there.'

'It's arbitrary. That it happens to be there.'

'Yes. It's arbitrary. But it's so. Can you imagine me, in a nice house in a nice district? Can you imagine it?' She was looking out of the window as she spoke: she turned on him, again aggressively, and said, 'I can't afford this case. I can't pay my solicitors. It'll ruin me. I can't afford to defend myself. Financially, spiritually, either way, I can't afford it. I'll have to get out. That's all there is to it. I won't give, so I'll have to go.'

He was dazed by her ugly, meaningless logic. He wanted to ask her to marry him, immediately. He even thought of getting down upon his knees. Instead, he said,

'Look, Rose, you mustn't give up so easily. Why don't you try talking to Christopher about it? Why don't I try and talk to him for you? He can't mean this, he can't mean to have done this to you. He wouldn't know what to do with the children if you gave them to him.'

'You mustn't talk to him,' she said. 'Please. I know what he's like, he's as stubborn as I am, you'll never get him to change anything. He's fixed, he's set. And if he says he wants them, he'll make himself have them. Like the divorce. He didn't want me, he hated me, but he wouldn't let me go. He'll take them from me, he'll take them, whether he wants them or not.'

'But don't you *see*,' he repeated, with a fitting note of exasperation, 'that no judge in the country would *let* him take them?'

'Ah yes,' she said, gazing at him, with a mysterious, mad, perverse, elevated smile upon her face, a smile quite awful in its unnatural dignity, 'ah yes, but I *give* them, you remember, I *give* them.'

And there she stood, pale, irradiated. Then, as suddenly, she moaned, and started to toss her head about, and her hands flew to her hair, and started to tug at it. He leapt to his feet, left his desk, went across to her, took her arms, and gently dissuaded her: her arms were as stiff as sticks, her hair where she had pulled at it stood in clumps, she was not there in the flesh. He held her arm, through her raincoat, and propelled her to the chair, and sat her down: she stumbled clumsily, as though disconnected, and sat as though the joints in her legs had been folded together by his propulsion, like the blades of a penknife. He stood by her, a hand on her shoulder: she stared ahead, unseeing. He did not know what to do with her: she had gone quite out of reach. He would have offered her a drink, if he had had one, but could not risk leaving the room in search of one, so he did nothing but stand there, trying to think of something to say to her. He was helpless, there was nothing he could offer, reason she had rejected, and he couldn't follow her in her nonreasoning. What was she seeing, with those blank eyes?

Whatever she saw, she did not begin to tell him, because the telephone rang. He had asked the girl not to put calls through, but he could not leave it ringing. It was Jefferson, wanting to see him, or so he said, urgently. I can't come at the moment, I'm busy, said Simon, but while he was trying to explain that he would come later he saw Rose get to her feet, and start mechanically to flatten down her hair, preparing to leave: before he got off the phone she was at the door, and had opened it. It opened on to the outer office: the secretary was watching.

'Don't go yet,' he said. 'Don't go, I'm sure there's something we can do.'

'There isn't,' said Rose, dully. 'I'm sorry I troubled you. I'm sorry.'

He couldn't make a scene, he couldn't detain her. She smiled at him, a little frozen smile.

'Goodbye,' she said.

Anyone else he would have accused of taking pleasure from his helplessness.

'Goodbye,' he said. 'I hope you'll get in touch with me, before you do anything.'

'Oh yes,' she said, absently, 'oh yes.'

And off she went. He watched her go: he went to his window and watched her cross the courtyard below. The distance ached and widened, as she shrunk and withered from his sight. He could have recalled her, he could have shouted, he could not comprehend how he had let her go: and relentlessly, inevitably, she grew smaller, and went away. It was not optical, the impression of her going: it was more that she shrank on his grasp, as her bony shoulder had sunk like a dead bird beneath his hand. He had failed her, he had done nothing for her, and now she turned the corner, her plastic bag slung over her wrist, her hands deep in her pockets, her head bent as though walking into a wind. Hunched and private. He knew that way of walking, a posture of indifferent pain, a shrugged confronting of a hostile element. It was his own.

It was a cold day, for June. A light rain fell. Looking out of the window still, herself gone, he was surprised to see no leaves falling for the light was autumnal. He thought of Easter, and the snow in Cornwall, and the man who had not been Christopher, bearing the child upon his shoulders through the gathering blizzard: he thought of Rose, and Emily, and their children running around in vests, and the chickens and the armchair. It was a Friday: the next day was the beginning of the Whitsun weekend, another unwelcome holiday, and it was about this that Jefferson had so inopportunely wished to consult him: some case that might require attention during the vacation. If he had not rung at that moment, perhaps some saving word would have come to his lips? Perhaps he would have kept her there with him, have thought of some way of convincing her? Perhaps, perhaps. It was not likely. How dreadful it is, he thought suddenly, that children are born of two parents, that they are the property of two parents with equal claim, that they do not spring fully grown from the brain, as Athene sprang from Zeus. What a ghastly mistake in evolution, for man to have attached such significance to identity, when he is condemned for survival to partition. Because, like Rose, he could not convince himself that the children were hers alone. He remembered them in the car with Christopher, laughing: later, proudly describing its gadgets. Christopher himself, alone, plotting, brooding, playing legal games in a mockery of the care of which he was deprived. He thought of the judgement of Solomon. A chancery judge, in despair over an impossible case, had invoked the ghost of Solomon: in genuine misery, a kindly old grandfather, he had said, I have not his wisdom, and the newspapers had derided him for a decision taken in the darkness of impossibility. But a decision had had to be taken. And so Rose, the true mother perhaps, would leave the baby kicking there, in the chalk circle, unable to resist a rival claim.

ROSE WALKED. She was not sure where she was going, she walked blindly, through unfamiliar streets. Her head ached and stormed. She had known it would come, she had felt it coming for months, and here it was: quietly she repeated herself, I will live through it, I will live through it. But it was bad, it was worse than she could have imagined. Her head split. If someone had taken a hatchet and split my skull, she thought, I could not suffer more. I feel the blood running in my brain, from this internal wound. My brain is wet with blood. It pours through where my mind is, I bleed, I bleed, I bleed. Let them not tell me we are material beings, it is in the spirit that we know pain, it is in my head, my spirit, it is there, I feel it. I am cut into two by the axe. I bleed, she said, I will live through it, she said, as her feet followed one another on the wet pavement.

She emerged upon the Kingsway, and walked into a coffee shop. It was one where she had been with Konstantin: he had called it the Snake Café, because he had thought that its sign, portraying a swirl of smoke arising from a cup, had been a picture of a snake. She queued, shuffling, as though unable to lift her feet: took a salad, a cup of coffee, sat down at a glass-topped table on a high uncomfortable stool. She stared into space at the street outside. She saw not the street, but an airport. The airport was in Africa, in Gbolo: it was where she was. She had just got off the plane, and she sat there in the lounge, with nowhere to go, sick and ill from the journey. She saw herself there, as from a distance: herself, sitting there in her mackintosh, with a suitcase at her feet. It was a vision so strong, so real, that she knew she must do it, that there she would be. But how could she be there? She should never have allowed herself to admit this image, it had formed itself slowly and dreadfully, the details gathered round it inexorably: she had tried to blot it out, she had reasoned with it, but its power was stronger than she was. The passport, the plane, the money, the ticket, the departure, the objects in that suitcase. It was a vision, and how could she know whether it was a temptation of God or the Devil? Twice before she had had these visions, and they had been made flesh. She had seen herself marrying Christopher, in defiance of all reason, and it was vision that had walked her to the registry office: the image of herself doing it had been too strong for her. Then again, later, she had seen herself signing the cheque. She had seen her hand writing her signature. God, she thought, had held her hand. He had propelled her fingers. Rose Vertue Vassiliou, he had written: and the oblong piece of paper had been taken from her, had gone up in smoke and fire. She had thought to have no more such visions, she had thought that she had found a humble way to survive them. She had thought, I am too old for these hallucinations, my next house I will not build upon the sand. But it too had crumbled. What is it, what is it, she asked herself, as her coffee grew colder, what is it that forms these acts for me, and what can I do, since they come to me, but submit to their promptings?

She worked it out: she would plan it in detail. She would consult the flights, the necessity for injections. She would find reasons. I will go there, she said, I will live there quietly till the money comes through, I will take a job if I can get one, and by the time the money comes through I will know what to do with it. I will be sensible, this time, I won't let it be burned, I'll find out first where it's needed, where it can be used. And then I will have done what I must do. And by then, I will know how to make myself useful. And by then, also, I will have travelled further than I will ever travel here, the ways of loneliness and extremity, I will voyage into that dark interior, I will satisfy this spiritual craving, I will see what it is like, that other world, the world of destitution, I was made for it, and there, in that hideous dark misery, which now, here, I cannot imagine, but which there could not deny itself to me—for what else would there be, nothing, nothingness—there I should see it, the unimaginable. It is there, it calls me, I have only to walk towards it, I myself. It is in me to go that journey, so how can I refuse it? Chosen, I was, to go those ways, or they would not so call to me, they would not lie open before me. If I do not go, I will wither and perish for not having gone. I cannot survive my own rejection of this image. It gathers in the darkness of my soul. It is my only chance to appease God himself, who so pursues me with these suggestions, who sends after me his fierce angels with their clattering wings. It is sacrifices that God has always demanded. He demanded Isaac. On the hilltop, the innocent. He shall have my children. On that dingy airport, where I shall be ill, and wretched, and lonely, he shall have myself. And there I shall find him. It is the only way to find him. There he will be, in that loss and solitude, in those nights of anguish. There I shall go. Not many people go there, but to that land I shall go.

She contemplated the vision. It seemed real, it seemed solid, it breathed life. And then, to test it, she conjured up the image of her children. They too seemed real and living. Incompatible, incompatible. She could not make them lose colour, her children, their faces would not fade on her, they were as real, as insistently real. Her mind started to divide again, sickeningly: the pain started up again. She had read once that the mind is indeed in two halves, and that some people have the halves divided, so that the right hand truly does not know what the left hand is doing. She experienced division. But the two sides did not obliterate each other, they collided, they continued to co-exist. It was unendurable. She could feel a cold sweat standing out on her skin. She prayed for the angel that appeared to Jacob. Oh God, oh God, she prayed, release me, be merciful, send me an angel with a sword, tell me what I must do. Restore me, restore me, I cannot endure a moment longer. They will cry if I leave them, God, they will cry for me, I love them, they love me. Take away your message. Take it away.

But God was not particularly merciful. All he sent to her was another tag, leading to the desert.

(It was largely desert, Ujuhudiana, an unfruitful land. Cracking plains of mud, dryness, dust, where small people had washed themselves humbly like saints in their own urine, stinking, defenceless. And over the border slouched Man the Murderer, swinging his long arms.)

If ye will not give up wife and mother and children to follow me, he said, unhelpfully, cruelly, ye shall in nowise enter into the kingdom of heaven.

I must be mad, thought Rose, shaking her head, eating a mouthful of lettuce. I should see a psychiatrist.

I don't want this vision, she thought, crossly. I really don't want it. It's silly and useless. What good is twenty thousand pounds to an economy like that? My other vision was quite good enough. Living in Middle Road, like a quiet person. What was wrong with it? Was it that it had got too agreeable? Was it not melodramatic enough? Perhaps it is the melodrama that is the temptation, after all. Could I not convince myself that it is my own neurosis that prompts me? Be reasonable, now, you know it is neurosis. What else could it be? Look at your background, woman. Look at the spectacular useless-ness of every gesture you have ever made. Why do you think this new one will be any better? It is nothing, it is part of the pattern. You could break the pattern now, if you tried. You could sit it out, as Simon said. You could resist. You could, now you are a grown woman, refuse to listen. Blot it out.

The woman in the airport paid no attention. She sat there grimly, refusing to be dislodged.

You realise, of course, what you've done, said Rose, mother of three children, to that unpleasant martyr, that faithless missionary. You've simply constructed for yourself the most horrible renunci-ation your mind can conceive. That's all you've done. It's silly, it's pointless.

But the woman in the airport looked up from her dusty shoes, with a tight dismissive smile of contempt, and said No, no. I didn't construct it. Christopher and God constructed it, they connived at it, they left me nothing else to do, don't you remember?

I don't believe you, said Rose.

Ah, said the woman. Refuse to believe. Abandon me. The choice is yours.

Oh God, said Rose, munching her salad angrily. I don't care. You can die for all I care. I'm going to go back now, and soon I can collect Maria and Marcus from school.

And the woman rose to her feet, white and wailing. In Rose's mind she wailed, like a soul in hell. On the bottom right-hand corner of the day of judgement she wept and wrung her hands, across the continents.

ON FRIDAY EVENING, Simon sat at home. The evening seemed endless. The children were sitting up late, as there was no school the next day: he had promised the boy that he could watch the late sports programme. The girls were bickering, monotonously, over a packet of felt pens, each claiming it as her own, neither sure whose in fact it was, and whose had been lost. Julie was watching a play on the television, and doing some crochet work. It was much in vogue, crochet. Simon himself was trying to reply to a letter of his mother's: she had written to him the week before, which she rarely did, expressing interest in the USTK case, a desire that the family would visit her for a few days in the summer, complaints about the bad weather, assurances (which could only mean the opposite) that she was in good health. He could not concentrate on his reply, because the atmosphere in the room was restless. Julie had wanted to go away for Whitsun, and he had refused, saying it would be too expensive, so soon after Easter, but she knew as well as he did that the refusal was arbitrary, and in revenge she had been difficult about the possibility of visiting his mother. Her irritation conveyed itself to them all, without words. He sat there, staring at the sheet of paper on his desk, at the words: Dearest Mum, Thank you so much for your letter, I was glad to hear . . . He was thinking of Rose, and of the cowardly and utterly characteristic way in which he had let her go. He was insistent enough on some occasions: he had won a case he should have lost, when his sympathies had been engaged (he might as well now admit it) the other way. His sympathies had been engaged with Rose too: was that why he had let her go? Because the truth was that he had known what she had been talking about. Nonsense it had been in some terms, but it had made sense to him. He had had no right to answer his telephone and to allow her to escape. He should have taken her hand from the door and shut it. He should have declared himself. Irrelevant it might have been, his declaration of interest, for what could Rose want with his affection at such a time, but nevertheless he should have done it, because that was what he had been prompted to do. There was no point in behaving reasonably on such occasions. She had not behaved reasonably in looking to him for assistance and advice. She had wanted him to say something to her. She had shown some form of trust and he had betrayed it.

He wondered what would have happened if he had spoken. He constructed, shamefully, a situation in which he had done so. A fantasy, it was, an image. He had done it before. He said to her, in this fantasy: I love you, I admire you. And she responded, if not with emotion at least with relief, with pleasure, with some feeling. And then they would hold together, after this declaration: they would marry, they would set up house together, they would eat and talk and watch the television and discuss the world together. Where the children were in this fantasy he did not know: sometimes they were with them, all six of them, sometimes they had disappeared, along with Julie and Christopher, into the outer darkness. He saw only episodes, as though picked out by the unnatural spotlight of hope: himself and Rose sitting together quietly in her dingy house, or walking in the country, or visiting his mother (why this returned so insistently he did not know) or going together to a dinner or a party. Talking over the headlines in the paper. Discussing his cases. Africa. Trades Unions. Politics. Students. Other people. The future. And the ironic thing about these visions was that they were not at all, in terms of character, in terms of their own selves, improbable. He and Rose were similar, he knew it. She was not one of those sexual fantasy women in vulgar black underwear: she was, in person, no less and no more attractive than he was himself. And in character, in interests, they were alike. There was nothing visionary about an image of their conjunction. It was sober, real, possible. It would even be productive and useful. They would be a good combination, good companions. He thought of the marriages he knew, marriages that he admired and envied, based on a community of interest, a common purpose. Most of them were second marriages, one had to admit. And there was the fatal flaw. For how could one soberly, quietly, responsibly, ever build such a thing upon destruction? Upon dead Julie, dead Christopher, upon the weeping of infants? The Mexicans (he thought it was the Mexicans) used to cement the foundations of their edifices with the blood of slaughtered children, for their greater security. And that was a logic which he did not wish to pursue. Nevertheless, beyond some gap in time and action, he and Rose sat down to supper together, with books perhaps beside their plates upon the table, looking up from time to time to compare notes, smiling as they pushed each other the butter, salt or bread.

The play on the television ground to a morbid close. The two girls were pushed, protesting, up to bed. Julie accompanied them, saying she had no wish to watch what was coming, and Simon told Dan that he could sit up and watch Sportsnight with Sykes, after the News. He himself sat and watched the News. It was dominated, for him, by an account of a case in which an Italian father, who had been given custody of his baby in the magistrate's court, and refused it on Appeal, had disappeared to Italy with the child, saying that he had no interest in the British Law, he was going to keep the child, in Milan, and bring it up a good Catholic. The English mother was interviewed: I want my baby back, she said plaintively, to the man from the BBC. But it was as clear as day that getting the baby back, physically, was going to prove an immensely difficult task. Mr Calvacoressi had the weight of Italian public feeling behind him, as well as the undoubted advantage of having the child in his possession. What do I care for the Court of Appeal, he had told the newspapers. Simon watched the account of this with growing alarm. He got up, went out into the hall, and rang Rose. There was no answer.

He let the phone ring for a long time, not knowing how she could not be there. There was still no answer. She cannot have gone away, he thought. Anxiety mounted in him. He could not put the receiver down. But in the end he did so, and rang, instead, without allowing himself to think too much, Christopher's number, which he found from Directory Enquiries. Christopher, unlike Rose, replied. I've got to talk to you, said Simon, and Christopher seemed not at all alarmed by such an approach. Come round now, he said, I'm out tomorrow. All right, said Simon. And he said to his son, look, I'm just going out for a few minutes, put yourself to bed when the programme's over, won't you. All right, said Dan, absently, unsurprised, his eyes not leaving the set.

Simon, walking down the dark road, past the florid scented hedges, remembered suddenly that night in the winter, the night after he had first met Rose. He had gone out into the garden, he remembered it. That was what had done it. A minor act of eccentricity. It was that which had led him here. Too late now, not to have done it.

Christopher, when he opened the door, appeared to have been drinking. Simon shortly found himself drinking too. Christopher had made things easy for him, in a sense, by assuming without preamble and in part correctly that his visit was connected with Rose's receipt of his affidavit. I suppose I ought to feel sorry about it, he said, pouring himself another large dose of Bell's, but I don't, I don't think I do, I think I hope she sweats blood. For Christ's sake, said Simon.

'Well, what would you have done, if it had been you, and you'd read it?'

'I didn't read it,' said Simon.

'Why ever not?'

'I didn't want to.'

'Well then,' said Christopher, with a bitter smile—with precisely, a bitter smile—'you'd better read it now.'

'No thank you,' said Simon, primly, like a teetotaller refusing a drink: and for the first time Christopher turned on him.

'You stupid bugger,' he said calmly, 'you really want things both ways, don't you? You want to come round here and chat me up on her behalf, and at the same time you want to think I'm a violent, ignorant cunt, don't you?'

That was so exactly what Simon wanted that he wiped his glasses, sighed, had a drink, and took the sheets of paper that Christopher offered him. His eyes moved over them. He saw paragraphs about education, about suicide attempts, about opportunities lost, about poisoning children's minds against their father, about—and here he stopped looking, even—about other men. A man the children had talked about, called Anton. Another man called Nick. He didn't read it. He handed it back, he threw it on to the table between them.

'No, thank you,' he said. 'I really don't want to read it. I don't suppose it's the truth, and even if it were, I don't want to know; nor do I see its relevance.'

It sounded like a loyal husband's deceived statement. In the face of it, Christopher became almost apologetic.

'I've got evidence,' he said, 'I'm not making it up, you know.'

Evidence or not, said Simon, it was irrelevant. What seemed relevant to him, he said, was that Rose was in a state of such acute distress that she seemed positively unbalanced. I don't know what she'll do, he said, I rang her this evening and there was no reply. She said she was going away, she might have gone already. You've driven her to it, whatever she does, he said. She probably didn't answer her telephone because she thought it was me, said Christopher.

'Aren't you worried about her, at all,' said Simon.

'Let's ring her and see if she's there now,' said Christopher.

They rang, as though in collusion. There was no reply.

'Well, shit,' said Christopher, quite drunk by now, but not showing it particularly, his speech slurred and dull as it always was, 'what do you suggest I do, as a sensible serious person, as I see you clearly are? Only really sensible people wear glasses like yours,' he said, offensively.

'I suggest,' said Simon, 'that you forget about the divorce, and go back and live with her.'

He had thought about this deeply, on the short walk between the two houses.

'Do you really?' said Christopher.

'Yes, I do.'

'She wouldn't have me.'

'You should ask her, first.'

'I don't want to live with her. She's made my life a misery once, why should I go through all that again?'

'Because if you don't, worse will happen. You know as well as I do that whatever you've written on those bits of paper—and how you found a reputable solicitor to handle your case I can't imagine—that there's not the remotest chance of getting your children back that way. You know what will happen when that case gets in front of a judge, don't you? You're no fool, you must know. You'll be denied access. Rose will plead, if she's any sense, that you're unbalanced, and they'll believe her, and you'll never be able to see them again. You haven't a hope. So it's up to you. Either you simply drop the case—forget it—and I don't believe you'd be content with that, would you?—or you change your line of attack, and try to get her back. That way, you've a hope. This way, no hope at all. I'm saying this to you because I don't think you are vindictive, I'm giving you the credit of believing that you really are more interested in yourself and your children than in having your revenge on somebody you've already reduced to a state of unbelievable misery. So there you are. That's all I've got to say.'

'Well, that's very generous of you,' said Christopher, aiming at irony. Without success. 'Thank you for your advice. It's not every day that people take such an interest in my affairs. Or give me their free legal advice.'

The attempt was deplorable, hopeless, the real knowing certainty of manner all gone. Like a child he spoke, like an angry child. He rubbed his eyes, picked up his glass, put it down again. It was only by such a fall that one could measure how high the flight had been. His eyes were red with tears. He covered his face with his hands. 'Oh God,' he said, 'Oh God, oh God, oh God.' He wept, now, his medium rediscovered, fittingly.

'I'd better go now,' said Simon, rising to his feet.

'Don't go,' said Christopher, 'have another drink': reaching for the bottle, blindly, without looking, although it was by now empty. But Simon left, nevertheless, thinking perhaps that for once, having for once taken some action, he might perhaps have made some kind of point. He might even, beautifully to his own disadvantage, have done some kind of good. He took some satisfaction from the thought that any gain would be his own loss.

ON SATURDAY MORNING, Simon decided that he would do some gardening. He had depressed himself so thoroughly by reading the newspapers that he felt he had to do something. The newspapers, for a holiday weekend, had been full of unimaginable disasters. An earthquake in the Middle East had killed tens of thousands, and cholera was breaking out amidst the survivors: There was an account of a trial in the States over an alleged massacre in Vietnam. Three men in an iron works in Yorkshire had been killed by molten slag from a mobile ladle. A child in a mental home had fallen into a bath of scalding water and had died five days later of burns. There had been a twenty-car pile-up on the M1. Mr Calvacoressi said that it would cost his wife a fortune to reclaim her baby. So Simon dug his garden, struggling incompetently against the crude and violent efflorescence of early summer. He was not very good at gardening, having been brought up with a backyard and a few stinking geraniums in pots: they had smelt of tomcats, the geraniums, as though there had not been enough cats around without such an addition. He was never sure whether it was weeds or flowers that he was uprooting: he would give dogs mercury and willowherb the benefit of the doubt, and throw lilies of the valley on the incinerator. A few tags, culled from God knows what repository of folk knowledge, aided him: slugs are no good, worms are the gardener's best friend.

And as he dug, he thought about industrial accidents, and the cheeseparing of employers when it came to safety precautions, and a horrible case he had been involved in where a fire had destroyed a whole warehouse full of people because the management had barred up the safety exits to prevent their workmen slipping out for an unsupervised smoke on the fire escape. God could still kill more at a blow, but man was doing his best to emulate his acts.

The crazy paving was coming loose all over the place. He spent an hour digging the weeds out of the cracks, and then wished he hadn't, because it looked even worse without them. He started to mix some cement to fill in the holes and replace the loose stones: the children, attracted by this activity, came out and wanted to help, so he gave them some old spoons and knives and let them have a go, knowing that whatever they did would probably need re-doing later. He thought about Rose and the London Rocket, that rare and modest herb, and about a story she had told him about the peppered moth, which had evolved a black species to survive in the industrial landscape. Biston betularia, the Manchester moth, its lighter brethren dying, its blackened survivors clinging grimly to blackened walls and tree trunks. Perhaps such modesty was all one could hope for. No more spectacular species, the envy of predators, but a grimy race of uniform lowliness. What was man to hope for, after all? Spectacular injuries, amazing sufferings, or the grim squabbling of those who intend to continue, who do not intend to be picked off. A ladle of molten slag. Herbert Alfred Jowitt, out of a job. But not starving, of course, not shot in the back, or dying of cholera. Progress and evolution, what banal and adolescent preoccupations. The loose stones, irritatingly enough, would never fit back into the holes that they appeared to have come out of: it was like a gigantic jigsaw puzzle. The children found it amusing. So, in a sense, did he. And why not allow oneself such modest pleasures? His father had received his near-fatal injury while inspecting the safety mechanisms in the glass factory up in South Shields: he was telling the foreman that the women ought to wear hairnets at work when half a ton of machinery had dropped through the ceiling on to his head. It had been a famous victory, the women had worn hairnets thereafter. Nothing would drop on to Simon's head in Chambers, not even a dislodged cobweb, and nowadays young men were suing their employers for wrongful dismissal if told to have their hair cut for safety reasons. There was progress, certainly.

'I think,' said Kate, looking up from the excavation over which she was squatting, 'I think we ought to plant some little plants in these holes, Dad, don't you? Don't you think it would look pretty?'

'I've just dug a whole load of little plants out,' said Simon, pointing to the smouldering heap of grass and plantains and groundsel and dandelions.

'Yes,' said Kate, 'but those were weeds, we ought to plant some nice little plants, flowers and stuff. Couldn't we leave a few holes for some flowers?'

'What chance do you think flowers would have, with you lot thumping around and riding bicycles over them all day long?'

'If weeds would grow, why wouldn't flowers?' said Kate.

'Flowers are more delicate,' said Simon. 'I think.'

'Oh look,' said Kate, 'do come and look at this nice beetle. Come on, quick, before it runs away.'

And he was just about to go and look at the beetle when Julie appeared at the back door. Her hair was in curlers: they were going out that evening.

'Simon,' she said, 'there's a woman on the phone for you.'

'Oh,' said Simon. He did not ask who it was. 'Oh, all right. I'm coming.'

He wiped his hands on his trousers: they were covered with mud and cement. There was only one woman he could think of who would be at all likely to ring him, but when he went in and picked up the receiver it was not Rose's voice that answered.

'Hello,' said the woman. 'Hello, Simon. This is Emily here, Emily Offenbach. I had to ring you, I'm sorry, I couldn't think what else to do, I am sorry to disturb you at the weekend, but I couldn't think what else to do, and I had to do something.'

'That's all right,' he mumbled, waiting for her to continue.

'It's about Rose,' she said, 'I'm at Rose's, I can't stay here, I've got to get back to the children, and she didn't want to disturb you, but I knew you wouldn't mind—and you might even know what to do, I thought, which I certainly don't—the thing is, Christopher came round to collect the children this morning, very early, he was going to take them to Norfolk for the weekend, that was all arranged, and he took them off, and then half an hour ago Rose got a telegram from him saying he was leaving with them. Taking them out of the country. And we just don't know what to do about it, we don't know whether to take it seriously or not, and she didn't know who to ring or who to ask, so I'm afraid we thought of you.'

'Oh Lord,' said Simon. 'Oh dear. She'd better ring her solicitor immediately, I think, and explain it all to him.'

'She's tried,' said Emily, 'but it's the weekend, he's not in.'

'Has she got his home number?'

'Yes, we've tried it, but he's not there either.'

'Is Rose there? Can I speak to her?'

'She won't. She won't speak to anyone.'

'Oh well,' said Simon, making his mind up, for him, more or less instantly, 'I'd better come round and see what I can do, hadn't I?'

'Would you really? Could you really?' The relief in her voice was evident. 'Please do, I really don't know what to do, I don't know what to do with her, I don't understand this whole awful business, it's been dragging on for so long now, I simply don't understand what's happening, it's getting quite ridiculous . . .'

'I'll be round in half an hour,' said Simon.

'And what shall we do? Wait for you?'

'That's right. Don't do anything. You could try the solicitor again, perhaps he's just gone out shopping, but if he's not there wait for me.'

'It's very good of you,' said Emily.

'Not at all,' said Simon, politely, and rang off. Then, before he had time to worry about it, he went and told Julie that he had been called out urgently. She was so astonished that she did not have much to say, beyond the fact that he couldn't have the car because she wanted it and hers was in the garage.

'I need it,' said Simon. 'I'll give you a ring, when I know what I'm doing.'

'You'd better be back for this evening,' said Julie. 'We're going out, remember?'

He left before she had time to emerge from her surprise, pursued only by a wail of anger about being left with all the children at a weekend without a car. As he drove off, he looked at his watch: it was 11.20. If Christopher had, as Emily had said, collected the children early, he had had plenty of time to get moving.

He arrived at Rose's just after half eleven. Emily opened the door to him, the telegram in her hand. She gave it to him. It read:

AM LEAVING COUNTRY WITH CHILDREN AS LEGAL MEANS SEEM DILATORY AND DOUBTFUL STOP HOPE YOU ENJOY YOURSELF WITHOUT THEM AS MUCH AS I DID

'What a bastard,' said Simon.

'Lovely, isn't it,' said Emily.

The telegram was dated with the day's date, and had been sent at eight thirty in the morning. Emily said he had picked the children up at nine, so she assumed he had sent the telegram from home before leaving, but could not decipher the postcodes to be sure of this. 'And now,' said Emily, 'I've got to go, I'm sorry, I've got to go, I feel awful, leaving you like this, but I dumped all the children at a neighbour's and I daren't leave them there a minute longer, I'll ring you, shall I, and see what's happened? Rose is downstairs in the kitchen. What a lunatic that man is, he ought to be locked up. I'll ring you, shall I?'

And off she went, running down the street to the bus stop on the corner. Simon went downstairs, and there was Rose, sitting in the semi-basement on the old settee. She did not look up at him as he entered: staring at the floor, she said stiffly,

'I didn't want to ring you.'

'Rose,' he said.

She looked up, and then stood up. He walked towards her and put his arms round her and she leant against him.

'I'm so ashamed,' she said, into his chest.

'I'm so sorry,' he said, 'I'm so sorry. I should never have let you go yesterday.'

'No, no,' she said, muffled, quivering, leaning towards him and stiffening back in the same movement, 'no, no, I should never have come, I must have been mad, I should never have come.'

'Never mind,' he said, 'never mind.'

He held her in his arms, and stroked her tight shoulders. He had imagined holding her, often, and always in terms such as these: to reassure, to help, to console. It was on these terms that he had first known her. And he had imagined for himself satisfactory moments, such as this, such as yesterday when he had so badly failed. And in the projected images he had been glad, at last, to hold her, glad that she had turned to him, glad that grief had driven her to him. But of course it was not like that at all. Because what he had never allowed to have any reality was the degree and the nature of the crisis that would give her to him, that would lean her against him, as she now was leaning. She was too unhappy, he could not take any comfort while she was so unhappy. There was no satisfaction in it. He was too unhappy on her account. He should have known that that was how it would be.

'Never mind,' he said again, as much to himself as to her.

He was still holding the telegram. After a moment she backed away from him: they looked at it together.

'Do you believe it?' he said.

'How could one know?' she said. 'How could one possibly know?'

'Are the children on his passport?'

'Yes, they are. All three of them. We were going to France for a week, just after Maria was born, and we put all three of them in both passports. We shouldn't have done, I know. I knew it.'

'I'd better ring the solicitor again,' he said: she gave him the number, and he rang. This time he was in: he had been out shopping with his wife in the car. Rose sat and listened, while Simon explained who he was, and what had happened, and asked what ought to be done. She heard them discussing injunctions, and affidavits, and vacation judges, and the extreme difficulty of getting anything done at Whit weekend when judges and barristers are on golf courses, and airports are crammed with casual holidaymakers. What Simon could hear and she could not was her solicitor's deep disapprobation of the whole affair. What those two need is a psychiatrist, not a solicitor, he said, from time to time. He had been hoping to spend the day asleep in the garden, had Rose's solicitor. However, as the minutes ticked by, he managed to work up a little enthusiasm for the task ahead: he insisted on speaking to Rose, and explained to her that she would have to provide an affidavit explaining why she needed an *ex parte* injunction. She dictated the contents of the telegram to him, and this time could not miss the snort of indignation that Jeremy Alford gave, in his quiet house. All right, he said then, that's enough, I'll draft something, don't you worry. Just you sit and wait, I'll be back to you on the phone in a few minutes, as soon as I've got hold of the judge and Counsel. Don't go away, will you, I'll be needing you and that telegram.

'Perhaps it's all a mistake,' said Rose, at this point. 'Perhaps he didn't mean it.'

'I don't care whether it's a mistake or not,' said Jeremy Alford. 'I'm not taking any more risks with that man. I've had enough.'

'All right,' said Rose, meekly, and put down the telephone.

And then she and Simon prepared to wait. Simon made Rose a cup of tea, and told her not to worry. She looked at him anxiously, and tried to drink her tea. They were both thinking of the Calvacoressi case, though neither of them dared to mention it. After five minutes, the solicitor rang back saying that he had got hold of the vacation judge's private phone number from the duty officer at the court, and that luckily it happened to be Mr Justice Ward, an exceptionally nice man, who luckily happened to live conveniently near, in Highgate. So as soon as I've got hold of Counsel, I'll be back on to you too and we'll arrange to meet up together, he said. Lucky you're there to make sure she turns up, said Jeremy Alford to Simon. Yes, said Simon, looking at Rose, sitting on the chair arm, biting nervously at the quick of one finger, running the fingers of the other hand through her hair. I've just remembered, said Alford, in a low voice, about that Calvacoressi case. Yes, said Simon. I'm sure you're right.

After another ten minutes, he rang back and said that all the barristers in the relevant Chambers seemed to be out, probably in their country cottages. What on earth do I do now? he said. He was beginning to sound rattled. Simon was getting quite fond of him. Try them all again, said Simon. One of them is in a hotel in Weymouth, Alford said, I got the number and tried to get him paged, I was getting so worried, but they said he'd gone out for a walk with a packed lunch. Try some of the others again, said Simon, they can't all be out.

A quarter of an hour later, Jeremy Alford rang back and said he had got hold of Francis Morris, at his tennis club, and had persuaded him to meet him in half an hour at his own home in Barnsbury. If you drive Rose over here, he said, she can read the affidavit I've drafted, and swear it, and I'll get the order from Francis as well. All right, said Simon. Two minutes later Alford rang back and said for God's sake don't forget to bring that telegram, will you, we can't do anything without it.

So Simon collected Rose, and the telegram, and put them both in the car, and drove them down the hill to Barnsbury. It was a beautiful morning: London lay like a map from the hill top, green sewage works, Hackney marshes, towers, railways, council blocks, all guttering with glass and metal in the summer air. They passed the Palace, went down, over the Archway bridge with its wrought-iron work, and into Islington. The clock in the car said that it was now ten past twelve. An aeroplane flew overhead. Perhaps Christopher and the children were by this time high up over the Mediterranean. Rose asked, as they drove down Upper Street, what the injunction would mean: would the police arrest Christopher at an airport, should he still be in the country? How would they know who he was? How would they get the message? Simon found it hard to reply, because he did not really know the answers, though it suddenly struck him that he ought to have asked Rose, while she was still at home, if she knew her husband's passport number, which would surely be a help to the Home Office. Too late now, for she certainly wouldn't know it off by heart.

He had visions of the Sunday papers, covered with items about Rose and Christopher. He wondered if she had thought of that. It would make a pleasant Sunday distraction from the Turkish death toll. He wondered how the press got hold of such information. Jeremy Alford had said something about the press. It wasn't going to be very pleasant, he suspected.

When they arrived at Alford's house in Barnsbury, Alford himself was waiting on the steps for them. Their greetings were perfunctory: Alford hustled them into the house, where Francis Morris, gloriously dressed in white from his tennis, was waiting for them and drinking a glass of beer. 'Hello, hello,' he said, in a reassuringly fruity public-school voice: Simon noted himself feeling reassured, like any guilty party with a good defence, though he knew for a fact that Francis had more voice than brain. 'Well, well, well,' said Francis Morris, smiling blandly as though it were a party, 'quite a little drama, this time, Mrs Vassiliou?'

And even Rose smiled faintly, responsively.

'Never you mind, Mrs Vassiliou,' said Morris. 'We've been talking it over, Jeremy and I, and we think you've nothing to worry about, nothing at all. Even if he's already got the children out of the country, we'll get them back again. And as for the custody case, he's done himself in completely, hasn't he, Jeremy?'

'Yes, yes, that's right,' said Jeremy Alford. 'Now look, Rose, here's a copy of the affidavit, would you just read it through, and then I'm terribly sorry, we'll just have to go down the road to a friend of mine who's going to act as Commissioner for Oaths, so he can witness it.'

There seemed to be an air of urgency: Rose produced the telegram, read the affidavit, was marched down the road to a fellow solicitor who was lying in bed with flu, swore it, marched back again. And now, said Jeremy Alford, now we can go and visit the judge.

'What, all of us?' said Rose. She was so confused by now that she had no idea what was happening.

'Yes, all of us,' said Jeremy Alford.

So they all got into Simon's car, and he drove them back up the hill to Highgate.

Mr Justice Ward's house was an agreeable house. Perhaps it was the look of the house itself, as much as the feeling that they had reached authority, that calmed their jangling nerves—for the bonhomie of Francis, at first so welcome, had begun to appear forced, and Simon had started to wonder why the fool hadn't taken two minutes off to change out of his tennis things, they weren't really all that becoming, after all. Jeremy Alford was feeling guilty about having left his very pregnant wife cooking the lunch when he had promised her an easy weekend, and his guilt was making him irritable. And as for Rose, she simply didn't seem to know what was happening. She was clutching the telegram, Exhibit A, as though it were a death warrant. So the calming influence of the Ward house was much needed. It was an attractive but modest house, 1905, detached and homely, with flowerbeds in front of it and flowers in window boxes, and it had a particularly attractive fanlight. Simon was staring at the fanlight when Lady Ward opened the door, and he had to bring his eyes down sharply. Lady Ward was also homely: she breathed out a calming preoccupied competence. She was a little woman, with a large bosom, and she was wearing a green dress and an overall.

'Come in, come in, excuse my overall,' she said, smiling distractedly at them, flinging open the door. 'Do excuse me, I was just having a little clean-out in the kitchen, so nice to have the house to oneself for a change, I was really enjoying myself—come in, come in, Humphrey's in here, he's expecting you.'

'We're so sorry to disturb you,' Rose was beginning to say, as they were ushered into the drawing-room—'not at all, not at all,' said Lady Ward, 'it's what we're here for—' and disappeared promptly into the kitchen, unable to resist the lure of an uninterrupted fiddle with her own pots and pans.

Humphrey Ward looked, if anything, more benign than his wife, because less dotty. He shook hands, sat them down, took their papers, with a kindly concern, then offered them all a glass of sherry—'You could drink it,' he said, 'to cheer yourselves up, while I peruse these documents?'

'That would be very kind,' said Jeremy Alford who seemed to be acting as spokesman: Francis Morris had undergone a strange nervous eclipse, and Simon was acutely aware that his professional status was highly ambiguous, a fact acknowledged by a discreet, questioning, sympathetic glance from the judge himself. He was too delicate to ask questions, was Mr Justice Ward, so he poured them all a glass of sherry—all the glasses attractive, but all different, the ends of sets, a fact which seemed to attune agreeably with the whole room. It was a pleasant room, not particularly tasteful, not particularly elegant or luxurious, but comfortable, inhabited. Books lined the walls: house plants stood about, some bandaged and propped up by strange splints, like invalids, too well loved to be thrown out, others flourishing more cheerfully. The settee and chairs were large, old-fashioned, deep, and covered in a large flowered print. In one of the chairs sat Humphrey Ward, his scarcely greying head bent over the affidavit. He looked remarkably young for his post: perhaps the fact that like Simon he was dressed in his gardening clothes made him look even younger than usual. The khaki trousers (a wartime inheritance), the muddy boots, the coloured shirt, all inspired confidence: watching him, as he sipped his sherry, Simon began to remember facts about him, bits of gossip, lawyers' stories. He had sat on committees, he had belonged to organisations associated with penal reform, he had founded a hostel for ex-prisoners. A nice man, a conscientious man. And he had two daughters, that was right: one of them worked in a primary school, he knew somebody that knew her, in fact somebody was married to her, and the other daughter was on some Race Relations body. He must have grandchildren the same ages as Rose's children, whose brief history he was now reading.

When he had read all the relevant documents, Mr Justice Ward made no objection to signing the order. So that was that. They all sat back for a moment, not quite liking to think what to do next, because it was obvious, since nobody knew where Christopher was, that it was impossible to serve the injunction on him. Francis Morris requested leave to announce the making of the injunction in the press: the judge smiled gently and said that leave was not necessary, as technically the hearing of an application for such an injunction would be in open court. Ah yes, of course, said Francis Morris, annoyed with himself for the slip. I'd better get moving, then, said Jeremy Alford, I'd better ring up the evenings, and see if I can catch the late edition.

'No, don't do that,' said Rose, suddenly. She had been sitting very quietly, watching the little motes turn in the sunny air. 'Don't do that, I couldn't bear it, not all over the papers again.'

'Now come, Mrs Vassiliou,' said the judge, gently. 'Surely you'd better do all you can, at this stage, rather than regret it later? It's unfortunate, I agree, but it's the lesser of two evils.'

'But we've no proof,' said Rose, 'that he ever meant to do anything. Perhaps he was just threatening me. Perhaps he's been at my father's for hours.'

'That's an interesting point,' said the judge. 'Did anyone think to ring your parents to see if they were there?'

Nobody had thought, it appeared. So Jeremy Alford rang the number of the house in Norfolk, and enquired of a servant whether or not Mr Vassiliou and the children had arrived. Not yet, he was told, though they were expected.

'So we're none the wiser,' said the judge, sighing gently, and looking at his watch. It was by now after one, and the judge was doubtless thinking of his lunch.

'Well, we mustn't impose on you any longer,' said Jeremy Alford, 'I must go and ring the Press Association and the Home Office.'

'Do use my telephone,' said the judge, but without marked enthusiasm: so they all rose to their feet, and began to take their leave. As Rose was shaking his hand she quite suddenly burst into tears again, and stood there, holding his hand and weeping. There, there, said the judge, patting her on the shoulder, don't you worry, it'll all be all right, you wait and see, you go off and get yourself some lunch and forget about it for an hour or two, it's all safely in hand now, there's nothing more you can do.

'Perhaps she'd like a sandwich?' said Lady Ward, who had appeared quietly in the background, no doubt to remind her husband that it was time for his lunch.

'No, no, not at all,' Rose managed to say, through her tears: and Simon led her off. His last view of the Wards was of their worried, concerned faces, as they stood at the window together watching them go, before going into the kitchen, to eat their meal off the kitchen table, amongst the half-cleaned silver.

In the car, they discussed what to do next. Jeremy Alford was torn between a desire to stop at the nearest Xerox machine, take a copy of the injunction, track down Christopher and serve it on him in person, probably as he was about to board a plane for Cyprus at Heathrow airport, and a desire to go home quick, placate his wife, and eat his lunch. Francis Morris wanted to get back to his tennis club: his role was over. He said this so clearly that Simon heartlessly dropped him, with effusive thanks, at a taxi rank. He then took Jeremy Alford home. Mrs Alford dutifully offered Simon and Rose something to eat, but was highly relieved when they declined. She did not feel up to entertaining.

'We might as well leave it to you,' said Simon. 'We're better out of the way, really.'

'Oh, I wouldn't say that,' said Jeremy. 'You've been most helpful. I don't know what I'd have done without you.'

And he pulled a face at Simon, signifying, Rose is impossible, and Simon pulled one back, signifying, yes, I agree. Rose intercepted these looks, and managed to convey, humbly, that she quite agreed with both.

'Well, I'll take her home,' said Simon.

And so he took her home, having promised to communicate if anything happened at Rose's end, and to await communications from Alford himself. They got back to Rose's house in Middle Road at just after two. The whole process had taken nearly three hours. Time enough to arrive in the Middle East, more or less.

And in Rose's house, they sat down and continued to wait. Simon was hungry, but felt it would be indelicate to make too much fuss about it: Rose said she did not feel up to eating.

'I feel like a drink,' he said, after a while, 'have you got anything in the house?'

He did not think that a drink would be considered heartless: on the contrary, it would offer proof of suffering.

'Not a drop,' said Rose, bleakly.

And thinking of drink, and suffering, brought suddenly for the first time into Simon's head the memory of his visit to Christopher the night before, and it occurred to him for the first time that the whole thing might be his own fault, or at least as much his fault as

Mr Calvacoressi's. For had he not put the notion of the hopelessness of Christopher's case firmly into his head? And had it not been that, precisely, which the telegram had deplored?

In the end he had to get up and make himself a meal. Rose followed him and watched him, listlessly, as he fried a couple of eggs. Suddenly she said,

'I should never have set the police on him. What will they do, if they get him at the airport?'

'I don't know,' said Simon, and at that moment the phone rang. It was Jeremy Alford, saying that the police wanted to know if Rose knew her husband's passport number. Simon asked her, but she shook her head dumbly. He had a suspicion that she would not have said, even if she had known. When Alford had rung off, Rose returned to her point. She should not, she repeated, have set the police on him.

'Nonsense,' said Simon sharply. He had seen this coming. 'Nonsense. The decision was nothing to do with you, it was simply a consequence of his own illegal action. He shouldn't have taken those children out of the jurisdiction without leave from the court anyway. He hadn't the right.'

'Yes,' said Rose, 'but whose fault is that? If I hadn't divorced him he'd have had a right to take them anywhere. So it is my fault, isn't it?'

'No, it's not. At the time, you did what you had to do.'

He turned his eggs, neatly, and fried them on the other side.

'Yes, I suppose I did. But I sometimes feel that I ought to have gone on taking it.' She paused, then went on, hesitantly. 'You, for instance, you don't give up, do you? I think about that a lot.'

It was the first time she had ever said anything of that nature to him. He did not pretend not to know what she meant.

'It's not so bad for me,' he said.

'It's not so bad for you because you're a nicer person than I am.'

'You don't know anything about me.'

'Oh yes I do. And I'll tell you why you're so nice. It's because you never give anything away.'

By anything, she meant anyone. She was delicate.

'I haven't got much to give away,' he said, as he sat down at the table to eat his eggs.

'That's what I mean,' she said, and smiled, sharply, sadly.

They both smiled.

'It's a pity,' he said, finally.

'No,' she said, 'not really. It's a good thing, to be like you. There need to be people like you.'

'I've told you before,' he said, 'I only act out of a sense of obligation.'

'That's good enough.'

'Not for me, quite,' he said.

'Ah yes,' she said, triumphantly, clinching it. 'But then *you* are not what you are thinking of.'

When he had finished his eggs, she started again.

'There was a letter in *The Times*,' she said, 'the other day. Pointing out that charity is for the sake of the giver, to save the soul of the giver, not the receiver. I couldn't tell if the letter was serious or not. It's the classic view, you know. I read it again and again, and I couldn't tell. It's interesting, isn't it? Do you think one could save one's soul by giving away one's children? Or would the crime of parting with them be greater than the virtue of the gift?'

'I don't always follow you,' he said.

She laughed.

'I don't always follow myself,' she said. 'You should see what it's like, inside my head.'

And the telephone rang. They both started, nervously. Rose got up to answer it, but as she listened, she reached her hand out to Simon, and he went and listened with her: there were pips, then a child's voice, Konstantin's voice, calling from a call box.

'Hello, Mummy,' he said.

'Hello, darling. How are you?' She spoke neutrally, calmly, as though to a child on a cliff's edge or lodged in a high tree.

'I'm fine, Mum, I just wanted to ring to see how you were.'

'I'm fine, love, I've just had my lunch...' she hesitated, then spoke again. 'Where are you? Are you having a nice time?'

'We're having a great time, we've just been down Grime's Graves, we haven't got to Grandpa's yet,' said Konstantin, his voice tremulous with responsibility, offering circumstantial evidence—'we just went down these great holes to see the flint mines, and it was all little corridors, and Maria didn't like the ladder and cried, and Daddy had got this torch, and then we came up again and had lunch in this café, and I thought I'd give you a ring to...' his voice faltered, 'I thought I'd give you a ring to see how you are, and to tell you we'll be at Grandpa's soon. Are you all right, Mummy?'

'Of course I'm all right, it was nice of you to ring...' Her fingers tightened on Simon's hand, leaving marks. She spoke again, carefully.

'Where are you, then? Are you in a call box?'

'No, Mum, I'm in the café, the others went out to the car, I just came back again, I said I wanted to go to the Gents, but I thought I'd just give you a ring. It's that café just beyond Littlewell, Jim's Diner, we had bacon and eggs and beans and sausages. I'd better go now, I'll see you tomorrow, Mum.'

'Yes. Yes. All right, darling. Be a good lad, look after the little ones for me.'

'Bye, Mum.' And he rang off.

Simon and Rose looked at each other. 'Christ,' said Rose.

'Has he ever done that before?' said Simon, urgently.

'No, not really. He's rung from Grandpa's, once or twice, wanting to speak to me. But never like that.'

'Christopher couldn't have put him up to it, could he?'

'I don't think so. No, he sounded—oh God, he sounded as though he wanted to reassure me. What an amazing child he is. What a marvellous boy. Quick, let's ring up Jim's Diner and see if they were really there. What a child, he even gave me the name. Whatever do you think Christopher told him? Perhaps he didn't tell him anything, perhaps he just picked it up, he's so quick, that child, what a life we've led him—'

Simon meanwhile had got the number. They rang the café: the man said that a man with three children in a Jaguar had just left that minute.

'They're there,' said Rose. 'It was them. What a foul bloody liar that bastard is.' She spoke with affection and relief.

'We'd better ring Jeremy Alford and get him to tell the Home Office,' said Simon. And they tried to ring him, but the number was perpetually engaged. 'Perhaps he's taken the phone off, perhaps he's had enough of us,' said Rose, and they both laughed.

'You're sure it was really Konstantin?' said Simon.

'Of course it was. Didn't you hear him?'

'Christopher couldn't have put him up to it, could he?'

'No, of course not. Anyway, we know it was him, the café man said so. No, Konstantin's far too sensible to be put up to anything. Try Jeremy again. Perhaps there's time to stop all the papers.'

So they rang again, and this time he was in. Simon gave him the news: Jeremy Alford listened in silence.

'Well?' said Simon, as the silence continued.

'Well *what*?' said Jeremy Alford, crossly. 'Look, I've got rid of my own children, sent them off to my mother's for the weekend, and Shirley and I were going to spend a quiet weekend asleep in our deck chairs. And instead I have to spend my time running round in circles after a lunatic.'

'Sorry,' said Simon.

'I was just going to have a large brandy and go to sleep.'

'Really. I am sorry. Is there anything I can do?'

'No. Not really. Just keep Rose quiet, won't you. Don't let her do anything silly. No, you leave it to me.' He sighed. 'I'll get moving. Again.'

'All right,' said Simon, and rang off.

'What did he say?' said Rose, anxiously.

'He was relieved, of course,' said Simon. 'He said he'd look after it. There's nothing we can do.'

And they looked at one another. The afternoon sun was falling, obliquely, into the semi-basement room: a children's mobile, made of cork and straws, turned slowly, dangling between them, from the low ceiling.

'You'll get them back,' he said, 'by the end of the day.'

'Yes,' she said, 'I think so.'

She touched the mobile with her hand: it circled.

'We could go down there ourselves and get them,' said Simon. The idea had only occurred to him, that instant, but once conceived, it seemed the only thing to do.

'Could we?' said Rose. 'Could we really? Would you really take me?'

'I would like to,' he said. 'It would be good for us, to get moving. We've sat around here too much, today. We need a bit of action.'

'We ought to tell somebody where we're going,' she said, 'just in case.'

'I daren't ring Jeremy again,' he said. 'Let's ring Emily. We ought to ring her anyway, to tell her what's happened. And she can ring Jeremy, later on. When we've gone.'

So they rang Emily, told her what had happened, asked her to ring Jeremy Alford in half an hour: tried to ring Jeremy themselves, after all, guiltily, then, and got no reply. Oh well, forget him, said Simon, he's had enough of us today anyway. And so they set off, in the car, through North London, to the A10. Simon had completely forgotten to ring Julie: Rose reminded him, and made him stop at a call box, and he rang and told her a story, half of which was true, about Francis Morris and the police and an urgent job, and apologised profusely for not being back. She was quite nice about it, attracted as Morris had been by the note of urgency and priority. 'I'll tell you about it when I get back,' he said, and they drove on.

They even enjoyed the journey. It was the excursion they had once promised themselves. It was a relief to be moving, after sitting for so long in so small a space at the mercy of the telephone. Simon wondered at times whether they had not perhaps acted on foolish impulse, but there had been nothing useful that they could have done, in London. He did not think about what they would do at the other end, if they found the children there: he could not see himself participating in an abduction scene, and hoped it would not come to that. He was not at all clear about the legal position in which he or indeed Rose found themselves: the position was probably not clear in itself. There could not be many precedents for Christopher's actions. He had perhaps created one. That was what happened, when eccentrics embarked on litigation. The law would tediously unravel, in accordance with its own concepts, the crazy acts of neurosis. He thought of other litigants, other madmen, passionately attached beyond all reason to cases that they had no hope of winning: disputed wills, territorial struggles between embattled neighbours, angry wives suing long-defaulted husbands for shares in homes now given to newer mistresses. Such cases were never ruled by the mercenary instinct, though they might seem at the outset to be so: they sucked in money, sometimes every penny that the participant had, they sucked it into the mud of resentment and emotion, without a hope of final prosperity. There was a case currently being fought in his own field: two unions which had amalgamated years back, were now struggling to disentangle themselves, to the obvious detriment of both. The judge involved had called both parties childish, and so they were, but they were past caring: they hated each other, they did not care if both perished, as long as the point was made. The only difference in Christopher's case was that he seemed to know what he was doing, he seemed to recognise the grounds of his own behaviour, and had done from the beginning, from the moment when he had chosen to defend his divorce. It was that which made him dangerous. He did not even think he was right. And so it would have been a logical step, to leave the country with the children. Covertly, at a traffic light, he looked at the AA book. There were no ports from which he could leave, except Yarmouth and Harwich, and when Konstantin had rung he had been far enough from both. Though there had been a case, not so long ago, before Calvacoressi, of a father who had abducted his children, who had set off to sea alone with them in a rowing boat, and had waited there, bobbing idly up and down upon the waves, until the police had picked him up. A few hours of the children he had had, and had thereby lost them for ever. People were mad, people were strange beyond belief, as one could see from reading any newspaper. He had a fleeting picture of Christopher hiding with the children in the woods, or concealing them in the bottom of a flint mine. He put his foot on the accelerator. Norfolk was a huge county, much larger than he had thought, and Rose's family seat was right at the other end of it. The traffic was bad, too. They would not get there before the early evening.

Rose, for her part, could not help enjoying the drive. She went out so little: it was months since she had been out in a car. She was sure, now, that she would find the children safely at the other end: she ought to have had faith in Konstantin, she should have known that he would not allow himself to be abducted, he was too considerate, he cared for her too much. Her pride in him was immense. She knew exactly why he had rung her: he had picked up from Christopher some threat or menace—possibly even a spoken threat—and had rung to tell her that it was all right, that all was as it had been planned, that they would be safely at the house as they had said they would be, that he would make sure that it was so. So she sat back, and watched the fields passing. It was a road she knew well, a road she had not travelled for years. She was trying to work out how long it had been, when Simon said,

'It must be a long time since you came this way.'

'That's just what I was thinking,' she said. 'I can't remember how long. I've only been once or twice since we were married.'

'When did you last see your father?' he said, and they both laughed at the classic question.

'I can't even remember,' she said. 'It would be strange, to see him again. Perhaps I should. I think my mother is there too. She's not there often, but she doesn't mind it, in the good weather. Perhaps I should see them.'

'I meant to go and see my mother this weekend,' he said, 'but I didn't get round to it. I keep thinking, I would like to take you some day to meet my mother. I don't know why.'

'Do you think she would like me, your mother?'

'She doesn't like anyone much. I was thinking more that you might like her. She's an interesting woman. It would be good to find somebody who might like her.'

'I would like it very much,' said Rose.

And they were silent again, for a few miles. Rose started to think again about Christopher's affidavit. It had upset her dreadfully, to see her crimes catalogued. And yet, as with the divorce, she could not help knowing that the crimes which seemed, technically, most serious, had not been so at all. Her only true guilt lay in not having been able, enough, to allow Christopher to be. Whereas the suicide—an event, she knew, which judges must take seriously, as Jeremy Alford had done—had really been a very trivial matter. She had, it is true, in front of the children, swallowed a whole bottle of aspirins, in response to some particularly grinding session of abuse from Christopher: she remembered quite clearly the sequence of events that had made her do it. I can't bear this, I must leave, she had said to herself. I can't leave, because of the children, she had then said—Maria being still a baby, at the breast. Then I had better die, she had said, and had swallowed the pills. No, I had better not die, she had then instantly realised: she had gone to the bathroom, stuck her fingers down her throat, vomited up a lot of white powder, then rung the hospital and requested to have her stomach pumped out, just in case. The ambulance had been round in ten minutes, her stomach pumped within the hour—horrible rubber tubes, she recalled—and she had been back at home cooking supper within a couple of hours. One could not call that irresponsible: it had been a thoroughly practical piece of behaviour. And equally trivial had been her acts of sexual misconduct. She did not know how Christopher had brought himself to mention them. He knew quite well, for instance, that she and Nick hadn't spent an hour alone together in years, so the citing of Nick must reveal more about Christopher's attitude to him than her own. And as for the man called Anton, there perhaps again she had been technically in the wrong, because she had in fact slept with Anton, but only as the result of a most embarrassing misunderstanding, a misunderstanding so much in her own favour that she supposed she would never be able to bring herself to explain it to anybody. And how Christopher knew about it she could not imagine. Anton was a student, a rather elderly student refugee, who had arrived from Prague the year before after some political trouble, speaking very bad English: he had been handed on to her by an old friend, who had asked her to find him somewhere to live, because I know, he had said, that you used to deal in accommodation, didn't you? Rose, too polite to explain that she had given up dealing in such things years ago, had said she would do what she could, and Anton had arrived on her doorstep one night, filthy dirty and rather drunk, in an old soldier's uniform. She had never found out what he was doing in uniform. She had asked him in, and given him a meal, and said he could stay the night with her: they had talked, till very late, in a confused mixture of languages, about the reasons for his flight, and as they talked she knew perfectly well that she had not the faintest notion of what he was talking about, and that the language barrier would never permit them to get very much further. But she felt sorry for him: he was a small man, his face white and waxy and gleaming from fatigue, his hair cropped short—this seemed to enrage him more than anything, the indignity of his cropped hair, she did manage to make out that he would never dare to show his face in the glorious streets of decadent London until it had grown a little—and he was also good-humoured, in a bizarre non-verbal way. Every now and then he would roar with laughter and crack a joke to justify his laughter, in Czech or German. She laughed too, pleased to see him in good spirits, but she was amazingly tired herself, and knew she would have to get up in the morning to get the children to school, and was longing to get to sleep. At about three in the morning she could stand it no longer, and got up and said emphatically, 'I really must go to bed.' She had already explained to him where he was to sleep—she had given him one of the children's beds, and put two of them in a bed together—and she had thought he had understood the message. So she said good night, and went up and got into her own bed. Just as she was about to switch off the light, Anton opened the door and came in. She sat up again, about to ask him what he wanted, but was struck dumb when he started to take his clothes off. She said nothing: she lay there and watched, her mouth open in astonishment. She said nothing when he got into the bed, turned off the light, and grabbed her. In confusion, as he got on with it, she thought, Christ, perhaps he's been propositioning me the whole evening and I've been agreeing without being able to understand what he's been saying. She was far too polite to resist: she didn't want to offend him, and it didn't anyway seem very important. In fact, she had to admit to herself that she did find him rather attractive, in some obscene sexy way: his skin was all dirty and slippery, he smelt of railway carriages, and he made love in an exhausted, enthusiastic, noisy manner, mumbling and grunting and reciting bits of poetry in foreign languages and grabbing at her without finesse and laughing suddenly and unpredictably into her neck. It was confusing but somehow irresistible: as before, as downstairs, she never got the jokes, but she could not help laughing, with him and at him and at the absurdity of the occasion. His head was round like a bullet, with its shorn hair, and his body was short and compact like her own, but much more solid. He was a man of middle Europe, a man of cabbages and shabby uniforms and shabby politics, and he bitterly resented it. This was one of the jokes. He would clutch, every now and then, desperately, at his prison crop, and then collapse upon her, trying to demonstrate that his hair would grow, given half a chance. He mumbled of Trotsky and Mick Jagger. It went on and on and on. Rose was amazed. She had never known anything like it. It was all so sudden and so silly, and she could not imagine how it had happened. It was not the kind of thing that usually happened to her at all.

Afterwards, when he had fallen asleep, she worked out that he had probably mistaken her emphatic declaration of her need to get to bed for an expression of desire: her voice had certainly been unnatural as she had said it, because she had been embarrassed about deserting her conversational duties as hostess, when he had clearly wanted to go on talking all night. She discovered the next day that this suspicion was correct: in his version of the English language, to go to bed was an active verb, synonymous for going-to-bed-with, and he had truly thought that what she had meant had been, 'I must go to bed, now, with you.' And he had duly obliged. This wouldn't in itself have worried her very much, but Anton, having found such a welcome, was not at all keen to move on, and she didn't know how to explain that he had got it all wrong without offending him. She contemplated, the next day, a situation in which he would move in permanently, without her ever being able to communicate that he couldn't: of course it didn't happen that way, in the end she did manage to explain to him that he had better find somewhere else, citing the children as a reason. But he did tend to come back and hang around waiting for another invitation. She was careful never to mention the word bed again. It reminded her of the headmistress at her school, who had told her girls on no account to invite men into rooms where underclothes or stockings were hanging up to dry. They had laughed at her then, but how right she had been (the canny old spinster). The children must have told

Christopher about Anton. One could never explain such an absurd situation. She wondered whether to embark on explaining it now, to Simon, but decided it was impossible to tell the story right: however she told it, it would look like an apology, and she did not feel at all apologetic. She hadn't thought about Anton for months, until she saw his name in the typescript: the thought of him hadn't crossed her mind. In a sense, the whole thing was Christopher's fault anyway: she wouldn't have dared to be so hospitable with so little protest, if she hadn't been swallowing pills night after night, for fear that Christopher himself would come back and rape her. He had threatened to do this on several occasions, and had once actually done it, the week after the divorce: well, perhaps it hadn't been rape exactly, because she hadn't struggled particularly hard because of her fear of waking and upsetting the children. She had hated him for that more than for anything. But she felt she had deserved it. It had seemed, as Christopher himself had yelled at her, an appropriate punishment. And he had never dared to do it again.

As an adolescent, like most girls, she had had fantasies of rape. How disagreeable fantasies became, when translated into action.

She thought of Mr Justice Ward, and his worried look. He was a nice man, he wouldn't have minded that she had slept with Anton and swallowed a few pills. He would surely have understood it all.

Suddenly she started to laugh.

'What's the joke?' said Simon.

'I was just remembering,' she said, 'thinking of judges, a song the kids sing. They skip to it, listen.' And in a quavering, irritating, imitation child's nasal whine she sang,

'Fudge, Fudge, Call the Judge
Mother's got a new born *Baby*.
It isn't a girl, it isn't a boy
It's just a new born *Baby*.
Wrap it up in tissue paper

Send it down the escalator
First floor *Missed*
Second floor *Missed,*
Third floor, kick it out the door,
Mother's got a new born *Baby.*'

They both laughed. He nearly took her hand.

And so they drove, towards Branston Woods, and Christopher, and the children, and the home she had left for ever. She began to recognise landmarks: towns and villages where she had stopped for meals on previous journeys, familiar skycrapes, pine forests, the cathedral at Norwich. Gables, Flemish architecture. There were a lot of small animals dead on the roads: shrews, hedgehogs, voles, a weasel. Simon remarked on it, and she said, 'Yes, but there are so many dead because there are so many living, you know, they're not really being killed off, it's where you don't see them on the roads that there aren't any in the hedges.' She was remembering, suddenly, a surreptitious visit she had made with Christopher ten years before, not long after their marriage. Then, they had not dared to approach the house. She wondered if she would dare to do so now. Christopher had commented, as Simon had done, on the death rate on the roads. They had climbed over the wall, she and Christopher, like children, like thieves. And now he had a room there, kept for him, and all her things were gone.

It was well after four when they reached Grime's Graves and Jim's Diner. She explained to Simon about the graves: not really graves but caves they were, ancient flint mines, a whole network of them under the earth. She had been down, as a child, with a miner's lamp, but like Maria she had been frightened by the darkness and the narrowness of the tunnels. There were a lot of cars parked on the road that led off the main road to the Graves: it was a day for sightseeing, and the traffic grew heavier as they drove on towards the coast. As their destination approached, slowly, she began to get nervous, having no very clear idea of what they should do when they got there, and when they turned off the main road to cover the last ten miles she wanted the journey not to end. They were driving through woods, no longer the orderly evergreen plantations, but deciduous woods, thick with undergrowth, and she said, suddenly,

'It's a pity we can't stop and get out for a walk, it's so lovely here.'

Simon slowed down. He too was not looking forward to the dénouement.

'We could, if you liked,' he said.

'Would it matter?' she said. 'It couldn't make much difference, half an hour, could it? Would you mind?'

'I'd like to,' he said. He thought it was unwise, to stop and to waste time, but did not like to say so.

'I'll show you a good place to stop,' she said, and in half a mile they pulled up, into a gateway, and got out. On the gate it said, Private Woods, Keep Out. Rose pushed it open and went through. From the gate a broad green lane stretched between the trees. They walked down it, in silence, their feet sinking into the thick grass. Bracken and brambles grew under the trees. After a few minutes Rose turned off, through the trees: she seemed to know her way. He followed her. A hare, startled by their approach, leaped up and raced away from them, huge and bounding: a dislodged pheasant clattered noisily up almost from under their feet, giving them a reproachful look as it took off. In the trees, small birds sang and rustled: she put her hand on his arm, and pointed upwards, to a bird with a pink breast that was creeping up a tree trunk. 'It's a nut hatch,' she said. And then, as they stood still to watch, she said, 'These woods are mine, you know. All this land south of the house is mine. Those fir trees were all mine. It was put in trust for me, years ago. These woods are going to be replanted, with conifers. They get a big grant from the Forestry Commission, and tax concessions. There's nothing I can do about it, nothing at all.'

He did not know what to say. He looked around him, at her property.

'Ridiculous, really,' she said, 'that one can't get rid of what is one's own.'

They stood there, and listened to the rustling of the leaves. He thought of the backyard and the geraniums, of his abandoned crazy paving, of Rose's muddy patch behind her house in Middle Road.

'Why should you wish to get rid of it?' he said.

'I don't know,' she said, lightly. 'Because I can't enjoy it, I suppose.'

'I was digging my garden this morning, when Emily rang,' he said. 'I couldn't tell whether I was enjoying it or not.'

'You're very like me,' she said.

'But for different reasons.'

'Yes, yes,' she said. 'You have risen in the world, and I have sunk. How curious it is.'

There was a sentence in his head, which said, 'If I had been free, I would have asked you to marry me,' but it did not seem useful to utter it. They stood there a moment longer, listening, and then they set off back again. The density of the trees, all so various, all to him so unnamed, amazed him: they trod on an immense abundance of small plants, on fungi purple and orange and brown. From a heap of rotting leaves grew a huge thing, a foot tall, with a large head and a curling fringe: she pointed at it, and said, 'That's called a lawyer's wig, that one. They're said to be edible, but one wouldn't like to try.' A little further on, just before they rejoined the green avenue that led to the gate, Rose stopped sharply and gave a cry: she had walked into a dangling stoat, hung from a tree by string. They stood and looked at it: she was trembling, trying to brush the touch of it out of her hair. It dangled there in the slight breeze, dry and stiff, utterly dead, killed twice over, trapped and hung, its wicked face pointing skywards, its long body lengthened by suspension, swinging from its natural gibbet. It was not rotting: it seemed mummified, dried out by exposure, archaic, pagan.

'It frightened me,' she said, smiling apologetically, tucking her hair back into its pins.

'If I had been free,' he said, 'I would have asked you to marry me.'

They both stared at the little corpse, strung up as a warning.

'Ah,' she said, gently, tenderly, 'ah yes. What a nice time we would have had. I too have thought of it, you know.'

And without looking at each other, they went back to the car.

WHEN THEY ARRIVED at the gates of the house—large, ornate iron gates, set between stone gateposts topped by worn sneering stone beasts—they stopped in astonishment and alarm. A great commotion seemed to be taking place: dozens of cars were parked, a man in an overall was directing traffic. Their first thought was that it must be the police and the press, that disaster had preceded them in some way, so utterly unexpected were all the signs of activity, but a moment's inspection made it clear that it was no such thing. A yellow poster was stuck on to one of the gateposts: it said BRANSTON HALL. WHIT SATURDAY, NATIONAL GARDENS SCHEME. OPEN TO THE PUBLIC BY KIND PERMISSION OF MR AND MRS BRYANSTON. 2.30—7.30 P.M. TEAS.

'Well, well, well,' said Rose. 'What an extraordinary thing.'

'What on earth *is* it?' said Simon, trying not to catch the eye of the man in uniform, who was beckoning him forward.

'It's their open day,' said Rose, 'I'd no idea. They only do it one day a year. It's in aid of district nurses. What on earth shall we do now?'

'I didn't really know what we were going to do anyway,' said Simon.

'We could just drive in,' said Rose.

'Do you think the children will be there?'

'Of course they will. How could they be kept away from fun like that?'

'And if they *are* there,' said Simon, 'what are we going to do about them?'

'I don't know,' said Rose. 'We could just steal them away quietly, if we could find them on our own. Or you could have a word with Christopher. Tell him there's an injunction on the way, or something.'

'*You* can have a word with Christopher,' said Simon. 'He's your responsibility, not mine.'

'I daren't,' said Rose. And they both began to laugh, helplessly.

'I could do with a nice tea,' said Rose. 'Do you think we're too late? I missed my lunch. So did you, more or less.'

'Why don't we just pay our two bob and go in and have another think? That man won't let me hang about here much longer, he's got his eye on me.'

'Why don't *you* go in? Nobody would know you, you could do some reconnaissance for me.'

'I won't go in by myself. I daren't. Christopher might shoot me.'

'Don't be silly, even if he saw you he wouldn't know *I* was here, would he? If you saw him, you could just say you were sightseeing.'

'What on earth would I be sightseeing here on my own for?'

'You might,' she said, looking at him, smiling, remarkably gay, 'you might be doing it out of sentiment. Out of affection for me.'

'An unfulfilled passion for you,' he said.

'More or less,' she said.

'Well, I won't,' he said. 'I'm not coming in without you.' He seemed, for the first time in years, to be saying what he meant as he meant it. The sensation was extraordinary, as though a clamp had been taken off his head.

'All right,' she said. 'I didn't really expect you to, you know. I'll come with you. Perhaps I could disguise myself. I don't know why, I always knew I'd come back one day in disguise. What can I do for myself, to make myself look different?'

'You could wear my glasses,' he said, 'but I can't see very well without them. Or there might be some sunglasses of Julie's somewhere.' He rummaged in the glove compartment, and produced some sunglasses, and a silk Dior headsquare with orange and brown blobs on it.

'It won't suit me,' she said. 'It won't go with my things.'

'It's not like you to be so choosy,' he said, and she humbly put them on, and inspected herself in the driving mirror.

'Marvellous,' he said, contemplating the Julie/Rose image. The bright clear orange tan and white looked very strange round Rose's unassertive, unpainted face: it was made to go with lipstick, and her features inside it looked lost and pale. 'Marvellous. Your own mother wouldn't know you.'

'It's to be hoped she won't,' said Rose. 'We could have a recognition scene, later, in the drawing-room or the library or the rose garden. Come on, let's go.'

So he drove up to the man, and gave him his four shillings, and was directed to a parking place just inside the gates.

'I feel a fool,' said Rose, getting out of the car.

'You can't imagine how foolish I feel,' said Simon, and they set off down the drive towards the house. It was a late eighteenth-century house, described in the leaflet which they had been given as unpretentious, but to Simon it looked pretentious enough. It was built of a lovely yellow beige brick: the front of the house, which they approached, had four bays, with tall slim decorative pilasters, and round arched doorways opening on to a lawn and terrace. The terrace overlooked a sunken garden with a pond and a fountain playing. The house was delicate, weathered, domestic. The windows of the upper storey, the scrolls at the tops of the pillars, the blind arches, the plain pediment, spoke of simplicity and harmony. Rose, as they walked up the drive, took Simon's arm, and explained to him its history: it had been built when the family was peculiarly prosperous, owing to marriage into a rich slave-trading family—(and now maintained, she said, by another rich marriage, but that was beside the point)—and it had been an act of defiance against its near and monstrous neighbour, Holkham Hall, a building deeply deplored by the locals for its hideous use of white-yellow brick (here so attractive and mellow, there so crude and unnatural), for its *folie de grandeur,* its marmoreal classicism, its squat Palladian squareness. It had been ungrateful, really, said Rose, to be so rude to the Cokes, because after all they had drained the land, but the Bells had determined that their country house should be all that Holkham was not—elegant, domestic, tree-surrounded, English, charming. No one could call Holkham charming, she said, we must go there one day, but this, this is charming, isn't it, and look, they've even got the fountain to work, it hasn't played in years. Her voice could not help but take on colour: she clung to his arm. She was happy, she was happy that he liked her at least, and holding his arm she felt, how much I have missed simply this, an arm to hold, a person to walk with. There's a lovely herb garden, she said, you must see it, in the rain it's so beautiful, I used to go and sit there in the pouring rain, and you must come and see the stables, you must see it all. And all the time they both looked out nervously for Christopher with a gun, for the children, for police descending in a helicopter.

Tea was being served on the terrace. Rose, seeing the woman who was pouring out from the huge tin tea pot, turned away, and said, 'That's Mrs Graves, oh dear me.'

'I'll get you a cup,' said Simon, and he went off to get cups of tea and sandwiches. Rose sat down on the parapet. She looked down at the sunken garden, and the roses, and the lilies in the water. Two women next to her were talking about the place they had been to the week before, a Jacobean house in Suffolk, where there hadn't been anything to eat but dry biscuits, though it had advertised Teas. This is what I call a tea, said one of the women, eating scones and rock buns and a ham sandwich. Rose could hardly prevent herself from taking some kind of credit. Simon, returning with a plateful of food, said, 'I asked your Mrs Graves if the family were at home. And she said yes, they were all here.'

'What did she mean by all?'

'I don't know. I didn't ask her. I felt as though I were enquiring after royalty.'

She smiled. 'You mustn't hate me for this,' she said.

And he suddenly thought of where she lived, and her ironing and the Ally Pally, and Africa, and Eileen's baby, and the chicken and the armchairs, and the extraordinary nature of her journey, and the distance she had travelled, and he said, 'No, no. How could I?' It was not possible that she existed, and there she sat, eating a buttered scone, in a silk headsquare that looked incomparably too rich and too showy for her modest features and her unassuming spirit. Nature had made her that way, nature had made her unremarkable, an ordinary person: fate had capriciously elected her to notoriety: and she had made the painful journey back to nature by herself, alone, guided by nothing but her own knowledge, against the current. There she sat, her bare legs crossed neatly, a Vinyl sandal dangling from the arch of her dusty foot, brushing the crumbs tidily from her brown skirt, a paying guest. He watched her: she was a vision kindly bestowed. She finished her scone, put down her paper plate on the wall beside her, looked up at him, and said,

'What shall we do? What should we do, now?'

'We'd better go and look, I suppose,' he said.

'I don't know where to begin,' she said, slipping down from the wall to join him. 'Where do you think they would be? Outside or inside? I don't think we're allowed inside, they don't open the house.'

'We could start with the outside,' he said. 'They're more likely to be out, on a day like this. You show me where to go.'

And they set off together, arm in arm again, through the garden, looking at this and that as they went, listening to snatches of overheard conversation, reluctant to waste the simple pleasure of walking together. There were a lot of people: the fine weather and the Bank Holiday combined had made for a good turn-out. The gardens were looking well, better than Rose had remembered. A special effort had been made for the public, she said. There were plenty of children running about, nagged by mothers to keep off flowerbeds, but none of them were her own. The grounds were extensive: there were plenty of places to look. They tried first the nearer places: the lawns round the house, the rose garden, the herb garden, and then hesitated between a long grass avenue leading between clipped hedges to an undramatic ha-ha, and the kitchen garden, which lay to their right, behind a high brick wall. And as they hesitated, Simon caught sight of the children. There they were, all three of them, miles away, climbing back into the garden over an ill-concealed fence at the far end of the avenue, small with distance and perspective, but unmistakeable, the one fair-haired child and the two dark ones.

'There they are,' he said, 'look, there they are,' and they both stopped and stared.

'We'll go and meet them,' she said.

And they walked to meet them, down the green path. The children were running, growing larger as they came, and they did not see Rose until they were within a few yards of her: then they recognised her, and shouted, and ran towards her, and she let go of Simon's arm and ran towards them. He watched them meet: he watched them come back towards him, clinging on to her, laughing, chattering. She was smiling: apologetic, slightly ashamed, but smiling. They met, at the geometric intersection of two avenues: green roads led off to right and left, before them the false rising perspective, behind them the house and its stone parapet. The meeting seemed to go on for ever, in that exposed spot: or wave after wave of it occurred and reoccurred, as though time had broadened endlessly to describe it. His mind was marked with green stripes: they crossed and crossed it. The high green hedges froze in a crest, about to break: the smell of trodden grass surged and rose and surged again. The planned and geometric grandeur stiffened and oppressed him: it was too much, too much intended. He looked for cover. There was no cover. They were intended to walk, down the very centre, back to the house.

On the way back, Marcus and Maria told Rose about Grime's Graves, and how frightening and exciting it had been: Konstantin walked a little apart, quietly, having formally acknowledged Rose's thanks for his phone call, asking no questions, worrying no doubt about what wheels he might have set in motion. Simon wondered about what they should do next. He had never really expected that they might discreetly escape, but any confrontation was inconceivable. Though the set seemed built, designed centuries ago, for confrontation. This is how the rich plan things, he found himself thinking: they arrange nature, they design it for their grandiose passions, and once a decade, perhaps, they fill in these great designs. Intersections, perspectives, the intolerable pretensions of those who think themselves free to operate. Rose gardens, shrubberies, ornamental lakes, the landscapes of the idle soul. The lake of disaffection, the spring of hope, the alleys of reunion. Once, at Oxford, on a summer night, he had looked out of his bedroom window across the college gardens, awakened by a dry thunderstorm, and there lay the garden, formal, beautiful, carefully maintained, lit by ray after ray of a pale amazing watery green, each leaf picked out, each flower blanched with immortality, everlasting flowers, and through the garden wandered, lit also by these fabulous shafts of light, the oldest fellow of the college, a mad old man in his nineties, wandering alone as he often did, walking off through the trees into the distance, landscape and figure gathered up together in some convulsive effort of significance, some delusive allegory of the soul. Then, deeply moved, he had stirred himself bitterly to rejection, protesting against this mocking beauty, this folly of grandeur, this arbitrary, exclusive illuminating shaft of light: and so now, too, he protested, against the very shape of the trees themselves. For what was the point of any virtue, any grace, if it was not of the common lot, there could be no beauty behind a gate marked Private, let them trample around on the flowerbeds, all of them, any of them: there was a hymn they had sung at school, it came back to him often, it said, The grass is softer to my tread, because it rests unnumbered feet, sweeter to me the wild rose red, because she makes the whole world sweet: and so it was, that was precisely so, as Rose had always known. And Rose's own rejections—her stumbling, her pallor, her renunciations, her Vinyl sandals—they appeared to him as the human, as the lovely, as the loving, as the stuff of life itself.

He heard her voice: irritable, querulous, pacifying. She was trying to comfort Maria, who had burst into tears of rage because Marcus was teasing her because she had cried down the flint mine; 'Don't be so *mean*, Marcus,' she was saying, and 'Don't be so *silly*, Maria,'—plunged back into the everyday, ignoring the high folding clipped hedges, the impressive destination. He listened to her, and they faded away. 'Maria,' she said, 'if you don't stop yelling I shall *hit* you.' And then she turned to him and said privately, 'Simon, quick, tell me, what on earth are we going to do?'

'I don't really know,' he said.

'Could we just take them home?' she said.

'We could try,' he said.

But it was too late, because there, walking towards them from the house was Christopher.

THEY MET HIM in the rose garden in front of the house. They converged, and met. The children stood about nervously. Christopher stood there in his dark glasses and stared at them, saying nothing. Simon did not dare to open his mouth. It was left to Rose to speak. She drew breath to do it, and then gently exhaled it, and started again. There was some line to deliver, she knew, but she could not find it. Finally, she let out a little sound that was half a moan and half a laugh, and said, 'Oh dear, oh dear, oh dear, oh well, never mind.'

'Ah,' said Christopher.

'Well, well, well,' said Rose.

And they all started to move, setting off as though by agreement towards the house.

'Well,' said Christopher, as they moved forward, 'as you're here, you'd better come in, I suppose.'

'Thank you,' said Rose. Then she started to laugh, and said, 'There's an injunction out against you, you know. Whatever an injunction may be.'

'Is there really?' said Christopher, pleasantly.

'Oh Christopher,' she said, 'what an absolute fool you are.'

'I suppose I am,' he said, 'but never mind. It's all over now.'

And over it appeared to be. Christopher had given in: his manner perfectly conveyed his concession. As he held open the french window for them, he turned to Rose and said,

'Why on earth are you wearing those ridiculous glasses?' and she said, 'They're my disguise, they're Simon's really, I'll take them off if you don't like them,' and she took them off and put them in her pocket. And there they were in the drawing-room, all six of them.

'Why, look who's here,' said Simon in astonishment: and there, sunk into two large chairs, sat Jeremy Alford and his pregnant wife, Shirley, in the gloom at the other end of the room. They were drinking gin and tonic.

'What on earth are you doing here?' said Jeremy, sounding as though he did not much care.

'Well, it's obvious, I'd have thought. What about you?'

'Equally obvious.'

'Don't let's talk about that kind of thing,' said Christopher, blandly, smiling. 'Let's all sit down instead. As I was doing already, with your nice friends, when it was reported that you were in the garden.'

'You have spies.'

'Oh yes, everywhere.' He was standing by the fireplace: the room seemed dark and murky, after the bright evening outside.

'We could tell the children to go off and play,' said Christopher, 'if you trust them out of your sight.'

'I don't know if I do,' said Rose.

'You're all right as long as you can see me,' said Christopher.

'I don't know about that,' said Rose. 'You might have agents all over the place. I know you. I don't trust you. You might have a yacht moored in Holkham Bay, for all I know.'

'I haven't,' said Christopher. 'I hadn't even thought of it. Too shallow, anyway.'

'What had you thought of, may I ask?'

'Nothing, really. I just wanted to give you a fright.'

'I knew it. I knew it. Well, you've really done yourself in this time. With all those injunctions and things. I can't stop them now, you know. Can I, Jeremy?' Jeremy smiled, embarrassed.

'No, I don't suppose you can,' said Christopher.

'Don't you care?'

'Not really. I'd had it anyway, hadn't I?'

Nobody answered him. The children had drifted off to the other end of the long room, sensing trouble. Simon wondered whether he should go away like a child and leave them to it, but did not know where to go to. The absurdity of the situation was so total that he gave up on it, happy to stand there like a stooge, even beginning to hope that Christopher would soon get round to offering him a drink.

'Let's have a drink,' said Christopher, reading his mind, and knowing he had read it, from the way Simon, relieved, met his glance. So he went over to the sideboard and opened a door and poured some drinks. The children, reassured by this comforting normality, slunk back and started begging for Coca-Cola, and were supplied. They all sat down.

'Are my parents here?' said Rose, after a while.

'Yes, they are. Your father's somewhere about, he was selling pot plants in the conservatory. You didn't see him?'

'We didn't try the conservatory. And where's mother?'

'She went to lie down. She didn't like all the people.'

'We were helping with the teas,' said Konstantin, 'but Mrs Graves told us to get out of the way, because Maria kept dropping the plates.'

'No, I didn't,' said Maria, and started to wail again.

'I'd better see them, I suppose,' said Rose. 'Do you think they could bear to see me?'

'I'll tell you what,' said Christopher. 'Why don't I tell them I was expecting you both? Why don't you stay the night?'

Rose looked at Christopher: really, she thought, in the end, one had just got to take him, and that's that. Her spirit, for the first time in years, moved to acceptance: she felt it embark for that final flight, she imagined it might one day rise and reach and settle in the clearer air.

'All right,' she said. 'Why not?'

'I can't stay,' said Simon. 'I must get back.'

'You must stay,' said Rose.

'You must stay,' said Christopher, 'you can't leave us, you daren't leave us. Why don't you all stay? Mrs Alford?'

'No, no, we can't possibly,' said Jeremy, a note of reluctance in his voice. 'We really must get back. Mustn't we, Shirley?'

'I suppose so,' said his wife, pulling herself to her feet. She was a small woman, with small tired features. 'I daren't stay too far away from the hospital, at the moment. We must get back.'

'I'm very sorry,' said Christopher, charming, helpful, moving forward to pick up her bag, take her arm, open doors for her—'I'm very sorry, to have caused so much inconvenience. Won't you have another drink, before you go? Do stay a few more minutes, and have another drink.'

Shirley Alford looked up at him. She looked a mild little woman, her hair a streaky silver yellow, her face soft and drained by pregnancy, frail, like an early daffodil, the delicate tissues of her skin dried by the process of gestation, soft and delicate, little lines round her eyes, blanched like a primrose too much exposed to a rough spring, as she had been too much exposed to exhausting, successive pregnancies, and the arduous life of a middle-class mother with a professional husband, standards to keep up, small children to tend unaided: strained, she looked, and overburdened, docile and fragile, subdued by her condition, but she looked at Christopher with a shrewd knowledge, and she said, in a voice utterly undestroyed, and robust, and decisive, the voice of one who will give birth and recover, with the next season of life, she said, 'Well, well, well,' she said, 'you really have got a bloody cheek. That's all that I can say.'

And she turned to her husband, and said, 'Come on, Jeremy, let's go.'

And at the sound of her saying, absolutely out, what they had all been thinking, they all smiled, even Christopher.

'You must forgive me,' said Christopher, unwilling to admit defeat. 'I must have ruined your weekend.'

'Not at all,' said Shirley, with dignity. 'You ruined one day of it, that's all. I daresay we shall make up for it tomorrow.'

And she walked firmly out of the room, saying goodbye to Rose as she went. Simon followed them: in the hall, he said to Jeremy,

'Well? What happened?'

'I served the injunction on him, of course,' said Jeremy Alford. 'He didn't even look at it. He just shoved it in his pocket. I made him get it out again and read it, so at least he knows what it's about. But I wouldn't let him out of your sight, if I were you. Did you come up to collect the children?'

'Yes, I suppose we did. Was that all right?'

'Very sensible. I was wondering if I ought to take them back to London myself, but Shirley didn't fancy having them bouncing around in the car.'

'Well, it's a bit much,' said Shirley. 'After all, I've got one bouncing around inside. And I went to great lengths to get rid of the other two. So I don't see why I should spend the time with other people's.'

'This'll be your third, will it?' said Simon.

'Yes, that's right,' said Shirley Alford, proudly. 'It's a good number, three.'

In the drawing-room, Rose was sitting down, looking out of the window. She turned, as Simon entered.

'You could stay, please,' said Rose. 'I'd like to stay. I think I ought to stay. And I can't, unless you do.'

'Perhaps your parents won't be very pleased if I do?' said Simon.

'Oh, they won't mind,' said Christopher. 'Why should they mind?'

And so he agreed to stay: Rose said she would ring up Julie and explain, and he thought that he might as well let her, as he was incapable of doing it himself, and there seemed to be little point in not burning one's boats, so clearly had this gathering constituted itself as a finale, as a dénouement, as a conclusion with no prospects. So Rose lifted the receiver and rang: he could hear every word she said, he could hear the note of confidence, of intimacy, of appeal, of gathering friendliness, and into his mind swam shadows of future meetings, rendered now inevitable: Rose and Julie, exchanging domestic secrets, sitting together on the settee, meeting with cries of delight at parties, Rose invited as an asset to dinner, Rose taken over, Rose obliging and willing to be of use, Rose uncritical and innocently pleased. It could have been worse, it could well have been worse.

Rose put the phone down and turned back to them. 'She says that's fine with her,' she said, 'she said not to worry at all. She sends you her love.'

'Ah,' said Simon.

'Have another drink,' said Christopher, 'and I'll go and look for my father-in-law.'

'Don't go,' said Rose. 'Send Konstantin. Konstantin, go and look for Grandpa. He can't still be in the conservatory, can he?'

'Oh, I don't know,' said Christopher, 'he gets quite carried away by this kind of thing.'

'But everyone's leaving,' said Rose, crossing to the window and looking out. 'Everyone's going home.'

'He'll be somewhere about,' said Christopher, and the children went to look.

'What a curious room this is,' said Simon, finding time to look round him.

'Yes,' said Rose, looking round herself. 'You can see why they don't let the public in the house, can't you? Amazing bad taste, my family have always had. Or rather non-taste. They just keep what they've got and shove it where it fits. The pictures are supposed to be quite good, but they somehow don't look very nice, do they?'

Simon looked at the pictures. A large Canaletto hung gloomily over the mantelpiece, flanked by a Gainsborough, a Claude, and a large painting of a cottage garden. The cottage garden dominated strikingly, sucking the others into its style in a curiously persuasive way. On the wall between the two long windows hung an Italianate crucifixion and a painting of the flaying of Marsyas, of sickening realism. On the end walls were family portraits, the older ones of some distinction, the more recent ones of monstrous banality. Rose as a small girl stood in pastels holding a small dog in front of a Wendy house. By her hung a framed dingy sampler by an ancestress of hers, one Cassandra Vertue, aged eight in 1810: the cloth was grey brown and greasy and damp with age, the flowers faded, and the motto in dirty yellow cross stitch said sadly but triumphantly; after Horace: QUOD POTUI, PERFECI.

The furniture showed the same eclectic principle of selection. Sheraton and mock-Jacobean huddled together in an overcrowded way: the settee and chairs were modern Maples, and the wall-light fittings were plastic mock candles with plastic dripping wax, and looked as though they had come out of Woolworths. The central chandelier was too large to have come out of Woolworths, but it suffered from proximity. On the mantelpiece stood a varied assortment of objects—some rather fine silver gilt candlesticks, a wooden troll, a pottery jug with flowers in it, an Aspreys clock, a china dancing-girl, and a Dr Barnardo's collecting box of some antiquity. The carpet was densely patterned and a little worn. It was impossible to tell, in such surroundings, whether it was quite pleasant or quite appalling.

'It hasn't changed much,' said Rose. 'I wasn't really allowed in here, when I was little.'

'They let the children in now,' said Christopher.

'So I'm told,' said Rose. 'I used to wonder why.'

'It's because I insist,' said Christopher. And then, with a new thought, he turned to Simon, and said, 'Look, about this injunction. What is it supposed to make me do?'

'An injunction is to stop you doing something,' said Simon, stiffly.

'Ah yes. That's right. I had one to stop me seeing Rose.'

'Pity you didn't obey it,' said Rose.

'And this one is to stop me taking the children out of the jurisdiction, is that right?'

'That's the idea. They're waiting to serve it on you in all the ports and airports of the country.'

'You exaggerate, surely.'

'Yes, I probably do. It's not really my field, you might say. Though at times I feel I'm becoming quite a specialist in it.'

'And what will they do with this injunction, when I tell them I've no intention of taking the children anywhere?'

'I think you have to appear in court. And give an undertaking.'

'And what will happen to my lovely custody case?'

'Nothing.'

'You mean it'll just grind slowly on?'

'Naturally.'

'I thought I might hurry things along a little.'

'No, I doubt it.' Simon was too polite to mention that he had lost the case decisively by his action.

'Amazing, really. The processes of law. So unruffled and so unperturbed. They just go on and on, with the same basic data, no matter what happens after the case is set in motion. One can't stop them until they've ground up the last little bit. And it's no good telling them that things have changed, that there are all sorts of new circumstances, they just carry on, then start again!'

'In that,' said Rose, sharply, swilling a little whisky crossly round and round in the bottom of a glass, 'in that, they rather strikingly resemble you.'

'Neither of those statements is really quite accurate,' said Simon.

'No, maybe not,' said Rose. 'But you must admit, he's created the law in his own image. You heard him.'

'I have a natural passion for justice,' said Christopher, refilling his glass, smiling blandly. His shirt was of white and blue stripes, in an embossed silky material, with small flowers raised in the pattern. He looked very relaxed, he had plimsolls on his feet and moved about silently.

'Ha. Justice,' said Rose. 'May you lose every case you ever embark on.'

'I probably will. And that will doubtless be justice. But I do like things to be gone into thoroughly. Don't you?'

'Not really,' said Rose. She finished her drink in one swallow. 'No, I can't say I do.' She began to pace up and down, turning from the window in time for them to surprise a look of anxiety on her face as she heard the door open. And there was Konstantin, leading her father by the hand.

Simon had seen photographs of him, in business sections of newspapers, but had not been prepared for the fact that he was so small. He looked little taller than his grandson: he also looked very unhappy at the prospect of an encounter with his censorious and prodigal daughter. His face, squarish and red-veined, had an unnaturally deep flush: he looked stubborn and angry, the last person to be able to handle the scene with any grace. At this point Simon would have given anything just to disappear, but it was too late. He looked at Rose: she was still standing by the window, blushing painfully, unable to move or speak. Her father looked at her, grunted, nodded curtly at Simon, and moved over to Christopher, who poured him a drink. He took the drink, sniffed at it, then put it down and said, 'I don't want that, thank you,' in a tone of indignation. Christopher seemed used to such treatment. In a way Simon was relieved by his manner: it would have been worse to find Mr Bryanston pleasant and reasonable, it would have been too much a judgement of Rose, and he had been apprehensive, on this score, for since knowing Rose he had heard, he had listened for stories of Mr Bryanston, and many of them had made him out to be a jolly old fellow, a card, a joker, a philanthropist, even. He had been suspicious of the stories, knowing the way that they gather around the wealthy and the great, with little regard to truth, invented to soothe the conscience or aggrandise the teller: but nevertheless he had worried. He did not want to picture Rose, even in her distant childhood, even pardonably, as wilful and capricious. He wanted her to have told him the truth. He need not have worried. The reality, this time, justified her, as the reality of Christopher had not. Mr Bryanston was clearly a mean and rude old man. He waited for what he would say next, and after a moment or two he growled, roughly in Rose's direction,

'You won't have seen your mother yet. She's lying down.'

'No,' said Rose, moving an inch or two forward into the room. 'I hope she's well.'

'What's it to you if she's well or ill?' said her father.

'Perhaps we've come on an inconvenient day,' said Rose, politely.

'You might have given us a bit of warning,' said her father. 'What do you expect me to do now? Kill the fatted calf, eh?'

'It was me that persuaded her to come,' said Christopher. 'Don't blame Rose, it was me that persuaded her.'

'Very nice of you, I'm sure,' said Mr Bryanston, and went back to the table and picked up the drink he had so abruptly rejected.

'This is a friend of mine, Simon Camish, Father,' said Rose. 'He very kindly drove me up.'

'Pleased to meet you,' said Mr Bryanston. The accent of the Midlands was pronounced in his speech. He shook Simon's hand, then sat himself down on the Maples settee.

'I hoped they might stay the night, Pa,' said Christopher. His manner towards his father-in-law was ingratiating in the extreme, but underneath the subservience he had a curious dominating confidence. He had no expectation of being refused.

'They can do what they like as far as I'm concerned,' said Mr Bryanston, putting his short legs up on a wooden footstool. He had clearly no intention whatsoever of trying to accommodate the drama of years: that job could be done by others. He was used to having jobs done for him. Remembering the way he had treated his daughter, Simon felt that a note of apology would not have been out of place, but it was clear that one could wait for it for ever. Rose, for her part, moved forward, and herself sat down.

'The garden's looking very nice,' she said.

'It'll all be trampled into mud,' he replied.

'How did the pot plants go?' said Christopher. He, alone of all of them, looked amused. He was enjoying himself, he knew he could play them: and indeed he managed it, within ten minutes he had them all talking about gardens and gardeners, the price of rebuilding walls, estate duties, forestry commissions, tax concessions. Mr Bryanston, having discovered that Simon was a lawyer, started to interrogate him about his views on investments, trusts, and bequests, a subject that seemed peculiarly unfortunate in the circumstances: after a while Rose got up and left the room, ostensibly to go and explain about dinner to the cook, and Simon found himself, far from condemning her, sympathising with her more and more. If this was the kind of conversation she had overheard throughout her childhood, it was hardly surprising that she had found a way out. And yet it was, perhaps, not ill-meant: he thought it more than likely that her father was a man of such limited human feeling and imagination that it simply had not occurred to him to ask himself how such a conversation, at such a time, would strike her. Rose had said to him once, speaking of her father, insensitivity beyond a certain point is sadism, and he had disagreed, thinking that people cannot help their natures: but perhaps she had been right. On the other hand, this man clearly needed people to talk to, he needed to ramble on about his financial affairs, it was a matter of emotion to him, and perhaps it was sadism in Rose, to refuse her participation? Rose thought there was a law above the human law, and that the indulgence of one's father was not a primal duty.

Christopher, on the other hand, participated all too well; curiosity as to how he had managed to reinstate himself so thoroughly, after such a bad beginning, was completely satisfied by the sight of him in action, eagerly, mystically intent on the subject of tax-deductible investments, doing quick calculations on the corner of the newspaper, discussing with passionate attachment proposed government policies for stimulating investment in overseas projects. The real world, this is, thought Simon, thinking of the money coursing like sap through the veins of England, and yet Christopher managed to transform it into a moonlit jungle. An extraordinary talent, he had, for transforming the most obdurate facts into a dense forest of personalised intentions and heroic achievements. The balance of payments blossomed into beauty beneath his fingers. No wonder his father-in-law liked him. Who could help liking somebody so attached to one's own interests, so helpfully enthusiastic, so redeemingly involved? After Rose, what a support he must have become. His father-in-law ate out of his hand.

Dinner that night was one of the most curious meals that Simon had ever sat through. Mrs Bryanston arrived at the last moment, pale, sharp-featured, wrapped up in a beige camel-hair dressing-gown, a woman so compellingly negative that it was an effort to force oneself to speak to her at all. She greeted Rose with such indifference that one might have supposed they had seen each other regularly once a week. Her husband ignored her completely, and when, occasionally, she spoke to him, he did not even reply. She asserted herself once during the evening, ringing a little bell that stood by her plate to summon the woman who waited on them: when the woman arrived, Mrs Bryanston said querulously, 'What did you give me this for?' and handed back a perfectly un-exceptionable plate of apple pie and cream, of which she had already eaten half. There was no explanation: the woman meekly removed the plate, as though used to such behaviour. Rose from time to time tried to speak to her, but achieved little response. So the conversation continued between the three men, with Rose quietly eating: Simon glanced at her from time to time, her head bent over her plate, her dry fingers pulling at a piece of bread, submissive, quiet. Where had she come from, how had it happened? People do not grow out of nothing, they do not spring from the earth. Somewhere in this house, in these two disagreeable ageing people, in this dingy dining-room, lay the grounds for her fantastic notions. He felt almost as though there must be some spirit, some clue, hovering in the air around them. Perhaps it was the spirit of desolation that hovered with dark wings and a vacant spiritual gaze over the polished wooden dining-table. It had brooded over her, as a small child, it had blessed her and inspired her. He tried to imagine what it must have been like, as a child, living in such a place, with such parents. He had little idea of what might be expected to happen to lonely girls reared in country houses: perhaps Rose was not the first to nourish delusions of virtue. Her history was singular, freakish, whereas his own seemed to represent a common lot. And he thought, suddenly, how strange it is, that here I sit, in the kind of house that my mother used to take me round on an entrance ticket, insatiable sightseer that she was, here I sit, and I am actually condemning the meal as ill-cooked, the decor as ugly and depressing, as though I had a right to judge, as though I knew better.

When the meal was over, Mrs Bryanston retired immediately to bed. Her lack of interest in life had afflicted them all: it was a disease, a mildew, which oppressed even strangers. Simon noticed that even Christopher had more or less given her up, though he had managed to get a faint flicker of a smile once or twice during the meal. He remembered Rose saying that she only appeared to be animated when really ill: once she had had an operation, which had excited her, and once she had broken her arm, a drama which she had enjoyed even more. But her norm of ill-health was too monotonous to afford her any satisfaction; she had cried wolf so often that her claims for attention were treated with little respect.

Her withdrawal from the scene had the immediate effect of cheering everybody else up: even Rose's father blossomed into something like joviality, at the prospect of a drink in the drawing-room without her. He became positively hospitable, asking Christopher several times if suitable arrangements had been made for Rose and Simon, asking Simon to stay on for a few days, telling Rose that she should come more often and that Konstantin ought to have his hair cut. His bonhomie, it was true, was somewhat sadistic in nature: he took pleasure in expressing concern for Rose by pointing out that the hem of her dress was coming down, and in telling her that she had been a fool to divorce Christopher. The delicacy of this latter subject deterred him not at all: he told her she was a fool to leave a man who would do and was doing so well for himself. She listened, and offered no defence: it would have been difficult to do so, for the case was not argued, it was flatly stated, with what Simon considered amazing, gross effrontery. They listened, the three of them, politely, to his discourse on human relations: he was clearly a man accustomed to delivering monologues, for when anyone tried to agree with him or question him, he ignored the contribution completely, starting to talk again through it as soon as he could think of anything else to say. Simon suddenly remembered whose manner it was that he recalled: it was a judge, now dead, whom Simon had had the misfortune to meet at a professional dinner, and whose pace of conversation had been deliberately designed to embarrass and wound the younger men around him. Simon had hardly been able to believe his ears when a senior colleague had said, on the old fellow's departure to the lavatory, 'Ah, he's a wonderful man, what a character, he's one of the most humane people I've ever worked with.' If that had been humanity, thought Simon, then God help the rest of the profession.

Mr Bryanston moved shortly from human relations to industrial relations, a subject which stirred him even more. Simon listened with growing satisfaction. Living as he did in a self-consciously progressive world, exposed only incidentally, in hotels and trains, to the voice of opposition, he found it reassuring to hear it, in all its glory. So many industrialists expressed themselves with such urbanity, demonstrating what was after all a historic connection between civility and exploitation, that it was a relief to hear the undisguised truth. At least one could thus see that it was a real division of interests at stake. Some men, even self-made men like Rose's father, had so picked up the tones of reason that it was hard to believe that it was not the national interest alone that they had at heart. But Mr Bryanston gave himself away. He spoke of the workers as though he were a mill-owner in a nineteenth-century novel, even delivering himself of the classic view that the fact that he himself had started work collecting scrap metal in a handcart was a perfectly adequate reason why workers deserved no sympathy at all— a view which showed a mental leap so precarious, so ibex-like, from crest of unreason to crest of unreason, that one could not but sit back and admire his magnificent, gravity-defying arrival. He spoke of strikes, of which two were notably in progress, one amongst the makers of surgical equipment, the other amongst the makers of certain bits of machinery which were impeding Mr Bryanston's own productivity: Simon, used to the emotive cries of sympathy for those about to perish for lack of a scalpel was pleased to note that

Mr Bryanston did not care twopence for such innocent victims, and that all his sympathy was reserved for his own loss of profits. He did, it is true, try to elevate this personal concern to the level of national interest—and indeed it probably was a matter of national interest, it was hard to deny it—but it was gratifying to see the roots of his concern so unselfconsciously laid bare. Healthy, tenacious roots they were, too, deep sunk, able to survive a little soil erosion. No amount of exposure impeded such force. After a while, Simon, unable to resist stirring it a little, asked Mr Bryanston what he thought of the surgical equipment pay-claim: Mr Bryanston stopped, snorted, grunted, unwilling to bend his mind away from his own affairs, but equally unable to refuse such an invitation, and finally said, 'Wicked, that's what I call it, downright wicked. Utterly selfish. If I had my way they'd all be deprived of medical attention for the rest of their lives.' Simon enjoyed this reply immensely: surprisingly, Mr Bryanston noticed his enjoyment, and reverted instantly to the safer topic of the way he had settled or failed to settle his own wage claims. As he went on, Simon found himself thinking with real affection of his own father-in-law, a genuinely modest man and a genuine exploiter, a man still so much of his own background that he knew how to get money from it with a perfect artistry. He had preserved a fellow feeling for his victims. He knew how to play on them because he was of them, he designed his brochures for them with a knowing eye. He was humble, because knowingly corrupt: he would never boast that others could simply choose to do likewise if they had the wit, he knew the others too well to claim it. Mr Bryanston had forgotten what the others were like, if he had ever known or cared. His memory was full of holes, and that perhaps was why he was perched up there on his solitary eminence, his Alpine peak of national interest, on a nasty snowy little rock of illogic. While down below, abandoned by thought, unjustified by human concern or even, at this stage, by personal ambition, the machinery ground away, the objects rolled off the conveyor belts, the profits ebbed and flowed, the shop stewards wrangled, the workmen carried on working, and every now and then somebody fell into a ladle of molten slag.

And yet, for all that, one couldn't help thinking that Mr Bryanston, after Mrs Bryanston, was rather a relief. At least he had something to say for himself, even though it was rather shocking. He was something rather than nothing, and after Mrs Bryanston in her dressing-gown this was a considerable step up in the scale of humanity. He ate, he drank, he had held his grandchild's hand and tried to sell a few pot plants for the district nurses in his conservatory: he had even, once, at dinner, passed Simon the salt. I've eaten his salt, thought Simon, I'd better stop judging him and worrying about him, there's no point in trying to relate wealth to personality, I have known that for years. Nearly a century and a half stand between me and the possibility of understanding such a relation, I had better give it up. So he finished his drink, quietly, as Rose was doing, and looked at Rose instead. He wondered what she was thinking, and if, ever, in her thoughts, she included him.

ROSE, HERSELF, was thinking that nothing had changed. It was all as it had been, dreary, oppressive, painful beyond belief. Hearing her father talk business was like hearing some old record replayed. How Christopher puts up with it I cannot imagine, she thought, quelling in herself the faint hope that Christopher might have discovered something tolerable, that he might be able to translate for her, into terms that she could understand, some aspects of grace. She would never have admitted it, but the fact that Christopher, whom she had once loved, had become close to her father, had not condemned Christopher, but had on the contrary given to her father's image a pale gleam of hope. She felt now that it had been illusory. She remembered the one act of imagination that her father had even directed towards her—when, all those years ago, he had summoned her to his study in the London house and asked her if she had got herself involved with the Communist Party. She had thought then, perhaps after all he knows who I am, perhaps he would recognise me if he met me on the street. She had later recognised, humbly, that his concern on this score could hardly by any light have been construed as affection. But it had nevertheless cheered her: better to be recognised as a link in a chain than not to be recognised at all. Sometimes she worried about the nature of the link—not that she had joined the Party, not that she had ever had much to do with it—but it was a link all the same, the simple link of reaction. She had reacted against what she had heard, as a child: she had become other. And where therefore was the transcendence? (Others might have been interested in the credit, but she was not: it was justification she sought, not gratitude.) Whence had come illumination, and why to her? At times she tried to trace a more natural connection between herself and her parentage, discovering in herself her mother's hypochondria with every sore throat, her father's inhumanity with her own preference for the total as opposed to the individual. I, like him, she would say to herself, am stubborn beyond belief, I too am partisan, it is simply that accident has forced me to take the other part.

But she did not believe these reasonings. Transcendence loomed over her head like a great owl.

Once, the winter before, crossing the park, a jay had creaked slowly across her path, noisily, heavy, flying low, from tree to tree, a few feet away, its plumage dull pink and barred and ominous, its flight heavy with cold. So exiled it had looked, so blundering.

The reaction, of course, had not been entirely unaided. There was always Noreen to be remembered. Somewhere about this house, so long unvisited, hovered the memory of Noreen, the witch-woman, with her unwanted, dour, true revelation, that revelation which had become almost sweet with time. Later, that night, she would go and trace it. Somewhere must lie the relics of the past, in the bottom of a cupboard or a wardrobe, in a broom closet, in a tea chest or a suitcase or an old box. The children had found, over the years, some of her things, and had brought back to her sad objects, old paintboxes, scrap-books, some wooden hens pecking on a board, a broken weather-house, a cross-stitch purse full of little plastic rabbits. Upstairs, there would be something that would bring back Noreen and her illuminations. The rooms were all different, now, of course—her own old room had been made over to Christopher, and the children slept all three in what had been the schoolroom. She had been put for the night in what had been Noreen's room, at the end of the corridor, while Simon was in the best guest room. Mrs Graves had told Rose this, in the kitchen, when Rose had gone to ask about dinner. Asking about dinner had made Rose feel so miserable, in so familiar a way: she knew that it would make no difference to the people in the kitchen, to be asked to provide an extra two meals, to be asked to make up a couple more beds, she knew that they were paid to do such things, that they could leave if they wanted to, that they were often asked to do much worse things with less notice and in less polite a manner, and yet nevertheless such a wash of embarrassment had poured over her, as she stood here clumsily and nervously, ill at ease, that it had transported her back twenty years, to the humiliation of being half-employer, half-servile child, treated by the staff with a mocking deference, and yet at the same time privileged to hear their complaints, their moans about her parents and the employing class in general, a tenant of both worlds, belonging to neither, recipient of the confidences of each about the other, and therefore all too painfully aware of the mutual contempt that reigned between them. It was these years, perhaps, that had made her so neurotically incapable of relying on the services of others: she recalled the relief that had filled her when she had discovered that it was possible to get through life cleaning one's own shoes, cooking one's own meals, washing one's own pants, that it was not a law of nature that decreed her to suffer for ever the humiliation of having these things done for her by people who despised her. She had met enough people, now, to know that others did not necessarily feel as she did, and that only lack of finance prevented a great many more women from employing each other to wash each other's underwear and make each other's beds. At first she had found this incredible, impossible: she could not believe that people of her own generation, nice people like Diana, really meant it when they sighed over the colonial life at dinner-parties, sympathising with returning members of the British council, or Shell, or OUP representatives, for their diminished staff. Nor would she believe the rueful, courageous complaints of these returning ladies—'Ah well, I suppose I'll get used to doing my own cooking,' these women said, smiling bravely, knowing that the women at home would not be pleased by too great a show of reluctance—but Rose herself so deeply assumed that these women *must, could only be* pleased to have got rid of the dreadful burden of shoe-cleaners and houseboys and nannies and ayahs (or whatever the word was) that it took her years to notice that it was the tone of regret that was in fact genuine, not the somewhat forced courage, and that the sighs of the Dianas of this world were not uttered through politeness to guests from different climes, understandably out of touch with the moral codes of Europe, but through genuine and sincere envy. Diana too would employ eight women at ten shillings a week if she could: Diana too would relinquish gladly those lovely jobs, the ironing and the cooking and the gardening, to anyone whom she could afford to pay to do them.

There had been one occasion on which she had found somebody to agree with her attitude, an occasion which at first sight seemed to bear out her suspicion that it was at root historical, neurotic. At dinner one night, talking to a group of women about au pair girls and charladies and their strange ways, one of the guests (sensing, perhaps, Rose's silent dissent) had turned to Rose, quietly, and said, you know, the trouble is, I can't employ this woman I've got now, any longer, I can't bear it. She looks like my own grandmother. She was in service, my grandmother, and when I see this woman on her knees in my kitchen, I feel as though I've put my grandmother down there to scrub my floor. I'll have to do without. Rose, to this, had revealed her own hesitations, trying to produce neurotic reasons for them as this other woman had done, each trying to condemn herself for abnormality, but they did not manage it. Uneasily and yet reassured they eyed each other, knowing the truth, relieved to find at least one to share it, meeting in the middle, one who had seen too much domestic employment from the upper side, and one who had seen too much from the lower, and both of them knowing that there was no justice in it and not enough pay. It had been an interesting meeting.

It was possible, of course, that the staff at Branston House had been a peculiarly dissatisfied lot. Rose's parents had never been very agreeable to work for. The gardener alone had any enthusiasm for the place, and carried on resolutely with his tasks, coming into the kitchen for a cup of tea every now and then. Rose would have liked him, had she not been so frightened of him: she liked to watch him doing things, digging, planting, trimming, and would hang around, afraid all the time that she was in the way. He, for his part, would have liked to talk to her, if she hadn't been such a sheepish little thing. But whenever he spoke to her, she started, and would then run off, as though afraid to be noticed. When she was older, a mooching adolescent, she would pluck up more courage, and would ask to be allowed to help: he didn't really like imparting his mysteries, having a deep suspicion of Mr Bryanston's horticultural notions, but he felt sorry for Rose, recognising that she was hardly on her father's side, and would invent little jobs for her to do. Once he came across her in the stables with her pressed-flower book: she showed him, politely. Ah, they're weeds, he said, which was all he could think of to say, but he was impressed nevertheless, and used to look things out for her occasionally. She, by this time, knew as much about it as he did, and had to be kind to him when he produced, triumphantly, some specimen she had collected years before. Oh thank you, Mr Cook, she would say, how nice. They both liked these almost mute transactions.

But apart from the gardener, the rest of the staff found their chief pleasure in grumbling. They did not even aspire to the mock, paid cheerfulness which some personal servants consider their duty: they soon found out it was not called for. There were times when Rose, at her lowest, would admit to herself that she would willingly, like a despot, have payed for a little kindness, for a little interest, a little flattery. Some of the most humiliating recollections of her life were memories of having tried to bully Noreen into showing a little tenderness. (Later, she thought it had been a blessing, not to have been offered substitutes. She had preserved at least the ability to distinguish.) Only once or twice in her life had she ever submitted to a servile, professional emotional approach: she recalled one of them now, with amusement and embarrassment, as she watched Christopher across the room, talking to her father about strikes and Industrial Relations, for Christopher had been there at the time, it had been just after the birth of Maria, at home in her own bed. Her cousin Sonia, who still preserved a certain affection for herself and Christopher, related largely to the gallant way in which Christopher had handled her on Folkstone quay, had sent them as a gift for the baby a large maternity nurse with a little dog, to look after mother and child for a fortnight. Rose had been horrified, for there was no room in her little house to establish so large a lady, and no possibility of being able to provide for her the standard of living to which she was accustomed, but she had been too weak and too polite to send her away again, and had struggled bravely, from her bed, to placate the nurse and Christopher and the dog and the larger two children, saying to herself, please God, please God let her go away soon and let me hold my baby.

The nurse, to be fair to her, had accepted the amazing domestic scene with the sang-froid of one constantly parcelled from house to house, and said cheerily from time to time that she had seen stranger sights in her time; she did her best to cope, unlike Christopher, who lost his temper and sulked. He did not want this strange woman in his house, he kept saying crossly and in earshot:

she filled the place up, one couldn't turn round without banging into her, she was a complete waste of money. I'm not paying, said Rose. No, but she eats, doesn't she, said Christopher, you should see what she eats. Don't be such a mean bugger, said Rose, and burst into tears, weak from childbirth, from the endless reminiscences of Nurse Williams, from the frustration of not being allowed to hold her own new lovely daughter except to feed her—and even when she was feeding her, Nurse Williams would be there, sitting in the rocking-chair, telling her how to do it (as though she hadn't reared two on her own already) telling her about impacted breast ulcers, asking her questions, and then telling her not to talk because of upsetting the flow of the milk when she struggled, occasionally, to answer. It had, to Rose, been a beautiful illustration of what people suffer at the hands of their own laziness. The interchange about Nurse Williams eating too much had been overheard by Nurse, who had been hanging around outside the bedroom door: she burst in, to make it clear that she had overheard, and found Rose weeping. Now then, now then, Mr Vassiliou, she said, what are you doing, upsetting a nursing mother, we can't have that, can we: and Christopher had sworn, and said he was leaving the house if he couldn't have a chat to his own wife in his own bedroom without strange women barging in, and had then gone out.

At his departure Rose had continued to weep, largely through fury at being left alone with Nurse Williams, but Nurse, in some quite extraordinary manner, so utterly professional and capable that Rose would never afterwards quite credit that such subtlety had come out of such a hulk, had managed to persuade Rose that it was rage with her husband that had made her cry, that men were like that, that husbands were really incredibly selfish, notoriously ill-mannered, that all wives were long suffering, that she, Nurse Williams, had seen it all, and that Rose had every right to weep her heart out when treated so badly by so boorish a man. And Rose, to her utter amazement, found herself as though hypnotised, reaching out her arms to this large woman, and being clasped to her uniformed bosom, where she wept like a child: she, who never touched except those she loved, she, who had never been allowed to weep, had never wept on a maternal bosom in her life. When Christopher came back, finally, drunk, she had told him about it, giggling, at midnight, describing the starched and glossy swell that had met her hot cheek, and the sense of corruption that had overcome her as she succumbed to so gross and yet so subtly manipulated a manoeuvre. We'll get rid of her, said Christopher. No, no, don't do that. She is going soon anyway, said Rose, cutting her toe nails, thinking how nice it was to be able to reach them so easily again, now that the baby was born. Put up with her, Christopher, please put up with her. She was on bad terms with Christopher, at this stage in her marriage, and all the insults that Nurse Williams could have thought to heap upon him, as a representative of the race of husbands, would probably have fallen short of the lurid truth, but nevertheless she felt tenderly towards him, for a day or two, tenderly, for having betrayed him in a nurse's arms.

She smiled to herself, remembering this. Christopher, bored by her father, caught the smile, and said, 'What are you laughing at?'

'I'm not laughing,' said Rose, 'I was just remembering Nurse Williams. I don't know why. And how glorious it was when she left.'

'Why on earth were you thinking of her?' said Christopher, and Rose, whose thought processes had been in fact quite different, suddenly wondered if she had perhaps remembered that incident because then, as now, she had felt a similar softening, at a time when she had no cause to feel it. She ought, perhaps, at this moment, to be at the depth of her outrage and indignation: he had behaved appallingly, dreadfully, irresponsibly: and yet, ever since meeting him in the garden, she had been feeling (in the peace of victory) a slight forgiveness.

'I don't know,' said Rose, untruthfully. 'Wasn't she amazing? Do you remember that horrid little dog? Nurse Williams,' she said, turning to Simon, 'Nurse Williams was this woman who came round when Maria was born, I can't tell you what a strange person she was...'

And she continued to describe Nurse Williams, and Simon was able to contribute reminiscences of his own, about a maternity nurse that Julie had engaged, in all seriousness, for her first child, though not for subsequent births, for she had subsequently found that Hampstead, unlike Newcastle, did not consider such adjuncts either necessary or chic, and had thereafter relied on the Nappy Service, a baby-sitting agency, the local clinic, a useless au pair girl, and a tame family doctor. Mr Bryanston listened to these domestic anecdotes with some impatience, though he tried to smile at the story of the day when Nurse Williams tried to air the baby clothes in the oven and forgot about them: he made a few attempts to bring the subject more within his range, but finally gave up, rather sadly, to let the young people talk. Rose noticed his face fall, as he lapsed into silence, and was surprised to note that she had even noticed: he must have been enjoying his talk with Christopher and Simon, he must have been thinking that he was making a good impression, he could not like the suspicion that they were relieved to turn from him to Rose. This attempt at insight startled Rose: she could not remember that she had ever seen him as a separate person before, and although it was not surprising that she should do so now, for the first time, after so long an absence, it nevertheless gave her a faint shock, a shock which was intensified and made distinct when he rose to his feet (a small elevation, it is true, what a little man he was, and he seemed to be shrinking) and said, 'Well, I'd better get to bed. Can't sit up all night.' He said this in a tone of deep dissatisfaction, locking his hands behind his back, rocking on his feet, staring at them all nastily, and Rose remembered that these were the very words, unchanged, identical, with which he had announced his departure on every evening that she had ever spent with him: it had always enraged her, the malignant gloom with which he would survey the room he was about to leave, the sugges- tion of accusation towards whoever else were there, as though they had been forcing him to stay up against his will, the note of command, which implied that everybody else had better follow suit immediately and do likewise. In fact, Mrs Bryanston, when she had been at home, had always risen at this announcement and silently left the room: so, too, had Rose, until one day in her last year at school she thought that she would try to sit it out. So she remained seated, her head bent over her book. 'Aren't you coming?' her father had said, surprised, and Rose had shaken her head, without looking up. And that had been that. She always stayed up after that, on principle, and her father's only gesture of protest was to switch off all the lights in the room except the one on the table where she sat. But he continued, every night, to repeat his parting shot; and Rose had continued, every night, to tremble and shiver inwardly as she heard the repeated words. And suddenly, this evening, after so many years, hearing them yet again, unchanged, it occurred to her that he said them possibly not out of ill-will, but because he could not think of any other way to leave the room. A thousand times one can suffer and resent, but the thousand and first time monotony, however staunchly resisted, becomes endearing after all. Really, thought Rose, whatever has come over me, I sit here forgiving them all, have I been wrong all this time, or is it that I have got tired of resentment?

They all got up to wish him good night. When he had left the room, Rose looked at the other two, who were already, in the relief of his departure, pouring themselves another drink, and saw that it would be the easiest thing in the world to settle down to an evening of tears, drink, remorse and confessions. Perhaps, she thought, I could even get Simon to talk. And the thought of it, the phrasing of it to herself in those terms, made her shy away out of a delicacy she could not understand or name: she had gone far enough, there was no farther she could safely go. So she too, like her father, declared her intention of going to bed. And went. She had a sense of some appointment more significant than confession, which awaited her upstairs.

On the way up the stairs—a wide, curved staircase with wooden treads, and an iron handrail, the house's best feature, which she had rarely ascended as a child, preferring the back staircase—she remembered the last night she had spent in the house. It had been the night before her departure to France with Sonia. Twenty years old she had been, and she had been mad with love and grief. Out of her mind with sorrow. She tucked the fact away into a little shelf of her mind. She would get it out later and have a look at it. It might afford some interest. Meanwhile, it was Noreen that she had on her mind.

She was to sleep in Noreen's bedroom. As a child, she had not been allowed in Noreen's bedroom: it had been like the staff room at school, out of bounds, mysterious, and admission to it signified some signal honour or disaster. Her curiosity about it had become so intense that once, when she knew Noreen had gone down to the village, she had crept in to have a look round. Everything here had seemed so significant, so concealed: the pale green silky watery bedcover, the sausage-shaped cushion on the bed, the ruched nightie-holder, the green basketwork chair, the green china dog on the mantelpiece, the framed print of a vase of flowers on the wall. She had stayed there only a moment, but her attraction towards it had become so strong that she made a habit of going there whenever she knew Noreen to be safely out of the house: her boldness had increased with her sense of security, and she had taken to opening drawers and gazing in awe at the neatly folded underwear, the silky blouses, the handkerchiefs, inhaling passionately the dry smell of lavender, the smell of moth balls, the indescribable cotton salty hygienic womanly smell of sanitary towels, which lay in a neat blue shoe bag in the bottom drawer.

Outside the door, now, she paused, standing there on the landing, she paused: recollection assailed her so sharply that she shivered, her feet would not move, she felt that a step more would take her across the threshold of time itself, into the dreadful past. The smell was in her nostrils: threatening, attractive, illicit. The green of the basketwork chair assembled itself in her mind: pale, washed, thirties green, and yes, on the green curved edges there were woven scallops, and they were faintly touched, yes, that was it, they were touched with a fading, much rubbed, washed out gilt. Basket scallops. It was too much to fear that the chair might yet be there: it must have been relegated years ago to an attic, or given away to a maid. Eau de nil, faint and poisonous, a colour that suggested in itself a lethargic indolence, a languorous repose, almost voluptuous, and yet which, in conjunction with Noreen herself, had managed to exhale self-denial, rigour, restraint. It swam before her, shaping itself now into a chair, now into the bedcover, now into the china dog with popping eyes (a powder container, the dog had been, but Noreen wore no powder) now into a dressing-gown of limp loose woven shiny fabric, embroidered in chain stitch lilies, lilies which had lain, one each, on each of Noreen's flat sulking breasts, breasts too flat to fall, which had yet fallen, only to rise again, just in time, almost elegantly, on either side, beneath the cross-over sash tied wrap, below the wide lapels. And there stood Noreen, within the green envelope, herself, as she had been twenty years and more ago, a woman of the thirties, herself in her thirties, her permed hair looking like an advertisement in a fly-blown neglected shop window, her lips thin and disapproving, and yet, like her bosom, not quite unattractive, her cold eyes and large high nose with a look of a goose about them, though why one should associate that particular association of features with a goose, that most unanthropomorphic and vicious creature, Rose did not know. Frightened, a little now, by the vividness of the ghost she had summoned, looking with some surprise at the exact spot, half-way down the corridor, her feet firmly on the Turkey carpet, where she had paused to meet it, as though she had expected the present to have dissolved from around her, she thought, almost, of going downstairs again, on the pretext of fetching a book to read; but instead went on, the few yards more, past the door of the room where the children were sleeping, and opened the door of Noreen's room itself.

It was, of course, unrecognisable. It had become a junk room, in effect: there was a bed, which had been made up, and clean thick towels had been put out, in the adjoining bathroom, but the bathroom was almost inaccessible, so full was the room of odd bits of furniture, bookcases, chests bulging open with old curtains, little occasional tables, pictures standing on the floor with their faces to the wall. One of Mrs Bryanston's nightdresses had been laid out upon the bed, an act of gentility which looked out of place amidst so much disorder. Seeing it, Rose was almost waylaid into speculation about why her mother had married her father—family pressure, apathy, greed?—as she sat down on the bed by the empty nylon gown, its stiff arms folded across its empty heart in a pious, neat gesture of prayer, but she could feel this as a false trail, she hesitated at the turning and went on down the corridor of memory, finding a clue in those crossed arms and angled elbows, praying, was it, yes, she used to pray, Noreen had taught her to say her prayers, Our Father which art in heaven, and she still prayed, occasionally, not incessantly as she had done through childhood, but every now and then a natural or man-made calamity would push her imperiously to her knees, a massacre, an earthquake, a drowning, and she would implore justice, mercy, intercession, explanation, not praying any more for herself, as she had once so futilely done, not even aware that she had ceased to do so, wondering even as she knelt whether there were any use in such genuflections, and yet pushed down as certainly as if a hand had descended on her head to thrust her from above, crushing her hair and weighing on her skull. And what it came to was this: did God, despite the fact that Noreen had believed him to exist, exist in fact, or not? Ha, she said to herself, that's it, I've got it: she was nearly there, and yes, she was there, the memory of standing in Noreen's room, a wicked intruder, silently observing empty clothes and full drawers, had brought back to her yet another act of disobedience, earlier in time than those silent visits, but similar in nature, it had been a day in winter, a wet rainy day, she could not have been more than six at the time, though it is hard to date events, but she remembered the dress she was wearing, a dark blue and red woollen check with a sash sewn into the dress, she had worn it on her sixth birthday. It had been raining all day, wet gusts of rain, squalls and sudden silences, and she had grown tired of watching the rooks rise and swirl from the bare trees in their huge wet eddies; the acute boredom of her childhood had seized her so passionately that she had ached in every bone, and had set off, desperate, to find some act so desperate that it would distract her mind from the dullness of total despair. The thought of going into Noreen's bedroom had not at that age occurred to her—perhaps Noreen had not yet moved into the house, perhaps she was still living in the village, visiting daily, she could not remember—but she was as strongly tempted by her parents' rooms, also forbidden ground. They were away from home, her parents: her mother abroad for the winter, her father in London, so there would be nobody to see her, if she crept in quietly. So up she went, and shut herself in, and proceeded to inspect the objects on her mother's dressing-table—cut-glass powder bowls, silver brushes with bristles too soft and yellow to brush, little pots and jars with silver gilt tops. There was no jewelry about except a broken string of pearls: everything else had been locked away. Rose put the pearls on and pulled a few faces at herself in the glass. She also powdered her nose with a large pink musty-smelling powder puff. Then, feeling boredom creep up behind her again like a wolf in a story, she leapt up with a pretence of eagerness that was really fear (a pretence for herself alone, there being no other spectators)—and made off into the bathroom. There she fiddled with the shower and fingered the face flannels and drank some water out of a tooth mug, and finally drew, mesmerised, closer and closer to her father's box of razor blades.

She knew about razor blades. Mrs Amery in the kitchen had a razor blade with which she sharpened pencils to write shopping lists. Rose had often watched the soft curved shavings fall. And she had wanted to have a go herself, but Mrs Amery would never let her: in fact Noreen and Mrs Amery had had words about that razor blade, Noreen contending that it was not a suitable object to leave lying about, even out of reach on the top shelf of the dresser, whereupon Rose had asked why razor blades were so dangerous, and Noreen had replied that such a blade would cut you as soon as look at you. This curious phrase had given the razor blade, to Rose, a peculiarly active potentiality, and she had spent much time gazing up to the shelf where she knew it to lie concealed, hoping it might take it into its head to look at her and leap down. She could not help feeling that Noreen had maligned it, that it could not possibly be as dangerous as Noreen implied—for so many things were not, wet grass was not, for instance, nor fresh bread, nor fruit cake, nor wet socks, nor cold milk, nor reading with a torch under the bedclothes. Being as yet neither blind, rheumatic, nor choked with permanent indigestion, Rose had decided, at the age of six, that Noreen consistently overestimated the dangers of the natural world. And now, finding herself alone with a packet of blades, she decided that she would put Noreen to the test. Carefully, nervously (for after all Noreen might have been right), she opened the box, and took out a single blade wrapped in an envelope of paper. Slowly she unwrapped the paper: it was greasy, the blade inside was covered with the thinnest film of grease, ready for action, delicately preserved. She held it between the flat of her finger and thumb, naked. She watched it. It did not move, it did not tremble. She was, in a way, disappointed: she had half-expected blood to flow as soon as she had unwrapped it, from some unspecified part of her body. She expected it to leap from her hand and attack her, like a magic sword which needs no master. Cut, cut, Noreen would say, rubbing her magic lamp in her cottage in the village, and the blade would fly from between Rose's small fingers and attack her, at the distant command.

Instead, it remained disappointingly, reassuringly inert. Rose stared at it. I'm a fool, she thought (which she wasn't, not nearly as foolish as her fears suggested) of course it can't cut me if the edge isn't touching me.

And so, carefully, she took hold of the blade in a firm grip, and applied it to the ball of the thumb on her left hand. At first she expected blood to leap to meet the blade, as fire leaps from the smokey wick of a candle to meet a lighted match, but what happened was in a way even more startling. The blade touched the thumb, barely touched it, simply rested on it, she could feel nothing, no cut, nothing (and perhaps at this point she pressed a little harder, she could not remember)—and then, suddenly, quite suddenly, blood was flowing, oozing, pouring, dripping from her thumb. She dropped the blade in terror. It was true, it would cut as soon as look. The blood poured. There was no pain, no sensation, She calmly turned on the tap and put her thumb under it, for the wound was nothing in the scale of childhood, which spends most of its time bleeding, bruising, falling, thumping, grazing: and as she stood there, her thumb growing colder and colder, it went thump thump in her head, the pulse of her dying thumb with its little whorls turning whiter, and she knew that it was all true, everything that Noreen said, rheumatism, rotten teeth, blindness, hell fire, devils, torments, betrayals, endless burning, the rack, the wheel and the screw, and oh help, even remembering it now, years later, it all came pumping back, horror after horror, the flaying of Marsyas hanging in the drawing-room, all that bleeding flesh and sinew and Apollo's grinning face, dead rabbits, a child with its hand caught in its butcher father's mincing machine, decapitations, My Lai, horror and bleeding and damnation, she had seen nothing on that tour of Europe but horrors, Saint Ursula and her virgins all dying on the shore, blood spouting from their necks, the loving detail of their severed carotid arteries, crucifixions with Christ bleeding and green, twisted on a flaming hillside in the blackness of man's unutterable wickedness, and worst of all that piece in the Grunig Museum called the Judgement of Cambyses, where a corrupt judge was being flayed alive before Cambyses and his impassive court, mesmerised she had stared at it, the open flesh, how could he have brought himself to paint it, day after day, week after week, the painter, from what model could he have taken such a subject? In the same room had hung David's Baptism, calm, delightful: in the foreground grew violets and spring flowers, perfect, fragile, hopeful. Christ's feet in the water, with the gentle water and the yellow flags, but they had crucified him, they had driven nails through those feet.

So, it had all seemed true. Razors cut, Christ was crucified, man was wicked, Hell was open. It is even true, thought Rose, ruefully, sitting quietly on the bed, it is even true that wet grass gives one rheumatism. She had suffered from rheumatism all her life, a legacy from disobedience, aggravated by the damp of the semi-basement at Middle Road, but surely initiated here, on the damp lawns, in the sodden undergrowth. It had all come about as Noreen had predicted: there had been no appeal from her darker pronouncements. And it being so, thought Rose, sitting there, thinking a thought that had come to her a million times, it being so, what can I do, what can I do to be saved? She smiled even, visibly, as the words came into her head, they were such old familiars, and she had so long abandoned hope of salvation through faith or through works, they had appeared in so many guises, the words, desperate, anguished, weeping, mocking, flippant, or as now rather sad and worn and ghostly: and yet, suddenly, it came back to her, perhaps through the influence of the room, or perhaps through a book in the bookshelf opposite her, on which her eyes must have been vaguely focussed, and which now, in a fusion of attention and memory, revealed itself to be the old nursery copy of *Pilgrim's Progress,* that fierce companion, that bitter solace. What shall I do to be saved, Pilgrim had said. It had been her favourite book. The journeys, the hazards, the faith-created mirage of a heavenly city. Frightened, a little, she got up off the bed, and went over to the shelf, and took it out: crouching, unwilling to commit herself to sitting down with it, she turned the pages. There they all were, Apollyon, Faithful beheaded, the Slough of Despond, the river, and all the trumpets sounding for him on the other side. Next to the book, stood *Grace Abounding to the Chief of Sinners:* she got that down and looked at it. That too she had read too often, and there it still was, that dreadful account of neurosis and woe. She had marked passages, as a child, as an adolescent: there were the pencil marks. Bunyan grieving for his sin, praying for grace, worrying old scriptures as a dog worries a bone, worrying whether he could be one of the elect, worrying about the birthright of Esau. She had marked heavily one paragraph: it said:

'Now I blessed the condition of the dog and toad, and counted the estate of everything that God had made far better than this dreadful state of mine and such as my companions was: yea, gladly would I have been in the condition of a dog or horse, for I knew they had no soul to perish under the everlasting weights of hell for sin, as mine was like to do ... I saw this, felt this, and was broken to pieces with it ...' and she had written, *see page 59,* and looking, obeying her past self, she saw that she had underlined

'... and after long musing, I lifted up my head, but methought I saw as if the sun that shineth in the very heavens did grudge to give light, and as if the very stones in the street, and tiles upon the houses, did bend themselves against me; methought they all combined together to banish me out of the world; I was unfit to dwell among them. Oh, how happy now, was every creature over what I was; for they stood fast and kept their station, but I was gone and lost.'

Gone and lost, gone and lost. Yes, that was the way it had been. How easy it was to underestimate what had been endured. Oh, how happy now was every creature. For years of my life, Rose thought, I remember it now, I would have changed place with any living thing. One forgets the dreadful pain, the conviction that one is marked. I used to wake in the mornings, at the age of what— nine, ten?—and pray to fall asleep, pray to die in my sleep, pray to be utterly deprived of consciousness. The very stones I envied, for they were innocent, and could neither do nor suffer wrong. How slowly I learned to live, to make myself forget.

Grace Abounding. She stared at it. It still frightened her, there was something in it still, some power for pain, even though she had confronted the words that Bunyan wrote—suppressed words, no doubt about it, she had suppressed them, wisely enough, because seeing them again now she knew that she knew them by heart. But had not thought of them for years. The mind, as well as its own torments, has its own remissions. She turned the pages again: and there it was, the final blow, the lurking horror, as disagreeable as the caterpillar she had once pressed by accident in her flower book. But this was no caterpillar, it looked innocent enough, it was a birthday card, used, one might think, as a bookmark, marking the lines, I was bound, but he was free: if God come not in, thought I, I will leap off the ladder even blindfold into eternity, sink or swim, come heaven come hell, Lord Jesus, if thou wilt catch me, do, if not, I will venture for thy name—a statement of heroic neurotic nonchalance that expressed more or less Rose's present theological position. The card, in marked contrast to the text, was cheerful and floral: it showed a bowl of flowers in a cottage window. Rose, seeing it, blushed. She felt the blood in her face, her hair gently rising. It was a card she had bought for herself, to send to herself, on her fifteenth birthday, when she was away at school for the first time. The misery, the humiliation. Birthdays had been a big thing at her boarding school: there was a special tea, for each birthday child, and the whole school would sing Happy Birthday. The child was allowed to put her cards on her dressing-table (usually denied ornament) and to open her gifts in the morning, after breakfast, instead of going straight to class. This system, agreeable enough in some ways, had produced a ferocious atmosphere of competition: girls boasted of the quantity of post, the lavishness of gifts, the warmth of ovation from the school. Rose dreaded the approach of her birthday from the first week there. Impossible to conceal the date, as she had once thought of doing: birthdays, in the dearth of other interesting topics, were a subject for endless discussion, and were easily discovered from the school register. She dreaded it. Even the least conspicuous, least friended girls received a respectable pile of post on their birthdays, from family, from friends at home. Rose knew that she would receive nothing. For weeks she lay awake at night, wondering how she could endure the humiliation, the surprised glances, the tactful enquiries, the sadistic sympathy. She lost her appetite, she could neither eat nor sleep, and her hair began to drop out. She developed a huge bald patch in the middle of her head: Sister said it was alopecia and asked Rose if anything was worrying her. No, said Rose, and brushed her hair over the patch so that it did not show. One night, lying awake, she thought, I could buy myself a card, and write in it a false name, and post it, and that would make sure that I had at least one card on my birthday. The idea had seemed brilliant and corrupt. I can't do a thing like that, she told herself, I can't, I really can't: and when, on their weekly visit to the shops, she found herself secretly buying the floral card, she told herself that it was not for herself but for a friend. As the days passed before her birthday, she struggled with temptation: she felt it behind her, as Bunyan did, pulling at her clothes. It would be so simple, to send the card, to claim a friend in the town, to be mysterious and discreet about her: it was surely an act morally neutral, a legitimate act of self-protection, a reasonable compensation for a sin in no way her own? Who would blame her, who would not pity her, if they knew the truth? Why should she suffer, needlessly? It was not as though one card would rescue her: she would still, receiving one card only, be an object of contempt, she would have achieved no dramatic success by fraud, she would have deceived nobody.

But, finally, she did not send it. She could not bring herself to do it. Honour, pride and honesty prevented her. Never mind, she said to herself the night before, trying to get her feet warm in the icy bed, never mind, never mind, never mind, it is only you that will suffer, Rose Bryanston, think of that, let that be your comfort. And it had comforted her, to a degree. To those that suffer is given the strength to endure suffering, she said to herself.

In the morning, in fact, she did get one card. It was from her parents. It had never crossed her mind that they would think of sending her one. Later, she wondered why she should ever have supposed that they would not.

Her hair grew in again, after this episode. Quite quickly. It was as though, having endured exposure, having endured exposure of all those bitter years, and having survived it, she had somehow won some shadowy victory. She had been right not to send herself the card. Bunyan, like Noreen, had been right. One has to keep on watch, while eating, while chopping sticks, while refilling one's fountain pen. Strait is the gate.

It had all worked out all right, after all. Amazingly enough. She had been miserable enough in these last thirteen years or so, she had been through some bad moments and some long trials—literally long trials, now she thought about it—but had never since her childhood felt that blind horror and despair. Never, since the age of eighteen, had she woken in the morning and wished to have died. She had wished to die, but that was another matter. A state of grace, in comparison. Never, since she first met Christopher.

Ah, Christopher. One could think what one might think about Christopher, but at the very least he had filled in the time. He knew how to stave off boredom, did Christopher, he knew how to keep things on the go. Even separation and divorce he had rendered more intimate than many marriages. Ever since she had first set eyes on him, in that paper-filled Bloomsbury basement. She had loved him, certainly—the last night she had slept in this house, her last night in England, she had been ill with love, ill with longing, she had wandered round the garden in the evening, surveyed from the house suspiciously by discreet embarrassed custodians, gazing at the flowers, pale and ominous and swollen in the dusk, gazing at the high hedges, at the muddy water in the pond and the leprous gold fish, not gold, but an unpleasant pale pink, like mullet on a slab they were in the evening light, wandering aimlessly in a static frozen garden, knowing that the time would never pass until she should see him again, coming at one point to a standstill, transfixed, gazing at a flowering currant bush by the garage, each flower dripping red blood like a bleeding heart or a strawberry fruit pastille, she had turned to ice, it too, the bush, burning like a message, had frozen, each flower, each leaf, each twig instinct with eternity, a horrible hush, a horrible pause, a silence, a stopping of the blood in the middle of the evening, before it all began sluggishly wearily to flow again, infinitely slowly, but at last wearily moving like the sluggish fish, and a slight breeze had moved the flowers of the currant bush, disturbing their spectacular significance—oh yes, she had loved him, certainly, that had been it, that had been love. But there had been more to it than that, he had not let her slip away, and when love had perished in its usual fashion he had kindly replaced it with all other kinds of distractions. Amazing, really. It was so obvious that she herself had been the kind of child to grow up incapable of relating: insecure, cold, undeveloped, guilt-ridden. What freakish providence had given her Christopher, so obsessed by the thought of possession that he refused to let her reject him? His desire to grab—herself, children, money, even parents-in-law— had proved too strong for her will to renounce. Interesting, really.

She began to get undressed. Getting undressed and thinking of Christopher had made her suddenly nervous. It was the first time she had slept under the same roof with him since the divorce. What if he wandered along in the night and attacked her? What if he took it into his head to drive off with the children in the small hours? He seemed to have taken his defeat quietly, even amicably, but one could not be sure. She stopped getting undressed, and put on her mother's nightdress over most of her underwear. The more she thought about it, the more extremely likely it seemed that he would make some kind of overture. He had stayed downstairs drinking with Simon: they were both probably drunk by now,

Christopher through remorse, and Simon through nerves, poor thing. She looked at her watch: it was very late, they could not both still be down there, they must have come up to bed. What a pity, really, that she could not marry Simon. She had had visions, herself, of marrying Simon and going off with him to other places and trying to be the person that she might have been. The touch of his arm, his stiff chest as she had leant against it, the silk of his wife's scarf had interested her. It was satisfactory, that he, a serious person, had thought of marriage too. Such satisfaction would have to be enough.

It annoyed her, to think that Simon and Christopher might become friends. It amused her, to find herself annoyed. It made her feel much better, to find herself amused: and in a moment of confidence, she jumped out of bed, thinking that she would go and see if the children were all asleep, and have a look round to see how their room had been decorated. She had been wanting to do that all evening, on one level, on her most ordinary functional level, but had been too depressed and waylaid by Bunyan. To hell with Bunyan, she said to herself, as she opened the door; then repenting, no, no, not to hell, poor Bunyan, the last place for him, too dreadful, and thinking of the hideous possibility of a hell in which an actual Bunyan might actually for ever roast, she made her way along the corridor to the children's room, smiling to herself and at the same time ludicrously sorry that she had had such an awful thought. The children were sleeping in the old schoolroom, which looked over the stables: a pretty room it had been, where Rose and ill-equipped governesses had stared at one another in paroxysms of yawning and boredom. One of them used to give her throat sweets, little hard black pellets. Sometimes she used to get three or four in a morning. What a thrill they had been, what huge excitements, what momentous events, how they had alleviated the monotony, black stars in a white waste of text-book dullness.

Outside the door, Rose paused. She didn't really want to wake them, but they were all going through a good phase, from the sleeping point of view, so she pushed open the door and went in. There they all were, Marcus and Konstantin in twin beds, side by side, Maria in what had been her own old bed—painted with roses and rabbits, it was—under the window. Maria, as usual, was flung about all over the place, her legs sticking out, her arms widely distributed, her head falling off the bed, her mouth open. Rose pushed her back. Konstantin had almost disappeared from view under the sheet and a blanket: even in hot weather he liked to be well covered up. Marcus was lying quite sweetly, with his head on the pillow where a head ought to be. There was a smell of socks. They had clearly profited from the evening's unusual drama by going to bed without a wash. Their clothes were all in a heap on the floor: she picked a few of them up, looking round as she did so at the new white paint, the posters on the walls (Christopher's taste, all informative ones, a taste securely affected by her own), the curtains with stars on, the gummed iridescent stars, faintly luminous, that had been stuck on the ceiling. It was nice. It had been done nicely. One could not blame them for liking it. Their swimming things had been laid out in a row on the chest. They must be intending to go for a swim in the morning. She hoped it would be a fine day again.

She was just about to leave the room, curiosity satisfied, when she had a moment of panic, thinking she could hear somebody in the corridor outside. She stood still and listened. There was certainly somebody out there. It could, of course, be anyone—her father, checking on the locks, as he sometimes did, her mother, wandering aimlessly about, one of the staff. No reason to suppose it was Christopher. But still, she preferred to wait a few moments, with the children as chaperones. Whoever it was had bare feet or slippers, and was walking very quietly. The footsteps stopped, and she had the impression that whoever it was had also stopped to listen. Very quietly, she took a few steps forward, till she could see through the crack in the door hinge. At first she could see nothing of interest: only the long corridor, with doors opening off it, and only a thin segment of that. The landing light was on: she had switched it on herself, on leaving her bedroom. But she was certain somebody was there, she sensed it. She pushed the door slightly, to widen the angle of the crack, feeling slightly foolish in her caution: the manipulation, the quiet, the sound of the children's breathing, reminded her of those days when they were small babies, when she would creep out of the room on hands and knees, having rocked them to sleep in their cradles, terrified of rousing them again. Konstantin and Maria had been the worst: Marcus, the desirable middle baby, had always slept well. If she pushed the door just a little further, she would be able to see the whole corridor: she pushed, risking a creak. And there was Christopher, as she had suspected, bare foot, in his trousers, and a black vest. But he was not standing outside her door. He was standing outside Simon's. Listening.

She watched him. At first she could not think what on earth he was doing there, but it came to her in a flash, after a moment or two of speculation. He was listening to find out if she was herself in there with Simon. It was logical. He might have tried her room first and found it empty, or he might have leapt to conclusions and gone to Simon's first. Either way, it was her he was listening for. She wondered how long he would stand there, before giving up and going away. It was clear that she herself could not risk going back to her own bed: she could always get in with Marcus, if it came to it, she was thinking, when suddenly she saw Christopher recoil, quickly, from his station, in a flurry of movement, but not quickly enough, for Simon flung the door open, and Christopher had not had time to get away. Simon was still fully dressed. Like herself, he had not risked undressing. He had had no intention, like Christopher, of being seen without his trousers, and had had the good sense to note that the night was not yet over. What an acute man he is, she thought. I really like him.

Simon, in his doorway, stared at Christopher. Christopher, though no longer with his ear to the keyhole, looked not particularly pleased at his discovery, and was not quick enough to pretend that he had just been walking along the corridor on the way to a bathroom or bed. He looked, in short, guilty, which provoked Simon to say, 'Where on earth are you going?'

Christopher looked aggrieved, thought hard, and then said, 'I might ask the same of you.'

It was quick, but not quick enough.

'I wasn't going anywhere,' said Simon. 'I heard you scuffling about out there, so I came to see.'

'You must have been listening bloody hard,' said Christopher, relaxing slightly, recovering from the slight inelegance that had overtaken him.

'I was,' said Simon.

'What were you listening for?' said Christopher.

'I don't know,' said Simon, and smiled. 'What were you?'

'Ha,' said Christopher.

'Well you were wrong, weren't you?' said Simon.

'She's not in her room,' Christopher started to say, but Rose had divined his words, with an accuracy of instinct that surprised her, and stepped innocently out into the corridor, judging that so far she could pretend to have heard nothing, but not for much longer. Both their heads turned sharply at the sound of the door, in comic alarm and unison. Smiling bravely, happy in the opacity of her mother's nightdress, she advanced upon them.

'Hello,' she said, confronting them. 'What are you two doing? I thought you'd gone to bed hours ago.'

'What were *you* doing?' said Christopher. And Rose, fully intending to say, looking at the children of course—a reply at once plausible, creditable, and true—suddenly, for no accountable reason, speaking out of some unpremeditated, mad, lying part of herself—the part that had made rows and hurled insults and ruined her marriage—found herself looking at Christopher and saying, 'I was avoiding you, of course.' As soon as she had said it, she repented: her reply had hurt Simon, and had both annoyed and gratified

Christopher, none of which had been her intention. It had been a fatal admission—fatal to admit that she was aware that he might have been looking for her, fatal to admit that even so dim a connexion might still exist. And having said such a thing, she could not think quickly enough to see what she could possibly do next. Clearly she could not return to her own room, but where else could she go? She could not stand in the corridor all night.

'Hell,' she said, rather crossly. Christopher was looking at her in a way she did not at all like. She had even thought of throwing herself on Simon's hospitality, wondering if it would be unkind to him to do such a thing, when Simon himself spoke.

'Why don't you both come in for a bit?' he said, 'since none of us seems to feel like sleeping. I've never had such a splendid bedroom to invite people into before, it seems a pity to waste the opportunity.'

Rose accepted gratefully, Christopher with a nod of the head. They went in. It was, as Simon said, a splendid room, the best guest-room. Rose had forgotten how splendid it was. It was papered with an original hand-painted paper, covered in Chinese foliage and birds and flowers and butterflies: there was a story that the artist, unsatisfied with his first attempts, had returned time after time to add extra items, until he had finally gone too far. Too far he had gone, perhaps, from the strictly aesthetic viewpoint, but the results were certainly interesting. There was a large bed with hangings, and some agreeable furniture, lacquer and inlay, which actually went with the wallpaper. By what miracle of neglect it had been allowed to remain there Rose did not know, but there it still was. Rose sat herself down on a couch by the bed, Simon and Christopher both sat on the bed.

'You could even have a drink, if you wanted,' said Simon. 'Look. I've never seen that before. I've read about it in books, but I've never seen it.'

And he pointed at the table by the bed. On it stood a cut-glass decanter, on a silver tray, accompanied by a Wedgewood biscuit barrel with a silver lid. The glass was not quite up to standard, but the general effect was pleasing.

'He must have liked you,' said Rose. 'Pa, I mean. He wouldn't do that for everyone. Did you give him some useful legal advice?'

'Not a word,' said Simon. 'I just listened.'

'Ah well, that would do. You look so intelligent, when you listen.'

'Would you like a drink? Either of you?'

'What is it? Brandy or whisky?'

Simon reached over, took the top off the decanter, and sniffed. 'I don't know,' he said, 'it's hard to say.' And he handed it to Christopher.

'Whisky poured into a brandy decanter, I'd say,' said Christopher. 'Typical. Never mind. It all does the same job.'

So, irresistibly, inevitably, they all settled down for a drink.

An hour or two later, they ate all the biscuits, with such avidity that Christopher went down to look for some more: while he was out of the room both Simon and Rose thought of saying to each other that Rose could on no account be left alone with Christopher, and did not bother to say it, for each realised that the other must be aware that this was so. Rose had already decided on her plan for getting through the night: she would fall asleep, there, where she was, her feet tucked up on the couch, her head resting quite comfortably on a petit point cushion. She would let Simon and Christopher talk, and she would fall unobtrusively asleep. They were quite happy to talk. Christopher she knew well enough; once under way as he now was, he would not stop, he would talk till the morning if given a chance. And Simon, though possessed of less natural energy, would probably not mind doing it for once. It was, after all, Sunday in the morning. No work, no school. Her eyelids drooped. The wallpaper was predominantly red, on a white background—a thin, dark wine red, hard and deep, like the red of the new wood of dogwood or sumac, a colour in nature that filled her with delight. Red trees, thinly branching, red flowers, with red butterflies and red birds perched delicately around, defying gravity. Once she had seen a heron alight on a treetop, elegantly, and the thin tree—a sapling it was, only—had bent and crumpled under the bird's weight, and the bird had had to flap up, clumsily, with an angry flutter, like the angry backward look of a man whose chair has collapsed beneath him. These painted birds were far too large for their elongated reedy insubstantial painted perches. But they would never fall. Silly, really. She yawned, and Christopher came back with a packet of Garibaldi biscuits and the remains of the apple pie from dinner, and he and Simon launched once more, relentlessly, into their discussion of which had been worse, poverty in the North East with a paralysed father and a genteel mother, or poverty in Camden Town with a crooked father and a Greek name. Both claimed immense sufferings, agonising humiliations. Rose listened, yawned again, and shut her eyes. Whatever they had endured, Simon and Christopher, they were real survivors, they had a winning ticket. As she had herself. There was no need to worry about either of them. And this thought, in itself consoling, led her inevitably to the nameless multitudes. They still implored. But she was too tired to attend them. And so, to a detailed description of working-class diet—oatmeal stew, bread and dripping, bloaters, tripe—she fell, at four in the morning, asleep.

THE NEXT DAY, Rose felt surprisingly well. She woke early, to find the decanter empty, and Simon asleep, still dressed, on top of the large double bed. Christopher had disappeared: she assumed he had gone back to his own room to sleep, then wondered if he had run off with the children. But he had not, for she could already hear them, having their breakfast downstairs. She went back to her room and washed quickly, noting that the towels were too thick to be serviceable—she hated a really thick fluffy towel, they left bits all over her, she much preferred the threadbare ones she had at home, fraying and hard and rubby. She dressed and went downstairs, feeling the curious weightless airiness that often possessed her after lack of sleep or excess of drink. It was most agreeable. Christopher was down already, helping the children: he too was cheerful, and claimed to have been up for hours. After a while Mr Bryanston and Simon also descended: Mr Bryanston was inclined to be annoyed about the absence of Sunday papers, and complained for some time about the erratic delivery of the local paper boy, who sometimes forgot them altogether. 'It's probably a strike,' said Simon, 'they're always striking these days.'

Well, it's annoying, said Mr Bryanston, I wanted to read about Wilshaw. And then he cheered himself up by telling them all about Wilshaw, a friend of his who had made a fortune in Readymix concrete, and who, not content with that, had expanded into the building world with disastrous results. He had crashed, spectacularly, the week before. I knew it was coming, I knew it was coming, said Mr Bryanston, unable to conceal his delight: he had reached the stage of life where news of the disaster of friends, like news of their deaths, is no longer a gloomy reminder of mortality, frightening in its sudden shadow, but a cause for self-congratulation, for gratitude for one's own personal survival. He engaged Simon and Christopher for some time in reminiscences about his old friend Wilshaw, now so satisfactorily bankrupt: I've known him for forty years, he said, and I always knew he'd come unstuck somewhere. From this subject, he could slip easily into his favourite discussion, which consisted of speculation as to whether it is harder to make one's first hundred, one's first thousand, one's first ten thousand, or one's first fifty thousand. Rose had heard this often, but not for so long that it had almost the charm of novelty. Christopher was a real sucker for it, he was mesmerised by it, he could not let it go. Even Simon seemed mildly gripped, and suggested that it would make a good board game, like Monopoly. Mr Bryanston was delighted with the suggestion, his mind flying already to marketing possibilities.

He was so delighted by the attention he was receiving from Simon and Christopher that he then, without much logical connection, moved on to his other favourite discussion—perhaps they were only linked in his mind by the pleasure which he took in each—which was a pondering upon the infinite variety of human physiognomy. All these millions and millions of people in the world, he said, and no two of them alike. The thought clearly awed him. It was a metaphysical concept which intrigued and perplexed and excited him. Rose had never forgotten this theme. As a child it had seemed to her banal and boring beyond belief, as any topic introduced by her father must be, and she had been irritated by the endless repetition of the same phrases, the indisputable nature of the argument, the lack of originality in the thought. Though human noses, eyes, teeth, chins and so on might be endlessly various, the thoughts of Mr Bryanston were not. But there was no doubting the sincerity of his awe, in face of the multiplicity and differentiation of human souls. It was as sincere as her own was, when she contemplated the ending of space. And, hearing him say it all again, now, after so long, she could not help but think that after all her father was right. It was a staggering thought. So many people in the world, and no two alike. It was indeed a fact of true philosophic significance. Snowflakes, she heard, had the same quality. But atoms presumably not? Molecules not? She did not know. Konstantin started to argue with his grandfather about identical twins and genes, and they would have been there all morning, had not Marcus and Maria insisted that it had been promised that they could go down to the sea and collect cockles and have a swim.

So they went to the sea. Simon protested at first, saying he should get home, but it was decided that he should drive Rose and the children down in the afternoon, Christopher accepted this without objection: he seemed to have lost all interest in his attempts to create trouble. He mildly offered to drive them all to the sea, on the grounds that Simon would be driving all afternoon, and because, he said, his car was bigger. It was bigger. Simon sat in the front, and Rose and all the children sat in the back, and there wasn't even a squash. Simon was wearing an old pair of trousers of Christopher's, and boots: he had been warned that it was muddy. Rose was wearing some boots of Konstantin's: their feet were the same size, though would not be for long. The road was quite busy, as it was Whit Sunday, but they turned off it, eventually, through a gate, and the big car bumped over the muddy furrows of a field, towards the sea. Christopher parked, at the far end of the field, and they all got out. The sea lay ahead, but inaccessibly distant, across acres and acres of green marshy flats. Beyond the green, miles away, one could see the yellow deserted sweep on the sand. There was nobody in sight, except two figures, small with distance, picking their way through the marsh.

'However do we get across all that?' said Simon, gazing at the vast expanse.

'We walk,' said Rose, smiling. 'It's all right, really. It's lovely. When you get to the sands, there's nobody else there at all, it's lovely.'

After half an hour's walk, Simon could see exactly why there would be nobody else there at all, at the other end. It was very heavy going. At first it was reasonably dry underfoot, though the little track they followed was crossed by innumerable little ditches and dykes, some bridged by planks, encrusted with red mud, others left to the improvisation of the pedestrian. But as they progressed, it got wetter and wetter: the dykes filled up, presumably from the tidal flow of the sea, and the texture of the solid ground itself became damp and boggy. It would have been easy enough for an unencumbered adult, alone, but they seemed to have a lot of equipment with them: bathing things, buckets, a picnic, a primus stove. And moreover the children kept falling into holes, even Konstantin, who was big enough to know better—it was ambition that trapped Konstantin, for he kept trying to jump over ditches and ponds, miscalculating, and falling in. Maria and Marcus, after the first twenty minutes, were in a state of extreme misery, yelling, moaning, begging to be carried, saying they were frightened of the crabs, of which there were indeed a great number at large, saying they wanted to go home, saying their feet were wet and that their legs ached, and in general behaving like children. It was in vain for Rose to yell at them irritably that it was they that had wanted to come in the first place: the children yelled back, with extreme simplicity, that they had changed their minds. Too late to go back, shouted Rose. Then Rose started to shout at Christopher, blaming him for the children's behaviour, for the route chosen, for the gear with which they were burdened: Christopher in turn yelled back that it was her fault for making them town children, whose fault was it if they couldn't face a bit of mud, certainly not his. It was all very domestic. They floundered on: Simon finally ending up well in front with Konstantin, which seemed as useful a place to be as any, for he was able to keep up Konstantin's morale by asking useful questions about crabs, cockles, purple flowers, and other interesting aspects of the journey.

'You see this green stuff,' said Konstantin, pointing at the greenery through which they were walking.

'I do indeed,' said Simon. 'It would be hard not to, there is so much of it, and one had to pay such close attention to the ground, on this kind of terrain.'

'That's samphire,' said Konstantin. 'We're having it for lunch.'

'Really? Is it edible?'

'Of course it is. You just boil it up, that's all. It's delicious. Samphire sandwiches, we're going to have. You needn't, if you don't want to. But you ought to try it.'

Simon bent down and picked a few sprigs. Now that he thought about it, he had heard of samphire: it came in *King Lear*. There was a man in *King Lear* who gathered samphire. A dreadful trade, Shakespeare said it was, and Simon had always assumed it was dreadful in the sense of dangerous, like collecting birds' eggs off cliffs, but he now saw it was dreadful more in the sense of muddy and disgusting. It was quite interesting stuff, extremely green, and branched and succulent. It was, in fact, so piercingly green that it was almost luminous with greenness: it glowed with colour. He nibbled a bit, experimentally. Konstantin, looking back, caught him at it, and said, 'It's not nice raw, it just tastes of salt, raw.'

'Yes,' said Simon, in complete accord.

'Don't give up, Simon,' said Konstantin, cheeringly. 'We're nearly there. Just over this next ridged bit, and it turns into beach.'

'Thanks,' said Simon.

He trudged on. Renewed wails from Maria caught his ear: looking back, he saw that Christopher had at last given in and picked her up. She was sitting on his shoulders, her muddy boots dripping down the front of his shirt. Rose was chivying Marcus, who had dropped his towel in the mud, and who was complaining about having to carry it now that it was so dirty.

'Don't be so bloody *feeble,* you awful child,' she was yelling at him, 'no *of course* I'm not going to carry it for you, you can carry it yourself, it's not my fault you dropped it, is it? Come on, for God's sake, we're nearly there, come *on,* can't you.'

'It's all muddy,' Marcus said, for the fifth time.

'Oh shut up,' said Rose, and strode on, leaving him.

Simon looked ahead again, and carried on. Konstantin was by now at the top of the ridge, outlined against the blue sky. Simon was just thinking that the part of the picnic he was carrying was excessively heavy, and that he would have preferred to fast than carry it, when Konstantin gave a shriek of delight, shouted, 'We're here, we're here,' and disappeared out of sight over the top. Inspired, Simon scrambled after him, and up to the top of the bank. And there, at last, was the sea, which had been lost to sight, through a trick of the landscape, for the last hundred yards. And all the swelling empty beach, yellow and brown and reflecting the blue sky from large swirls and washed and watery inlets. The sea was miles away still: the beach was enormous, miles of it extending around them, vast, ahead and on either side, untrodden, beautiful. Standing on the top of the bank, Simon turned and beckoned to the others, shouting, 'We're here, we're here'—and one by one they arrived, and took in the landscape, and shed their ill-temper as though walking into a fabled land, where children will cry no more, and adults will no more wrangle. They put down their burdens, and the children capered off, running wildly, and they stood and stretched and smiled, and took off their boots, and felt the wet firm sand.

Such a mood could not last unbroken—there was dispute about the exact location of the picnic site, some of them feeling it feeble to sit down so close to the frontier, some refusing to move an inch further. Marcus managed to enrage Konstantin by flapping at him with his muddy towel: Konstantin hit Marcus, Christopher hit Konstantin for hitting Marcus, Rose shouted at Christopher for hitting Konstantin, and then at Maria for smiling so smugly because the other two children were in trouble. They were all hungry. In the end they tramped for another ten minutes, towards the sea, and settled themselves down on a high bank by a wooden post. The beach was strange, undulating, full of curves, crossed by inexplicable dips and channels, here hard and flat to the feet, there dipped and rippled in lumps that rose painfully against the instep. Rose, opening the packets, beginning to distribute the picnic, explained that it was one of the best beaches in the district for cockles, but that few people used it, because it was so inaccessible. Miles away, on the horizon, they saw the two tiny figures of the men who had preceded them: they were cockling, bending and stooping in the hot sun at the eye's limit. We'll get some ourselves after lunch, she said, or they can while we have a sleep. She was beginning to feel tired: the sun, the sandwiches, the fresh air, the lack of sleep the night before, were all telling on her. She roused herself enough to boil up the samphire, a job done to amuse the children, bending over the primus, watching it green and bubbling: Simon, watching her, thought of the holiday in Cornwall, and the watercress that had grown in the stream by the sea, and his mother's views of watercress. His mother would not like the idea of eating samphire unwashed, either. He was not at all sure that he did himself, it was one thing to nibble the stuff experimentally, it was another to treat it as a foodstuff, and put butter on it, as Rose was now doing.

'It's quite like asparagus,' she said, proudly, as she handed him his portion.

'Yes,' he said, and ate it up. It wasn't bad, eventually. But he was relieved to learn that the cockles, as they required soaking, would not be cooked and consumed on the spot.

When they had all finished eating, the children went off with their buckets to look for a cockle bank, unable to sit still for one moment except while in the act of feeding themselves. Their bitter complaints of fatigue had been entirely forgotten: so too had their ill-will. Rose, Simon and Christopher took off some of their clothes and lay out in the sun, staring up at the sky, Simon was thinking, how like children adults are, they squabble and fight because they are hungry or tired or cold, but they lose the faculty for forgetting, forgiving. They nourish their resentments. The thought was banal, it did not quite satisfy him. What I am really thinking, he said to himself, is that there is nothing much wrong between Rose and Christopher. She accepts him, now.

Rose, for her part, was thinking Oh God, how can I face it. It may seem all right, now, in the sun for an hour or two, with Simon to keep the peace, but if he weren't here we'd have been in the shit already, we'd have quarrelled about the way I distributed the sandwiches, about the way we each treat the children, we'd have been locked right now into some bitter ideological dispute about this empty beach and the relative merits of Southend and conservationism and Fabian pamphlets and expanding economics and Galbraith. I can hear it going on in my head, that dreary bitter row. I am like a child, I can no more keep my temper than a child can, I can no more resist provocation than a child can.

I want to go home, thought Rose.

Christopher was thinking, she's stubborn, but she'll give in. Twenty-four hours of space will have been enough. She'll never want to endure that squalid little dump again. How can she? How can she?

He really did not see how she could.

Rose was thinking, I want to go home, I want to be home.

Then she fell asleep. They all fell asleep.

They woke at the return of the children, laden with cockles, excited, triumphant. I picked *millions,* said Maria, and the boys conceded that she had not done too badly, at all. Rose felt again the sensations of childhood, the fingers sinking into the wet sand, the cockle, a little knob, its hiding place revealed by the small breathing hole in the surface above. It had never seemed very cruel, catching cockles. One couldn't feel much emotion about a cockle. There was always a nasty moment in the pan, when they started to put their grey and orange tender feet out and walk about, but that was all. They weren't very vulnerable, cockles.

After a while they all went swimming, except for Simon, who said that he hated the sea, meaning that he didn't like to be seen without his trousers. The sea itself was nearly a mile away: the children lost interest in reaching it, and made do with lagoons and lakes, that the tide had left. Rose and Christopher set off for the open sea, but they too gave up, swimming for a few minutes in a deep channel, then returning, shivering, complaining of the cold. While they were dressing, Simon looked out across the water, and saw suddenly, quite close in, a yacht, sailing northwards. It was a pretty sight: white, with white sails. He pointed it out to the children: they all turned to watch its progress. 'Lovely, isn't it?' said Christopher, drying his hair elegantly, staring out through his dark glasses—he had swum in his glasses. 'I'd like a yacht.'

'Why don't you buy one, Daddy?' said Konstantin.

'It'd be fun, wouldn't it?' said Christopher, idly, quite innocently, or so Simon thought: but Rose turned on him with a look of fury, and said sharply, 'Piss off, would you?'

There it was, in a nutshell, their domestic life. Rose, distorted by rage from all her virtues: Christopher, idly provocative. Simon felt a chill in his bones: he shivered.

They set off back, shortly, having watched the yacht out of sight. The picnic bags were lighter to carry, but the swimming things heavier, because wet, and the buckets were full of cockles. But the route seemed shorter, going home; as routes always do. On the way they paused, on a little wooden bridge over one of the deeper crevasses: there were two boys, fishing for crabs with a string and a bent pin. The crabs were so intent on destruction that they would cling to the pin with only the merest suggestion of a bait to tempt them. The boys put them in a large pail. The pail was nearly full. 'What do you do with them, when it's full?' asked Rose, gazing at the heaving mass. 'Oh, we just put 'em all back in again,' said one of the boys, and smiled happily. 'Then we catch 'em all over again.'

It seemed a satisfactory arrangement, to both boys and crabs, endowed with the repetitive futility of joy. As they moved away from the ditch, Rose found herself walking between the two men, on the widening, hardening track—they were nearly back now, to the solid ground—and said suddenly, 'Once I saw a corpse, in that ditch.' She had only just remembered it, and was surprised by the effect that her words produced: she hastened to correct herself. 'Well,' she said, as they continued to look awed and horror struck, 'I didn't actually *see* the corpse, I just knew it was one, if you know what I mean.'

'Not at all, we don't know,' said Simon. 'Tell us more.'

'Well,' said Rose, 'I was out here one day, on my own I was, I must have been quite old, about sixteen or seventeen, and I was walking with Jack's dog, a Dalmatian she was, a really nice dog, and anyway just as I was going over that bridge back there the dog disappeared. I called her, but she was barking away, and had obviously found something interesting, so I went after her, and there she was a bit further up this creek, getting all excited about a sack.'

'A sack?'

'Yes, a sack. It was a very wet, muddy sack, and it was carefully tied up with rope, and it was half in half out of the water. The dog was mad with excitement, she kept whining, and nosing and scratching at it. It was just the right shape for a corpse. And I remember saying to myself, I bet that's a corpse in there. And then I got the dog away and put her on the lead till she forgot about it.'

'Didn't you tell anyone? Didn't you ring the police?'

'No, of course I didn't. The thing is, I didn't really think it was a corpse. I mean, I thought it was, but I didn't think it really was. But the more I think about it now, I think it probably was. It was a good place to dump one after all. And what else could it have been?'

'How very odd of you, not to have told anyone.'

'Do you think so? Perhaps it was. Do you know, I haven't thought of it from that day to this. I didn't even remember on the way out this morning. I only remembered when we stopped to talk to those boys.'

'It could have been a sheep. Or a cow.'

'Who would put a sheep or a cow in a bag and tie it up with a rope and dump it? Anyway it was too small for a cow. It might have been a sheep.'

'Perhaps it's still there. Shall we go back and look?'

'The skeleton, you mean? No, I don't think so. I didn't look any closer that last time because I was afraid it was what it was. Why look for trouble? Mrs Sharkey once found a dead baby in a carrier bag in a ladies lav in the park. She wished she hadn't looked, you know. She said to me, if only I wasn't so nosy.'

And reminiscing in such a vein, it was in a way a shock, and in a way somehow unsurprising, when they came in sight of the car, and found it accompanied by a police car, and two policemen, who were standing at the edge of the ploughed field deep in consultation.

'They've found your skeleton at last,' said Christopher. 'Taken them a long time, hasn't it?'

'It's not my skeleton they've come for,' said Rose, putting two and two together rather quickly. 'It's you.'

And at that they all stopped, because it was obviously true. The children were way behind, lagging again, poking in ditches and kicking stones. The adults looked at each other in alarm, until Rose started to laugh.

'They won't take me away, will they?' said Christopher. 'After all, I haven't done anything.'

'I should think they'll lock you up for ever,' said Rose. 'And serve you right.'

'However did they track us down here?' said Christopher. 'And more to the point, why ever did they bother? You two haven't been engaged in any criminal activities, have you? Simon, what on earth do you think is going on?'

'I really don't know,' said Simon, truthfully: he had forgotten all about injunctions and contempt of court orders in the warmth of the afternoon. He could not imagine what those two policemen were up to, standing there in a field. Had they come with a writ of attachment for Christopher? Was he about to be taken off to jail before their very eyes? Surely not. He hadn't even done anything. The more one thought about it, the clearer it became that he hadn't done anything, except send a threatening telegram. It was even by now his official day for seeing the children: Sunday. It seemed, on reflection, that everybody had panicked in a ridiculous way, lawyers included. How harmless he looked, Christopher, standing there with a bathing towel round his neck and a string bag in his hand.

But then, so had Mr Calvacoressi, on the television on Friday night. He had looked harmless enough, until he had got talking. They were all under his shadow, all of them. He had spread panic through them all—father, mother, children, friends, vacation judges, barristers, solicitors, the lot—and now, from the look of it, the police as well had panicked, the Home Office too had lost its calm. Such is the force of precedent, the king-pin of the law.

They stood there for a few moments, hesitating, the two separate groups, in the bright sunlight. The turned earth of the massive furrows glinted blue back to the sky: the earth itself was blue. The police had noticed them, were studying them—noticing, too, the children, now running up behind.

'Come on,' said Rose. 'We'd better go and see what they want.'

And she made her way across the field towards the two cars, stumbling on the uneven ground. The two men followed her. As she approached, the police began to look extremely uneasy: they communicated indecision. It was reassuring.

'Hello,' said Rose, cheerfully, bravely, nervously, arriving in range. 'Is anything the matter?'

The policemen, curiously, did not answer. They looked by now acutely embarrassed. One of them coughed, the other kicked at a pebble. The younger looked reprovingly at the elder, who coughed again, cleared his throat, and with a note of agonising effort managed to speak. His words had the air of being picked at random.

'You do realise,' he said, 'that this field is private property, not a parking lot?'

The younger policeman exhaled a breath of relief, and shot his colleague a glance of deep admiration. The spokesman himself, having spoken, appeared remarkably pleased with himself, quite suddenly: his anxious gloom gave way to a certain jauntiness and enjoyment. Rose, for her part, was quite enchanted.

'But of course, of course,' she said. 'We know it is. It belongs to Mr Cooper. He doesn't mind us using it, we've been using it for years, he really doesn't mind.'

'You live round here, then, do you?'

'I used to,' said Rose. 'My parents do.'

'Well, that'll be all right then,' said the policeman. He was smiling broadly, as at some private amusement, and at the same time giving Christopher a funny look. 'You'll excuse us asking, won't you. We have to keep an eye open, with it being holiday time. You wouldn't believe the damage we get.'

'That's quite all right,' said Rose, opening the car door, bundling the children in. The policemen were still standing there, as they drove off, over the bumps and furrows. They were laughing. One of them slapped the other on the back, and they were laughing.

'*They* were up to no good,' said Rose.

'No,' said Christopher, 'I think you're wrong. I think they thought we were up to no good. They probably thought I'd dumped the car in the field and was abducting you all on my private yacht.'

And they all laughed, but not more loudly than the policemen in the field, for that—owing to the Sunday papers, and crossed messages from the Home Office, one about illegal immigrants and one about a threatened kidnapping—was precisely what they had thought. And while they were slapping each other on the back, the little white yacht moored on a deserted stretch of beach a few miles north and landed ten bewildered Pakistanis.

THEY ALL MET UP AGAIN at the end of the week, on Friday, in Court. The Law Courts were being cleaned: dust sheets draped the stony corridors, and giant vacuum cleaners lay like snakes upon the ground, lending the place a festive, temporary look, reminiscent of a display in a marquee. There was something festive in the reunion. There they all were, Mr Justice Ward in his wig, looking very small on the bench, his large size dwarfed by its dimensions: Francis Morris in his wig, the ends of which stuck out smartly and wildly like a lobster's white whiskers into the sunny air: Christopher's counsel, his solicitor, an unexplained black man in a wig, Christopher himself, Rose, Julie, Emily, Jeremy Alford. Jeremy Alford's wife had had her baby: it was a boy, welcome after two girls. Christopher, Rose whispered to Simon and Julie, had sent Shirley

Alford a huge bunch of flowers. Isn't he *awful,* she whispered to Julie. Awful, yes, said Julie, but there were worse ways of being awful. Yes, I suppose so, said Rose.

Rose had got to work on Julie, during the week. Or had it been the other way round? It was no longer possible to tell, thought Simon, but it had happened. And explanations had, of course, been necessary. She had probably done the right thing. She had an instinct for these things.

Mr Justice Ward was explaining the nature of the injunction to Christopher's solicitor who was listening politely and humbly, as well he might. He was consulting his papers, he was saying that the custody case was due to be heard by his colleague Menzies in three weeks' time, and that it would be a good idea if time were saved by having the Welfare Officer's Report, which had been ordered months before, ready by that date. It is more than usually important, Mr Craddock, he said, that the case should be disposed of soon. These are children we are dealing with, not building sites, you know. Yes, my lord, of course, my lord, said Craddock. And now, said Mr Justice Ward, perhaps your client would step into the witness box for a moment, I want to make quite sure that he has understood the meaning of the solemn undertaking that he has been required to give the court.

And so there stood Christopher in the witness box. He too listened politely, and nodded his head intelligently. He had been subdued, since the press had got on to him. He had himself hidden the Sunday papers, that morning in Norfolk: he had got up early and shoved them all under his mattress. They had been full, once more, of the Vassilious: Greek abducts children: Vassiliou makes trouble again: More Drama for Ward-of-Court Heroine: More Thorns for Rose: Another Calvacoressi Case: Divorced Greek steals Heiress's children: the papers variously declared.

He had not been able to conceal their contents for ever: his father-in-law had got hold of them in the end, and he had not been very pleased. Neither, it is true, had he been very angry: he had forgiven him, but not without some unpleasantness. And now the press were on to Christopher all the time. He had moved out of his flat, into a small hotel in South Kensington, and was trying to keep himself out of the papers. He had called on Simon, one evening, and stayed for a meal, at Julie's insistence. He seemed lonely. It was hard to resist the notion that he was lonely, and penitent. There he stood, looking sad and remorseful, agreeing with every word that the judge said, apologising for his behaviour. Behind him the usher stopped cleaning her nails, and looked up, idly, as Christopher said, 'I assure you, my lord, I never at any point intended to abduct those children. I assure you. I would never take any action without the court's consent.'

'In that case, Mr Vassiliou,' said the judge, blinking and peering, 'in that case, what a pity it is that you wasted so much of the court's time. And gave some of us, if I may say so, a rather unquiet weekend.'

'Ah well,' said Christopher, 'I'm sorry about that. I didn't realise what a trouble it would cause. Though it was, in some ways, quite a useful experience.'

'What do you mean by that?' said the judge. But Christopher would not repeat it, was reluctant to explain himself. I meant nothing, he said, I did not mean what I said. I meant only that now I know where I am. You may say that I have been wasting the court's time, I cannot help feeling sometimes that the court, with its extraordinary delays, has been wasting mine. It is reassuring to find that things do get moving, when they have to.

Mr Justice Ward was amused, despite himself, by this.

'Oh yes,' he said, in quite a friendly tone, 'we can get moving when we have to. And I can tell you, if you make another move either to remove the children, or to threaten your unfortunate wife with removing them, you will find yourself in prison in no time. You know what that means, don't you?'

'Yes,' said Christopher, smiling dourly. 'Yes, I've been through this before.'

And he looked, from the witness box, at Rose.

And that was that.

'You'll have no more trouble from him,' said Jeremy Alford, as they stood out in Fleet Street and waited for a taxi. 'He wouldn't dare.'

And he was right. The case came up before Mr Justice Menzies in three weeks' time, as had been predicted, and Mr Justice Menzies, who did not much care for Rose, nevertheless found himself obliged to admit that Christopher might be an even worse prospective guardian for his own children. 'Really, Mr Craddock,' he said, glaring at him angrily, as though Christopher had broken the rules of some club by smoking in the wrong room, 'really, I should have been very much more inclined to give your client a favourable hearing, had it not been for his irresponsible behaviour over the Whitsun weekend. I am afraid I cannot take his application very seriously, in view of the way he himself has acted.'

He did not mention the fact that when the Welfare Officer had called on Christopher, Christopher had been an hour late for the appointment, and had nothing to show as suitable accommodation for three children but a small single room in a hotel in Gloucester Road, full of whisky bottles. (When the Welfare Officer had called on Rose, she had felt guilt because she was reading the *Guardian* instead of scrubbing the floor.)

The judge did not like to dwell too much on all of this. He did not like Rose. He managed to convey that if Christopher had not proved himself even worse, there were things in his affidavit about Rose that he would have taken very seriously indeed. Jeremy Alford, listening to this, trembled: for was it not Menzies who had, in similar cases, rudely dismissed medical and psychiatric evidence, pouring contempt on expert witnesses? He had once given custody to a father, because his wife was living with her lover: the father had been a most unsuitable parent, a religious maniac, a vindictive and violent man. Menzies had dismissed the family doctor's evidence on these matters as an impertinence. There had been an outcry, at the time, but he had got away with it. Jeremy Alford wondered if he dared do it again. But he did not. He gave Rose the children: he said she could keep them. When it was over, it was obvious that he could not have done anything else. The Welfare Officer, a nice woman in her fifties, had liked Rose immensely. They had had a long conversation about the problems of the district, ending up with a discussion of the prospects of Mrs Sharkey's Eileen's baby. Both agreed that they were poor. They had shaken their heads, over a cup of tea, and liked each other, and the Welfare Officer had said firmly to the judge that the children were perfectly happy and well-cared for with their mother.

'You'll have no more trouble from Christopher,' said Jeremy Alford, again, standing there on the pavement, hailing a taxi with his umbrella, a strong wind tugging at his raincoat.

But within a year, Christopher had moved back into the house in Middle Road.

IN A WAY, Simon said to himself, eighteen months later, when he had got used to it, we ought to have expected it. What else were they to do? It had not much surprised him, even at the time. Looking back, he took comfort in recalling his lack of surprise.

The new situation even had its conveniences, from his own point of view. It was not as though Rose and Christopher were happily reconciled, warmly reunited. They still had their problems, and one of the results of their new arrangement was that they seemed to need company and support. The two families, the Camishes and the Vassilious, saw quite a lot of each other. This improved the quality of Simon's domestic life immensely. Julie invited the Vassilious to dinner constantly, and they often accepted. They also met, with the children, at weekends, from time to time, and organised an occasional excursion to Kew Gardens or Hampton Court. Christopher taught the Camish children to roller skate. Julie taught Rose to crochet. Rose seemed genuinely fond of Julie, and Julie, responding to affection, merged a little more happily in Simon's mind with the image he had once had of her.

In fact, in some ways Julie seemed to be becoming what he had once taken her to be: as she grew older her mannerisms began to suit her better, she became better looking, it seemed that she had managed to achieve her childhood ambitions, she had managed to become smart, and generous, and worldly. She had become an attractive woman. He caught glances directed towards her, at dinnerparties, and could now see that they expressed admiration. Perhaps they had always done so, and he alone, guiltily, had misinterpreted them. It was he alone that had thought, when people had thanked her for gifts or hospitality, that the thanks contained an element of mockery. It had not been so, perhaps. People liked her. They liked her company. Rose liked her. They would talk together on the telephone for hours, like real women, and Julie would come back to him and report what Rose had said.

Things were better, domestically, than he had ever hoped. He even began to enjoy his social life, now that one or two of his own friends were included in it, Julie had become more gracious towards his interests.

Indeed, the new régime was so successful that Diana, who had in a sense initiated the whole thing, was heard to remark in exasperation that it was all Simon Camish's fault that the Vassilious had gone back to each other. He couldn't have stood the strain of the real thing, she said, but he's quite happy propping them up and watching and helping and acting as mediator. Well, let them be, said Nick. He had given Rose up long ago. But Diana could not quite let them be. Her relinquishing of Simon was more recent, she did not like to see Rose playing so successfully the role in which she had cast herself. It's a great mistake, she said, a kind person aggrieved as much by her own pique as by her cause for pique, it'll do them no good, you wait and see, you wait.

And of course there was some truth in what she said. It worried Simon greatly. Julie had improved, in his mind, it was true, but

Rose had deteriorated. Christopher's effect upon her was not for the good: she became increasingly querulous, strained, irritable. She and Christopher would quarrel, even in public, for no reason, idly, bitterly, tiresomely, and Rose always emerged from these disputes without credit. She appeared, she was, petty, vindictive, resentful. Simon had thought, at one time, that these evidences of her unhappiness would have gratified him, but as he watched, he knew that he was losing more than he could gain in secret pleasurable knowledge. He was losing her: she was being destroyed, before his eyes. And yet he accepted what she had done. He accepted her terms, completely. What else could she have done?

He waited, patiently, as everyone else waited, for Rose to announce that she and Christopher were buying a new house. It was inevitable that they should: they could not go on living where they were. And with the announcement, thought Simon, I will know that that is it: she will really have made the sacrifice, she will have lost.

He waited, but the announcement never came. At first, as the months passed, he thought, she is winning some victory in there, behind those threadbare curtains. She is sticking it out, meaninglessly faithful she is loyal to her vows. But then he began to notice that things were changing. It was not only Rose herself that was changing, it was the whole district she lived in. By some freak of fashion, it was coming up in the world. The process was at first so slow that it was almost imperceptible: but once noticed, the signs were clear, they multiplied, the change accelerated. Sale notices appeared on house fronts: whole streets were bought up, painted up, resold. Property prices soared. Rose's own house tripled in value, while she did nothing but sit in it. The less traditional branches of the middle classes moved in: an actor, a journalist, a publisher, a civil servant, a lecturer in sociology, an antiquarian bookseller. Front doors were painted black and khaki and ochre and sage. Lace curtains and decorative little wrought iron gates disappeared: the prams on the street got shabbier, the windows dirtier, the glimpses of wallpaper more expensive, and the shop on the corner began to sell French cigarettes. Some of the Greeks stuck it out: there were still a few houses with the bricks painted red and the pointing picked out in other colours, but their number was not increasing, as it had been. But then the Greeks were on the whole fortunate enough to own their own houses, so they could not be dislodged. It was the tenants who began to disappear. Once the landlords latched on to what was happening, out they went, all those who could be legally evicted. Mrs Sharkey's tenancy was protected by law for the first year of the improvements, but she knew she was going to have to get out in the end. 'I can't complain,' she said, 'I've only been paying a pound a week for the whole house. That's why the roof leaks. There's fungus as big as my fist growing out of the ceiling upstairs. You can't complain, at a pound a week, can you?' Mrs Sharkey was lucky, she was on the list for a council flat and was given one when her rent was increased. It was on the tenth floor, and she moved in there with her two sons, her daughter Eileen, and her granddaughter. At first she was quite thrilled with it: Rose, visiting her, was vaguely depressed by her enthusiasm for the new kitchen and the small square rooms and the mini-balcony where she was not allowed to hang her clothes or keep budgies. Then, being Rose, she reproached herself for this mean, romantic response. I'm a fool, I'm a fool, said Rose to herself. But after six months Mrs Sharkey was fed up with the flat: the plaster was cracking, the lift never worked, she missed talking on the front steps, she missed her neighbours, she missed Rose. Rose felt reassured. She sat there and watched the baby, bumbling about in a caged, listless way, now getting on for three years old, and listened to the story of the flat's disadvantages, and the drama of Eileen. Eileen, despite her lack of scope and her boring job in the bedding factory, had managed to go even more to the bad. Rose found this exhilarating, though she could not have said why. Eileen had got herself mixed up with a group of flashy would-be pop singing would-be Hells Angels boys who hung around in the pub on the council estate. A modern pub it was, called, for some reason, Prester John. It was a depressing spot, though one could see that the architect had made every attempt to integrate it into the landscape. It had a forecourt, where stone mushrooms served as seats, and plants grew out of pots from a topsoil of fag ends. Sitting in this forecourt on a stone mushroom one summer evening, Eileen had been shot in the leg. She had not been aimed at: the youth responsible had been aiming at Terry Monk from the Balls Pond Road. But he had been a bad shot, and Eileen had received the bullet in her thigh. It had cheered her up no end. She had been in hospital for weeks: Rose, visiting her, had found her elated, transported, her heavy face deeply transfigured by pain and notoriety.

In her brushed nylon turquoise frilled nightgown, she had sat there, with one jug of flowers by her bed, the queen of the estate. Her dark skin lowered under the pale pretty frills, decorated, satisfied. And she and Rose, looking at each other, had recognised, together, that her fate had not neglected her, that God was not as careless as he had at times seemed to be: he had sought her out and marked her down, as though she had been worth his personal attention. Mrs Sharkey didn't see it that way. But even Mrs Sharkey had found Eileen weigh less heavily on her mind, since the accident. At least now I know what I'm worrying *about*, was how she put it to Rose. Rose knew exactly what she meant.

And so it seemed, perhaps, as though fate itself had intervened on Rose's behalf and saved her from being rehoused. Christopher could hardly object to Middle Road as it now was. Even Harringdon Road school had gone up in the world: inspired by Rose's example, one or two middle-class mothers had risked entrusting their children to its unknown dangers, and Maria had quite a little entourage of fashionable friends. Miss Lindley had left: times had changed, Miss Lindley's skirts had dropped from the top of her thighs to her ankles, and Miss Lindley had moved on, out and on, to darker regions, more primitive lands of conquest. She was now assistant head of a school in Finsbury Park: she spent her evenings running a language centre for parents of immigrant children. Tireless, she was. Rose had lost touch with her. She had not time for Rose.

Simon watched, anxiously. He saw Rose's house repainted on the outside, he saw Rose taken off for a summer holiday in Italy, he saw her depart for weekends in Norfolk, he saw her offer him drinks as though whisky were not three pounds a bottle. He heard reports of her remarks at dinner-tables not his own, he heard that she had been seen gambling with Christopher at Emilio's, he heard that she had been seen laughing at the theatre, at a charity concert asleep, at a Private View drunk. He even read a letter from her in a weekly, about Women's Liberation, protesting against some comment about a friend of hers, saying that women seemed incapable of taking into consideration the fact that men (not women only, but men) were naturally fond of their own children, and questioning the virtues of the new matriarchy. (It hurt him a great deal, that letter: not only the implications of its sentiments, but the indelicacy, so unlike her in so many ways, of having written it at all.) He saw her drawn into a new life, unable to reject her new neighbours, as tediously involved in their different deprivations as she had been in Mrs Sharkey's, and more mercilessly, because more intelligently exploited by them. He saw her fight to send Konstantin to a state school—fight, bitterly, disagreeably, crazily, and win. (Simon's own eldest had started at Bedales. What could he do? The child was impossible, the child was psychotic.) He saw Konstantin flourish, politely, watchfully. He saw Rose's hair turn paler and tarnish, like old metal. He watched. He watched like a hawk, for signs of cracking, for signs of ruin, for signs of decay. He needed her, he needed her more than ever. He watched her clothes, to see if she would spend money on herself. He watched her hair, to see if she would have it done, at three guineas a time. He watched her face, and the lines of it, to see if she would betray him. He watched for scars and bruises, but all he saw was the tightening of the skin on her cheekbones, the whitening of it round her eyes, a new maze of crowsfeet when she smiled. If she was bruised, it was in the soft flesh he could not see, the soft flesh he had never seen. If she bled, she bled internally.

Nobody ever mentioned the next instalment of the money due to Rose, the next thirty thousand pounds that would eventually come her way. It was as though it did not exist. Occasionally he thought of it. It hung over her, a threat as vague as death and as real and as trying, and one could no more ask, what will you do with it, than one could ask, how will you die, what will be the manner of your dying, do you hope to die in a state of grace. There was nothing to do but wait.

He watched the inside of her house, the rooms of it, the rooms she lived in. Breathlessly, over the years, he watched. They changed, a little. They did not change much. Such love, such salvation, he felt, at the sight of each object that remained in its place. The tea caddy. The tin tray. The armchair. The shabby cat. Sometimes things went—the settee, she decided one day, was past bearing, and he stood with her and Emily all one Saturday afternoon, waiting for the rag-and-bone-man with his painted cart. I can't stand it, I can't stand it a moment longer, said Rose, laughing weakly, hysterically, looking at her watch, pummelling the awful old thing with its black and brown and orange patterned unbelievably filthy bulging ripped shiny prickly covering, hitting it till dust a century old flew out of it, the dust of North London, sacred and creaking, horsehair poking out of it, wadding seeping out of it— it's foul, she cried, I can't stand it, get it out, get it out, committing sacrilege, of course, giving in, she the unconquerable, betraying disgust, she the unshockable—get it out, there he is, she said, and there he was, they heard his cryptic cry, his mysterious wail, and there was his shabby pony outside the window, his cart hand-painted, oh, the age was dying, and in those dingy corners you could hear its death rattle, as Rose Vassiliou and Emily Offenbach and Simon Camish opened the basement window, and heaved the ancient settee out into the area, because it was too big to go through the door, because it had been in that room for generations. The old man didn't want it, they had to give him five bob to take it away, and oh, well rid of it at the price, said Rose, looking round the room, that now looked empty, empty without it.

What on earth shall we *sit* on, now, she said, some minutes later. And being penitent, it was some time before she replaced the old settee.

SIMON, SUSPICIOUS, calling that winter (a Tory Government, a new Industrial Relations Bill, decimal coinage, a new world later) calling on another Saturday, remembering the clouds of dust rising into the summer air, found them there, Rose and Emily, sitting on the new Habitat settee. And his suspicions glared, gathered. She was wearing a new fur coat, Rose was. What would she do, would she comment, would she apologise? A child had opened the door to him: they were to go out, he had brought two of his children, he was late, Rose and Emily were waiting for him, Julie had gone to the cinema, Christopher was abroad on business, and he and Rose and Emily were to go to the dog show at Alexandra Palace. And there was Rose, sitting on her new settee in a new fur coat. She looked up, and he came into the room, as the children opened the door for him, she looked up and smiled at him. 'Simon,' she said, 'hello, how are you, how are things?'

'All right,' he said, 'all right, I'm sorry I'm late.'

'That's all right,' said Rose, 'there's no hurry.'

And he looked at her, at her treachery. He looked at Emily. Emily had grown so beautiful with the years that it was now almost unbearable, one could hardly bear to gaze at her, so moving were the marks of time and beauty. Her hair had streaked, had turned grey and white: it was thick and heavy, she wore it untidily pinned up, a brown pin holding it, coarse and drooping, sinking from the pin with the weight of years, and her skin, once brown and sallow, had faded and whitened, her lips were almost blue, so had the pink retreated, her eyes were etched in red and blue lines of amazing

416

splendour, her whole face was lined and carved and withered into beauty, her hands too were marked with age, their veins courageously upstanding, their nails blue with a fine withdrawal. She seemed the image of time, triumphant, vindicated, conquering but conquered. Beside her Rose looked pale and delicate. They could not have survived without each other, and they had admitted him to their secrets. He looked back at Rose, and of course there she was, her coat a moth-eaten old thing she had picked up at a jumble sale, and as she rose to her feet, as she shouted for the children, as they gathered themselves together, bags and baskets and children and hats and scarves and boots, she turned to him and said, 'What d'you think of my new coat, Simon? Smart, isn't it? I found it in a cupboard at Branston and it seemed a pity to *waste* it, and then I got worried because I think I once signed a pledge about rare creatures, but it's so incredibly old and dead, one couldn't really call it a rare creature, do you think?'

'Christopher says it's *wolf* skin,' she said, as they went through the door and up the steps, 'but I think it's more likely rabbit. Wouldn't you?'

They went up to the Palace. Even the Palace had changed. There was an artificial ski slope now, on one of the hills, and there was talk of all sorts of developments—hotels, art centres, God knows what. The view was still the same, except for a few new tall buildings, like the one housing Mrs Sharkey. There it all lay, London, the roof tops, Hackney marshes, the railway lines, the fair delusive green spongy fields of sewage. 'Bloody cold, isn't it,' said Marcus, casting a perfunctory glance at the panorama, and they agreed, and went in.

Rose had been promising Simon a dog show for years. With immense satisfaction he formulated to himself that sentence. For years, now, she had been promising to take him to a dog show at the Palace. He had known her for years. There she was, slightly ahead, a child dragging on one arm, her hair tumbling on to her fur coat shoulders. She turned to him, she smiled. 'I've been meaning to bring you to one of these for *years*,' she said, 'but don't expect too much fun, will you? It's an awful bore, really.'

'I'm enjoying it already,' he said.

There was a strong smell of dog. Under her guidance, he had seen other events there—a jumble sale, a chess competition, a roller skating competition, a London Festival Drama for Schools Exhibition—but never yet a dog show. There were all the dogs, in the big hall, standing around rather carelessly with their owners. Most of them were Alsatians. 'Don't for Christ's sake walk on the dog shit,' said Emily, yanking a child firmly to one side, as it was about to put its foot in it. The dogs looked bored and angry. So did their owners. Emily had been too late with one of the children: scraping its shoe crossly on a step, she told them about Iceland where dogs were illegal, Reykjavik, the only civilised capital city in the world. 'All dogs should be shot,' said Emily, loudly, and the children bristled and whispered and giggled, thrilled by her audacity, shocked and embarrassed by it at the same time, half expecting the dogs or their provoked owners to leap angrily at her throat, half proud of her evident heroic disdain.

In fact, it became obvious, when they had wandered around for a quarter of an hour or so, that there wasn't much going on. It was a very second-rate dog show. There were some quite interesting small dogs in cages: Maria and Simon's youngest managed to work up a little fake enthusiasm for some malevolent Pekinese, but were easily corrupted by the elder ones, who wanted to go and look for something to eat. 'I can't face it, I can't face it,' said Rose, wanly, as they drifted off.

'I'll go,' said Simon, politely, 'I'll go and cope with them.'

'They can look after themselves,' said Emily. 'For God's sake.' And she led them off firmly, leaving the children in the cafeteria, to the other end of the large hall, and sat down and got her newspaper out of her pocket, and started to read. 'Peace and quiet,' she said, 'we might as well enjoy it while we can.'

The back of the hall was banked with steps. Wooden steps, thick with dust, reached upwards. It must once, Simon thought, have been some kind of auditorium. Emily was sitting on the bottom step, indifferent to the dirt. Rose looked around her, looked upwards.

'Let's go and sit at the top, up there,' she said. 'It might look more interesting, from up there. You never know.'

Emily did not look up from her paper. She was reading about how to peel whole oranges and stew them in caramelised sauce. Emily hated cooking, and she always read recipes, to enrage herself. She could get quite emotional about recipes. She took them as personal affronts.

'Come on,' said Rose to Simon, as she started to climb. The steps were steeply banked. He followed her. The room grew lighter, as they climbed up: there were windows in the dome of the hall, letting in superior light. With each step the dog scene fell into shape below them. The dogs and their owners, harmlessly employed. Simon looked up at Rose. The light fell from the windows, the winter sun fell on to her pale hair, shafts and slanting planes of it, and he could see all the dusty motes in the bright air, and her hair itself, falling on to the points of her fur collar, fell into a thousand bright individual fiery sparks, the hair and the fur meeting, radiant, luminous, catching whatever fell from the sun upon them, stirring like living threads in the sea into a phosphorescent life, turning and lifting, alive on the slight breeze of her walking, a million lives from the dead beasts, a million from her living head, haloed there, a million shining in a bright and dazzling outline, a million in one. She walked ahead, encircled by brightness, she walked, and turned and stopped.

'Let's sit down here,' she said.

And she sat there, in the thick dust, and he sat by her, and they looked down at the hall beneath them, with its wooden boards and its traditional amusements.

'It's a bit shabby,' she said, 'isn't it?'—leaning forwards, her elbows on her knees, her chin in her hands.

'I like it,' he said.

'Do you remember,' she said, 'that day when we went to see the chickens and the armchair? I said we would come to a dog show then, I remember.'

'It's good,' he said, 'that we did what we said we would do.'

'One doesn't always,' she said, frowning. 'Things don't always work out as one expects,' she said.

She was thinking of Christopher. She had never spoken of Christopher to Simon, since his return to her: she had maintained an honourable silence. There were many things that she had wanted to say—now, as she sat there watching the dogs below, she thought of some of them—but she had never been able to say them. She wanted Simon to understand. She wanted him to think well of her, not to judge her harshly, but could not state her own case without treachery. She could not acquire his esteem without begging for it, and thereby forfeiting a right to it. So she kept silent, hoping that he would do her justice, in his mind. She desired his approbation, passionately. It was her strongest emotional need, and one that by its very nature she could take no move to satisfy. And the greatest threat to his fair judgement of her was one of the qualities in him that she most loved, which made her trust him, which made her admire him and seek his friendship: for it was his own diffidence: a man like him, how could he ever guess, correctly, at what she truly felt—and why, in any case, should she want him to know it? Since Christopher's return, she had lived in various kinds of misery, but she knew that nobody, not even Simon, would credit her distress. He would credit, perhaps, her sense of loss, because he had seemed to acknowledge what it was that she had, on her own, her way of life, her peace of mind, but she suspected that he, like others, would think that she had gained more than she had lost. He will think, she thought bitterly, he will think, as everyone thinks, that I am lucky to have Christopher back again, that I wanted him all the time, that I played my cards and won, that he came back to me ostensibly on my terms to vindicate me, but in fact on his own, to support me. She was ashamed, she was humiliated, by the thought that others might think so of her—that they had seen her as a deserted wife, humbly and gratefully accepting her husband's return, chastened, accepting, glad to re-admit him to her house and her life and her body. She knew how the world saw Christopher: she knew how Simon must inevitably see Christopher: the successful man, the delicately achieved man, the man who cannot be rejected, the man whose power overcomes more rational hesitations, the man who awarded blows through love, the man who cannot be denied. They saw her, in consequence, as the woman who had tried to do without him, who resisted him on one level to succumb more deeply on another, to accept him more fully for his transgressions. She hated this picture of herself. The picture of Christopher she did not mind, for it bestowed on him a little of the dignity that she truly, deep within herself, feared that he might lack. She would connive with the world to protect him: but why should her good name suffer, in her connivance? She saw no way out. She had taken him back because she could not bear to keep the children from him: why should she be so silenced, so compromised, by her own act? And it was not only in silence that she suffered. Her whole nature was being corrupted by her deep resistance to Christopher, by the endless, sickening struggle to preserve something of her own. She had become irritable, nagging, shrewish, difficult: she quarrelled with Christopher, in public, over the least issue, and at home, though she was able to prevent herself from becoming violent, she could not bring herself to be pleasant or placid. She had never made that leap into the clearer air. She looked back with bitter regret to those exhausting days of peace, when she was on her own, alone, lonely, when she would put the children to bed and then sit up herself a little while with a book, and then go quietly to bed. They seemed endowed, those days, with a spiritual calm that it had been a crime to lose. And now she lived in dispute and in squalor, for the sake of charity and of love. She had ruined her own nature against her own judgement, for Christopher's sake, for the children's sake. She had sold for them her own soul, but it had not been a downright transaction, over and done with, the soul handed over like a little parcel as St Catherine's was, to purchase food for the flock—no, the price she had to pay was the price of her own living death, her own conscious dying, her own lapsing, surely, slowly, from grace, as heaven (where only those with souls may enter) was taken slowly from her, as its bright gleams faded. Oh yes, she knew it had been narrow, her conception of grace, it had been solitary, it had admitted no others, it had been without community. That made its loss no less real to her. At times she tried to persuade herself that she was mistaken, that her decision to live with Christopher was not only right but also, beneath all her resistance, satisfactory to her: at times she came near to persuading herself that this was so, that she enjoyed strife or would not endure it, that she enjoyed his bullying or would not condone it. But she could not keep up this pretence for long: she would catch herself out. As she had done, now this week—for when he had said he was going abroad on business for a fortnight, she had not been able to conceal from herself the waves of relief, of physical and mental relief that swept through her. No Freudian subtlety on earth could have persuaded her to mistake that relief for dismay. The relief at the thought of two weeks without him had been overwhelming, shaming, vindicating, triumphant. For fourteen days she could go to bed in innocence, and get up without fear. And if this was so, if this was how it was, then her decision to take Christopher back (measured, thus, in terms of anguish, of suffering, of justifying pain) must have been right. She had been right to take him: no ulterior weakness of her own, no sexual craving, had prompted her to do so, she had done it in the dry light of arid generosity, she had done it for others. Her duty, that was what she had done. For others. For him, for the children:

Though that, of course, was another matter. Since Christopher had come back she had been much less pleasant to the children. She had shouted more, she had made an issue out of everything, she had lost her temper several times a day. Really, there was no knowing what one should do. To yell at the children, angrily, I'm doing this for you, you fools, could hardly be good for them. Perhaps she would grow out of it. Perhaps in the end she would settle down. Live through it. Get over it. It was so embarrassing, seeing people like Simon register her ill-temper. He never missed a thing. He was over-sensitised, poor Simon, to displays such as her own. She wished she could tell him that she was feeling better this week, because Christopher was away. But how could she commit such an indiscretion, how could she betray one man to another? So many times, she had wanted to ring him, had wanted to complain, of something Christopher had said to her, of something he had done — she had wanted to reinstate herself, through complaint, through exposure. But of course it could not be done. She and Christopher were together now, husband and wife, unable to bear witness the one against the other.

She turned to Simon. He was lighting himself a cigarette, absent-mindedly: he offered her one. She declined. She had had a bad throat, for the last week.

'What do you think, Simon,' she said, 'do you think one can sell one's own soul, in a good cause?'

'You have some archaic concepts,' he said.

'Yes, I know,' she said. She had seen her soul, suddenly, as she spoke: it was dark and crying and bloody, like a bat or an embryo, and it was not very nice at all, not an agreeable thing, and it flapped and squeaked inside her angrily whenever Christopher touched or spoke to her. Let it go, let it go, strangle it, burn it. The warm daylight of love she would aspire to, oh she would make it, though her nails were torn, her knees barked with hanging on; and the harsh clanging of her own voice, the sounding of righteous brass and the clanging of the symbols of her upright faith-demented ideologies, she would silence them all, she would learn to do so. The sun fell and the dust danced in it, and the smoke from Simon's cigarette turned in it.

'I often think I'm a foul bitch, you know,' she said, pleasantly, conversationally.

From the hall below them, a dog barked, irritably. Another answered, then another: barks, followed by long drawn out slow echoing moans and howling. They both laughed, at the ridiculous melancholy sounds. Then they got up, disturbed, slightly, by the uproar, thinking of children and rabies and babies savaged in their prams by fierce Doberman Pinschers—not that they had any babies, either of them, they were long past the baby stage, but nevertheless one could not really rely on the good sense even of ten-year-olds. They stood for a moment, looking downwards, then started to descend, together, and as they went Rose told Simon about a job that she had been offered, and how pleased she was, it was a British Council job looking after all the Ujuhudanians who came to Britain and vice versa, and he wasn't to laugh at her for being so enthusiastic, she knew it must sound dull to him, but it was interesting to her, and not to mention it to Christopher yet because she hadn't dared to tell him because he was sure to laugh even if Simon was polite enough not to, she really was very pleased and looking forward to it, she hadn't even applied, she'd been offered it, through Jenny Ward who worked at the Home Office. Ujuhudiana was becoming an interesting place at last, she said: they'd discovered copper there, but of course they couldn't afford to mine the stuff themselves, they'd have to get the South Africans and Chinese and Americans and God knows who else in to do it for them, but they'd get royalties off it, at least, and there were people coming over already, to study engineering, hoping they'd be able to join in when they got down there, in a few years time. I might even get over there myself at last, she said. What do you think, Simon, she said, do you think it's a good idea, looking at him earnestly, pale and washed out now she had descended from the sunny regions, her hair as dull as the dead fur round her neck, and he did not know if she meant the job itself, or her whole life, but he said yes, yes, it seemed all right to him, it seemed a good idea, an excellent idea, he would look forward to hearing about it, and he meant exactly that, he would look forward to hearing, over the months and years, the things that she would have to say.

And so they went down, to collect the children, and Emily. Emily stood up and folded up her newspaper: her coat was thick with dust, and she hit at it, viciously, with the folded paper. She had moved on from the recipes: she had been reading a piece that had upset her, about population explosions and car accidents and lemmings running into the sea. The thick yellow-brown dust clung to the black fabric, and she stared at it, and said, as they moved to meet the children, who were waiting for them in the doorway with their bags of pop corn and crisps, 'I don't know, I don't know, I don't know. Life is real, life is earnest, and the grave is not its goal, dust thou art to dust returneth was not spoken of the soul. It's all very well,' she continued, thinking of Malthus, looking with distaste at the dogs and their owners, 'but the whole *world* is turning into dust. People are like rats. Look at them, rats. We'll start living in the sewers, soon.'

They moved out, on to the high terrace round the building. The cold wind had dropped: the sun shone. The huge yellow building stood behind them, mad, shoddy, decayed. The children begged for a twopence to look through the telescope, and Simon gave them one. They stood there, the three adults, on the parapet, and looked at the view, and looked back at the Palace, with its odd shabby Corinthian pillar, its peeling plaster caryatid, its yellow bricks, its ugly Italian parodies, its bathos, its demotic despair, and then looked back at the view, where houses stretched, and tower blocks, and lakes of sewage gleaming to the sky, and gas works, and railway lines, effluence and influence, in every direction, all around, as far as the eye could see. It seemed that Emily was right.

They felt the cold chill of her reading, and she said, leaning on the stone by the eroded perfunctory sphinx, 'It's not the dogs that should be shot, it's the people. Look at it. Just look.'

'We've got no right to talk,' said Simon. 'We've got three children each. We should be the first to go.'

Rose was silent. She edged along the wall, a little, away from them. She did not want to speak, she did not want to offer her hope to their scorn, she did not dare, and she did not like talk of shooting, even from Emily. They were probably right, she was almost certainly wrong. There was no knowing. I will leap off the ladder even blindfold into eternity, sink or swim, come heaven come hell. Like a rat, swimming through the dirty lake to a distant unknown shore. She shivered, the cold wind blew, her throat ached. She looked along the wall: one of the lions had been broken, since her last visit. She went up to it, to see closer. It was hollow, the lion: shabby, weathered, crudely cast in a cheap mould. Half of its head was missing. It was hollow inside. She peered inside the hole: there were two concrete struts instead of intestines, and somebody had placed carefully inside it a Coca-Cola bottle, a beer can, and a few old straws. She was glad there was nothing worse. A few straws lay crossed before its noble feet. She remembered the beasts on the gateposts at Branston: elevated, distinguished, aristocratic, hand-carved, unique, with curled sneering lips and bared fangs. She looked back at the shabby mass-produced creature before her: it was one with the houses, the streets, the dog show, the people. Half its head had gone. It was one of many. Somebody had written on it, years ago, in red paint: SPURS, they had written, and the red paint had dripped and run, spattering its heavy jowl like old blood. But it was a toothless lion, any boy could draw on it. She peered at it, closely. It was grey, it looked as though it were made of grey brawn—small specks and lumps of whiteness stood out in the darker background, diamond shaped flecks. She wondered what it was that it was made of—cement, concrete, plaster. And the Palace itself. What a mess, what a terrible mess. She looked back at it. It was comic, dreadful, grotesque. A fun palace of yellow brick. She liked it. She liked it very much. She liked the lion. She lay her hand on it. It was gritty and cold, a beast of the people. Mass-produced it had been, but it had weathered into identity. And this, she hoped, for every human soul.